Also by Tate James

DEVIL'S BACKBONE
Dear Reader
Watch Your Back
You're Next

MADISON KATE
Hate
Liar
Fake
Kate

HADES
7th Circle
Anarchy
Club 22
Timber

Watch your back

TATE JAMES

Bloom books

Published by Bloom Books, an imprint of Sourcebooks
P.O. Box 4410, Naperville, Illinois 60567–4410
(630) 961-3900
sourcebooks.com

Cataloging-in-Publication data is on file with the Library of Congress.

Printed and bound in the United States of America.
LSC 10 9 8 7 6 5 4 3 2 1

This book is dedicated to Pizza Shapes, the superior shape, with honorable mention going to Chicken Crimpy.

Barbeque has no place here.

Chapter One

ELDERS' COUNCIL REPORT CAME THROUGH LAST NIGHT. THE FIRE THAT
DESTROYED THE OLD SCIENCE HALL AT NEVAEH ALSO KILLED ONE OF THE
JANITORIAL STAFF. THE MAN RUSHED IN TO TRY TO EXTINGUISH THE BLAZE
AND WAS PINNED BY A FALLING BEAM.

MY FRIENDS ARE KILLERS...AND THEY DIDN'T EVEN KNOW WHAT THEY
WERE DOING. IT MAKES ME WONDER WHAT THE FUCK I'M RESPONSIBLE FOR.
WE ALL NEED TO KEEP OUR DISTANCE FROM ASHLEY.

FROM NOW ON, I'M DOCUMENTING ANYTHING AND EVERYTHING OUT
OF THE ORDINARY. JUST IN CASE.

N. ESSEX, DECEMBER 15

My phone buzzed on the bedside table, pulling my attention away
from the show I was watching in bed. Heart in my throat, I reached
out of my pillow nest to grab the device. Disappointment washed
through me faster than I could even acknowledge my silent hope
when I saw the message was from Meg at my old job and *not* any of
the people I hoped to hear from.

Biting my lip, I opened her message and sighed. She was asking if I was back in Panner City for Christmas and if I wanted to pick up any massage shifts at Serenity. It was a tempting offer…just walk away from this depressing, anxiety-ridden life in Prosper and return to my old one.

A sharp knock on the door interrupted my melancholy daydream.

"Layne! Your mom wants you to actually get out of bed today. Go downstairs and make an appearance or something." Nate's tone was pure frustration and I extended my middle finger at the door… as if he could see it.

When I didn't reply, he gave a long sigh, then knocked again.

"I know you can hear me. Either go downstairs and put on a smile for our parents, or they're likely to stage an intervention instead of Christmas dinner tomorrow." He said it in a low growl, clearly trying not to be overheard by either of our parents. "Please."

It was that afterthought that broke me. His voice cracked over the word, and a moment later, his footsteps faded away, making my eyes burn with unshed tears. I wasn't the only one hurting—it wasn't fair to act like I was.

"Fuck," I whispered, pressing pause on my newest obsession show—a delicious enemies-to-lovers dubbed into English from German—and threw back my blankets. "God damn it, Essex."

I fucking hated when he acted like a human and made me feel bad for him. But facts were facts: Heath was more than just a friend to him; he was practically his brother. No matter how much I was aching in the chasm left by Heath, it had to be a hundred times worse for Nate.

Dragging my ass out of my cozy nest, I stumbled through to the attached bathroom. After everything at school with the fire—and *Heath*—I'd wanted to crawl into a hole and never come out. Mom had lovingly bullied me into taking my exams, which I barely remembered even doing, then she and Max welcomed me home. Although I suspect they weren't anticipating I'd disappear into my room and not surface again for days.

It'd been two and a half weeks since the fire. Since…

My throat tightened, the memory of Heath's lifeless body hanging from the middle of his room flashing through my mind for the ten-thousandth time. Tears filled my eyes and I screwed my lids shut, refusing to let the tears fall. I'd done enough crying, and it wasn't changing what had happened.

"Pull it together, Layne," I whispered to myself, wiping my eyes with the heel of my hand, and cranked the shower on high. If I was making an appearance to convince Mom I was okay, then I needed to shower.

Trouble was…I hadn't been even remotely okay since the moment Heath hung himself.

Fuck. I couldn't do this.

The tears spilled over and I crumpled to the bathroom floor, sobbing.

How long I stayed like that, I had no clue. All I knew was that one minute I was drowning in my own puddle of grief and guilt, and the next Nate was turning off the unused shower and lifting me up off the floor.

"I'm sorry, Ash," he muttered, carrying me back to my bed. "I shouldn't have pushed."

My only response was a sniffle as I buried my face in his neck. He sighed, placing me down in the middle of my pillow fort, then tucked me in and turned my show back on.

"I'll tell Carina you've got a cold. Take your time."

He was gone, shutting the door softly behind himself before I could even clear the fog from my eyes and thank him. Which only made me feel worse for thinking he was the devil himself.

Eventually, I mentally bullied myself hard enough to get out of bed again. This time, I did everything possible to *avoid* thinking about Heath as I went through the motions of showering, washing my hair, and dressing in clean clothes.

"Ashley, baby, Nate said you weren't feeling well?" Mom

exclaimed as I dragged my feet into the kitchen where she was baking cookies with Max's help, or his company at least. Mom seemed to have parked her new husband on a stool with a cocktail in front of him. Not surprising considering she was a baking control freak.

I forced a smile as Mom brushed off her hands and grabbed me in a hug.

"I'm okay," I mumbled. "Just, um, allergies." Despite the fact that it was the middle of winter, literally snowing, and I'd never had hay fever in my life.

Mom let the lie slide, knowing perfectly well how heavy Heath's decision weighed on my shoulders. She just hugged me tight, and I breathed a little easier when she let me go.

"Join me for a drink, Ash?" Max offered, indicating his creamy cocktail. "Brandy Alexander. Very festive."

I gave a weak smile and shook my head. "Thanks but…no. I'm not a brandy kind of girl."

"Come help me with this gingerbread dough, honey," Mom suggested, gesturing me farther into the kitchen, but her endearment stabbed through my chest like a knife.

My breath caught and my stomach dropped, remembering the day I'd tried to give Heath a nickname. I sucked at nicknames, but he was so sweet…

"What did I say?" Mom asked, her face stricken as she stared at me.

I wet my lips, trying really fucking hard to hold it together. Words were failing me, though. How the fuck did I explain that I was utterly shattered inside, the broken pieces of me cutting up my organs with every breath?

"Ashley," Nate said from the doorway, jerking my attention away from my mom and her hard questions. "Help me hang these lights?" He held up a string of Christmas lights, but his expression was hard and tense. Like him or not, he got what I was going through.

I nodded quickly and murmured a *be right back* to Mom before hurrying out of the kitchen once more. Nate said nothing as he led the way across the living room to where the enormous sixteen-foot Christmas tree sat decorated in the corner.

"You okay?" he murmured, draping the end of the lights over the fireplace mantel.

I drew a deep breath, fighting the instinct to lie. Nate, for all his flaws, didn't buy my bullshit. "No," I admitted. "Are you?"

He shook his head, jaw clenched.

Somehow, weirdly, that made me feel better. I wasn't alone in my grief.

"Your mom really loves Christmas," he commented after some moments of silence. "Has she always been so…" He trailed off with a bewildered glance toward the kitchen. Peals of my mom's laughter echoed through to us, and it made me smile slightly.

"Always," I confirmed. "Or as long as I can remember, anyway. It used to be because my dad was away so often but always came home for Christmas, so she wanted to make it special. Then it was like she was overcompensating once they split."

Nate just nodded and said nothing, continuing to arrange the string of lights that were totally unnecessary in the already opulently decorated room. Mom had always been big on Christmas, but this was a new level, even for her. It looked like Santa had exploded in the middle of the living room and splattered every surface in festivity.

Sometime later, as I sat on the sofa and offered exactly zero assistance on the Christmas lights, the doorbell rang, and Nate shot a curious look my way.

"Have you heard from the guys?" he asked, his mind obviously going to the same place as mine had. They'd shown up unannounced on Thanksgiving—would they do the same for Christmas?

I wet my lips and shook my head. "Nothing." Not that I'd tried terribly hard. After Heath hung himself in their apartment, we'd all fallen apart. Grief and guilt drowned all of us, and once Nate explained the weird trance situation and their involvement in arson

5

and manslaughter—once Royce and Carter realized they'd had no control over their actions—it'd all gotten worse.

None of them trusted themselves anymore. Paranoia had taken the reins with an iron grip, and I'd barely seen any of them since—not even Royce for sleepovers. Instead, an honest-to-fuck bodyguard was hired to sit outside my dorm room—to say I was pissed off would be an understatement.

The only reason Nate was talking to me now was our parents.

Max must have answered the door because echoes of his enthusiastic greeting traveled through the house to us, and I shrugged. "Have *you* heard from anyone?"

Nate's pinched expression suggested that he had and that he just didn't want to tell me. I had guessed I was the only one being avoided like the plague, but it still hurt to know I wasn't wrong.

"Ashley!" Max called out from the entry foyer. "Your Christmas present arrived early!"

Confusion saw me rise to my feet and head in the direction of his voice. A small spark of hope ignited in my chest, growing with every step, but I was totally taken aback when I saw who stood in the marble foyer, brushing snow off his sweater.

"Dad?" I squeaked, frozen in shock.

His weathered face lit up in a bright smile. "Hey, baby, merry Christmas." He opened his arms, and I launched myself at him. His hug closed around me, and I sobbed into his cashmere sweater, which was still lightly dusted in snowflakes.

"What are you doing here?" I mumbled into his chest, my face wet with tears all over again. "I thought you couldn't—"

"Mom said you needed a hug," he told me in a low whisper, "so if my boss asks, I've got cold and flu symptoms and put myself into self-isolation. All right?"

A slightly hysterical laugh bubbled out of me at the absurdity of him flying from South Sudan just to hug me. Then again, my dad was that kind of guy…for me, anyway.

"Stuart, you made it," Mom said from behind me, and I reluctantly let him go.

Dad shot me a wink, then offered Mom a much quicker hug and cheek kiss. "Wouldn't miss it for the world, Cara. Is that gingerbread I smell?"

Mom rolled her eyes but her smile was undeniable. Even Max was grinning, not betraying even a hint of jealousy at having my mom's ex-husband in his home. The three of them seemed...comfortable.

I watched them head through to the kitchen, unable to wipe the smile from my own face even when Nate cleared his throat to pull my attention.

"I should have guessed," I admitted with a small headshake. "Gingerbread is Dad's favorite and Mom hasn't baked it since their divorce."

Nate said nothing back, just gave a small nod. But as I passed him to follow the adults, I could have sworn a small smile touched his lips.

Chapter Two

ASHLEY IS NOT OKAY. SHE'S BLAMING HERSELF FOR WHAT HAPPENED WITH HEATH, AND WE'RE ALL TOO SCARED OF OUR OWN HEADS TO REASSURE HER OTHERWISE. ROYCE WON'T EVEN TAKE MY CALLS, SO I CAN'T ASK HIM FOR HELP. DICK. MAYBE CARTER CAN DEAL WITH HER INSTEAD. I SURE AS FUCK DON'T WANT TO.

N. ESSEX, DECEMBER 24

For the first time in weeks, I slept soundly. After sitting up late chatting with my dad and crying way too much over Heath, I'd finally fallen asleep on the sofa in front of the flickering fireplace. When I woke, I was tucked up in my bed once more and the crisp smell of laundry detergent said my sheets had been changed. Probably Mom.

The sadness was still there, like a permanent mark on my heart, but I could breathe.

Putting myself into the shower seemed easier, knowing both my parents—and Max—were here in the house and there was nothing they couldn't fix. Right?

Christmas music tinkled through the house, and sounds of laughter chimed like bells as I made my way downstairs at a leisurely midmorning time. The kitchen was empty, but I quickly found the three parents in the living room. Mom sat on the floor under the enormous tree, surrounded by what seemed like hundreds of carefully wrapped gifts, and the pure happiness on her face was impossible to ignore.

On the sofa, grinning back at her, both my dad and Max sat side by side. Dad held a steaming mug of something—probably cocoa since he didn't caffeinate—and Max had his arm slung over Dad's shoulders. It was cozy and I hesitated, suddenly questioning whether I was interrupting something.

"Good morning, sweetheart!" Mom sang out, seeing me hovering in the doorway. She scrambled up off the floor and skipped over to hug me warmly. "Merry Christmas, Ash. How'd you sleep?"

"Um, really well," I admitted.

Dad got up from the sofa, kissing me on the cheek, and Max ruffled my hair affectionately. All three of them were...really fucking happy. It was slightly disconcerting, considering the dynamic.

"Good morning, Nathaniel," Dad called out, and I glanced over my shoulder to see a sleepy, scowling Nate running a hand through messy hair. "Thanks for your help getting this one up to her room last night. My back isn't what it used to be."

I blinked my confusion. Did he mean me?

Nate just shrugged and made a vague motion toward the kitchen before disappearing once more.

"Um, I'm going to get some coffee," I murmured, already retreating from the postcard scene in front of me. A heavy yawn rolled through me as I made my way into the kitchen, finding Nate already hovering over the coffee machine like it was his one true love. "You gonna share?"

He shot a sleepy glance my way, then shrugged. Apparently he was nonverbal pre-coffee. I sighed and plucked a piece of fruit off one of the enormous breakfast platters laid out on the counter. If I had to wait him out, I would.

A moment later, he deposited a mug of fresh, hot coffee in front of me.

I blinked at it, confused and wondering if he'd spat in it while he retrieved a bottle of gingerbread syrup and whipped cream and delivered those to me as well. All without a word.

"Thanks," I murmured, unsure what his motivation was.

He shrugged again, turning his back on me as he made his own coffee. *Weird, grumpy asshole.* I sweetened my coffee the way I liked, then added way too much cream before returning to the living room.

Dad was quick to make me a spot beside him on the couch, and Max bellowed for Nate to join us for presents. After a short pause, he emerged from the kitchen once more and took a seat as far from the rest of us as possible. A frown dipped his brow as he eyed the adults in the room, squinting at them.

"Are you all wearing matching pajamas?" he asked with an edge of disdain.

I flicked my gaze back to my mom and dad, then to Max…and sure enough, they all wore different style variations of the same cheery Christmas fabric. Confused, I glanced down at myself and gave a short sigh of relief to see I was not partaking in the crazy.

"Don't mind him," Max said with a grin. "Nate's never been a morning person. Here, Ash, this one is for you." He tossed me a squishy parcel and I caught it one-handed so as to protect my coffee.

"Thanks," I murmured. "Um, I didn't really do much shopping this year…" I'd bought Mom and Max a couple of things weeks ago, but since everything that'd happened with Heath, I just hadn't been able to force myself into shops with all the happy people and joyful music.

"We don't need anything," Mom said with a warm smile. "Having you both here is all we wanted." She reached out for Max's hand as she spoke, and he kissed her knuckles with love overflowing from his eyes.

Practically gagging on the sentimentality of the moment, I handed my coffee to Dad and cautiously opened the present in my lap. Then grimaced.

"Oh. Um. Thanks?" I unfolded the soft Christmas pajama shirt and held it up in stunned disbelief. They really had got us all matching jammies.

Nate made a coughing sound that could have easily been a stifled laugh, and I shot him a glare.

"Don't worry, Son. We have one for you too," Max laughed, tossing a present in his son's direction. Nate caught it, then offered an almost painfully forced smile in return.

I smirked, enjoying the fact that I wasn't being singled out. "Go on, Essex. Open it."

Nate reluctantly did as he was told, forcing another pained smile as he revealed his own set of the gingerbread man jammies.

"Put them on!" Max enthused, smiling wide at the two of us.

I shook my head, suddenly feeling the overwhelming pressure to actually play happy family rather than simply observe it with confusion and disdain. "Um, I'm actually not feeling so great…"

Mom's face instantly creased with concern, and a sharp stab of guilt lit my chest. "Oh, honey, are you still not feeling any better? Did you check for a fever?"

She reached out as if to check my temperature, and I slithered off the sofa and out of reach, practically choking on my own lies. "Yeah, um, I thought I was better but I guess not. I'm just going to step out for some fresh air, if that's okay?"

I made it halfway out of the room before Mom made a confused protest.

"Ash—" she started.

"I'll join you," Nate announced, cutting Mom off and giving me the opportunity I needed to escape. I didn't actually expect him to join me; I assumed he was just using my exit as a convenient excuse to also dip out of the weird Hallmark scene they had going on under the huge tree, so I quickly grabbed a coat and stuffed my feet into a pair of boots.

Throwing open the back door, I inhaled the frosty air deeply, then stepped out onto the snow-covered lawn. My footsteps crunched and squeaked over the snow, and a small smile touched my lips.

"Wait up," Nate called out, and I glanced over my shoulder. He'd just stepped out of the same door I'd used and was hopping on one foot as he tugged a boot onto the other. He'd tossed a coat on, but it was open and his T-shirt had more than a few holes in it. Hardly appropriate for the weather.

I shook my head and continued my crunching across the lawn. "Why?" I replied, unable to hold my tongue or my curiosity.

"I said I was coming with you?" His crunchy steps came quicker than mine, like he was hurrying to catch up.

I rolled my eyes skyward. "I'm aware. I didn't think you—" I broke off with a frustrated huff. "Why are you following? You know full well I'm not sick."

"Aren't you?" he muttered, seemingly under his breath but when I jerked to a stop and glared daggers, he held up his hands in surrender. "Look. I just…don't think you should be alone."

My eyes narrowed. "Like you fucking care."

His brows lifted. "I do. Don't ask me why, I find you utterly infuriating and a stone-cold bitch for playing with my friends' feelings, but for some cursed reason, I actually do care if something happens to you, Ashley."

Bewildered, I just stared back at him for a moment. Then a deep shiver snapped the tension and I shook my head. "Bullshit. You just want to stay in Max's good graces by acting the part of a compassionate big brother." Turning away, I hugged my arms around my body and stomped across the snow-covered lawn, farther away from the house and all the soul-crushing happiness inside.

I didn't deserve to feel happy. Not after how badly I'd failed Heath.

"That statement couldn't be further from the fucking truth," Nate muttered quietly behind me, but I shook it off and continued my determined hike through the snow. After a few moments, he sighed. "Where are we going, Layne?"

"*We* aren't going anywhere. Fuck off." I was being a grouchy shit again, but the farther I got from the house, and away from the snow globe of Christmas magic our parents were desperately trying to create, the worse I felt. The guilt and regret were once more weighing me down and I just…wanted to be alone.

That wasn't true.

I didn't want to be alone—I wanted to be with Heath.

Nate didn't say anything back, but he also didn't go back to the damn house. Short of tossing him over my shoulder and carrying his snarky ass back, there wasn't much I could do other than just ignore him.

So that was what I did all the way to the edge of the small lake at the back of Max's property. It was frozen solid, but I wasn't foolish enough to go wandering out onto the ice, so instead I dusted off the bench seat and sat my depressed ass down.

A moment later, Nate took the space beside me and the two of us sat there in dead silence for what felt like hours. It was probably only a few minutes, though, before cold sunk through my sweatpants and a little shiver set into my skin.

"So…" Nate broke the silence, seemingly totally comfortable despite the rips in his shirt literally exposing his skin to the frigid air. "Do you wanna build a snowman?"

My head swiveled as if I were in the fucking *Exorcist* and I eyed him with bewilderment—and a touch of concern. "Are you on drugs?"

Somehow my question shocked a genuine grin to his pretty lips and he shook his head. "I wish. This would all make a shitload more sense if it was all a fucked-up acid trip, wouldn't it?"

I grunted, hugging my arms tighter. For once, we agreed.

"Have you told Max?" I asked after several more minutes of silence. "About...the fire, I mean?" Obviously Max knew about Heath. Everyone knew. But the shit that happened before? We hadn't discussed it. At all.

Nate heaved a sigh. "No. Have you told Carina?"

A scoff escaped me as I shook my head. "What the hell could I possibly tell her? That your friends are responsible for arson and manslaughter but had no idea what they were doing? That they somehow sleepwalked their way through that whole process and have zero recollection of ever being there? That you nearly—"

"Okay, I get it," he snapped. "Same reason I haven't said anything to my dad. Fuck me, if he knew..." He shook his head with a small groan. "His moral compass is way too true north. He'd make us report it all to the police and put his faith in the justice system. But how the fuck would we ever defend ourselves when we have no clue what even happened?"

I swallowed hard, nodding my understanding, then pulled my knees up to my chest in an attempt to warm myself. "So what do we do now?"

A small huff from Nate made me turn my face back toward him. His brow was deeply furrowed, tension lines bracketing his tight lips. "We? Nothing. You need to stay the fuck away from the rest of us until..." He trailed off again with a shrug.

I arched one brow, waiting for the rest of his statement. Until what? Until someone else committed suicide? Until they were all dead? A thick lump of terror choked me and silenced my protests, but the tears welling in my eyes told him where my mind had gone.

Nate's answering gaze was pure agony.

"I'm sorry, Ashley," he said softly, barely louder than a whisper.

I bit the inside of my lip, desperately trying to hold the water-works at bay. "This isn't fair," I croaked in response. I didn't want to stay away, and I hated the professional security guard that'd turned up at my door that first night I spent back in my dorm. Royce had taken all his things and left a stranger in his place…and I harbored more than a little bitterness toward him for that fact, even though I understood his reasons.

Nate didn't disagree with me. He just hung his head and ran a hand over the back of his neck, like he was at a loss for what to even say. That made two of us.

Distantly, and only because of how incredibly quiet it was sitting there in the snow, I heard a car engine coming closer. Which was weird, because it was Christmas Day and we had no other family.

"Do you hear a car?" I asked, in case I was just imagining shit. Which wasn't outside the realm of possibility, all things considered.

Nate's gaze snapped to mine and he cocked his head to the side, listening. "I do. Are you expecting anyone?"

A bitter laugh bubbled out of me. "Oh sure, one of my dozens of friends are coming to hang out and gossip about our love lives. Oh wait. That's right. My only friend hasn't spoken to me in weeks." Not that I blamed Carly for that fact—she was dealing with a lot. But still, it hurt to be dropped so very quickly.

The car engine came closer still and, a moment later, cut off. Followed by the sound of a car door slamming. With a sigh, I pushed back to my feet. May as well go find out what other insanity our parents had arranged in a valiant attempt to salvage our first Christmas together.

"You're wrong," Nate said quietly as I stalked back across the frozen ground toward the house. "Carly isn't your only friend." He gave me a long look as I glanced over my shoulder, then shifted his gaze away. "Royce is still your friend… He's just scared shitless of hurting you."

There was something weird in the way he said Royce's name, but I shook it off. I could already hear Max's enthusiastic greeting from within the house, and my curiosity got the better of me. I ignored

Nate and stomped back into the house, leaving little blobs of snow on the wooden floor as I kicked off my boots.

"Ash? Nate?" Mom called out. "Is that you? Come in here! Your next present just arrived."

I stifled my groan and made my way toward the foyer, picturing anything from a sports car to a live tiger waiting out front in a giant bow. But neither of those options would have shocked me quite as much as what I found waiting by the front door.

"Merry Christmas, Ash."

Those three words, that voice I'd thought I might never hear again—it damn near killed me. A sob ripped from my chest, and I threw myself forward, no longer in control of my own actions.

Thankfully, he caught me, his strong arms wrapping around me like he was made to hold me.

I sobbed into his chest, now utterly sure I was hallucinating, and he just stroked my hair as he chuckled with a sound so warm, rich, and real. So...Heath.

Chapter Three

Heath looked good. I mean…really good. He looked like he did the day we met, back in Panner City when he inappropriately propositioned me for sex after a massage—calm, confident, rested. If I didn't have the vivid memory of seeing him hanging, lifeless, from a makeshift noose, I'd never guess that, just three weeks ago, he was suicidal.

I couldn't seem to let him go. Even as Carly hugged me, whispering a nonspecific apology, I still clung to his fingers, utterly terrified that if I let go, then he would disappear and this would all turn out to be yet another fucked-up dream sequence. Or delusion.

Sometimes I questioned whether anything was real…or if I was locked in a padded room somewhere, playing out a whole life inside my broken mind.

Heath gave my hand a squeeze, and it snapped me back to the present.

"...staged a jailbreak from the facility using inflatable banana suits..." Carly was saying and I tilted my head to give Heath a confused look.

He just smiled back at me and shook his head. "That was her intended plan but then I explained to her that I wasn't being held against my will and was perfectly capable of discharging myself anytime I wanted."

Carly gave an exasperated sigh. "My plan would have been way more fun. Royce would have rolled with the banana suit."

I flinched slightly at the mention of Royce, and Heath's grip on my hand tightened.

"Are you staying to eat with us?" Mom asked, breaking the awkward tension that'd just settled over us. "We have plenty of food! Almost like Max anticipated we would have extra guests..."

Nate chuckled and clapped Heath on his shoulder. "Dad always expects three extras on all holidays. Good to see you, bro."

Heath's fingers left mine as he returned the dude-hug, and I desperately tried to swallow back the small gasp of fear that I'd see him disappear in a puff of smoke.

"You okay?" Carly asked quietly, bumping my shoulder with hers as Nate led Heath through into the snow-globe living room.

I blinked, frowning as I shook my head. "No. I'm really not."

She just gave a small nod. "I'm sorry I haven't been around. Heath was only allowed limited visitation during his recovery and I'm basically the only family member he doesn't hate."

I had nothing to say to that. On the one hand, that was perfectly understandable and I couldn't hold it against her. If he'd have let me be there, I'd have dropped everything and everyone to give him my total focus. But on the other hand…why Carly? Why not Nate or Carter or Royce? Or me? Why didn't he want me?

At a loss for a reply, I just gave a tight smile and headed through to the living room, where Dad was introducing himself to Heath. Which made me blink twice, because I'd totally forgotten they'd never met. Did Dad know that Heath and I had been sort of dating before he tried to kill himself?

Awkward and uncomfortable, I started toward the single armchair across the room from the enormous sofa, but Heath quickly grabbed my wrist, tugging me to sit on the lounge with him instead.

His fingers intertwined with mine, holding me tight even as he responded to Mom's offer of coffee and brunch with an enthusiastic acceptance. A heavy breath of tension escaped me, my shoulders sagging as I squeezed his hand back, leaning my shoulder into his broad side.

Maybe it wasn't a delusion after all. Or maybe I was just further gone than I realized. Whatever, I'd take whatever I could get at this stage. Just a few weeks ago I thought I'd never hold his hand again…

"I missed you, Ash," Heath whispered, leaning down so his lips brushed my ear while he spoke.

My heart seized and I needed to swallow past the choking emotions before I could croak a weak reply. "I missed you too, Heath." More than I could even put into words.

He brushed a featherlight kiss over my cheek, then gave a small sigh. "We need to talk."

Fuck. Those four words made my heart drop right out of my ass, and a cold chill set into my bones. I couldn't even find the words to respond because it was all I could do not to cry. We need to talk? That was never good.

The doorbell rang but it only dimly registered somewhere in the back of my mind. Whoever it was couldn't be more important than the fact Heath was unquestionably about to break up with me on Christmas Day. Shit, was that even a thing? We weren't dating

19

exclusively. He knew full well Carter and I had—past tense—been involved as well. So maybe he just wanted to say he was also seeing someone else?

That thought made me almost throw up, selfish bitch that I was.

"Oh shit, the whole gang is here!" a familiar voice said, snapping me so hard out of the depression spiral that I almost blacked out.

"Royce?" Stunned didn't even begin to cover how I was feeling. Especially when I glanced past him to the handsome, expensively dressed, and scowling Brit who'd just followed him inside. "Carter? What the—"

"Stew, have you met the rest of my boys?" Max asked my dad, cutting off my stunned question like he hadn't noticed the extreme tension that'd just flooded the room.

Dad crossed the room to greet Royce and Carter with firm handshakes, and I scrubbed a hand over my eyes. Now I was sure I couldn't be delusional because not even my imagination was this wild.

"Um, I'm going to help Mom," I mumbled, slipping my hand out of Heath's and making a lightning-fast retreat out of the living room while avoiding all attempts at eye contact from Carter. Royce hadn't even tried. He hadn't even so much as glanced my way when I said his name.

Mom was busy making coffee and humming a Christmas carol under her breath when I came in, but she turned a bright smile my way as I grabbed a water glass. "Everything okay, hon?" she asked with a touch of concern. "Are you still feeling unwell?"

I jerked a sharp nod, filling my glass with ice water from the fridge dispenser. "Yeah. Not great. Did you, um, did you know all the boys were coming today?"

She arched a brow. "Heath and Carly, yes. Carly called me a couple of days ago to suggest it. Are Royce and Carter here too?"

I hummed my affirmation as I sipped my water. Carly wandered into the kitchen a moment later, giving me a long look before asking Mom if she needed help with anything.

"I might just go lie down for a bit," I murmured, thinking that surely no one would notice if I slipped away for a bit. I just... Christ, my head was a mess. All I'd wanted for weeks was to see Heath alive and well, to get the whole gang back together and have everything go back to normal. But now they were here and the tension was fucking suffocating.

I'd rather be alone.

Before I could escape the kitchen, Carly physically blocked the exit with her arms crossed and a frown marring her brow. "Ash. Quit it."

My eyes narrowed as my temper flared. "Quit what? I have a cold, so I'm not feeling well."

Carly rolled her eyes. "You do not, you big liar. Snap out of the sads, girlfriend. Heath needs this today. Okay? He needs us all together and acting like nothing happened. He needs normal right now, and more than anything else on this whole damn planet he needs you. So turn that frown upside down and help me carry those platters through for brunch. By the look of things, Max was expecting the big eaters to show up."

Stunned, I just stared at her, mouth open and eyes wide like a fish.

She sighed and smoothed a hand over her ponytail. "And I know I've been a shitty friend lately, which I really am sorry about. Between Heath and exams—which I did horribly on, by the way—I just kept failing to text back. I'm sorry."

I wet my lips, shaking my head a little. "And you blamed me... didn't you? That's what you said, at the hospital that night. That it was my—"

"I didn't mean it," she whispered with heartfelt regret. "I was scared and angry and...I lashed out. Ash, you know I never actually blamed you. If anyone was responsible, it was the three guys who literally lived with him...not you."

She'd already left me a choked-up voicemail the day after making

21

those accusations, apologizing for her words, but it still stung. And I was pretty sure that had contributed to her ghosting me ever since.

"Should I…maybe give you two some space?" Mom asked with an uncomfortable smile. "I can leave…"

I shook my head, my lips tight. "No. It's fine." Because despite the hurt, Carly had a point. Heath needed this…so I would suck it up and pull on my big-girl panties. Biting my cheek, I turned back to the enormous array of food and picked up a platter.

"Ash…" Carly groaned. "Don't—"

"It's fine," I snapped back. "We're fine. Okay?" I met her gaze, glaring hard and begging her silently to just let it the fuck go. We would be fine…eventually. But right now, things were raw and sensitive. The best I could do was exactly what she asked: not running away when Heath needed normal.

Returning to the living room with the platter of pastries, I busied myself setting up the huge low coffee table for everyone to graze at their leisure, while Max handed all the boys gifts from under the tree. He'd definitely known they'd all show up sooner or later.

"If they don't all get the matching pajamas," Nate muttered quietly as he appeared beside me with a fresh coffee in hand, "I'll start a riot."

I snorted a laugh despite my mood and shook my head. "If they try to make us wear them for a group photo, I'll start a riot. Did you know our dads were friends?"

Nate shook his head. "Nope. I'm just as weirded out as you." He held out the coffee. "This is yours. You look like you need it."

He returned to the lounge to chat shit with Carter while I sipped the coffee. Surprisingly, he'd already sweetened it, but he'd used what tasted like butterscotch schnapps, rather than my usual syrups.

Fuck it. He was right. The very faint buzz from my spiked coffee helped me relax enough to paste on a smile and rejoin the sofa as everyone ripped into gifts and snacked on the brunch platters. Heath pulled me back into sitting at his side, confusing the fuck

22

out of me, but I didn't pull away when his arm draped around my shoulders.

When I put my empty mug down at some stage, Nate just wordlessly collected it and disappeared back to the kitchen. Five minutes later I found myself warming my hands on a fresh—spiked—coffee and my smile came more easily.

Was it a healthy coping mechanism? Fuck no. But I made a mental note to finally book a therapy session for the new year and took another sip of my drink.

Chapter Four

WHY AM I BEING SO FUCKING NICE TO ASHLEY? SHE IS CLEARLY WEIRDED OUT BY IT, AND SO AM I. AND YET...I FEEL KIND OF SORRY FOR HER. SHE SO OBVIOUSLY BELIEVES MY FRIENDS CARE ABOUT HER, AS MORE THAN JUST MY INCONVENIENT NEW FAMILY MEMBER, BUT SHE'S WRONG. WE'VE ALREADY DISCUSSED IT. ASHLEY NEEDS TO GO, AND THAT'S THE ONLY OPTION...SO WHY DO I HAVE THIS SLIMY FEELING IN MY GUT?

N. ESSEX, DECEMBER 25

It took some time—and several coffees—but I eventually relaxed enough to enjoy the day with my friends and family. The parents seemed determined to make it a perfect day, and I had to guess they also understood how much Heath needed it. The food was incredible—Max was a great cook—and during dessert, Dad whipped up a batch of his peppermint martinis that somehow ended up with Carly and me both drunkenly sobbing in the bathroom as we apologized to each other for being crappy friends.

Wisely, we both then opted for a little nap to sober up, and when we woke a few hours later, the house was much quieter. I gave Carly my fluffy robe to wear, then wrapped myself up in a blanket to head back downstairs. The snow had started falling again outside, and the fireplace crackled in the living room.

The four guys were all sprawled out on the sofas, awake but silent. Just…existing.

"Hey there, sad elves," Heath greeted us with a slow grin spreading across his lips. "You two get all the emotions out?"

"Along with half a swimming pool worth of tears," Nate murmured with the ghost of a smile. *Prick.*

Carly snorted. "Don't be jealous that girls can talk out our differences and move on from them like mature adults. No fist fights necessary."

"Just a bit of vomit in the shower," I added with a wince. "It's cool, though. I cleaned it up."

Heath laughed and it was possibly my favorite sound in the whole world. I stepped over Royce's legs propped up on the coffee table and took the vacant spot at Heath's side, snuggling in.

"Where are the parents?" Carly asked, flopping down into an armchair, then groaning. "Ew, I think I'm hungover already."

Carter tossed her a bag of corn chips. "Eat something. They went out to that party Max mentioned, told us not to wait up."

"Are the three of them—" Royce started to ask, but both Nate and I cut him off with a sound of protest in unison.

I shook my head, grimacing. "We don't know. We don't *want* to know. Gross."

"Agreed," Nate grunted.

Royce snickered. "I'm just saying, Carina was all kinds of dolled up and—"

Nate threw a cushion, hitting Royce square in the face to shut him up. Thank fuck for that too. I desperately didn't want to picture my mom as the meat in a fifty-something-year-old sandwich.

"How are you feeling?" Heath asked me in a low voice, his arm draped comfortably over my shoulders as I rested against his side. "Do you need some water?"

"Or aspirin?" Carter added, smirking from his relaxed position perpendicular to us.

Pouting slightly—because I really didn't feel so great—I shook my head. "I'm fine. I never realized how strong my dad's peppermint martinis were, though."

"Probably has something to do with them being almost entirely vodka," Heath mused. "Anyway, it's good you're here now and sober…ish. We need to talk about some serious shit before your parents get back."

Fuck. Inhaling sharply, I sat up straighter. "Um…" Was this when he told me we were done? Or that he couldn't stomach sharing me with Carter? Not that that had turned into anything, since both Carter and Royce had ghosted me even harder than Carly had.

Heath wet his lips, running a hand through his hair, messing it up in such a sexy way. "This is hard to say but…" He paused and I held my breath, bracing to have my heart broken. "…what do you guys know about hypnosis?"

Huh?

"Hypnosis?" Royce repeated thoughtfully. "Like…when I snap my fingers, you'll act like a chicken?"

Heath chuckled. "Yeah, something like that."

Hypnosis? Oh. Oh. The serious talk wasn't about our love life, and holy shit, I was officially the most self-centered bitch on earth. Here's Heath, having just survived a suicide attempt and subsequent rehab, wanting to talk about the very scary shit that went down at Nevaeh…and I was fixating on whether he liked me or not.

Wow.

"You okay, Spark?" Carter asked quietly as Royce responded to Heath with an anecdote about someone he knew who used hypnosis to quit smoking.

I bit my cheek, trying to quell my embarrassment as I nodded. "Yeah, fine. Just…hungover, I think."

He gave me a sympathetic smile, then pushed to his feet with a stretch and groan. "I'm grabbing a drink. Anyone want anything?"

"A lobotomy," Carly moaned from the fetal position she'd curled into on the armchair.

Royce grinned. "Carly wants another peppermint martini. I'll take another beer."

Carter left the room and Heath cleared his throat. "So…I take it no one really knows much about hypnosis then?" He glanced around at everyone, including me. I shrugged my response and he gave a thoughtful hum. "Yeah, me neither."

"So why ask?" Nate sat forward in his seat, elbows on his knees. "Do you think…?"

Heath wet his lips again, seeming more nervous than I'd seen him…maybe ever? "Don't you? Look, it sounds farfetched and a bit fucking sci-fi, but one of the other guests at Sunshine Valley Center suggested it as a possibility, and I have to admit, it sounds plausible. I've done a little bit of research and I think maybe this needs investigating."

"By guest you mean inmate, yeah?" Royce teased.

Heath scoffed. "It's not a prison. Patient, if you must be clinical about it. Yeah, look, it wasn't any of the doctors that suggested it, and when I mentioned the possibility in therapy it was kind of brushed aside as borderline fictional. But…they also haven't given me any better explanations."

Carter returned from the kitchen, handing out beers to all the boys even though only Royce had asked for one. To me, he passed a can of ginger beer and a packet of salty crackers.

"Thanks," I murmured, sitting up a little straighter so as not to spill all over Heath. My head hurt for sure, but I was a million times better off than Carly. Just remembering the mess she'd made in the shower made me wince.

27

"You know anything about hypnosis, Carter?" Royce asked, slouching back with his fresh beer.

Carter gave a small shrug, sitting back down. "Nope."

"Look, right now it's the best explanation as far as I'm concerned," Heath said with an edge of frustration. "It makes a shitload more sense than whatever the fuck the Sunshine Valley therapists think is going on."

That caused a barb of worry to tighten in my chest. "What do they think?"

Heath glanced at me, then sighed. "Something about sleep psychosis and poor impulse control."

My nose wrinkled. "How do they explain multiple people having the same sleep psychosis at the same time?"

He ran a hand over his face with a groan. "They can't because I didn't tell them about the fire. It was bad enough, convincing them that I wasn't going to try to kill myself again without admitting that my friends and I are responsible for a man's death."

"And that none of us have any recollection of even being there," Carter added with a grimace. "Good thinking."

For some reason, my gaze shot to Nate, and I caught him staring back at me with his brow furrowed in concern. We were the only witnesses to the fire, and it'd taken a lot to convince Royce and Carter that they had, in fact, been responsible for the arson.

"What did you tell them, then?" Nate asked, echoing my own thoughts.

Heath took a sip of his beer, clearly sorting through his thoughts. "As much as I could without being put back into involuntary admission. That I'd been having increasingly violent dreams and waking up with unexplained scrapes and bruises…that I couldn't shake the feeling I'd been involved in something bad and that I was scared I'd end up hurting someone I really care about."

His hand shifted to the back of my neck as he spoke, and his fingers flexed ever so slightly at the end of his statement. He was scared of hurting me. I leaned into him, trying to silently remind him that I was fine.

"Okay, so that's why they're dismissing your hypnosis idea, I guess…" Nate mused aloud, his fingertips drumming his knee thoughtfully. "And they've just drawn the logical conclusion that you decided it was safer to…you know…"

"Kill yourself," Royce filled in when Nate floundered. "You decided it was safer to kill yourself, so you didn't risk killing Ashley."

Fuck. The tension in the room was so thick, you could cut it with a knife, and when a log on the fireplace popped, Carly gave a little scream.

Heath gusted out a sigh, running his hand over his hair even as his fingers flexed on my nape.

"Okay, Royce, a little tact goes a long way," I said, sitting forward to put my drink and snacks down. "There's no need for snark."

Royce swung his gaze to meet mine for the first fucking time all day, and I sucked in a breath at the anger simmering beneath the surface of his gray eyes. "Ashley, *tactfully*, this isn't about you. It's about our best friend and why the fuck he thought suicide was a better choice than asking us for help. Why he thought we were so useless, we couldn't possibly get him help when—"

"Enough!" Heath barked. "Royce…don't fucking speak to her like that. This wasn't about Ash. Not entirely, anyway. And if we're out here pointing fingers and casting blame, you all knew I was sleepwalking. It's why you insisted on staying as Ashley's roomie for so long and didn't let me stay over. So don't act like this is all such a shock."

Holy fuck. The conversation was going downhill real fast, and somehow, I was at the center of it again.

That's when Carly started laughing—just a little giggle that turned into more of a chuckle as she tried to stifle the sound. "Sorry," she chortled. "Sorry, it's not funny. It's not. I swear, this is a very serious subject, but you know you're wrong, right?"

29

"Wrong about what?" Heath asked, since she was speaking to him. She shrugged, flicking a quick glance at me. "That's not the reason Roycey wouldn't let you stay over."

"Okay, thank you, Carly," Royce drawled, rolling his eyes. "Sounds like you're still under the influence of peppermint martinis. Let's stay on topic, yeah?"

"Hypnosis could explain why none of us were aware of our actions," Carter said thoughtfully, not having paid much attention to the friction flaring in the room. His phone was in hand, and he'd been scrolling something. "The thing is, we don't really have any symptoms or even hard evidence to put against it. Only the fire, but if you guys hadn't physically seen us there…would we have ever known?"

Heath nodded firmly. "Exactly. So, doesn't that beg the question of what else we've been responsible for? If no one saw anything, then how the fuck would we know? I have a horrible feeling I was there in the forest with Ash that day she got kidnapped. I just… It might be overactive imagination like my therapist says but someone dumped her out there. What if it was me?"

A cold chill ran down my back. I'd blamed Nate at the time, but things were different now. I didn't believe he wanted to hurt me like that. Not consciously, anyway.

"I think it's something we need to look into," Carter agreed. "But now that Royce has brought the subject up with all the grace of a bull doing ballet, how are you doing? Are you going back to the rehab center after the holidays?"

It was a good question. Regardless of the reasons…Heath had still tried to kill himself.

"No," he replied after a beat, "I'm okay now…I think. Honestly, I'm having a really hard time understanding my own reasoning for what I did. It's all just murky in my memory."

"That'd be the brain damage thanks to lack of oxygen," Royce muttered.

Irritation flared in my chest. "Royce, shut the fuck up." I glowered at him, and he glared back. Apparently, his shit attitude extended to me as well as Heath.

"Ignore him," Nate advised. "He's just masking his emotions with dickishness. We were all really worried about you, bro."

Heath shifted in his seat, his hand moving to the curve of my waist like he was having a hard time letting me go. "I was worried about me too, to be fair. When I woke up in that hospital room and they told me what I'd done..." He blew out a long breath, shaking his head. "I can't explain it. I really can't. But I don't want to try it again, if that's what you're worried about."

"It is," Royce snapped.

Nate threw a cushion, smacking Royce in the side of the head and knocking his beer out of his hand. "Shut up."

"Look, it's a valid concern," Heath said with a shrug. "I don't know what pushed me to that point so I can't sit here and say with a hundred percent certainty that it won't happen again. I don't know what else to say... Do you want me to go back to rehab where I'm being monitored?" That question was aimed at Royce, who looked like he was genuinely considering it.

Carter thankfully seemed to be the voice of reason, though. "Of course not," he replied firmly. "But would you be okay if we just keep you from being alone for the time being? Until we can do more research on the whole hypnosis thing?"

I hated to admit but...he was talking sense. Maybe it wasn't just for Heath's sake, but for all of us, to alleviate worries.

"Good thing he already has someone to share a bed with tonight then, huh?" Carly drawled with a suggestive grin my way.

Royce scoffed a bitter laugh. "Yeah, because Ashley kept such a close eye on him last time. No. Heath, you're bunking with me tonight."

Ouch. I guess Carly wasn't the only one who'd blamed me after all.

"At least now I know why you've ghosted me these last three weeks," I muttered, cheeks flaming with anger and embarrassment. Royce heard me, despite how quietly I'd said it, and his sharp gaze speared me as effectively as a javelin.

Carly hummed a thoughtful sound, pretending not to notice the tension. "Technically, if Heath had been with anyone else, the night could have ended a lot worse. Nate, didn't you say it was Ash calling your phone over and over that woke you up? Or...broke the trance or whatever?"

Nate nodded, then stood up. "Right. There's only one solution for this, then." He exited the living room, leaving the rest of us confused as fuck in his wake.

"Uhhh...anyone else feel like he finished that conversation in his head?" Royce asked, showing the briefest flash of the Royce I thought I knew. The fun one. The one who didn't look at me like I was the devil incarnate.

We didn't wait long before Nate reappeared with a huge armful of neatly folded linen. "Royce, quit being a dickhead and go get pillows. We're all sleeping down here tonight."

Speechless. Nate had officially rendered me speechless because it was a solution I'd never have thought of. So I silently got up and went to fetch all the pillows and blankets out of my own room to help set up our sleepover.

Everyone pitched in with moving furniture around and dragging mattresses out of guest rooms, and within half an hour, we'd become thoroughly carried away and set up a whole blanket fort to sleep in.

It was well past midnight by the time we all settled down—me snuggled into Heath's arms—with the twinkling lights of the tree acting as a night-light. Somehow, it was the perfect end to what'd turned into a pretty magical Christmas day.

Chapter Five

THE DEVIL'S BACKBONE SOCIETY WANTS TO EXPEL HEATH. THEY'RE CLAIMING THAT ATTEMPTED SUICIDE GOES AGAINST THE REPUTATION AND ETHOS OF THE SOCIETY AND THAT HIS TREATMENT IN THE MENTAL HEALTH FACILITY CASTS A STAIN ON THE SOCIETY. I NEED TO FIX THIS SOMEHOW, WITHOUT SOUNDING COMPLETELY INSANE MYSELF.

N. ESSEX, DECEMBER 27

For two days, we all camped out in the living room, eating snacks and watching movies inside the enormous blanket fort, which only grew more grand once Max and my dad saw it the next morning. It was peaceful and cozy—and never going to last.

After those two amazing days, the blanket fort was packed away.

"So what happens when we head back to campus next week?" Carly asked as we folded the last of the sheets. "Are you coming back, Heath?"

He nodded, seeming more relaxed and comfortable in his skin than I think I'd ever seen him. "For sure."

"We are installing some new security features at the apartment," Carter added, watching Heath warily. "Just alarms and shit to alert us if anyone sleepwalks."

It was a smart idea, but I was dubious as to whether it'd work. If all of them were under the same hypnosis, like they had been the night of the science hall fire, then would an alarm be enough to snap them out of it? I wasn't so sure. But I also had no better suggestions.

Anxiety clawed at me as the guys all packed their bags to leave, words sticking in my throat. I wanted to know if things would change or if we'd go back to how it was. Would Royce still ignore me? Would I have a stranger parked outside my room as security? Or had we decided I was no longer in any danger from the Devil's Backbone Society and therefore permitted to resume normal college-dorm living?

I wanted to ask. But I was too scared to hear the answer, so I bit my tongue as Mom hugged everyone and they left the house. To my surprise, Nate also left with the guys, but I didn't realize until after they were gone.

"He has some society business to take care of," Max told me quietly when I asked. "Making sure Heath can keep his place without participating for a while."

I frowned, staring out at the empty, snow-covered driveway. "Why would he even want to stay in the society? What's the point? Surely, they can do dumb rich-kid shit without the cloaks and masks?"

Max sighed. "That's not what the DBS is all about, Ash. I know it might seem like it, with all the parties and silly pranks—nice work on the duck game by the way—but it's about more than that. Former DBs make up some of the world's most powerful and influential leaders and for any college students with aspirations of grandeur, they can't afford to be cast out." He shrugged, like it was just the facts of life. "Anyway. What are you going to do with the rest of your day? Your dad suggested maybe ice skating on the lake?"

I frowned, confused by his explanation. Did Heath have aspirations of grandeur? I wouldn't have thought so but then again, maybe I didn't know him all that well. I didn't really know any of them that well.

"Um, yeah, that sounds nice. Dad used to take me skating every Christmas when I was little." Then I paused and offered Max a lopsided smile. "You can join us if you want?"

The smile that he sent back was full of warmth. "That's nice of you to offer, Ash, but I'm a hopeless skater. No, you spend some time with Stew before he has to fly out. I'll take Carina shopping, since I know she loves the chaos of sales days."

She really did. My mom was an odd breed, genuinely enjoying the bedlam of a big sale in a department store. She used to drag me out of bed early on Black Friday just to experience the mayhem, not even to buy anything.

I tried my best to push the anxiety of the secret society, the guys' distance, and Heath's mental health all aside to focus on my dad. He needed to fly back to South Sudan soon, and I didn't know when I'd next see him.

For the rest of the day, we skated—thanks to the new ice skates I'd just got for Christmas—and baked more gingerbread cookies, then ate them all before they'd even cooled. We did all the things we used to do when I was little—before his work took him away for so long and before Mom decided it was easier without him around.

"Can I ask you a question?" I finally plucked up the courage as we cleaned up our baking mess that evening.

"Of course you can, sweetheart. What's on your mind?"

I avoided eye contact, focusing on drying the mixing bowl he'd just washed. "What's going on with you, Mom, and Max? Do you guys…have history?"

My dad gave a startled laugh, grabbing a dish towel to dry his hands. "Well…if I may answer your question with another question: What's going on with you, Heath, and Carter?"

My face flamed. Carter had kept a respectful distance the whole time he'd been here, but he'd taken every opportunity to eye-fuck me and make suggestive comments when he thought no one was listening. Apparently he was wrong because my dad had sure as fuck noticed.

I cleared my throat. "Touché. Let's leave it at that."

Dad laughed, tossing his head back. "Good choice, kiddo. Let's leave it at that. Now, are we making popcorn and watching one last Christmas movie before I go?"

"Only if it's *The Grinch*," I replied, heading for the pantry to grab some microwave popcorn.

"Nothing less!" Dad replied.

When Mom and Max came home a little later, she complained about our choice of movie—the Whoville Whos gave her the creeps—but they both joined us nonetheless.

Weirdly…I was a little sad that Nate hadn't returned. Which was extra odd because he drove me fucking insane most days and was downright unpleasant on the rest. But it felt a little empty without him lurking around like a scowling house cat.

Saying goodbye to Dad before dawn the next morning was hard. Just as Max and Mom drove away to drop Dad at the airport, Nate's truck passed them at the gates on his way back in.

I waited, my arms folded around myself in the frosty predawn air.

"What?" Nate asked as he slammed his door and glared up at me standing in the doorway.

I bit back the urge to toss insults, because I genuinely wanted answers and it was Nate's style to withhold information if he was riled up. "Is everything okay?" I asked instead, keeping my tone civil.

He quirked a brow as he drew closer. "Okay with what?"

I rolled my eyes, already irritated. "With the society shit. Max said—"

"Max shouldn't have said anything," he snapped back, towering over me and causing me to tip my head back to hold eye contact. He gave a small frown. "Have you always been this short?"

36

I was just in socks, having gotten out of bed to say farewell to my dad, but I didn't exactly wear heels every day. "I'm not short, you ass. I'm average height." According to Google, five foot three was perfectly average, but when Nate was a whole foot taller…yeah, it did feel pretty short.

"You're short as fuck, Ashley. And you're freezing. Go inside, idiot." He said it with a scowl, but his voice lacked any real harshness.

I tilted my chin back farther, holding his gaze defiantly as I stood my ground. "I'm fine. Did you fix things for Heath? Are they kicking him out?"

Nate's brows rose. "Wow, my dad really got chatty. Society business only concerns society members. Which you, Layne, are not. Now are you letting me inside, or do I need to know the secret password?"

Amusement sparked in my chest against my better judgment. "Yes."

"Yes?" he repeated, confused.

"Yes, you need to know the secret password. Or you can tell me what happened with the society instead?" I shifted my weight because I really was shivering but also determined to block him from passing until I got the answers I wanted.

He scoffed a short laugh, running his hand over the dark scruff of his jaw. Then instead of just telling me what'd happened—like a rational human being—he grabbed my waist and lifted me clear off the ground.

A startled squeak escaped me, and I instinctively gripped his biceps for balance as he took several steps forward into the foyer of the house, kicking the door shut behind himself.

"Short and light. Makes for a shitty gatekeeper, Layne." He put me down on the marble floor and tugged off his leather jacket. "Are you going back to bed or do you want coffee?"

My jaw was basically on the floor as he hung his jacket on a hook and kicked his boots off.

37

"Since when are we making each other coffee?" I spluttered as he swaggered through to the kitchen with me trailing behind.

"If you don't want one, just say so."

Dickhead. "I do want one. I'm just confused."

"And short," he added under his breath but still loud enough that I heard him. "Don't read too much into it, Layne. I'm making coffee for myself so it's not a big deal to make you one too."

I mean, sure, that was logical, and if it were anyone else, I wouldn't be questioning their motives quite so much. But given the general animosity between us, I was now second-guessing all the coffee he'd made me in the last few days. Was he spitting in it?

"Are you going to tell me anything about the society stuff?" I asked instead, refocusing on the important.

Nate shook his head while concentrating on the coffee machine. "Nope. It's need-to-know only, and you, reckless shithead, do not need to know. Caramel or chocolate syrup?"

"Rude," I grumbled. "Caramel, please."

He went about making our drinks, and I leaned against the counter while trying to think of another tactic to get information.

"Why do you all want to be in the Devil's Backbone Society anyway?" I asked, attempting a roundabout approach. "Do you have delusions—I mean, aspirations of grandeur in your future? Politics or something?"

Nate scoffed. "You reckon I'd make a good politician, Layne? I'm weirdly offended. And I'm not talking about the DBs with you."

I rolled my eyes. "Why? Because I didn't want to do all your dumb initiation games? I still did the duck thing, didn't I? So aren't I technically part of the cult too?"

Nate sighed. "Yes. Against my better judgment, technically you are. But you're nowhere near the level that grants you the information you're fishing for, so just quit it. Heath will be fine—we'd never let anything bad happen to him." As soon as those words left Nate's mouth, he stiffened and his expression tightened, clearly thinking how his friend had nearly died recently.

"You didn't let that happen, Nate, and you couldn't have done much to stop it," I said softly, recognizing the guilt etched across his face. "But that whole thing is why I want to know what—"

"On the contrary, Layne, that whole thing is exactly why you should have nothing to do with this." He slid my coffee across the counter to me, then picked up his own. "Heath's choice to attempt suicide was strongly tied to his feelings of guilt and fear of hurting someone. You. He was scared he'd end up hurting you, Ashley. So bear that in mind when we return to campus. Maybe Heath would be a lot happier and safer if you weren't around."

Surprise and confusion stilled my tongue. Was he blaming me? Or warning me of something?

"Food for thought," he muttered, then took his coffee and headed into the living room. A moment later, the sound of the PlayStation booting up echoed through the house and I retreated to my bedroom to think about what he'd said.

Maybe I did need to consider keeping my distance…for Heath.

Chapter Six

Reality TV was my best friend. I couldn't have told anyone what exactly happened in the shows I spent the days after Christmas watching; all I knew was that I couldn't stop. When the TV asked if I was still watching, I took great offense. Of course I was! I needed to know what the pretty Mormon moms would do in Vegas, dammit.

"What are you doing?" Mom exclaimed, startling me as she turned off the TV, plunging the living room into darkness.

Confused, I sat up from my couch nest. "Mom, what the—"

"Do not finish that out loud, Ashley Layne," she scolded, flicking on the bright overhead lights. "Why are you still here on the sofa in your dirty jammies? We leave in twenty minutes!"

"Huh?" I rubbed my gritty eyes. "Leave for what?"

The look on her face should have been enough to snap me back into action, but I was way too groggy from my TV binge. "Ashley. It's New Year's Eve and we are going to a party at the Covington Hotel. Get up. Shower. Get dressed. Now!"

I exhaled heavily with relief. "Oh, that. I told you yesterday, I don't want to go."

"Same," Nate agreed, dropping onto the couch beside me and grabbing my half-eaten bowl of popcorn. "I told Royce I'd battle him in *Call of Duty* tonight while the servers are quiet."

Mom's eye twitched and I stiffened up. We were in trouble. Big trouble.

"Nathaniel Essex, Ashley Layne, I was not asking you if you wanted to come to this party, I was telling. You do not have a choice. Sometimes, I understand we don't always want to do the things our parents ask us to do and that it's frustrating." Her tone had mellowed into a sickly sweet…gentle parenting voice. I shuddered. "So we're going to take those messy, angry feelings, and do you know what we're going to do with them? Hmm?"

I swallowed, glancing at Nate.

He winced, his jaw tight. "Whisper them to our hand and hold on to them for later?" he guessed with a growl underscoring his words.

Mom smiled, fluttering her lashes. "That's right! Good boy, Nate. Now off you skip, shower first, then get dressed. Max and I will be waiting with the car out front in half an hour. Chop, chop!"

Her glare hardened when she shifted attention back to me. "You too, missy. Move it." No sunnily sarcastic gentle voice for me. Rude.

I sighed but accepted defeat as I hauled my ass up from the couch. "I don't have anything to wear," I grumbled in a weak final argument, already heading for the stairs to do as I was told.

"I bought you a dress and left it in your closet," Mom called after me. "Matching shoes too. Hurry up!"

I groaned as I dragged my feet up the stairs, and Nate glared as he passed me with those long legs of his.

"Your mom is a psychopath," he muttered.

I snorted a laugh and nodded. "Yep." But I loved her anyway.

A quick sniff of myself verified why Mom had specifically mentioned showering several times, and a glance in the mirror told me a simple freshen up wasn't enough. I needed to wash my hair to detangle the bird's nest I'd somehow grown. Shit. No way would half an hour be enough to get party ready but Mom would have known that.

Resigned to my task, I scuffed my feet into my bathroom. I kept my actual shower as quick as possible, even with the need to shampoo and condition. It was blow drying and styling that took the bulk of my time because my hair was long and thick.

Even so, I did my best to haul ass and slapped on my makeup as fast as humanly possible while my curls cooled.

"Ashley!" Mom called up the stairs when I emerged from my bathroom a solid forty-five minutes after her thirty-minute warning.

"Five minutes!" I yelled back, spotting the white garment bag draped over the end of my bed with a shoebox beside it. The designer name—Portia Levigne—seemed familiar but I couldn't place why.

Inside the garment bag, I found a gorgeous bloodred, beaded cocktail dress with drop shoulders and a flirty skirt. It fit beautifully, like it was made to measure, despite the fact it had to have been off the rack for Mom to have picked it up today.

"Pretty," I whispered, running my hands over the bodice as I inspected my reflection in the mirror. Turning back to the bed to grab the matching shoes, I paused. A tiny little resin duck sat on top of the shoebox and I picked it up between my fingertips to take a closer look.

"Where the fuck did you come from?" I murmured, frowning like I expected the little red duck to reply. Then Mom yelled my name again and I jolted back into action. *Shoes first, ponder ducks later.*

A quick knock on my door made me roll my eyes as I fiddled with the delicate buckles on the red satin heels.

"Patience is a virtue, Mother!" I snapped in frustration.

"Just me," Nate replied as he pushed open my door. "Are you—" He broke off abruptly and I looked up at him in irritation.

"What?" I barked, sweeping my hair back from my face. "I'm nearly ready—tell Mom to chill the fuck out."

His brow arched, then he gave a small headshake. "I'd rather wax my own balls than tell your mom to chill the fuck out. Need help?" He gestured to the fiddly, little buckles I was trying and failing to fasten around my ankles.

My frustration gusted out in a huge sigh. "Yes. I do."

I expected some kind of snarky response to that, where he told me tough luck or something and left me to fend for myself…but he didn't. Instead, he silently crossed the room and knelt in front of me, taking one foot into his lap.

"What are you doing?" I asked, my voice coming out in a breathy whisper for some stupid reason.

He said nothing, just deftly threaded the strap into the delicate clasp and fastened it. Then he shifted to my other shoe to do the same before looking up at me with a shuttered expression.

"You need to lose the necklace," he finally said, his tone oddly dark. "Earrings are enough." Then he straightened up and brushed his hands down his suit pants. "I'll tell Carina you're almost ready."

Words failed me as I watched him slip out of my room once more, and I blinked like an owl for a solid moment. What the fuck was that all about?

Confused and off balance, I stood up and crossed back to the full-length mirror leaning against my wall. Grasping my necklace in one hand, I shifted it off my chest and squinted at my reflection, then cursed and took it off entirely. Nate was right—the dress was more striking without the distraction of a necklace.

With a sigh, I returned the necklace to my jewelry box in the bathroom and grabbed a clutch purse for my lipstick. Then I hesitated and scowled at my reflection before quickly swapping my peachy nude lipstick for a deep scarlet to match the dress.

43

At the last moment—and for no discernable reason—I tossed the little red duck in my purse before heading downstairs to the waiting limo.

"Ashley, you look stunning," Max gushed as he held the car door open for me.

I grinned, feeling a hell of a lot more put together than I had an hour ago in my sweaty jammies. "Thanks, Max. You scrub up all right yourself."

Nate was already seated in the back and handed me a glass of champagne when I settled into the seat beside him. "We can dip out early," he said quietly, clearly not wanting Mom to hear him. "Just make an appearance and pay lip service to the Covingtons."

Surprise had my eyes widening. "I thought it was just at their hotel?"

Max overheard that as he settled in the seat beside Mom and the car started to roll down our snow-lined driveway. He spent the next little while explaining the relationship between his company and the major international hotel chain family.

I'd have been lying if I'd said I listened to everything, but I smiled and nodded as I sipped my champagne and otherwise just relaxed for the rest of the drive into Prosper City.

The presence of actual paparazzi outside the hotel when we pulled up was a surprise, but given the guest list Max had mentioned, it made sense. There were actual celebrities, A-list movie star guys like Brodie Keller and Steven Harrison attending. It was basically the Met Gala on New Year's in snow-covered Prosper City. Wild.

I hung back as Max smiled, waved, and greeted dozens of people on our way into the hotel, introducing them all to his beautiful bride as Mom blushed and laughed.

"This is full-on," I admitted under my breath when Nate offered to take my coat as we paused at the cloakroom. "I'm surprised the guys aren't here. Isn't Heath's dad some big-deal rock star?"

"That's his uncle, Zeth, and his cousin…also called Zeth. Older

Zeth did a lot of drugs." He handed over our coats to the attendant and took the claim ticket in exchange. "Also his family sort of figured a party like this wasn't the best environment for him right now."

I rolled my eyes. "He didn't overdose or anything. It was... depression, I guess?"

Nate shrugged. "Rehab's rehab as far as tabloids are concerned."

Max and Mom handed over their own coats, then gestured for us to follow them through to the impressive ballroom of the six-star hotel. I marveled at the impressively high ceilings, then grinned when I eyed the huge crystal chandelier in the center of the room.

"Are you thinking what I'm thinking, Spark?"

The words were whispered directly into my ear, and I couldn't help the grin that spread over my face. His hands circled my waist even as I spun around to get a better look.

"Carter Bassington Junior...what are you doing here?" But fucking hell, I was happy he was.

His dark brows lifted. "You didn't know I was coming? But you wore my dress..." His gaze dropped lower and one of his hands traced the beaded neckline. "And it looks even better on you than I could have imagined."

My jaw dropped for a moment, then I laughed. "The duck. I should have known."

"You really should have," he agreed, a sexy smile playing across his lips. "When Nate mentioned your mom might make you attend this party, I knew I had to show up. No way was I leaving these lips unkissed at midnight."

Just as Carter dipped to brush a kiss on my mouth, someone called out his name, and I groaned my frustration.

"Later, Spark," he promised with a smirk, then released me to respond to the guy.

With a sigh, I accepted a glass of champagne from a passing waitress, then drifted over to where Mom was raiding a canapé table. She shot me a wink, then handed over a mini tart.

"Try these," she mumbled around her mouthful. "They're kale but actually taste good. Trust me."

Trust me. Fucking hell, my mom knew me better than I knew myself some days. Trust me, she said, and she very rarely ever let me down. So I ate the kale tartlet and loved it, just like I loved the fact she'd forced me to come to this opulent party instead of staying on the couch.

"Love you, Mom," I mumbled as she handed me some other tiny food to sample.

She beamed back at me, pure happiness radiating from her very pores. "Love you too, Ash. Now, go dance with Carter. He can't take his eyes off you."

Christ, she was right again. My breath caught as I locked eyes with Carter across the dance floor, and I was powerless to resist when he gestured for me to join him. We really badly needed to hash things out and figure out what was happening with me and Heath…but for right now, it was just us.

Chapter Seven

I WAS KIND OF HOPING CARINA WOULDN'T FORCE THE ISSUE FOR NEW YEAR'S EVE. THE IDEA OF STAYING HOME WITH ASHLEY WAS NOT AS UNPLEASANT AS IT SHOULD HAVE BEEN. WEIRD.

N. ESSEX, DECEMBER 31

I danced with Carter for far longer than I had anticipated. Long enough that my feet hurt by the time we stumbled, laughing, to the bar for refreshments.

"Lean on me," Carter murmured, wrapping his arm around my waist as I wobbled in my heels, trying to take pressure off my toes.

I smiled up at him, accepting the help because it felt good to be in his embrace. "I'm glad you're here tonight, Carter."

"You already said that, while we were dancing," he replied with a chuckle, then ordered us a couple of margaritas from the sharply suited bartender.

I perched on a barstool, taking the pressure entirely off my feet for a moment. "These shoes are beautiful," I told Carter with a groan, "but they weren't made with comfort in mind."

"High heels never are, Spark. You look utterly stunning, though." He stepped in close, his fingertips trailing over my collarbone and then gently gripping my chin to tilt my face up. "Most beautiful woman in the room."

"You already said that," I teased, smiling, "while we were dancing."

The bartender slid our drinks over then, and we took a few minutes sipping the sour cocktails while Carter pointed out various guests that he knew fun facts about. And by fun, he meant things like who was cheating on whom and what outrageous businesses other guests were rumored to be moonlighting in.

"Oh, I love this song!" I exclaimed when a familiar tune came on. "Wait, this is Seventeen Daggers, isn't it?"

Carter nodded. "Yep, sure is. Come on, let's dance again. I like having my hands on you." Another sexy wink that made my insides go all fluttery.

I finished my drink, then groaned as I put weight back on my feet. "Carter…"

"Come on, Spark baby, one more song," he murmured in my ear, that sexy accent rolling over me like a caress, "and then we can dip out and I'll eat your pussy in the back of my car to start the New Year right."

Well, shit. With an offer like that, how was a girl to refuse?

Carter knew he had me, whirling me out onto the dance floor, where dozens of other couples and groups were enjoying the music. The song playing was a ballad, a slower, more romantic melody than the band's usual rock style, and it was beautiful. Better yet, Carter was an incredible dancer and led powerfully as we waltzed around the room.

Only a minute or so after we started dancing again, Nate bumped into us with his familiar dance partner.

"Suzette?" I asked, recognizing my mom's friend. What had Carter called her at the rehearsal dinner? Cougar Suzette.

"Ashley, darling, you look gorgeous," she told me with a slightly tipsy smile.

"Hey, Bass?" Nate said with a tight expression on his handsome face. "Remember Prague?"

Carter groaned. "Yeah…I remember." He sighed, then leaned in to kiss my cheek. "Sorry, Spark, he's cashing in a favor." Then he released me and offered a hand to Mom's friend with a gallant smile. "Could I steal you for a dance, Suzette love?"

Before I could voice a protest, Carter had whirled Suzette away and I found myself face-to-face with Nate.

He quirked a brow and put out his hand, palm up. "Shall we, Layne?"

I huffed a small sigh, because it would be petty to refuse. "What was that all about?" I asked, taking his hand and letting him lead me back into the dance.

He cast a glance over my shoulder, presumably to Carter and Suzette. "Your mom's friend is a little too handsy for my liking. Carter is more tolerant than I am."

Well, shit, I didn't like the idea of that. I scowled, craning my neck to try to see whether Cougar Suzette was being inappropriate with my man, but it was a sea of sharp suits and sparkly dresses on the dance floor; they could've been anywhere.

"Are you having fun?" Nate asked, pulling my attention once more. "Better than eating that pint of strawberry ice cream in your jammies in front of the TV?"

I pursed my lips, trying to hold back a smile. "On par," I murmured, then caught sight of Carter across the room. He was smiling his charming smile, but it lacked warmth. "Did you know he was going to be here tonight?"

"No," Nate admitted, spinning me in a quick twirl. "But I should have guessed when I saw you wearing a Portia Levigne Sanguine dress."

I frowned, confused how that would have tipped him off. "You're not going to give me a lecture about how I need to stay away from your friends for their own good? Because everything I touch seems to turn to crap?"

Nate's lips tightened, his gaze heavy for a moment while he seemed to ponder his response. Then he shook his head slightly. "Not tonight. Carter will push you away all on his own, Ashley. He doesn't need my help."

Irritated—because deep down I knew he was probably right—I pushed out of his hold and stepped back. "You're an asshole, Essex. You can't let anyone be happy, can you?"

He rolled his eyes. "Don't be dramatic, Layne. I'm only telling you the truth. I figured you'd appreciate some honesty." Grabbing my hand a little more aggressively than needed, he jerked me back into his embrace to continue dancing.

I gritted my teeth, trying to pull free without causing a scene but he wasn't giving me any good options. "Let me go," I snapped.

"Don't be a child. We're just dancing." He paused. "Besides, if you let me go, Suzette might come back and I really, really don't have the patience to fend her off." He pulled me closer still as he said this, his hand firm on my lower back.

As annoyed as I was with him, I also felt a little bit protective. Suzette was twice his age and should know better, so I huffed a frustrated sigh and loosened up a bit. I even went so far as to loop my arms around Nate's neck. His death grip on my waist relaxed instantly, instead holding me gently.

"Thank you," he whispered on an exhale.

I mumbled a grudging "Whatever."

The music ended after not much longer, and, then all of a sudden, the whole room was calling out the midnight countdown in excited unison. I had totally lost track of time and had no clue we were so close to the New Year already, and there I was with my arms draped around Nate's neck.

Startled, I loosened my grip but he didn't move away.

"...two...one...Happy New Year!" the whole room screamed, but I just stared at Nate in confusion. Why was he still holding me so close? Why was he looking at me like that?

"Happy New Year, Ashley," he murmured, his brow creasing with a frown.

My lips parted, intending to return the sentiment, but Carter took that moment to appear—somewhat breathless—and grab me out of his friend's embrace. Before I could say a single word, his lips crushed to mine in a kiss so desperate I nearly forgot where we even were.

"Sorry I was late," he whispered in a husky voice some moments later when our kiss eased off. "Happy New Year, Spark."

Dizziness swept through me as I curved my body into his and kissed him again. I couldn't get enough of Carter Bassington, even when he was a giant twat-waffle.

"Bass, did you know your mom was at this event?" Nate asked from somewhere nearby and I groaned as Carter broke away from my lips abruptly.

His hands steadied me when I stumbled, but his whole mood had shifted dramatically. "She's fucking what? I thought she was in Milan!"

Nate shrugged, rubbing the back of his neck. "She's over there talking to Max right now." He tipped his head toward the bar, and Carter physically flinched. Then cast a panicked look to me. The woman speaking with Max was beautiful, elegant, and every inch the Bassington matriarch I had pictured when Carter spoke of her. She was cold.

"Ah," I said with a sinking realization. "I see."

"It's not—" Carter started to protest, his eyes darting to his mother like a cornered wolf. "Nate?"

"On it," Nate replied with a tight nod. He reached out and took my hand in his, giving me a tug away from Carter. "Come on, Layne. I'll take you home."

It was on the tip of my tongue to protest and insist I wanted to stay. Even if Carter was too ashamed to let his mother see me—for valid reasons, considering the possible murder charge—I could have insisted I wanted to stay at the party. But I didn't because, without Carter, I didn't want to be there. So I let Nate grip my hand firmly in his own and lead me quickly out of the glittering party.

We paused at the foyer, and by the time our coats had been retrieved, the limo had pulled up out front, ready to drive us home.

Neither of us spoke as we climbed in, and it was several minutes before Nate blew out a long breath and raked his fingers through his deep brown hair, messing it up.

"Are you okay?" he asked, shocking me as thoroughly as if he'd just quacked like a duck.

I scowled. "Do you care if I am?"

His gaze snapped to mine, his expression hard. "Contrary to what you think of me, Ashley, I'm not a total prick. I'm trying to warn you, for your own good. Case in fucking point right back there. Carter's mother—"

"I already know," I snapped, breaking eye contact because I was fucking sweating under his intense scrutiny. "He told me."

Nate's soft chuckle was anything but kind. "I'm sure he did."

I hated that he sounded so sarcastic, but I also didn't want to keep dwelling on the whole messy affair. Carter was already so fucking hot and cold as it was—maybe I needed to draw a line in the sand soon. I wondered what Heath would say...

Refusing to rise to Nate's bait, I huddled into the corner of the car and closed my eyes. It was a twenty-minute drive, and I'd have rather taken a nap than make small talk with him. Or worse, have him spend the whole drive making me feel like a stupid, naive twit for not seeing the red flags.

I saw them. Every fucking time I was around Carter, I saw the red flags. I just didn't care...or at least that was what I told myself.

A shiver trembled through me, and Nate muttered something

under his breath about stubborn women before draping his jacket over me. I bit my lip, holding back the instinct to say thank you and settled in for a quick nap thanks to the silence in the car.

Chapter Eight

I'M UNEASY ABOUT RETURNING TO CAMPUS. THE GUYS HAVE BEEN IN
CONTACT EVERY DAY AND HEATH SWEARS HE'S READY TO RETURN, BUT...I'M
WORRIED. SOMETHING CAUSED THE SLEEPWALKING OR HYPNOSIS OR
WHATEVER HAD HAPPENED LAST SEMESTER. WHAT IF IT HAPPENS AGAIN?
WHAT IF HEATH HURTS HIMSELF AGAIN AND THIS TIME WE'RE NOT THERE
TO CUT HIM DOWN?
 WHAT IF NEXT TIME HE HURTS SOMEONE ELSE? OR I DO? NONE OF US
ARE IMMUNE...EXCEPT MAYBE ASHLEY...

N. ESSEX, JANUARY 3

"You're back!" Carly squealed, tackling me in a hug as I tried to
unlock my dorm room door. "I was worried the gloomy guys were
going to make you stay with them or worse."

"What could possibly be worse?" I joked, laughing slightly as I
hugged her back. "How was your New Year, anyway? You're tan as
shit, girl." She and Heath had spent the last week on a beach somewhere in the Caribbean for a family get-together. Carly had kept me

up-to-date with photos daily, but Heath had been uncomfortably silent.

"It was…a lot quieter than yours. Have you spoken to Carter since then?" She followed me into my room and flopped down on my bed. I'd called her the morning after the party and told her all the juicy details.

I shook my head, unzipping my suitcase on the floor to unpack. "Nope. Nothing."

Carly scowled, her chin propped up on her hands. "Well, that's a bit shit. Have you tried contacting him?"

"No. I'm leaving the ball firmly in his court for this mess. I honestly thought with how strong he'd been coming on, he must have sorted things out with his mom. Apparently I was wrong." I sighed, trying really hard not to admit just how hurt I was by Carter's silence. "To be blunt, I'm sick of his hot-and-cold shit."

"I don't blame you," Carly said, agreeing. "How were things with Nate? You guys spent a lot of time together over the holidays."

That was a loaded question. How were things with Nate? It was hard to say. In some ways he'd been blowing hot and cold worse than Carter, but at the same time, he'd been inexplicably supportive and stable over the last few weeks. It was confusing, to say the least.

"We're tolerating one another," I finally said, "but I still don't trust him as far as I could throw him, if that's what you're worried about. I haven't forgotten what a slimy fuck he is."

With how civil Carly had been toward Nate lately, it was easy to forget he'd broken her heart in the past. That he'd cheated on his girlfriend with her, then let the mean girls drag Carly through the mud for his indiscretion. Last I checked, Carly hadn't been the one in the wrong since she wasn't dating Paige.

My friend puffed out her cheeks, then gave a long exhale. "So. About that."

I raised a brow, giving her my full focus as her face pinked. "Yes…?"

55

"Heath let me in on a few top-secret facts while we were on vacation. He sort of mentioned about how like, you and me are besties and how he and Nate are basically brothers and it wasn't fair to keep the negative energy running…" She was rambling, which made me all the more curious about what point she was dancing around.

Turning to face her fully, I abandoned my clothes sorting. "Spit it out, Carly."

Her brow pinched. "So, he swore me to secrecy so you can't tell anyone."

I grinned, shaking my head. "Okay, sure. Tell me."

"So that thing with me and Nate last year… Apparently he didn't cheat on Paige. They had broken up like a month before, but Paige was refusing to admit they were done. Then she found out he was with me at that party and faked a pregnancy to reel him back in."

My jaw dropped. "And he just…let you get treated like a cheap whore for a year and never spoke up to clear the air? After Paige faked a pregnancy? Ew. You know what, though? That doesn't even shock me. It took Heath how fucking long to finally admit nothing happened between us when we first met."

Carly groaned, scrubbing her hands over her face. "I know. It's not exactly a redemption, is it? But on the other hand, I do feel a bit better knowing I was not actually facilitating his cheating and Paige is probably certifiably crazy. Also, and I cannot stress this enough, I am glad Paige did what she did because Nate and I never would have lasted. In hindsight, I really wasn't into him."

I snickered a laugh. "Just using him for the dick, hey? You hussy. But I get it, and it's good that Heath told you…eventually. Douche move for Nate to never tell you, though."

Carly shrugged. "I thought the same, but when I went back to really think about all the bullshit from Paige and Jade, part of me wonders whether Nate was really aware of what was going on. They're sneaky little bitches."

Frowning, I turned back to my unpacking and kept my

mean-spirited comments about Nathaniel Essex to myself. Carly was being too generous in thinking he didn't know what hell his girlfriend was putting her through for the last year. Wasn't she?

"So…what's the situation this semester? Will Roycey be moving back in here?" Her tone was teasing, and I shook my head.

I hadn't heard from Royce since he'd left Max's place with everyone else after Christmas, so I seriously doubted it. "Unlikely," I murmured. "I think their main focus is on Heath and the whole…you know…hypnosis-sleepwalking-brainwashing thing. I am getting the distinct impression that they'd quite like it if I disappeared."

My friend scoffed. "As if. They basically worship the ground you walk on, Ash. Have they tried to make you pick between them, yet?"

Surprised, I gave a nervous laugh. "Heath and Carter, you mean?"

Her nose wrinkled. "Sure. Heath and Carter."

"No…I mean, not really. But also there's no choice because Carter is being a shady fuck about this stuff with his mom, and I don't need any miscommunication plot lines in my life, thank you very much. And Heath, as much as it pains me to say…might be better off focusing on his recovery rather than jumping into a thing with me." Also, he seemed to be ignoring me.

"I don't love that," Carly muttered, pouting, "but that does sort of line up with what his doctors have said."

Well, that was news to me. I'd been letting Nate get into my head and guilt me about my part in Heath's mental-health decline, but if his doctors also thought we should be seeking a little more distance? Then maybe it wasn't the worst idea.

"Right," I mumbled. "So…where does that even leave me?"

Carly shrugged. "With Royce, obviously. Or me! I've never eaten pussy before but I reckon I'd be excellent at it."

I snort-laughed and threw a pair of rolled-up socks her way. "What tempting options. In case you forgot, friend, you're straight."

She rolled her eyes. "What's the saying? So's spaghetti until it gets wet?"

"Oh my god, stop it," I groaned, laughing. "But anyway, Royce is basically still not talking to me, so even if we weren't firmly in the friend zone—which we are—he won't even give me the time of day." I was rambling and kind of blushing because somehow she'd just put the idea of me and Royce into my head and I was remembering how nice it was waking up in his arms.

Damn it. No. We were friends. Or we used to be… Now I wasn't so sure we were anything.

A knock on the door interrupted the weird twist my thoughts had taken, and I hopped up to see who it was.

"Oh," I said, blinking up at the tall black man in a suit. "Hello?"

"Ashley Layne?" he asked, his expression totally neutral.

I nodded. "Yes, that's me. You are…?"

"Lionel Hughes, your personal security." He extended a hand for me to shake, and I stared at it stupidly.

The man had to be in his forties at least, and the suit screamed Secret Service, which was utterly ridiculous at a university. But more to the point…he was my *what?*

"Um…sorry, what? I didn't hire personal security."

Carly, understandably curious, scrambled off my bed and came to stand behind me as she took the man in. Lionel Hughes was, for lack of a better word, huge.

"I'm aware you didn't hire me, Miss Layne, but that's my job. I just thought I'd introduce myself, but otherwise you won't even know I'm here. Feel free to pretend I don't exist." His lips curled slightly, as though he was trying to force a reassuring smile and failing miserably.

I raised one brow, giving him a long look up and down. "Uh, I don't see how that would really work, Mr. Hughes. But let's circle back to my original point: I didn't hire you."

His brow dipped ever so slightly. "I'm aware."

"Okay…so who did?" I prompted.

Carly snort-laughed. "Ten bucks on Sir Carter Bassington Junior. This is his level of controlling."

The security guard gave no reaction, and I narrowed my eyes while waiting for his answer. When he said nothing, I folded my arms and tapped my fingers against my elbow. "I'm waiting, Mr. Hughes."

He cleared his throat, looking a little irritated. "Clients are confidential, Miss Layne."

Yeah, now my money was on Carter too. This felt like his sort of move. Well, I was done with his games. He wanted to play hot and cold, hiding me from his mother like a dirty little habit. Frankly, I was worth more than that.

"Thank you, Mr. Hughes, but no thank you." I started to close the door in his face, and he shot a hand out to stop me.

Now his brow really was furrowed. "I'm sorry, I don't think I understand. My job is—"

"Oh, I'm well aware," I said, cutting him off, irritation prickling my skin, "but I am declining your services. Please advise your client that I am not interested."

He shook his head, clearly frustrated now. "Listen, Miss Layne, I really don't think—"

"Mr. Hughes," I snapped, cutting him off again. "I do not need, nor want your protection. I am twenty-one and to the best of my knowledge, I am not medically unfit to take care of myself. If you persist in lingering outside my dorm room or following me around campus, I will have to report you for stalking and harassment. You're a grown man, Mr. Hughes. I don't give a flying fuck what your client wants. I am saying no thank you."

With that, I shut the door in his shocked face and spun to face Carly.

She stared back at me with eyes wide and mouth agape, then a moment later we both burst into laughter. There was really nothing funny about the situation, but the confrontation had me all hopped up on adrenaline and that shit did weird things sometimes.

"I can't believe you just did that," she chortled, flopping back onto my bed once more. "But also super-valid point about him looking like a stalker. As if a legit Secret Service agent is going to just blend into the background at a university."

I giggled, picturing Lionel Hughes in a varsity jersey and ripped jeans. "Yeah, no. Talk about drawing attention to myself. Also, better point, it's completely unnecessary."

That made Carly sober up a little and she screwed up her face. "I dunno, girl. What about the whole situation with being kidnapped and dumped in the woods to get hypothermia and potentially starve or freeze or be eaten by a bear? Maybe a bodyguard isn't so silly after all."

I shook my head firmly. "Nope. If I need one, then so does everyone here. No one tried decapitating me on a society retreat or burning me alive in a building fire."

She winced. "Okay, but did you forget the part where the decapitated guy was in your bed? It was clearly a threat of some kind, don't you think?"

Yes, I did think that. But none of it made sense...and I didn't truly believe I was meant to die in those woods. I just had a gut feeling someone knew that Abigail's diary entries would lead me out eventually.

"I just don't need a fucking bodyguard," I murmured, turning back to the task of unpacking. "If Carter is so worried, he's welcome to shadow me himself."

"Is he?" Carly asked, giving me a curious look.

I groaned, scrubbing my hands over my face. "No. Yes. I don't know. He's a dick, you know that?"

She grinned. "I'm well aware. And he's legitimately scary with his anger-management crap. But you don't ever seem intimidated, and by the sound of things, you're quite fond of his dick."

Now that she mentioned it, I hadn't seen that scary side of Carter in a while. It did make me worry that I'd forget, let my guard down, and get hurt all over again. I sighed and shrugged. "What was that offer about eating pussy again? Maybe you and I are the answer to everything."

Carly scoffed, grinning like a maniac. "You wish. My offer is already off the table! You should call Carter."

With that sage advice, she left me to sort out my room and blew a kiss on her way out. I should call Carter…and ask if he was the one responsible for Mr. Lionel Hughes.

Chapter Nine

THE DEVIL'S BACKBONE SOCIETY ELDERS ARE PUTTING PRESSURE ON FOR
AN INCREASED SOCIAL CALENDAR THIS SEMESTER. NORMALLY IT WOULDN'T
BOTHER ME, BUT I CAN'T SHAKE THE FEELING HEATH'S SLEEPWALKING IS
LINKED TO THE SOCIETY SOMEHOW. WE WERE ALL IN OUR CEREMONY
ROBES AND MASKS THAT NIGHT, WHEN THE SCIENCE HALL BURNED DOWN.
WHEN ASHLEY HAD SOMEHOW SNAPPED ME OUT OF THE TRANCE.
  FUCKING ASHLEY. WHY DOES IT FEEL LIKE SHE IS THE CORE OF THE
PROBLEM? OR IS SHE THE SOLUTION? I WISH I KNEW.

N. ESSEX, JANUARY 5

Carly practically kicked my door down first thing the next morning
to drag me out for coffee and breakfast. I was tired from staying up
way too late reading ahead in my Humanities textbooks while also
trying not to check my phone every five minutes. Was it really so
stupid of me to think Carter would reach out?

"Still nothing from Sir Carter, huh?" Carly asked as we walked
across the lawn toward the coffee shop. I hadn't even realized I was

staring at my phone until she said that, and I guiltily put it back in my pocket.

"Nope," I confirmed, shaking my head. "It's fine. I don't care."

Carly scoffed. "Liar. What about Heath? Are the guys back in their apartment?"

"Yeah, I think Heath and Nate got back over the weekend—Nate dropped me off yesterday—but no idea about Carter and Royce. They cut me off, remember?" I screwed up my face, trying to make light of a situation that was actually stinging something awful.

Carly sighed. "Stupid boys. What are you going to do about Heath? Has he said anything about what the doctors are advising?"

"You mean, has he ended things between us for the sake of his mental health? No. He hasn't. We haven't actually spoken since New Year's Eve, which sucks massively. But it means that I will eventually have to be the asshole, and I really don't want to do that. So…I figured I'd take the mature, adult approach to the whole thing."

She snorted a laugh. "Avoid it until it becomes a thing?"

"Yup." I nodded. "Exactly."

A car revved somewhere nearby, and some women screamed, making Carly and me stop in our tracks and look in the direction the noise had come from.

"Watch out!" someone yelled just moments before a car swerved off the road entirely, plowing through the bushes and heading straight toward Carly and me.

Before I could even register what the fuck was happening, someone body-slammed into me, grabbing me clean off my feet and carrying me some fifty feet before I could get a proper scream out.

"Put me down!" I shrieked, my instincts screaming at me that this wasn't someone I knew. It wasn't a hold I was familiar with in any way. It was too rough, too impersonal, too…professional. "Let me go!"

Mr. Lionel Hughes placed me back on my feet but didn't move

away. He just turned his huge back to me, his head swiveling as he searched for…what, exactly? Another out-of-control car speeding toward me? That'd be crazy bad luck.

"Miss Layne, we need—" he started to speak at the same time he grasped my biceps, clearly intending to drag me along with him.

"I think the fuck not," I snapped, wrenching my arm out of his grip. Or trying to. He was stronger than anticipated, or at the very least he'd been prepared for my resistance. All I managed to do was jerk against his iron grip pitifully. Then panic whipped through me as I glanced around. "Carly! Carly!"

It was total chaos where Mr. Hughes had just moved me from. The car had gone all the way across the lawn and crashed into a tree. People were screaming and running, and the front end of the car was so crumpled, there was just no way the driver was still alive. Carly was nowhere to be seen, though, and there were several people on the ground in various states of injury.

"Let. Me. Go!" I screamed, yanking my arm away with all my might. Mr. Hughes released me just a split second before I yanked, though, and I went tumbling to my ass on the lawn. I gasped, stunned for a moment, then I realized what had happened.

Mr. Hughes hadn't let me go. He'd been knocked back a few steps by Carter's fist, and as I watched he caught a second punch right in the nose before dodging a third.

"Carter! Stop!" I cried out, scrambling to my feet once more. He showed no sign of even hearing me, and Mr. Hughes had shifted his focus to defending himself…which surely wasn't going to end well. Mr. Hughes was a trained bodyguard who looked like he'd spent time in the armed forces or Secret Service or something, but Carter? He had anger issues and not so long ago beat a man to death in Paris, then dumped the body.

My panicked gaze flicked back and forth between them, but an agonized wail reminded me of the bigger issue at hand. The out-of-control car. The injured bystanders. Carly!

Deciding Carter could handle himself, I turned and ran back across the lawn, searching for my friend. "Carly!" I screamed, looking everywhere. "Carly! Where are you?"

I skidded to my knees beside a blond girl lying on the ground, an ominous pool of red spreading beneath her. My heart lodged in my throat as I reached out to brush her hair back.

"Ashley!" a familiar voice exclaimed.

I sucked a breath so sharply I nearly choked, looking away from the gravely injured—possibly dead—girl on the ground. The girl whose face I didn't recognize, and that revelation flooded me with sickening relief.

Carly was running toward me, shock and fear etched across her face as she grabbed me in a fierce hug. "Holy shit, Ash, I thought something bad had happened to you!"

"Me?" I squeaked, hugging her back tighter than a bear trap. "I thought the car hit you!"

"Close," she admitted with a groan. "I dove onto the path and feel like I will be one whole walking bruise tomorrow. Better that than the alternative, though." She released me, then reached out to check the unfamiliar girl's pulse. "Oh shit, she's still alive. Call an ambulance!"

I blinked like an idiot as I pulled out my phone. Call an ambulance? That would have been the smart thing to do. Why didn't I think of that sooner? Sirens already filled the air, and I figured others had called in the accident already, but still, this girl needed help. Badly.

"What happened?" I asked Carly after speaking with the 911 operator and being assured multiple ambulances were en route already. "That car—"

"Insane," she agreed, shaking her head with disbelief. The girl on the ground started to stir, moaning, and Carly shifted her focus to comfort her. "Hey, Jess, it's Carly. You need to stay still, okay? We've called for help, but please stay really still in case..."

Tears pricked at the girl's eyes, but she was lucid enough to understand. Her lips tightened and she squeezed her eyes shut in obvious agony. *Fucking hell.* Carly grasped her hand, murmuring soothing reassurances, and I looked over in the direction of the siren noises.

"I'll get one of the paramedics," I said, pushing to my feet and sprinting toward the street where they'd likely be pulling up. Just a moment later, two came speeding around the corner and pulled up quick when they undoubtedly saw the chaos.

There were lots of people needing medical help, but I had a horrible feeling about Jess's injuries, so I pushed, shoved, and pleaded to get one of the paramedics to accompany me back to her straightaway.

They went to work efficiently, strapping Jess into a neck brace and spinal board. She whimpered and sobbed quietly as they got her prepped, but Carly kept offering quiet reassurances to keep her calm.

"I'll go with her," Carly told me. "You should go back to our dorm. I'll meet you there?"

I nodded quickly, assuring her I'd be fine. Once the paramedics got Jess onto a stretcher and hurried her back to the ambulance, I turned to look for Carter and Mr. Hughes.

To my shock, they were still fighting it out. To be fair, it seemed more like Mr. Hughes was just deflecting blows and attempting to disengage while Carter looked like he genuinely wanted to murder the older man.

"Carter, stop!" I bellowed as I drew closer.

He paid me no attention, launching at the bodyguard with more fury as if Mr. Hughes's attempts to deescalate were enraging him further. Without really thinking my actions through, I rushed forward and physically placed myself between the two of them, then instantly braced for impact as I registered how utterly stupid that move was.

The blow never landed, though. Carter caught himself, his knuckles barely kissing my hair as he aborted the motion; then he

66

grabbed me with both hands on either side of my face and an expression of utter horror etched across his face.

"What the fuck are you doing?" he roared, giving me a little shake. His arms were so tightly flexed it seemed like his veins were about to burst, but his touch was protective rather than threatening. "You could have been hurt, Spark! You could have—"

"You weren't listening," I said, defending myself, trying to hide the way adrenaline pumped my heart like a bongo drum and my limbs trembled in shock.

His incredulous stare morphed into something undefinable. Then he crushed his lips to mine in a kiss that stole the breath from my lungs and turned my knees even weaker than they already were.

I didn't pull away, because I needed that kiss just as much as he clearly did. Kissing Carter was pure torture, but the kind I kept willingly entering into because it felt so fucking good even when it hurt.

"Carter," I murmured against his lips after his desperate kisses eased. "Why are you trying to kill your bodyguard?"

He withdrew an inch, brow furrowed with confusion. "My bodyguard? That guy? He was manhandling you. I heard you screaming for him to let you go and he didn't… I saw red."

I licked my lips, tasting his kiss there and craving more. "You do love red."

Mr. Hughes cleared his throat pointedly behind me, and I sighed as I peeled Carter's hands off my face. Then I narrowed my gaze as I looked between the two of them. "You didn't hire Mr. Lionel Hughes to be my bodyguard?"

Carter's expression was undeniably confused. "What? No. I've never seen this asshole in my life."

I shot the security dude a long, hard look but his answering stare was totally blank and unwavering. I sighed. "Whatever. Mr. Hughes, I appreciate your timely assistance, but I was quite clear with you last night. I do not want or need your services. Please pass that along to whoever the fuck your client is."

Not waiting for a response, I grabbed Carter's arm and started marching across the lawn in the direction of Dancing Goats coffee. Yes, I would head back to the dorms but not without some caffeine to settle my nerves first.

"Spark, wait," Carter said a moment later, gripping my hand as he pulled me to a stop. "Are you okay? You're not hurt?"

I shook my head. "I'm fine. You, on the other hand, are a fucking mess. What were you thinking, starting a fight like that? He's clearly a professional and you could have—"

"I was thinking that he was hurting you," he snapped, cutting me off. "You were screaming at him to let you go. I thought…" He trailed off, shaking his head. "I thought he was trying to kidnap you or something. I panicked. It was like Paris all over again, and I just…" He shrugged.

I got it, though. My anger evaporated and I squeezed his fingers with understanding. "Let's get coffee. Then maybe you can explain why I haven't heard from you since New Year's?" Or from Royce or Heath either, to be fair. But they hadn't shown up to sweep me off my feet at a fancy party, then dropped me like a hot rock when Mommy showed up.

Carter's brow furrowed. "What do you mean? I called you a dozen times. You blocked my number."

I scoffed, dropping his hand as I continued in the direction of coffee. "I did nothing of the sort. I thought surely you'd explain things or, I dunno, apologize, but the silence sort of put that final nail in the coffin, Sir Carter."

He jogged a couple of steps to catch up, then grabbed my hand again, jerking me to a halt. "Okay, we can discuss that nickname later—I don't hate it, by the way—but let's get this perfectly clear. I tried to call. I tried to message. Dozens of times. You. Blocked. My. Number. Spark. Did you seriously think I just didn't care enough to explain?"

"Bullshit," I snapped back. "Prove it."

His brows shot up. "Okay, then." He released my hand and pulled his phone from his pocket, swiping the screen with his thumb to bring up his message thread with me, then turned the device so I could see the long scrolling list of messages showing undelivered, interspersed with call not connected.

My jaw dropped. "What? I didn't block your number, though." But just in case, I pulled out my own phone and searched for the function listing all blocked contacts. Shock rippled through me as I read Carter's name on the list...along with Heath and Royce. "What the fuck?"

That explained a lot. A lot. But it didn't change the fact that I hadn't blocked any of them... And then it hit me. I'd fallen asleep on the drive home from the New Year's Eve party. I'd fallen asleep in the car, fully dressed in my fancy designer gown and heels, then woken up in bed wearing a T-shirt over my lingerie...with my phone charging beside the bed.

"Fucking Nate," I growled, my fingers curling around my phone and squeezing just like I'd like to have done to his neck. "I'm going to kill him."

Chapter Ten

0600: WOKE UP FEELING LIKE A BAG OF DICKS. CHECKED MOTION
CAMERAS TO CONFIRM I DIDN'T SLEEPWALK AGAIN. ALL CLEAR.

0630: CHECKED MY MESSAGES... STILL BLOCKED. HIT THE GYM.
DEADLIFTED 300LBS AND COULDN'T STOP THINKING ABOUT WHY
SHE HAS ME BLOCKED.

0830: SHOWERED AND ATE BREAKFAST—OVERNIGHT OATS WITH
BANANA AND MAPLE. BLACK COFFEE.

0930: LEFT THE ESTATE TO RETURN TO NEVAEH. CALLED HEATH
EN ROUTE AND VERIFIED HE WAS ALSO BLOCKED.

1100: ARRIVED AT THE APARTMENT. NO ONE ELSE HOME.
UNPACKED IN MY NEW ROOM—HEATH'S OLD ROOM. SEEMED
SHITTY TO MAKE HIM RETURN TO THE PLACE WHERE HE
ALMOST DIED JUST A MONTH AGO, SO I SWITCHED WITH HIM
DURING EXAMS. WHILE HE WAS IN RECOVERY. HOPE HE ISN'T
PISSED ABOUT IT.

1300: STILL BLOCKED. CARTER ARRIVED HOME AND TOLD ME
THAT ASH AND NATE WOULDN'T BE BACK UNTIL LATER IN THE
AFTERNOON. SOME SHIT ABOUT A FAMILY LUNCH.

1700: STOOD ACROSS THE ROAD FROM NEVAEH DORMS TO VERIFY
ASH WAS BACK. SHE IS.

Carter convinced me to still get coffee, since we were already so close to Dancing Goats, but we ordered it to go and he escorted me to his car once we collected our drinks. It was a sexy deep-red Koenigsegg Gemera, almost the color of blood—or, coincidentally, the color of the dress he'd bought me for New Year's Eve.

"New car?" I asked as he pulled out of the parking lot. It had that distinctive new-car smell, so it was a fairly redundant question, but I was suddenly all awkward and nervous, so it was the only thing that came to mind.

He shot me a sidelong look, one brow raised. Then the corner of his lips curved up. "Yeah, it is. Do you like it?"

I shifted in the soft, black leather seat and ran my hand over the dash. "I do. Does it go fast?"

Now his small smile broadened into a grin. "Spark, baby," he chuckled. "What do you think?" He punctuated that question with a sudden gear shift and burst of speed that flattened me back into my seat for a moment.

Crap. Why did that do tingly things to my lady parts?

"I thought you were more of a classic car girl," he commented thoughtfully, slowing to stop at a yellow light. I appreciated the fact he wasn't risking our safety just to show off.

I wet my lips, cursing the fact that my cheeks were warm with

71

an unquestionable blush. "I am a car girl in general. I have a classic because it was my dad's passion project and it was just kind of our thing to work on together. He couldn't exactly take it to South Sudan with him and it was being wasted sitting in the garage." I shrugged. "It's more of a sentimental car than anything. I can still very much appreciate these newer luxury cars."

Carter nodded thoughtfully. "You know Royce is totally obsessed, right?"

I snort-laughed. "With my car? Yeah, I know. He drives well, though, so I'm okay letting him borrow it every now and then."

Carter gave me another long look before the light turned green and he accelerated once more. "Right."

My phone dinged and I pulled it out to read the message from Carly. Then I gave a sad sigh at seeing her update.

"Everything okay?" Carter asked with understandable curiosity.

I shook my head. "The driver of that car died at the scene. Daniel Mahoney. Did you know him?"

"Yes…he was a DB," Carter murmured. "Do they know what caused him to crash?"

"Not yet," I replied, tapping out a quick reply to Carly, letting her know I was going to the guys' apartment, before putting my phone away. "His girlfriend was in the passenger seat, but she's in surgery right now. The girl Carly went in with is apparently still being seen by doctors too."

Carter grimaced. "First day back. Doesn't really bode well for this semester, huh?"

Fucking hell, I hadn't even considered that the car crash might be linked to the hypnosis stuff Heath had talked about. Surely it was just a coincidence? It was a conversation we needed to have, though. All of us.

"How's Lady doing?" I asked, changing the subject. "Who took care of her over the holidays?"

"Our downstairs neighbor, Mrs. Brown. She's well into her

eighties but likes to pretend she's only fifty. Real funny old bird and loves animals. She's got a chihuahua called Vera that Lady likes to play with." Carter softened when he spoke of his adopted dog. It was so unexpected after the mutt had been dumped in my room to cause havoc at the beginning of last semester.

I smiled, thinking how Carter was just a big softy deep down. Really deep down, below the bad temper, control issues, and arrogant entitled bullshit.

We arrived at the guys' building a few minutes later, and I noticed Heath's motorbike was parked in his usual spot when we parked. He'd been blocked in my phone too. Did he think I was ignoring him on purpose? Or had he taken his doctor's advice to distance himself from me until his mental health could recuperate fully?

Carter took my hand when we got out of his car, linking our fingers together as we crossed the concrete toward the elevators. I let him, because I loved touching him. Loved how safe he made me feel when he gripped my fingers like that. We stepped into the elevator and he backed me into the corner, balancing the tray with our coffees in one hand and lowering his head to kiss me...but I pushed him away.

My willpower was getting stronger every damn day, but that was a tough one.

"Carter," I admonished, giving a slow shake of my head.

His brow furrowed, his jaw tight. "Spark...please let me kiss you."

Oh my god, Carter begging? Dirty tricks.

I shook my head again with monumental effort. "You keep doing this, sucking me in with this thing between us." I gestured to the air between us as he stared straight through to my soul through my eyes. I could hardly breathe. "This electric attraction between us... it makes it impossible to think, and all my better judgment flies out the window. We are not in a good place, Carter, and every time I let you get close, it feels like I lose a piece of myself to you."

Sadness tainted his expression and he wet his lips. "Is that such a bad thing, Spark? I'd keep those pieces safe."

"I know," I whispered, my eyes burning with the sudden urge to cry, "but I'll never get them back. So where does that leave me when you eventually marry some European heiress that your mother approves of?"

Conflicted emotions swirled in his gaze, and he didn't immediately have a response to that question. Then as he parted his lips to speak, the elevator dinged and the doors slid open on the boys' floor.

Biting my lip to hold back the tears, I slipped past him and walked the short distance to their door with Carter silent and brooding at my back. He paused a moment with his key in the lock, glancing down at me with a dark look in his eyes.

"This conversation isn't over, Spark. I'm not letting go of you that easy, but you've raised good points. I need to think."

"Okay," I whispered, too choked up for any higher volume. But I didn't want the conversation to be over... I just wanted him to sort out his mommy issues and finally tell her to fuck off. I wanted him to fight for me and be proud to be with me, not stuffing me into a closet at the mention of his mother.

Then again...she was holding the threat of a murder charge over his head. Maybe I was being too harsh.

Carter pushed the door open, gesturing for me to enter ahead of him. As soon as I did, I was greeted by the wet, slobbery kisses of his mongrel street dog who was wearing an honest-to-fuck bow in her fur on top of her head.

"Aw, hi, Lady." I greeted the pup. "You look lovely. Mrs. Brown has taken good care of you. Look at that pretty bow."

"Mrs. Brown didn't put the bow in," Heath replied from the sofa where he reclined in a pair of gray sweatpants and nothing else. Totally shirtless. Fuck, he was sexy... His hospital stay had slimmed him down somewhat, but the muscular structure was still evident, and I'd bet anything he was hitting the gym hard to get it back.

I arched a brow at Carter, the only other logical culprit, and he shrugged. "Lady likes to look like a lady sometimes," he murmured, bending down to love on the dog.

I left him scratching the mutt's belly and crossed over to the sofa to sit beside Heath. "Hey, you," I said with a small smile. "So…uh…I don't totally know if you've tried to message me since New Year's, but it's recently come to my attention that I had you blocked."

Heath's brow arched and he set aside the Xbox controller he'd been using. "Yes, I noticed. That wasn't intentional?"

Carter scoffed, coming over to join us. "Oh, it was intentional, all right."

I rolled my eyes. "It wasn't me," I explained to Heath. "I just thought you were all ghosting me."

He frowned his confusion, glancing between the two of us as he puzzled it out. "Nate?"

"That's my best guess," I replied. "Is he here? I'd like to ask him to his face and figure out what the fuck he thought he was playing at."

Heath grimaced. "That part is obvious. He's a meddling shit sometimes. But no, he had an early class and usually stops at the gym before coming home. Paige was over here last night too."

A sharp jolt of irritation shot through me at that statement. "Why? Didn't they break up?"

Heath shrugged, running a hand through his messy, dark hair. "Yeah, but they've broken up heaps. It doesn't always stick."

Why the fuck did that thought annoy me so much? Was it because I knew she'd been sleeping with Royce behind Nate's back? Or maybe just because she was a horrible person and I didn't want to be stuck playing nice in social situations? Not to mention the secret Carly had filled me in on about Paige's fake pregnancy.

Yeah, that must have been it.

"I'll call him," Carter offered. "When he gets home, I'll pin him down while you slap him, Spark. You deserve a couple of free hits."

My lips twitched with amusement at that mental image.

Slapping Nate would be very cathartic… It was a tempting offer, for sure. "You'd better call Royce too. I think we have more to discuss than just Nate fucking around with my phone."

Lady whimpered at the balcony door, pawing at it, and Carter got up to take her outside. Heath took that opportunity and illusion of privacy to slip his arm around my waist and haul me into his lap, making me squeak in surprise.

"What are you doing?" I asked, stunned and a little hypnotized by his half-naked status as my knees straddled his hips.

A sly, sexy smile tilted his lips. "Making sure my feelings are crystal-clear, since you haven't gotten any of my messages." Then he slid his hand into the back of my hair and pulled my mouth down to connect with his.

I moaned softly as his lips caressed mine, his tongue slipping in to tangle with my very heartstrings. His strong fingers pressed against my skull, his other hand cupping my ass, and I suddenly became shockingly aware of the swell of his dick beneath my crotch.

Dimly I heard Carter talking to Lady out on the balcony and knew our time was limited. I'd just pushed Carter away in the elevator—it'd be a harsh slap in the face for him to come in and find me grinding his best friend on the couch. But I couldn't force myself to stop kissing Heath. His touches lit up every damn nerve in my body to the point I was sure I must be vibrating, and I wanted more.

He sucked on my lower lip, making me whimper with need, and my hands splayed out on his chest. He was already shirtless, and my imagination told me maybe he was commando underneath those sweatpants. If only I weren't in jeans…

Heath's fingers in my hair flexed, tugging on the strands in a way that sent a whole-body shiver through me, and I slid one hand up to his neck. Then he flinched so hard, our teeth knocked together.

My confusion only lasted the time it took to see where I'd just placed my hand. It'd been a month, but the mark still ringed his neck from where he'd hung, and my fingers rested directly over it.

"Shit," I hissed, withdrawing my hand like I'd been burned. "Heath, I'm so sorry. I didn't—"

He swallowed hard, his eyes haunted as he reached out and grabbed my hand. "No. I'm sorry." He very deliberately placed my hand right back where it was, covering his scar. Then crashed his mouth back to mine in an almost-feverish kiss, like he was trying to prove something to himself.

"Squirrel? What the fuck?"

Royce's startled question came just a moment before the front door slammed shut, and I damn near jumped out of Heath's lap like I'd been caught by my dad or something.

Carter chose that moment to step back inside with Lady at his heels and arched a brow at me in question. Without a doubt, my face must have been the color of a fucking tomato.

"Hey, roomie!" I greeted Royce with a weak smile. "Miss me?"

Heath sighed heavily and stood up from the couch, not bothering to try to hide the way his sweatpants tented from his boner. "Fucking cockblocker," he growled, heading out of the room. "I'm taking a cold shower. Don't start slapping Nate until I'm back!"

Royce's face was a picture of confusion as I smoothed a hand over my hair in a desperate attempt to look less like I was about to fuck Heath on the sofa.

"Why are we slapping Nate?" he asked, looking to Carter for answers.

Carter just shrugged. "Why not?"

Really, though, why the fuck not? He permanently deserved it, even without fucking around in my phone. Nate was a walking red flag and I guess, apparently, I was the bull.

Chapter Eleven

January 6

My doctors suggested I keep a journal as a way of "talking about my feelings" outside of the clinic, but it just reminded me about the journal Ashley found in her room, how Abigail had been documenting all the weird shit going on within the DBs during her time at Nevaeh, and it made me think it wasn't such a bad idea. Maybe this way, if anything else happens to me, it's in black and white that I am not suicidal. I am, however, willing to kill whoever has been fucking around in my head.

H. Briggs

"Okay, let me get this straight," Royce said, leaning forward with his elbows on his knees as he stared into my fucking soul. "Nate didn't just block Carter's number because he was a total douchewad at the New Year's party and acted like you were his dirty little secret—"

"Come on, man," Carter protested.

Royce flicked him an unapologetic glance. "Don't wanna be called a douchewad, don't act like a douchewad, Douchewad. But back to the point. Nate didn't just block Carter—he blocked all of us? Why? Also, how'd he get into your phone?"

I threw my hands up, frustrated with the whole thing already and Nate wasn't even back yet for me to yell at him. The more we talked about it, the angrier I was getting too. It was a massive invasion of privacy and downright petty.

"He kept going on about how I needed to distance myself from you guys, how me hanging around was detrimental to Heath's recovery, and how it was just safer for everyone if I left Nevaeh entirely. I guess when I didn't fall into line, he thought he'd cut me off from the three of you anyway and make it seem like you all didn't want me around?"

Royce scowled. "Why would he think that would work?"

I quirked one brow. Was he serious? "Um, maybe because you've basically been ghosting me since Heath…since the fire. It wasn't really a huge stretch to think you'd gone back to acting like I don't exist."

He recoiled like I'd slapped him. "I wasn't—That isn't what I—" He broke off with a sigh, scrubbing a hand over his face. His jaw was rocking some day-old stubble and it was a shockingly good look on him. Rougher than he usually looked. More rugged. "Yeah, okay. I can see the logic, I guess."

At that moment, the front door lock clicked, and a moment later Nate casually strolled in like he didn't have a care in the world. Hell, he looked downright smug. Wait. Ew. He looked like he'd just gotten laid.

"Carter, bro! What's with the SOS? I was letting Paige beg for forgiveness so this better be—" He paused when he laid eyes on me, seated on the huge leather sofa with my iced coffee in hand. "What the fuck are you doing here, Layne? Can't you take a hint?"

Scowling, I placed what little remained of my coffee down on the table, then stood up, walked across to where Nate had stopped in his tracks, reached up, and slapped him right across the face.

"Ow! What the fuck?" he exclaimed, reeling back in shock.

"That," I snarled, "was for fucking around in my phone while I was asleep, you entitled fuck nugget." Then I slapped him again because I could sense he thought I was done. Once again, my palm connected with a sting across his face. "And that was for taking my dress off. Creep."

"Whoa!" Carter exclaimed. "He did fucking what now?"

Nate glared daggers his way, then caught my wrist before I could deliver a third slap—this time just for the hell of it. "I was being nice, Ashley, considering it was a ten-thousand-dollar dress and covered in so many sequins it would have been like sleeping wrapped in sandpaper. Most people would try using a polite thank you instead of assault."

"That doesn't excuse your little hacking game in my phone, Essex!" I barked back, attempting to tug my wrist free of his iron grip. He didn't let go, though, instead using it to pull me a step closer.

His lips parted, but whatever he was going to say got interrupted by Heath returning from the shower. "Oh, come on, I told you not to slap him until I was back!"

Amusement cut through my anger like a crack of sunlight in a pitch-black room, and I fought to stop my lips from curling. "Sorry, honey. Heat of the moment and all that."

Nate's hard gaze cut from me to Heath, then over to Royce and Carter before he released my wrist with an abrupt motion. "I see we're all straight back to simpering over my stepsister again. Silly me for thinking you had more self-respect, Ashley."

My jaw dropped. "Excuse you? Self-respect? You blocked them in my phone!"

Nate shrugged, apparently totally unapologetic. "Okay…and so you thought the first opportunity you got, you'd go begging for attention and asking why no one had contacted you? Kinda pathetic, don't you think?"

The look he gave me as he headed for the kitchen was full of pity, and my blood fucking boiled.

"Okay, enough." Heath stepped closer, looping an arm around my waist as if to physically restrain me from going after Nate with violence again. To be fair, my fists were so tightly balled at my sides, I definitely wasn't thinking about slapping anymore. Nope, I was thinking about breaking his perfect fucking face. "He is deliberately trying to get a rise out of you, Ashes. Don't fall into his trap."

Nate snort-laughed. "Aw, are we all using cute nicknames now, Ashes? I think I'll call you...hmmm...how about Nevaeh Bicycle? Because apparently anyone can take a ride. Better double wrap your dick, Heath. Who knows what you might catch from that communal cum dumpster?"

This time, I didn't need to resort to slapping. Heath let me go, crossed the distance to where Nate stood in the kitchen, and dropped him with one solid punch.

"Ow," Nate groaned from the ground. "Yeah, I deserved that one."

"The next words out of your mouth better be a heartfelt apology to Ashley," Heath snarled, "or I'll let Carter have the next punch."

Geez, even I flinched at that threat. A quick glance Carter's way confirmed he was on his feet with fists clenched and a murderous look on his handsome face. Fuck, even Royce looked like he'd happily drown Nate in the sink right now.

"I apologize, Ashley," Nate gritted out, sounding shockingly sincere for once. "That was out of line and I'm sorry."

Heath looked at me, silently asking if that was good enough. I jerked a shocked nod his way, then scowled back at Nate, who was glaring daggers. "Apology accepted, but insult certainly not forgotten," I muttered, folding my arms.

After another tense moment, Heath extended his hand to Nate, who clasped it and let his friend pull him back to his feet.

"That was a hell of a punch, considering how scrawny you're

looking," Nate told Heath, offering a lopsided smile and a shoulder check as he headed for the freezer to grab an ice pack. Which then reminded me about Carter's face.

"Toss Carter some ice too," I instructed. Nate didn't question me, just lobbed a gel pack across to Carter, who caught it and pressed it against his purple cheek.

Heath huffed, folding his arms over his chest. He'd sadly put a T-shirt on after the shower, and admittedly, it was a little loose. He was far from scrawny, though. Just not quite as jacked up as Carter and Nate. Or shit, even Royce was rocking some serious guns at the moment.

"Why'd you block all our numbers in Ashes' phone, Nate?" Heath persisted, gesturing for me to rejoin Carter on the couch as he and Nate headed over to find seats. "You let us all think she was mad at us for something when you knew all along."

Nate shrugged. "Seemed like a good idea at the time. I'd had at least two bottles of champagne that night, to be fair. Besides, you were told by your doctor to avoid any romantic relationships for the next six months, while you're in therapy."

"So you thought you'd intervene?" Heath looked like he was seriously considering punching him again. "What gave you the fucking right, Nate? Last I checked, I'm an adult and can make my own decisions."

Nate snapped. No more blasé, no-fucks-given attitude. He totally snapped. "What gave me the right? Maybe the fact that I fucking care about you, Heath. I don't want to ever be responsible for cutting you down from a ceiling fan again. I don't ever want to be the one to give you CPR and try to bring you back to life again. How about that? Maybe, just maybe, if you weren't all tangled up in Ashley's shit, then you never would have done such a stupid thing."

For a moment, no one spoke. The silence was so thick, you could have heard a pin drop. Then Lady whined like she didn't enjoy the tension either, and Carter leaned over to scratch behind her ear reassuringly.

"You don't know that," Heath finally said in a quiet voice. "All of this could have played out exactly the same without Ashley's involvement. It still could happen again and have nothing to do with her. You're blaming her for shit that has nothing to do with her, except that you don't know who else to blame."

"Wasn't Ashley the one who snapped you out of the sleepwalking trance that night too?" Royce pointed out. "So it could be argued that we would all be in a much worse place right now without her."

Well. When he put it like that… If Nate hadn't snapped out of it, would we have found Heath in time to save him? Remembering how fuzzy and out of it both Royce and Carter had been, I couldn't be so sure.

Nate had a stubborn scowl on his face, though. Or I guessed that was what the expression was, considering half his face was covered with an ice pack. "That doesn't change your doctor's advice," he replied.

"I wish I never fucking shared that with you," Heath groaned, raking a hand through his hair. "It's irrelevant, anyway. My doctor said to avoid any new emotional connections that might be confusing during my recovery. This isn't new, Nate, and I can't just pretend I'm not already falling for Ashes just because it makes you uncomfortable."

I choked on my iced coffee. Gasped with the straw still in my mouth, inhaled liquid, choked. My face heated to a million degrees as I spluttered and gasped, and Royce watched me with the strangest expression on his face as tears streamed from my eyes.

Carter gave me a firm pat on the back, which did exactly nothing to help, but I quickly managed to get my shit under control again and wipe my eyes with the sleeve of my sweater.

"Sorry," I croaked. "Sorry, I, um, I wasn't expecting that." Fuck me, now all four of them were staring at me and I wanted to be literally anywhere but here. Except at the same time, I really wanted to be alone with Heath, so I could make him repeat that. Just for me. Preferably while balls deep inside me.

"Bro…" Nate said with a pitying head shake. "You can't seriously be falling for that." He gestured to me with an insulting sort of grimace.

Heath, on the other hand, looked at me like I was a goddamn queen. Pure adoration that was impossible to ignore. "Why not? She seems pretty perfect to me."

Oh Christ, this was too much. This felt like a conversation I shouldn't be sitting right fucking there for. Could I sneak out without anyone noticing?

"Dude…she's fucking Carter for one thing," Nate scoffed, and my face heated even more. I couldn't even say anything to defend myself because technically it was true…even with our chat in the elevator earlier, I was under no illusions that I wouldn't fall back onto his dick at some stage.

Heath just shrugged. "I've had plenty of time to make my peace with that. If I had to share with anyone, I'm glad it's one of you dickheads."

"Wow," I blurted out. "This has been…a lot. Um. Ah…can we possibly put a pin in this super awkward chat that feels way too personal for the current group setting? And maybe circle back around to the whole hypnosis issue that is the root of the conflict here? Let's, um, yeah, let's talk about that and stop talking about who is sleeping with who, yeah?"

"Whom," Royce murmured, correcting me. "Who is sleeping with whom, Squirrel. And while we're on the subject, I think it's best if we reengage our roomie arrangement. For safety."

"Seriously?" Nate barked, throwing his hands up.

I was pretty sure Royce was just fucking with him at this stage, but it did remind me to ask about Mr. Lionel Hughes. "Okay, wait, which one of you is responsible for hiring the bodyguard?" Because it wasn't Carter, or he wouldn't have punched the man for doing his job.

"What bodyguard?" Heath asked with obvious concern.

I gestured to Carter's face where he had the ice pack against his cheek. "The one Carter got into a fight with this morning after the car crash on the South Green."

"Wait, what?" Royce exclaimed. "What car crash? Why'd Carter get into a fight with a bodyguard? Catch us up, please."

I sighed, then my stomach rumbled. I'd grabbed coffee at Dancing Goats, but at the time my appetite had evaporated thanks to the near-death situation. Now, though? I was hungry as hell.

"You tell them," Carter said, dropping a very casual kiss on my hair as he stood up. "I'll make you something to eat."

It was a solid deal, so I nodded and then gathered my thoughts. Screw it, may as well start with Mr. Hughes showing up at my dorm room and go from there, so I didn't leave anything important out. We still couldn't rule out the car crash being part of the hypnosis thing, either. After all, the driver had been a DB, and according to Abigail, it all centered on the society.

Everything centered on the society.

Chapter Twelve

EVERYTHING FEELS DIFFERENT ON CAMPUS. I'M LOOKING TWICE AT EVERY
SHADOW AND FEELING EYES ON ME EVERYWHERE I GO. THIS SLEEPWALKING
THING...IT'S BIGGER THAN JUST HEATH. I FEEL IT'S BIGGER THAN JUST THE
FOUR OF US TOO. IS IT CENTERED AROUND THE DBS? OR IS IT THE SCHOOL?
BOTH? I HAVEN'T WANTED TO TELL ANY OF THE GUYS, BUT I'VE STARTED
HAVING WEIRD NIGHTMARES TOO. I HAVE A HORRIBLE FEELING THAT I WAS
INVOLVED WITH ASHLEY'S KIDNAPPING, AND IT MAKES ME SICK TO MY
STOMACH. SHE NEEDS TO STAY THE FUCK AWAY FROM US UNTIL WE CAN
WORK OUT WHAT'S GOING ON.

N. ESSEX, JANUARY 6

Carter wasn't joking when he said he'd make me something to eat.
Before I fully finished recounting the events of last night and this
morning, he'd made cinnamon buttermilk pancakes from scratch and
served them up with maple syrup, whipped cream, and strawberries.

"I didn't know you were such a chef, Sir Carter," I teased as I
slid down to sit on the floor so I could use the coffee table to eat on.

Nate snorted. "Is that a kink thing? Gross."

I squinted at him for a moment, confused about what he was talking about. Oh, he thought me calling Carter sir sounded like a Dom-sub thing, rather than poking fun of his British accent and affluent family. "I find it fascinating that you're constantly thinking about sex around me, Essex. Don't you?"

His eyes widened in shock, and I smirked.

"Both of you, cut it out," Heath scolded before Nate could retort to my snark. "Let's stay on topic. Do we know anything more about the driver of the car? Carter, did you see anything useful, like whether they were actively trying to hit Ashley?"

I startled at that and almost choked on the mouthful of pancake I'd stuffed in. Almost, but managed to swallow safely before continuing to react. "Was that a concern? That never even crossed my mind. I just figured it was the wrong place, wrong time."

Heath arched a brow at me. "Really? After you've been repeatedly targeted by someone posing as society hazing? I don't believe in coincidences, Ash. Not here."

Well, shit. That left me stunned and a little speechless as I thought it over. Surely that wasn't the case with the car crash, though. It was just a random…coincidence. Wasn't it?

"The driver was Daniel Mahoney. His girlfriend was taken to surgery," Carter informed the guys. "But no, I didn't see any of it. I arrived just in time to hear Spark screaming at the bodyguard douche to let her go and see him totally ignoring her demands."

"That explains the shiner," Royce mused aloud, then fist-bumped Carter as if to say nice.

Nate and Heath exchanged a long look, then Nate nodded. "He was a DB. So's his girlfriend, Zara. Can we get an update on how she's doing? Maybe she knows whether he was acting strange before the crash."

Royce nodded, pulling out his phone. "I'm on it."

"If this is hypnosis," Heath said thoughtfully, "then there has to be a common denominator. Someone pulling all the strings and planting the orders, right?"

My mouth was too full to contribute—Carter was a great cook—but I hummed a sound of agreement with that statement. I knew who my prime suspect would be, but it'd be interesting to see if he suspected anyone else.

"My money is on Dr. Fox," Nate said with a grimace.

Heath sighed heavily, his shoulders dropping. "Mine too. He is the logical culprit, right? He's a clinical psychologist. I had regular sessions with him after which I would often have shockingly bad headaches... What if he was using my therapy sessions to mess around with hypnosis?"

"Isn't that...too obvious?" Royce asked, scratching the back of his neck. "Like, surely he'd know that this would blow back on him if anyone ever worked out what was happening?"

I put my hand up so I wouldn't lose my train of thought while finishing my mouthful. "Um, do you all have therapy sessions with Dr. Fox? Because you were all sleepwalking the night of the fire."

"I do," Royce confirmed with a grim look. "But Nate and Carter don't."

Heath tapped his fingers against his lips for a moment, his gaze distant while he thought it over. "Okay...so it's not an iron-clad opportunity but I think he's worth investigating? Maybe just...a casual snoop around to see if there's anything incriminating in his office?"

"Heathcliff Briggs," Carter chuckled, "did you just propose breaking and entering? Royce is rubbing off on you."

Heath's answering grin was pure mischief. "Sure. Let's all pretend Royce is the only delinquent here. But yes, that's exactly what I'm suggesting. We gain access to Dr. Fox's office somehow and just take a little browse around. If we can even take a look at my own medical file, it can confirm whether my therapy sessions were bullshit or not, right?"

He had a point. Dr. Fox—if he was somehow involved in a weird hypnosis experiment—wouldn't bother fabricating therapy notes if he had no reason to think anyone would see them. Right? You wouldn't need fake notes with doctor-client confidentiality and all that.

"I'm game," Royce announced, clapping his hands together. "How, when, who, where?"

"He has office hours on Mondays and Tuesdays, but Wednesdays he teaches Neuropsychology over in Belford Hall with John Catton as his TA. That'd be the best opportunity, I think." Heath reached out and stole a strawberry off my plate, shooting me a wink when I scowled. "In the meantime, we can all keep our eyes and ears open for anyone else experiencing sleepwalking or…whatever. Agreed?"

The guys all murmured their confirmation of the vague plan, and I checked my phone when I felt a message come through. Carly sent an update about Jess—the girl who'd been hit—and I read it aloud for the boys to hear. She apparently had a broken pelvis and cracked skull so had been put in an induced coma until the swelling on her brain went down.

"Jessica Bentley?" Royce repeated, stunned. "Shit. She's basically the star player on the Nevaeh girls' basketball team. That fucking sucks."

That must have been how Carly knew her. She'd mentioned being a former basketball player when we'd met and clearly kept up with the team.

"Carter, can you drop me back on campus? I want to go pick Carly up from the hospital before my class this afternoon." I climbed to my feet and carried my dirty plate over to the kitchen to rinse off, like a good guest. The pancakes had all but disappeared. I'd been hungry, but it hadn't escaped my notice how immaculate the guys always kept their apartment. Carter had washed up all his cooking dishes straightaway too, so I didn't want to be the slob leaving a mess.

"Wait, why does Carter need to drive you?" Royce asked,

following me over to the kitchen. "What happened to the Firebird?"

I rolled my eyes, fighting a smile. "No one else keyed it, if that's what you're wondering. It's at my dorm. I just came over here with Carter because his car was closer to Dancing Goats."

"And she didn't bring any coffee for the rest of us," Heath added, his tone teasing. "I know, dude. I was offended too."

Royce frowned, shooting Carter a suspicious look. "Well, I'll drive you. I've got the same philosophy class as you this afternoon. We can pick up Carly on the way."

I shrugged, not really giving a shit who drove me so long as I didn't need to waste money on a rideshare while there were four perfectly good vehicles parked downstairs. Royce grabbed his keys and backpack, and Heath grabbed me for a not-so-brief kiss before we headed out.

Carter shot me a dark look when I glanced over my shoulder, and I shook it off. He knew perfectly well that my reasons for pushing him away were valid. He wanted time to think? He'd better think fast because Heath wasn't messing around anymore.

Royce was oddly quiet on the elevator down to their parking garage, and I couldn't help feeling like he had something on his mind that he was reluctant to voice aloud.

Once we were seated in the close confines of his car, I sighed and shifted to look at him. "What's going on, Royce? You seem… burdened."

A small frown creased his brow and he glanced over at me before shifting into reverse. "I'm fine," he lied.

I huffed a frustrated sound. "Okay, then. I guess we're not back to the way things were, then?"

His jaw clenched as he guided the car through the underground lot toward the ramp. "How were we, Squirrel? What are we supposed to be back to?" His voice held an odd level of seriousness that threw me off balance. Like I was meant to be reading between the lines and totally overlooking something important.

"I don't understand the question," I admitted. "We were friends, weren't we? At least, I thought we were…temporary roomies, but otherwise…friends?"

He said nothing back for the longest time, just keeping his focus entirely on the road and his driving, as though I weren't even in the car with him. Then after what seemed like an eternity, he sighed.

"Yeah, sure," he murmured. "We're still friends, I guess."

"You guess?" I laughed a little uncomfortably. "Okay, weirdo. How come your schedule changed this semester anyway?"

He gave a one-shoulder shrug. "It didn't, really. I was taking this class with you last semester in our doubled-up schedule and decided I liked it enough to officially enroll."

That made sense. I'd thought about doing the same in some of his courses as well but didn't want to add to my workload when the credits didn't apply to my degree. I was kind of pleased that he'd still be in some classes with me, even if he wasn't playing protection detail.

Which reminded me… "You definitely didn't hire my security guy, right?"

Royce shot me another sharp glance. "Definitely not."

"I assumed it was Carter, initially," I admitted, thinking out loud, "but the way he started a fight sort of verified that he had no clue who Mr. Hughes was…so did Heath do it? Why wouldn't he have mentioned it to me or at least to Carly if he thought I didn't wanna talk?"

Royce scoffed. "Maybe it was Nate."

I chuckled. "Sure. Because he cares so much for my safety. Oh, can we duck through the drive-thru?" I pointed to the fast food place coming up on our left. "Carly asked for chicken tenders and Texas toast."

"Yes, ma'am," Royce agreed, merging across to turn into the driveway.

We picked up food for Carly—and Royce—then continued on to the hospital where Carly was waiting outside for us to pull up.

"Roycey!" she exclaimed with a grin as she clambered into the back seat. "You're alive!"

He rolled his eyes, fighting a smile as she hugged his neck from behind his seat. "Of course I'm alive, drama queen. You texted me a middle finger emoji yesterday when I asked if you guys were back on campus."

Carly snort-laughed, buckling herself into her seat. "Yeah, you were dead to us yesterday for ghosting Ash. Right, babe? I got your back. But apparently bygones are bygones and all that? How fucking much did I miss today? How'd you two kiss and make up?"

"Mmm, last I checked," Royce replied with a mischievous smirk, "it wasn't me that Squirrel was kissing and making out with on the sofa."

Carly gasped a scandalized gasp. "What? Ash! You swore Carter was dead to us too!"

Royce snickered. "Heath, actually."

I groaned, scrubbing my hands over my face. "It was technically both of them. Just…eat your damn chicken. I'll fill you in later."

Carly gave a sound of protest, her mouth already full. Royce's hands flexed on the steering wheel, his knuckles white for the briefest moment before he glanced my way with a somewhat lopsided smile. "Don't be like that, friend. We want the gossip. Right, Carls?"

"Damn right," Carly mumbled around her food.

I sighed. The two of them wouldn't let me off the hook quite so easily. Besides, Carly needed to know about the blocked-number situation, so I wouldn't seem like quite such a pathetic bitch for forgiving their supposed ghosting that easily. Reluctantly, I filled her in about that, then gave both of them the dirt on Carter and Heath.

I kept Heath's intensely vulnerable confession of falling for me quiet, though. It felt too intimate to share, even though all the guys had been right there to hear it.

Carly chattered, squealed, and asked a dozen prying questions...
but Royce remained quiet. It was weird, but he was probably only
playing along to encourage Carly. He really didn't give a fuck for the
smutty details himself.

Or maybe he disapproved of me being involved with two of his
friends at the same time? The idea that Royce disapproved of, or
was disappointed in, my decisions caused an uncomfortable anxiety
to swirl through my guts, so I smoothly changed the subject for the
rest of the drive.

Chapter Thirteen

Heath told us we all need to keep a journal so there's a written account of...stuff. It's a stupid idea, though. If we are sleepwalking or hypnotized or whatever, then we won't remember. And if we don't remember, then we can't fucking write about it, can we? He's being stubborn, though, so I'm writing this to get him off my damn back. Maybe I'll just keep a running record of all the filthy things I want to do to Ashley instead... Yeah, that's a better idea. Especially now that she's keeping me at arm's length.

That won't last long. She likes me way too much, I'm sure of it. Then again, she likes Heath a whole lot as well. Will she pick him over me? Has she already? Fuck. I need to sort my crap out ASAP.

Jan. 7
C. Bassington

My bodyguard had been fired, apparently. He was nowhere to be seen when I returned to my dorm with Carly after class, and I nearly had a damn heart attack when my door opened well after I'd turned my lights out. It was just Royce, though. He shushed me, ordering me to go back to sleep as he slipped under the covers and erected our pillow wall as though the last month of weirdness and ice had never happened.

I wanted to call him on it and not let him brush it under the blankets so easily, but at the same time I was glad to have him back. So I shut my mouth and went back to sleep secure in the knowledge that my roomie was back.

The next morning, I woke up with the familiar warmth of Royce's chest under my cheek, and for an insane moment, I wondered what would happen if I didn't sneak away. What would he do if he woke up to find us all tangled up like lovers rather than friends? Probably give me no end of hell and tease me about having a crush on him, to which I'd blush as red as a damn fire truck because it wasn't untrue. Not that I'd admit it to anyone...not even Carly. I was already greedy enough with Heath and Carter.

So, biting back my baser instincts, I slithered out of his sleep-heavy embrace and silently fixed the pillow wall once more. Stupid unconscious need for snuggles was messing with my head.

By the time I got back from showering and getting dressed, Royce was gone. He'd texted me, though, letting me know he had an early lecture and that I'd snored.

Grinning, I sent back a middle finger emoji and told him he was a liar.

Carly and I headed out for coffee and found Heath already waiting, with coffees ordered, and the rest of the day went smoothly. Or smoothly in comparison to the car crash and student fatalities from the day prior.

The next morning Carly came barging into the shower while I was halfway through shampooing my hair.

95

"Um, good morning," I spluttered as she shoved her hand through the shower curtain to show me her phone. "What am I looking at here? Also, is your phone waterproof?"

"Of course it is, dummy, but read the message!"

Steam was fogging up the screen, though, so I sighed and leaned back to rinse my shampoo out. "Read it to me—it's too foggy."

Carly made a frustrated sound, then withdrew her phone to read aloud. "Zara regained consciousness last night and was questioned briefly by police. She told them that Daniel seemed totally normal. They were listening to the radio and talking about their plans for the afternoon, then all of a sudden he went blank like a zombie, then locked his eyes on some girl walking across the green and drove straight at her."

Shock rippled through me, and I rinsed my hair faster. "Wait, who was that from?" Because that was a whole lot of information that probably should be kept classified by the cops, wasn't it?

"Emerson, one of the basketball girls. She was at the hospital to visit Jess and overheard this all going on so just lingered to hear the rest. Ash, it sounds like Daniel was hypnotized, doesn't it?"

I'd filled her in on our discussion around Dr. Fox's possible involvement, and she was totally on board with the plans to investigate.

"Royce is in my room," I told her. "Go show him while I finish up in here." Because I still needed to apply conditioner and shave my legs. A girl had priorities.

Carly gave a startled laugh. "He is? Well, isn't that interesting?" She took off out of the shower before I could explain that we were just sleeping together…not sleeping together. *Ugh.* Better make it a speedy shower after all.

Back in my dorm room, I found Carly pacing the small space with her hands flapping around as she clearly talked through a conspiracy theory. Royce reclined against my pillows as though it was his bed, hair messy and shirtless. Fucking hell, he was a sexy man. Even more so when he turned those pretty green eyes my way and looked me over with an odd expression on his face. Annoyed? Aroused? What was that?

"Good morning, Squirrel," he murmured, his voice still husky from sleep. "Did you really tell Hurricane Carly to wake me up?"

I wet my lips, my pulse racing uncomfortably for some reason. Maybe it was the news Carly had just broken, making me anxious? "I didn't say to wake you up, but I definitely wanted to finish my shower without an audience." Carefully avoiding eye contact—for some fucking reason—I tossed my dirty clothes into the laundry hamper, then towel dried my wet hair a little more. "I assume she gave you the update about the crash?"

Royce yawned loudly, stretching his arms above his head and pulling my attention before he replied. "Yeah, it sounds suspicious as fuck. Reckon he does sessions with Dr. Fox too?"

That hadn't even occurred to me, but it was a valid question. Then I frowned. "You don't still have sessions with him booked, right?" Because he'd said he and Heath both did therapy with the professor in question.

A lopsided smile hit Royce's lips, and I found it hard to look away. "Of course not. I haven't done a session in ages, and Heath now has a new doctor from the rehab clinic."

"Uh…is something going on between you two?" Carly interrupted and I nearly flinched when I remembered she was there with us. "Because if I'm about to become third wheel in this relationship, I will need formal written notice."

I rolled my eyes and threw a pair of rolled-up socks her way. "Don't be ridiculous. Anyway, we are hitting Dr. Fox's office today, aren't we, Royce? While he's teaching?" Why the fuck was I blushing? *Stop blushing, Ash!*

Royce stretched again, then tossed back the blankets to swing his legs out of my bed. He'd taken to just sleeping in boxer shorts because apparently the dorm thermostat was cranked up too high, and Carly's pointed stare in my direction said she had things to say.

"Yup, after lunch," Royce confirmed, pulling on his jeans and tugging his black top over his head, hiding all those abs. "I've got to get to class, but I'll text you later, Squirrel."

"What about me?" Carly pouted, giving him a narrow-eyed glare as he pulled his shoes on. "Gonna text me too, Roycey?"

His answer was a sarcastic middle finger as he headed out the door. I busied myself with brushing my wet hair in the wake of his departure, until Carly loudly and very pointedly cleared her throat.

"What?" I asked, innocent as anything.

Her brows hiked so hard they were basically in her hairline. "Ashley Layne…were you not just telling me two days ago about how you'd made up and made out with both Carter and Heath again?"

"Yeah…your point?" I had a pretty solid feeling I knew what her point was, but I'd feign innocence as long as I possibly could nonetheless.

Carly's eyes bugged out and she gestured wildly to the rumpled bed that Royce had just vacated. "Do you want to explain that?"

I wet my lips, then realized…no one knew Royce had literally been sleeping in my bed all this time. Carly had thought he was sleeping on the floor, like how our little roommate situation had started.

"Oh. That." I turned back to my mirror to work out some stubborn tangles with my brush. "Don't read too much into it, Carly. He is very diligent about putting a pillow wall in place to maintain personal space. It's just not fair to make him sleep on the floor all the time."

She scoffed. "He doesn't have to sleep in here at all. That's his choice. What does Heath say about this? Or Carter, for that matter? I can't imagine he's thrilled about Royce trying to cut his grass."

I spluttered a laugh. "Excuse me? That's not—" I shook my head, not needing my reflection to tell me how red I just went. "That's not what's happening here. Royce is being a good friend, and none of us are comfortable with Heath sleeping here until we can be sure he's not sleepwalking anymore. So, it's Royce or Mr. Lionel Hughes..."

Carly cracked up, shaking her head. "Oh my god, you're so delusional. Okay, I've got to get to my Early Written Languages class. You gonna be okay on your own this morning?"

I rolled my eyes. "Don't you start too. That car could have been aimed at you just as much as me. Or Jess or fucking any of the other dozens of students on the lawn that morning."

"Mm-hmm, sure," she muttered unconvinced, "and Royce is just a good friend. Okay, bye. Text me later."

She left before I could insist again that Royce *was* just a good friend, and I groaned to myself once I was alone. She'd hit a little close to the bone on her question too. Heath had been really unimpressed to hear that our arrangement was back in place, and Carter had looked like he was going to punch a wall. Not that I was ever going to invite him to sleep over, considering our chat the other day.

"Messy, messy situationships," I muttered to myself as I hunted out my hair dryer. I didn't have any classes on a Wednesday so intended to spend my morning studying at the library before meeting the guys at lunch to plan our breaking-and-entering mission.

As much as I was frustrated by this constant shadowing that the guys were doing—not leaving me alone fucking anywhere, it seemed—a weird spike of fear hit me as I laced up my boots to leave the dorms alone.

"You're being paranoid, Ashley," I whispered to myself, trying to shake off the feeling. But...what if I wasn't? That glimmer of uncertainty was enough to have me text Heath to ask if he wanted to study with me in the library.

He replied almost immediately and invited me to the apartment instead. I chewed my lip, debating if it was a good idea or not, and he followed up with another message to say he was home alone. That was all I needed.

Perfect. I'll be there in 10!

His reply was just a heart emoji, and my stomach flip-flopped. In a good way, though. Butterflies were fun, and maybe I didn't need to study this morning after all. It wasn't until I started thinking about all the other things Heath and I could do that I realized how worked up I already was. Maybe I was ovulating? Seemed plausible.

.

Chapter Fourteen

WELL. APPARENTLY MY PLAN TO FORCE SOME DISTANCE BETWEEN ASHLEY AND MY FRIENDS BACKFIRED. NOW NOT ONLY IS SHE PROBABLY PLOTTING MY AGONIZING DEATH BY A THOUSAND PAPER CUTS, BUT THE GUYS ARE ALL DEFENDING HER. AS IF SHE NEEDS IT. LITTLE SPITFIRE CAN FIGHT HER OWN BATTLES. MY FACE STILL HURTS AND NOT JUST FROM HEATH'S RIGHT HOOK.

N. ESSEX, JANUARY 8

It felt good to be back in my own car. I hadn't driven in weeks, since before winter break, but my Firebird still ran like a dream. Heath had texted me the access code for their parking garage and directed me to park in Royce's spot since he was at campus.

When he answered the door, his hair was messy and once again no shirt was to be seen. What was with these guys being allergic to clothing? Not that I was complaining. I basically climbed him like a tree the moment the door shut behind me.

"This is better than studying in the crusty old library," he murmured between kisses, his hands gripping my ass as my legs wound around his waist. "How long do you have?"

"Ages," I replied as he carried me over to the huge leather sofa and laid me down carefully. "You're definitely home alone?" It seemed disrespectful as hell to fuck around if Carter was in the next room. Nate, I didn't really give a fuck about.

"Yup, all morning. Royce and Carter have class, and Nate's at the gym. I'm all yours, beautiful." He punctuated that point by kissing me so hard, I forgot to breathe. My fingers flexed against his strong back muscles, and my hips rolled against him as I silently begged for more.

He understood perfectly but gave a low chuckle as he braced his weight on his elbows on either side of my head to keep from squashing me. "Ashes, is this what you meant when you asked if I wanted to study? Because I could study you all damn day and not get tired of it..." He trailed kisses down my throat, then shifted his position to help me strip out of my sweater.

I grinned as he tossed it aside, then stared intently at my tits, still restrained in my basic black bra. I definitely hadn't had this in mind when I'd been getting dressed this morning.

"It's not," I admitted, "but I'm not mad about the change of plans. I was way ahead on my reading anyway." Then, because I was living for the way he was looking at me, I sat up just enough to snake my hand behind and unclip my bra. I slipped it off and tossed it across the room, where it landed on the TV.

Heath's groan was perfection as he cupped my tits in his huge hands. "I feel like I don't remember enough of our first time," he admitted in a dark whisper. "Like it was happening through a blanket of fog. I hate that I've lost the details...like how perfectly my hands fit around your incredible breasts...or how responsive your perfect rosebud nipples are..." He flicked his thumbs over the body part in question and I moaned at the sensation.

He dipped his head, taking one between his lips and sucking, his tongue flicking the tip and causing me to gasp with need. He was serious about studying apparently, and that required us taking our time.

"Mmm," he hummed as he released that nipple and swapped to the other. "This might take several intense study sessions to ensure no details are missed."

I grinned, my fingers threading into his soft, dark hair. "I'm okay with this." But at the same time, I was already so keyed up, I could easily come without even being touched down below. Nipple play never made me come, but apparently I just hadn't been with the right partner. Or maybe it'd just been way too long since I'd gotten off and I was ready to burst.

"Patience, little minx," he teased as I tried to tug on the waist-band of his sweatpants. "We've got all morning, remember?"

"Yeah," I agreed, already breathless, "but that just means we can fit in a repeat performance."

That made him pause, tilting his head thoughtfully. Then he smirked. "I like that idea. But there's something I've been wanting to do since the moment we met. Since that day I lay there on your massage table with the most painful boner known to man as you rubbed me down."

I shivered, remembering that day. I'd been so incredibly attracted to him, and then he'd rolled over to reveal that erection he'd been hiding... Fuck, I'd been tempted to take his shady offer. Way more tempted than I wanted to admit.

Heath kissed his way down my belly, then unbuttoned my jeans. I lifted my hips as he peeled them down, taking my panties along for the ride. It took a second to get them off entirely, then I was totally naked on the sofa in broad daylight for his inspection. It was a damn good thing I wasn't modest, or it could have been uncomfortable being so incredibly on display.

"Fuck," he moaned, then immediately sank his face between my thighs.

"Oh!" I exclaimed, my back arching as my fingers tangled in his hair once more, pulling him closer as his tongue penetrated me. "Heath, oh my god, uhhh…" I was way too tightly wound already to hold out under this kind of torture.

Heath was working with single-minded determination, though, eating my pussy like he was starving and sending me hurtling toward an orgasm at a million miles an hour. It was almost criminal how fast he was about to make me come.

"Technically," I panted, my voice shaking, "this isn't the first time you've done this." But I understood what he'd said before, that the events of the night we'd slept together were not clear in his memory.

He wasn't going to be distracted. His mouth shifted to my clit, sucking and flicking with his tongue while two fingers filled my pussy with a firm stroke.

"Oh, shit," I moaned, then my legs stiffened, my thighs locking around his head as an intense climax rocked through me. Waves on waves rolled from my core, sending tremors to every limb and causing my hips to buck violently.

Heath didn't let up, either. At some stage, he had to have stopped breathing, but he seemed fully determined to wring every last droplet of orgasm out of my pussy. Then when my thighs eventually loosened around his head, he withdrew his fingers to suck them clean.

"Fuck," I gasped, watching him as though from outside of my own body. Did he just make me astral project? Wild. "Please, Heath…I need your dick inside me."

His smirk was pure satisfaction as he pushed his sweats down, kicking them aside as I tried—and failed—to catch my breath and slow my racing pulse. It was a lost cause. Then he licked his lips and moaned like he was tasting the sweetest nectar on earth.

I watched the motion, spellbound, until his long lashes fluttered open and his hazel gaze locked on mine once more. "I want you to ride me," he announced, grabbing me by the waist and lifting me up as though I weighed little more than a wet kitten.

Fair, considering my pussy was drenched.

"Like this?" I murmured, settling my knees either side of his hips as he settled against the back of the couch in a seated position. His thick cock sat hard and proud between us, bumping against my mound as I found my balance.

Heath dragged his lower lip between his teeth, humming his satisfaction as he cupped my breasts in both hands. They were right in his face with this position, and he smirked up at me. "Perfect."

I chuckled, low and husky, as I rose up high and reached for his cock to line us up. "Shit, you're big," I whispered, my fingertips barely touching around his girth. No wonder he'd been so determined to make me come that hard first; he was making sure I was well lubricated to take him fully.

"You can take it, Ashes," he replied, kissing my throat. "I know you can."

I notched his tip at my cunt, then braced my hands on his shoulders as I lowered myself down. I took it slowly, savoring every millimeter as his huge cock stretched and filled me in the most delicious way.

"Heath..." I moaned, my eyes rolling back as my whole body flushed with heat and a shiver lit up my skin. "Fuck..."

His answering groan was music to my ears as he grabbed my waist and slammed me down the rest of the way until our hips met, flush together. "Ride me, Ashes," he ordered, his husky voice like a caress over my hypersensitive flesh. His hands grasped my butt cheeks, encouraging me to set the pace as my tits bounced in his face.

"Heath, oh my god," I gasped as I moved, sliding up and down his rock-hard length with increasing speed.

Then the fucking front door opened and I froze, locking eyes with the intruder.

His whiskey-brown eyes widened, his lips parting in shock as he took in the scene on the couch. Or what he could see of it from the doorway, which was likely just Heath's head on the back of the sofa

105

and my tits out on full display. It didn't take a genius to deduce what we were doing, though, even with the furniture blocking the best parts.

"Why'd you stop, Ashes?" Heath moaned, clearly not having heard the door. His hips bucked up and I whimpered before I could catch myself.

That noise seemed to shock Nate almost as much as seeing me there fucking his friend on the couch, and he visibly flinched. Then his brow dipped into a deep scowl and his lips twisted with a sneer.

"You have a bedroom for a reason, Heathcliff," he snarled, dropping his gym bag by the door and making his way toward the open-plan kitchen.

Heath—having just realized we had company—quickly tossed a throw blanket over our bottom halves, then covered my breasts with his hands. "Dude! What the fuck are you doing here?"

"I live here, dickhead," Nate snapped back.

Logically, I could appreciate the fact Heath was simply trying to preserve my modesty by covering my boobs with his hands, but my libido was roaring at me to finish what we started so I was having a hard time not leaning into his touch.

"You're supposed to be at the gym," Heath growled, shifting his hips in a way that probably wasn't intended to have the effect it had. Which was, of course, to draw another strangled little whimper from me as his cock twitched inside me. "Can you please…fuck off?"

Nate's gaze locked with mine again, and I bit my lip. Words were not going to be my friend right now. His gaze dropped to where my teeth sank into my lower lip, then his scowl darkened. "No. I came back to make a protein shake. If you wanted privacy, you'd have done this in your bedroom. Last I checked, this is shared space."

Fucking hell. Sweat was rolling down my spine now, and I rocked my hips in a desperate attempt to relieve some pressure. Was this what soaking was? Putting it in and not moving? It fucking sucked, for the record. I needed to come more than anything and I was quickly not giving a flying fuck who was watching.

"Jesus," Heath breathed, kissing the dip between my breasts. "Ashes, quit it. Nate, are you seriously going to stand there and watch?"

Nate gave a choked scoff. "As if. Layne is two solid seconds away from playing modest and leaving you with blue balls. She doesn't have the guts to fuck in front of an audience."

Anger burned through me at that, and my gaze whipped back to Nate's. He was staring right at me, like he was waiting for my reaction. He wanted to see his insult hit home and then probably laugh as I ran from the room, red-faced and embarrassed.

Well. Fuck that.

"Don't talk about me like I'm not right here, Essex," I replied, finally finding my voice. In fairness, it was husky and breathless, but there was no mistaking my irritation underscoring those words. "You don't know the first thing about me, and you sure as shit don't know what gets me off. Maybe I like the audience."

I was talking a big game, but the moment the words left my lips and I very deliberately started to ride Heath's dick again, I mentally panicked. Maybe I did like an audience? Because I was far from embarrassed right now, and I was insanely wet.

Heath groaned, his hands massaging and his fingers tweaking my nipples as I moved, rising and falling in his lap. "Ashes...holy shit. We can take this to my room if you want."

I shook my head, my eyes still locked with Nate's. "Nope. If Nate is uncomfortable, he can leave." Then I tossed my head back, closing my eyes and arching my back as I doubled my efforts riding Heath's huge cock.

It took longer than I anticipated, but right as I started to come— screaming—something in the kitchen smashed and the front door slammed. Just a split second before Heath shot his hot load into me with a gasping grunt.

"That was..." Heath murmured while panting and kissing my throat. "Amazing. But Nate is going to be a total dick about this later."

I shrugged as I snuggled my face into the curve of his neck, feeling way too post-orgasm floppy to give a good god damn. "Well, at least now he knows his dumb little blocking scheme didn't work."

Heath laughed, and it was seriously becoming one of my favorite sounds. His hands scooped under my ass again and he stood up with me in his arms, his dick still firmly lodged inside my dripping pussy. "Come on, showgirl. I want you to make good on that promise for round two before we need to break into Dr. Fox's office. Maybe even round three…"

I chuckled, clenching my inner muscles around him. "I'm a woman of my word, Heathcliff."

"And a closet exhibitionist too," he teased. "Good to know. Maybe this Carter thing won't be such an issue, after all."

Oh fuck. I liked that idea a lot more than needing to choose between them. The way my body reacted betrayed how much I liked it too, and Heath whispered curses as he laid me down on his huge bed. Good curses, though. He was definitely on board with the filthy ideas currently filling my head.

Question was, though: Would Carter be?

Chapter Fifteen

Keeping journals is fucking stupid. The only good to ever come from a journal was whatever clues Abigail left for Ashley. Even then, it sounds like her "record" was more like the ramblings of paranoia rather than a reliable information source. Maybe instead, I'll just keep a running record of all the times I've jerked off while picturing Spark. How many times I've had to wash those panties I stole from her in Paris because I can't stop using them to catch my cum. It's a filthy addiction...clearly I need to steal a few more pairs so I can rotate.

Jan. 8
C. Bassington

We all met up outside Cromwell Hall, where Dr. Fox's office was located, and sat under a huge oak tree as we discussed how to execute the breaking-and-entering plan. Or Royce and Heath discussed it. Nate just glared at me the whole time, and I very deliberately avoided catching his eye. Sure, in the heat of the moment, I was totally unashamed. Now? Different story. Carter must have sensed something going on, because he kept watching the both of us, like he was waiting for someone to start explaining the odd tension in the air.

Eventually, it was decided that Carter and Nate would head over to Dr. Fox's class to keep an eye on him and his TA, to ensure they didn't leave the lecture early for whatever reason. Royce had somehow gotten his hands on a copy of the janitor's master keys and Heath insisted he knew what to look for within the files more than anyone else. Me? Well, they tried to tell me to go to the library to study.

The laugh I spluttered when they said that almost saw me snort. "I'll be doing no such fucking thing," I informed them with a bemused smile. "But it's cute that you tried."

Royce threw his hands up with frustration. "Fine, you can go with Nate and Carter to—"

"No, she can't," Nate snapped. "She can go with you, or Carter can take her back to her room or something."

Heath smirked, shooting me a sly grin. "You can come with us, Ashes. This will be easy, anyway."

"Smart choice, Heathcliff," I replied with a grin of my own, tapping my index finger innocently on my thigh. His gaze followed the motion and he ran his tongue over his lower lip, understanding me perfectly. Sometime around the third time he'd eaten my pussy during our morning in bed, he'd left a bite mark and dark hickey on the inside of my thigh. Marking me, like a fucking caveman. I loved it too.

That was the spot I'd just tapped, and I could tell by the way he attempted to subtly adjust himself that he was hard again. The man had stamina, I'd give him that.

"Okay, clearly you two are fucking again," Royce muttered, pushing to his feet and stuffing his hands into his pockets. "Let's go and get this over with. I've got a date with Willa tonight and need to do some manscaping."

He stalked away before I could ask who the hell Willa was or make any jokes about his manscaping. But still, I didn't love the twist of anxiety in my gut as I accepted Heath's hand to stand up and follow.

"Who's Willa?" I asked, unable to keep the question to myself.

Nate snickered, a cold sort of laugh. "Jealous, Layne? Don't be so hypocritical." He swaggered away from us before I could ask what the fuck that was supposed to mean.

Carter sighed, then leaned down to brush a kiss over my cheek. "Willa is no one important," he told me, then took off after Nate at a slight jog.

If anything, his reassurance only worried me further. I turned to Heath with the question on the tip of my tongue, but his raised brow caught me in my tracks. Why was I fixating? Royce could date. Of course he could. We were just friends after all.

Biting my tongue, I swallowed back my weird mix of emotions. Heath threaded his fingers through mine, squeezing my hand as we trailed after Royce into the building. The two of us waited with our eyes on the hall to ensure no one saw us entering, but with the help of Royce's stolen key, we made it inside in no time at all.

"Where do we start?" Royce asked, tucking the key back in his pocket and looking around the neat office. His eyes lingered on the chaise lounge, and a frown creased his brow, his thoughts etched across his face.

"Hey," I said softly, touching his arm to pull his focus. "We'll get to the bottom of this. Maybe Dr. Fox is totally innocent?"

His answering smile was weak. "Yeah, maybe." He sighed and glanced at the banks of filing cabinets lining the wall. "Heath, you still know how to pick locks?"

To my surprise, Heath nodded. "Probably a bit rusty, but cabinet locks are a lot easier than doors." From his pocket, he pulled out a little case with honest-to-fuck lock picks inside.

Royce glanced over and grinned, then physically closed my gaping mouth with a finger under my chin. "We all grew up very rich and often got very bored," he explained while Heath went to work. "Sometimes our practical jokes required us to learn new skills. This one came in handy when we wanted to swap out all of the junior class report cards for ones with failing grades."

"The whole class?" I asked, bemused and honestly turned on as hell. Who knew Heath was a closet bad boy under that cinnamon-roll exterior? "Wouldn't that have been obvious?"

Royce shrugged, moving over to Dr. Fox's desk to poke around. "Yeah, but we didn't want anyone to actually think they'd failed. Just annoy our teachers a bit."

I chuckled at how them that was. "You guys were doing Devil's Backbone bullshit before you were even Devil's Backbone."

"Well, yeah," Royce agreed, flicking through some papers in Dr. Fox's desk drawer. "Our parents were all DBs when they went to Nevaeh. How's that lock going, Briggs?"

"Shut up," Heath grumbled, squinting at the little metal picks he was manipulating the lock with. "I told you I was rusty. You just need to be—aha! Got it." He withdrew the picks and slid open the file drawer with a triumphant grin.

For the next few minutes, the two of them sorted through the records, reading out names of people I suspected I'd never even met, pulling them out and stacking them into a pile on top of the cabinet. Among them were their own personal files and Daniel Mahoney's.

"So he was seeing Dr. Fox too…" I mused aloud when they added the now-dead student's folder to the stack. "What about all these other ones?"

"Society members," Heath informed me while Royce pulled his file from the stack and flipped it open. Then scowled.

"What the fuck? It's empty."

I crossed over to peer over his shoulder and verify what he was saying. The folder wasn't empty exactly, or that would have been evident by the lack of paper within. The pages themselves, though, were blank of all relevant information about their therapy sessions. The header and footer contained Royce's personal information, date of birth, student ID, all the usual stuff, as well as Dr. Fox's logo and details... but the bulk of the page where session notes should go? Blank.

Royce put his aside and grabbed another off the stack, flipping it open to find the exact same thing. "This seems... suspicious."

"Compare it to another file," I suggested, gesturing to the open filing cabinet. "Someone not in the society."

Heath pulled out another file and handed it over. When Royce opened it, the difference was unmistakable. Pages on pages filled with Dr. Fox's cramped handwriting in a blue ballpoint pen.

We looked through several more, then took photos of all the blank ones we could find. Every single one, the boys confirmed, was in the society.

"We should go," Heath murmured once we put everything back and he locked the cabinet again. "I feel like that's all the smoking gun we need at this stage, right?"

"Sure seems that way," Royce agreed, nodding.

On a whim, I grabbed the top page of Dr. Fox's notepad beside his computer and tore it off to take with us. When the boys looked at me in confusion, I offered a sheepish smile. "I saw it on a crime show. You can use a lead pencil to see what he was writing. I dunno, maybe something useful?"

The two of them grinned at me like I was being cute, so I rolled my eyes and tucked the blank sheet of paper into my pocket with a mumbled "whatever" before carefully easing the door open to check if the hallway was clear before we exited.

Heath called Carter as Royce locked the door behind us, and we made a plan to reconvene back at their apartment so we could talk in privacy. My car was parked behind Cromwell Hall, and the three of us headed that way without any discussions. It felt like there were eyes and ears everywhere, and I doubted it was safe to talk about anything of substance unless we were totally sure no one could overhear.

As we started across the parking lot, heading toward my Firebird, a group of girls crossed paths with us and two unpleasantly familiar women paused, eyes locked on my boys.

"Heath!" Jade exclaimed, her mouth rounding in fake shock. "You're back! We all thought—"

"Sorry, can't chat, we're busy," Royce interrupted, placing a hand on the small of my back to nudge me forward. Paige stepped in front of him, forcing him to either stop or bump into her. Regretfully, he didn't knock her on her ass…more's the pity.

She fluttered her lashes, a sultry smile on her lips. "I hope this isn't going to be awkward between us, Royce… I figure if Nate can move on, then surely you and I can too?"

What…the fuck was she talking about?

"You're delusional, Paige," Royce scoffed. "Nate doesn't forgive or forget so easily."

Paige just shrugged, coy as fuck. "Are you sure? He seemed like he was in a real forgiving mood on Monday. Or this morning, for that matter, when he pulled me out of class because he was so desperate for me." She licked her lips, innuendo clear as day. "I think you boys will be seeing me around the apartment more often, so it's probably best we all get along."

She reached out, patting Royce's chest in a condescending sort of way, and I acted without thinking. I grabbed her wrist and shoved her away so hard, she stumbled back a step, her vicious glare acknowledging my presence for the first time.

"You bitch," she hissed.

I glowered back, moving slightly to block her from touching Royce again. "Takes one to know one. I wouldn't get your hopes up about your future with Nate if I were you. Him letting you suck

114

his dick doesn't change anything, except his mood for like three point five minutes." I took a step forward, and satisfaction rippled through me when she backed up a step. "And don't even try faking another pregnancy to guilt him, or I'll personally expose your medical records for the whole damn school to see what a fake and a liar you are."

Paige's pretty face drained of color and her jaw hit the floor. I took advantage of her shock, grabbing Royce's hand and pulling him past the bitchy girl and her desperate sidekick. It was either leave or end up in a girl fight, and I really wasn't in the mood to get pulled into the university dean's office today.

"What was that all about?" Heath laughed as the three of us slid into my Firebird a minute later. "Also, remind me to scold Carly for spilling secrets."

I met Royce's eyes in the rearview mirror, checking that he was okay. He nodded back to me, a small smile on his lips. "Thanks, Squirrel," he murmured. "I honestly can't believe I ever fucked around with her. I've never liked her, even before we slept together."

I frowned, his words tugging at a new and unsettling thought as I pulled out of my parking space and started toward the guys' apartment. "Like...you never found her attractive or had a crush on her?"

Royce gave a sigh, running his hand through his hair and drawing my focus back to the mirror for a moment. "Yeah, I always thought she was pretty fucking insufferable. Fuck knows why I decided it was a good idea to sleep with her. I must have been drunk as hell."

Heath shot me a sharp look, and I nodded back. Clearly, he was drawing the same conclusions.

"I don't think you ever thought it was a good idea, Roycey," I said softly as I drove. "It sounds to me like someone planted the idea in your head and gave you no choice."

It was a horrifying thought, but considering what we'd seen so far, it was hardly the worst that hypnosis had done. Still, the idea that free will could be so thoroughly overridden filled my gut with anxiety. It was psychological abuse at best...and in Royce's case, it sort of felt like rape.

A deep shudder ran through me, and Heath squeezed my knee. None of us spoke for the rest of the drive, though, all lost in our own dark thoughts.

Chapter Sixteen

Carter and Nate beat us back to the apartment, and Carter was deep into his task of Lady's belly scratches when we arrived with the dark cloud of new speculations hanging over our heads.

Nate arched a brow in question and Royce made a beeline for the kitchen.

"I'm getting a drink. Anyone else want one?" He yanked the fridge door open, and the clink of glass bottles confirmed he didn't mean soda water.

"Yes," Heath agreed with a grimace, scrubbing a hand over his face.

Royce grabbed a second beer, then glanced over his shoulder at me where I still stood near the door. "Squirrel?"

I jerked a nod. "Yeah. Whatever you've got is fine." Not that I was a fan of beer, but after mentally acknowledging the extent of this hypnosis violation? I'd drink it and love it.

"What happened?" Nate asked, his eyes narrowed with worry as he looked between the three of us. "What did you discover in the office?"

Heath gestured for me to join him on the sofa, and I forced my feet to carry me over there while Royce deposited beers for everyone—Nate and Carter included—on the coffee table.

"It wasn't what we discovered in the office," Heath said with a small sigh, "which was a suspicious lack of evidence. It was the discovery that Ashes just stumbled over after we ran into your psycho ex, Nate."

His brows rose. "Paige?"

That brought a small smile to my lips. "You have more than one? Why doesn't that shock me?"

"She wanted to let us know that you guys are getting back together," Royce announced, clapping Nate on the shoulder sarcastically. "Congrats, man. When can we expect baby Essex to arrive?"

Nate jerked like he'd been struck, his startled eyes flicking to me before glowering at Royce.

"Chill, bro," Royce drawled, flopping onto the sofa on my other side and draping his arm behind me. Not on my shoulders, but if I leaned back, I could rest my head on his forearm. "Ash already knows about Paige's lies."

Carter cleared his throat, his bottle held between two elegant fingers as he met my eyes. "In somewhat of Nate's defense, Spark, he gave her the benefit of the doubt up until very recently. She was very convincing with her so-called miscarriage."

"Do we keep *any* secrets anymore?" Nate demanded, glaring daggers my way. "My business is none of your business, Layne, so I don't need your opinions."

I held up my hands defensively, shaking my head. "I hadn't said a damn word, and didn't intend to." At least...not to him. Paige deserved whatever came her way.

Royce gave a short laugh, probably thinking the same as I was, about how Paige looked like she'd seen a ghost when I called her on her bullshit. Then he covered the sound by guzzling half his beer in one go.

"After we exchanged some...polite words with your ex, we stumbled over the idea that Royce's, uh, misstep with her wasn't entirely of his own free will." Heath said it as delicately as possible, without calling it what it was. Royce fucked Nate's girlfriend behind his back. But our new suspicion that it was a hypnosis-planted idea... it felt more authentic. The idea that Royce cared so little for his friend? It wasn't him.

Stunned silence filled the room, and I watched Nate's expression intently. What was he thinking? That it was all bullshit made up to save face for Royce? Or...

"So...you guys think that hypnosis made Royce sleep with Paige? And without that...he wouldn't have been interested?" His expression was thoughtful, slightly shrewd, and his voice carefully even.

Royce finished his beer, then wiped his mouth with the back of his hand. "Not even the slightest bit. She always irritated me, and seeing her today made my skin crawl. Uh, no offense and shit?"

His skin crawled? That wasn't a normal reaction to seeing a consensual one-night stand.

Nate ignored the insult to his ex and shifted his eyes to me and Heath, then tipped his head to the side. "So to be clear, you're suggesting hypnosis could be somehow faking attraction between otherwise unattracted individuals? How interesting." His gaze turned mean as he locked eyes with me. "How confident are you, Layne, that Heath and Carter both wanted to fuck you?"

My initial reaction was that I wanted to throw my beer at him. But that knee jerk was closely followed by the ice-water dousing of uncertainty. If it was possible for Royce to be manipulated in that way, what proof did I have that Carter and Heath hadn't been similarly influenced?

The blood drained from my head, leaving me dizzy and my mouth dry. Nate's brow furrowed, no doubt seeing his words hit home in their intended way, and his lips parted like he wanted to say something more.

"It's not the same," Royce growled, interrupting before things could get any more out of hand. "No one here is being manipulated into their attraction to Ash and you fucking well know it. You're just so choked up on jealousy that you're grasping at straws."

I blinked at my usually lighthearted friend. Since running into Paige, his mood had turned dark, and there was no joking in his tone as he took swipes at Nate.

"Okay, this is getting out of control," I said quietly, trying to diffuse the fire we'd somehow lit. "And we're burying the lede. Heath, show them what we found in the files. Do you have a pencil somewhere? I want to try the notepaper thing."

He directed me to his desk, and I went to find it while he showed Nate and Carter the photos we'd taken of all the files. We'd made sure to photograph every society member's file that we could find, and some non-society members to offer a comparison.

I found a pencil in the top drawer of Heath's desk and carefully rubbed the lead over the notepaper page to reveal any indentations from a ballpoint pen writing on the page above. For a moment, I was disappointed. It seemed totally blank...or maybe I was doing the trick wrong?

Then, toward the bottom of the page, I struck gold.

Just one word: Hyperion.

"Does this word mean anything to anyone?" I asked, returning to the living room. "Hyperion? That's what was on the notepaper."

Royce grinned from where he was fetching another beer. "Nice work, Nancy Drew. I'm impressed."

I rolled my eyes but couldn't fight my satisfied smile. I liked when he was impressed. "Thanks. But it might just be the name of his erectile dysfunction medication or something equally useless."

"'Hyperion: Greek titan of heavenly light and watchfulness,'" Carter read aloud from his phone. "Why would a psychology professor be researching Greek myths?"

It didn't make sense. Then again, for all we knew, it could be a code word or a business name or...anything really. Nate muttered something about doing some research into the incorporated company database later when he was at his computer, and I remembered he had some skill with hacking.

The conversation started to go in circles about Dr. Fox and his objectives, until Nate's phone dinged and he groaned. "Shit, I totally forgot that was today," he grumbled under his breath. "Heath, come for a drive?"

Heath's brows hitched in question while he took a sip of his beer. "Where to?"

Nate tossed his phone down and ruffled his hair with his fingers. "Airport. Mom's flight arrives in half an hour, and I'm supposed to pick her up. You know how she is, dude, and she fucking loves you..."

Nate's mom? I'd never met her... Hell, I don't think I could even remember Max ever mentioning her. I sort of figured she was around but she wasn't active in Nate's life since the divorce.

Heath's nose wrinkled, and he shook his head. "Do I have to?"

Nate's response was a dark glare. "After the shit you pulled this morning? Yeah. You do."

Carter glanced between his friends, then suspiciously my way. "What'd Heath do this morning, Nathaniel? Did it have anything to do with the pair of Spark's panties I found under the couch cushion?"

Crap. That's where they'd been hiding. I'd had to give up when we were already running late to meet up with the guys at lunchtime.

"Fine," Heath groaned. "But I'm using the opportunity to ask your mom about hypnosis. She could have some really good insight, and god knows we can't trust anyone else on campus."

I blinked, confused as I looked at Nate with curiosity. "Your mom? Why…?" Why would she have insight on this matter?

Nate nodded with a shrug. "It's a good idea. She's a research psychologist," he explained for my benefit. "Spends most of her time working with some think-tank shit out in Silicon Valley but technically has tenure here as a professor, even though she's rarely ever here."

"She wouldn't…um, she wouldn't have anything to do with this, though…right?" I asked, uneasy for some reason. Coincidences didn't sit well with me. Or was I reading way too hard into this and Nate's mom could be a really valuable asset in our research?

Nate's brows rose, but he didn't seem to take offense to my implication. "No. She wouldn't. For one thing, she doesn't have any student face-time when she's here on campus. For another, she fucking hates Dr. Fox. He tried to have her fired for some ethics shit a few years back, simply because he wanted her job." Then he paused, his jaw tightening and his gaze darkening. "Not to mention the fact that she's my mother. Regardless of what poison Carina has told you about her, she's still my mom and would never hurt me. Or any of us."

My jaw flapped a couple of times before I managed to squeeze an apology out. "Sorry, I didn't… My mom has never even mentioned her. I just… Everyone feels like a suspect. That's all."

Heath rubbed my back reassuringly. "That's valid, Ashes. Nate's mom is a bit cold, but she's not a psychopath. Promise."

As I glanced around at the other guys, they all seemed to be in agreement, so I shrugged. "Okay, you all know her. Yeah, maybe see if she can offer any insight into what this is all about. Just…I don't know. Be careful not to say too much? Not that she's involved, but what if she says something to the wrong person and it comes back to bite us in the ass later?"

To my surprise, it was Nate who nodded his agreement. "That's valid. We will keep it vague. Got it, Heathcliff?"

Heath offered a mock salute. "Understood, boss. Are we leaving now? I'd better get changed."

Nate grinned, rolling his eyes. "You're such a suck-up, Briggs, you know that?"

Heath only took a few minutes to change into a collared shirt, then kissed me and promised to call me later before leaving with Nate. I frowned after them, chewing my lip as I worried about all the what-ifs of involving someone else in our little investigation.

"This is good," Royce said, shaking me out of my spiraling thoughts. "Nate's mom is supersmart and well connected in the academic space. Even if she doesn't know, she'll know someone we can ask. Come on, Squirrel, let's head back to your dorm." He pushed up from the couch and carried our bottles to the kitchen to trash.

I shook my head, giving him a narrow-eyed look. "For one thing, that was your third beer. For another, don't you have a date tonight? Willa, right?"

Royce winced and scrubbed a hand over his face. "Right. Willa."

Carter scoffed. "Go shower, bro. I'll keep Spark company."

For a moment, Royce stared at his friend with an unreadable expression on his face. Then he sighed and nodded. "Yeah. Cool." Then he disappeared down the hall toward his room, looking like he was carrying the weight of the world on his shoulders.

Alone with Carter all of a sudden, I felt my pulse start to race. Was this what a lamb felt like under the watch of a wolf?

"Oh, gosh, look at the time. I promised I'd meet Carly for dinner. See ya!" I quickly scooped up my car keys and made a beeline for the door while Carter laughed behind me.

"Coward!" he teased, but I was already out of their apartment with the door closing firmly between us.

Chapter Seventeen

January 9

When we were thirteen, we went to Keystone for a ski trip with Max as our chaperone. He was basically the only parent who would ever take us to do fun shit, instead of leaving us in boarding school year round. Day two of the vacation, Max broke his wrist trying to beat Royce in a snowboard freestyle competition and had to visit the medical center in Silverthorne for X-rays. While he was there, a blizzard hit and cut off the road. We were stuck in the Essexes' mountain chalet for four whole days with no parents to tell us no. I used to think that was the best week of my whole life.

It's not anymore. This one is. This week, with Ashley in my bed, underneath me, moaning and writhing in my sheets? This one, hands down, is the best week of my whole freaking life.

The only shitty part is how guilty I feel when I see the look on my best friend's face.

H. Briggs

To everyone's disappointment, Nate's mom didn't have a huge amount of useful information for us. According to Heath, she just verified the information we'd already found online for ourselves. That, for the most part, hypnosis couldn't force someone to go against their free will or morals. Which directly contradicted what was happening at Nevaeh…

The only thing she had said that we hadn't considered was that some military experimental scientists several decades ago had been trialing the combination of hypnosis with drugs to break through that internal moral barrier. She had no idea whether they'd succeeded or whether their research continued and emphasized that it was only academic gossip with no factual backing.

When the weekend rolled around, I was surprised—and apprehensive—to hear there was a Devil's Backbone event we were expected to attend.

I spent most of the day working—my first shift back at the Club spa—and somehow got talked into covering a gap between shifts, so found myself racing back to my dorm with barely half an hour to get dolled up for what was probably another black-tie event.

"How'd you get in here without me?" I demanded, finding Royce in a sharp suit—minus jacket—sprawled out on my bed, reading a book on his Kindle. "Actually, don't answer that. I bet you've had a key for months."

His flash of teeth told me that yes, he did, and yes, he was proud of himself. Another expensive-looking garment bag was draped over the back of my desk chair and, and in the seat, a matching shoebox.

"Carter is going to blow his entire inheritance on these dresses before he deals with his mom at this rate," I muttered, totally unsurprised but also all kinds of warm and fuzzy to see he was still thinking of me. He'd been noticeably absent most of the week, and considering how much time I'd spent at their apartment, I'd hoped to see him more.

Royce chuckled lightly. "Impossible. We need to leave in thirty minutes, though." He quirked an eyebrow as if to tell me to hurry the fuck up, and I rolled my eyes.

"Yeah, I know. Work was busy but I showered at the club already, so just chill while I do my makeup, all right?" I moved the garment bag and shoebox aside, briefly noting the little duck sitting on the box lid was blue this time.

I put some music on my little speaker to fill the silence while I sorted out my hair and makeup, so Royce didn't need to hear my stomach rumbling, but fuck I was hungry. I'd missed my lunch break thanks to multiple clients running late, and we definitely didn't have time to pick up a burger on the way.

Thankfully, I'd worn enough makeup lately that I had my routine down to a cool fifteen minutes. My hair took a whole hour to curl, thanks to the thickness and length, so I swept it up in a quick, simple high chignon and tugged a few wispy bits out to frame my face. All the while, it felt like Royce was watching me, but when I glanced over, his attention was totally engrossed in whatever he was reading.

Which made me curious. "What are you reading?" I asked as I spritzed my updo with hairspray.

"New release from my favorite fantasy author," he murmured, not taking his eyes off the screen as I unzipped the garment bag to see what gorgeous gown Carter had sent this time. "It's about shifters."

The dress was blue. I had been expecting red again, but maybe that was why the duck was blue? "Hmm?" I blinked, realizing Royce had answered and I wasn't really listening. "Sorry, this distracted me."

He glanced up from the screen, looking from me to the dress and back again. "Wrong size or…?"

I shook my head. "Doubt it." Carter was borderline creepy in how perfectly tailored all my dresses had been. "But Carter usually sends red dresses." Then again, it'd only been twice. Maybe it was just a coincidence.

126

Royce's lips twitched with the hint of a smile. "You should call him and ask."

That wasn't suspicious at all. I narrowed my eyes at him and sighed. "You're up to something. Cover your eyes—I need to get dressed."

This time he rolled his eyes. "We're not twelve, Squirrel. I think I can handle seeing your underwear without cracking a boner."

It was a valid point. And really, how were my bra and panties any different from a swimsuit? He was more than used to seeing my ass, anyway, since I often wore just a T-shirt and panties to bed with no bra. So I shrugged and pulled my T-shirt off, tossing it into my laundry hamper.

"Sorry, I wasn't listening before. What's the book?" I shimmied out of my leggings that I'd worn home from work and unzipped the glittering, blue gown.

Royce didn't answer for a moment, then cleared his throat as I stepped into the full skirt of the dress. "Uh, it's a fantasy book about shifters. Lots of romance. You'd probably like it…the main character has multiple love interests. Maybe you can relate."

I snickered. "Ha-ha, very funny. Zip me up?" I unclipped my bra and wiggled out of it before adjusting the strapless neckline of the gown to sit comfortably.

Royce put his Kindle down and shuffled off my bed to where I was presenting the back of my dress for him. His fingers brushed a teasing line up my spine as he did so, and I swallowed heavily to keep from imagining he'd done that on purpose. Obviously it was unavoidable with how snug the dress fitted.

"Thanks," I said, moving over to check my appearance in the full-length mirror beside my door. It fit beautifully, but then I expected nothing less from Carter Bassington. The way it pushed my tits up without a bra was pure magic, though, and even my brows rose at how obvious my cleavage was. "Does this look okay?" I asked Royce, spinning to face him and gesturing to my chest.

For a moment, I got no response. Nothing. Then he swiped a hand over his sunshine hair and shrugged one shoulder. "Yeah, you look good. Shoes will help you not trip."

"Thanks, genius," I grumbled, my cheeks heating. Was I a little disappointed that all I got was "you look good"? Yes. As conceited as it was, I kind of hoped Royce would find me more attractive, but if he didn't react to how my boobs looked in this dress? Yeah, we were deep in the friend zone.

I ducked my eyes away, sitting down at my desk to put on the midnight-blue satin pumps with dazzling jewel buckles on the toes. Then quietly searched through my paltry jewelry box for a simple necklace and matching studs. Nothing overpowering for the statement dress, just…something.

"Okay, shall we go?" I asked when I was ready, tossing my lipstick and phone into a basic black clutch. Royce stood up from his comfy position on my bed and pulled his suit jacket on before opening my door for me. I was still avoiding eye contact, weirdly embarrassed by my own reaction to his lack of reaction, but he grabbed my arm as I passed through the door.

I tried to pretend that I hadn't noticed, but he gave me a little tug to stop me. "Hey. You okay?"

"Mm-hmm," I lied, mustering up a smile. "Is Carly coming with us or meeting us there?" I gestured to her door across the hall, but Royce was watching me with a frown creasing his brow.

Eventually, he sighed. "If you say so. She's meeting us there. I think she's got a date."

My brows shot up in surprise. "Get out. Why did she tell you and not me? No offense."

Royce acted wounded, but it was with a smile on his lips. We slipped back into a comfortable zone as we made our way down to the parking lot where my Firebird was parked. Royce then proceeded to plead for my keys so he could drive, even offering to do my laundry in exchange. I didn't actually need the bribery—I hated driving in

128

high heels—but before I handed over the keys, I made him sweeten the deal with a promise of going for pedicures with me.

"You're so fucking weird," I chuckled as he caressed the steering wheel when the engine started up. "Your car costs more than I could earn in a lifetime, yet you always wanna drive mine."

"You can't put a price on a feeling, Squirrel," he murmured without any trace of humor as we drove out of the campus parking lot.

The party was being held in Prosper City, at one of the insanely opulent hotels where we pulled into valet. Carter had just pulled in ahead of us and waited by the foyer door as Royce handed my keys to an attendant and presented me with the claim ticket.

"Spark, you look…" Carter's gaze dragged over me from head to toe like he was undressing me in his head.

"Lovely," Royce finished for him. "Doesn't she look just lovely in blue, Bass?"

I smiled, shaking my head at his teasing. "Thank you for the dress, Carter. Why the change of color, though? I thought red was your thing?"

His gaze darkened, and his jaw ticked like he was clenching his teeth. "It is," he muttered, cryptically. "Heath and Nate are already inside. Let's head in." He offered me his arm, and I tucked my hand through without hesitation. I had to admit, these parties were letting me live out my Disney Princess dreams and I wasn't mad about it.

"You really do look stunning, Spark," Carter murmured, leaning down so his lips brushed my ear as we headed into the hotel. "But I prefer you in red."

Confusion saw me wrinkle my nose, but before I could ask why the hell he'd sent me a blue dress, I spotted Heath heading toward us with a devilish smirk and a distinctly blue pocket square tucked into his blazer.

"Ashes, holy hell, you're breathtaking." He took my hand, pulling me away from Carter as he dipped to kiss me. He restrained himself to a lingering peck, which my lipstick appreciated, and I

129

hummed with desire for more. "You wore my dress. I'm so glad—I thought maybe Carter would beat me to the punch."

"I did," Carter growled, stalking closer once more. "There were no other dresses in Spark's room when I dropped mine off earlier."

Heath's smug grin spread wider. "Weird." But from the corner of my eye, I spotted him and Royce fist-bumping behind Carter's back. Sneaky boys.

"Blue is your duck color?" I asked Heath, noting the info in my head. Red was Carter's duck that we'd used at that first society event I'd been invited to, but their colors must apply to more than just that one night. Carter was red, Heath was blue... "What's your color?" I asked Royce.

He shrugged. "That's one secret I'll never tell."

I snort-laughed. "Okay, Gossip Girl. Where's Nate?"

Heath wrapped his arm around me, his hand resting on my waist as we headed for the elevators where other black-tie-attired guests waited. "Upstairs already, with Jocelyn."

Surprise saw my lips part. "Nate's mom is here? Is...uh, is Max?" And my mom? Because that screamed uncomfortable situation, since I seriously doubted they had the kind of friendship that Mom and Dad still had. Surely Mom would have mentioned it if they were attending, though. I'd spoken to her just yesterday and told her I was coming to a party tonight with the guys.

"No, they're not attending because Jocelyn's here," Heath explained with a grimace. "I don't know how much you know, but their divorce was messy. It's better that they're not in the same room together."

Well, that was a relief. A pang of sympathy vibrated in my chest, though, thinking about how awful that might have been for Nate. He would have only been ten or eleven... Maybe that was why his bond with the guys was so strong.

130

Chapter Eighteen

I LOVE MY MOM, I REALLY DO. BUT SHE DOESN'T MAKE IT EASY. ESPECIALLY WHEN SHE WAS SO FUCKING CONCERNED FOR HEATH, ASKING HIM ALL ABOUT HIS RECOVERY AND SHOWING GENUINE CONCERN FOR HIS WELL-BEING. MEANWHILE, ALL I GOT WAS A DISMISSIVE SNIFF. SHE'S STILL PISSED THAT I BROKE UP WITH PAIGE, SINCE SHE'S FRIENDS WITH PAIGE'S MOM. TOUGH SHIT. I SHOULD HAVE DONE IT SOONER.

IM GLAD FOR HEATH, THOUGH. HE SEEMED TO GET A LOT OUT OF TALKING TO MY MOM ABOUT EVERYTHING HE WAS GOING THROUGH. I JUST WISH SHE'D SHOW EVEN AN OUNCE OF THE SAME INTEREST IN MY LIFE SOMETIMES.

N. ESSEX, JANUARY 10

It took us a few minutes to find Nate, and when we did spot him across the room with an elegant, tall woman with his same toffee-brown hair, he gave us a sharp head shake.

"I guess he doesn't want company," I muttered, turning my back on him and focusing on the three boys I'd arrived with. "So, is this just a party or do we have a silly challenge to complete?"

They glanced between one another, then Heath smirked and produced a little silk bag from his pocket and offered it to me. Somehow, I had a feeling I knew what I'd find inside but dipped a hand in to check nonetheless.

"Of course," I murmured, pinching one of the tiny little resin ducks between my thumb and forefinger. "What do we do with them?"

Heath took the little duck from my fingers and glanced around us. He spotted a waitress passing by with a tray of what looked like caviar on blinis and subtly deposited the duck directly onto one of the canapés without the waitress noticing. Then he returned to us, and we watched the little blue duck go for a little ride around the room.

"That's it?" I asked as the waitress disappeared to replenish her tray.

Heath shrugged. "Pretty much. Ducks that make it back to the kitchen get counted and tallied. If they get picked up by a guest, then they don't get back to the kitchen and don't get counted. The games stay simple at a party like this because the elders council don't want to get caught in the crossfire."

Royce and Carter shared a rueful grin at that.

"Ever since the elephant toothpaste incident at the graduation ball freshman year, he means. Rules changed after we ruined Dame Edith's vintage Valentino gown," Carter explained with an eye roll. "Most things can be replaced with enough money. Vintage couture cannot."

I had no idea what elephant toothpaste was, but it sounded messy. I eyed the next canapé tray heading our way and noted a tiny white duck riding on what seemed to be a smoked salmon tart. I had no idea whose duck it was, but if the objective was to get them into the kitchen to be counted, then surely a little sabotage was allowed?

Reaching out, I snagged the tart with the duck on top and grinned as I turned back to Heath and the guys. "Is that permitted?"

Heath barked a laugh. "Shit yes, it is."

"Had to be that duck, didn't it?" Royce murmured to Carter, who sent back a knowing smirk.

I quirked a brow at them in question, but Heath looped his arm around my waist to lead me away. "They're the competition now, Ashes. You're on my team tonight." He offered me the little bag of blue ducks, so I slipped the white duck into my clutch and ate the tart. "But if you're sabotaging, I'd love it if you targeted more of those white ducks."

I shrugged, dipping a hand into the bag to grab another blue duck. "Any ducks that aren't blue are fair game. What's the prize?"

"Does it matter?" Heath asked the question with genuine curiosity. He was right, though—it really didn't matter to me what the prize was if I had the glory of winning against Nate. "Carly just arrived, if you want to say hi?"

We made our way across the room casually, and I somehow managed to divest myself of three blue ducks along the way. I was feeling all kinds of pleased with myself as I greeted Carly and met her date—Edmund—until I glanced around and spotted Nate plucking one of my blue ducks off a roaming tray.

I scowled, and he met my gaze across the room with a sly smirk before pocketing my duck.

Dick.

"Hey, what color are Nate's ducks?" I asked Heath, interrupting whatever Carly was saying. She arched a brow at me with a pointed look, and my cheeks warmed. "Sorry, that was rude. What were you saying?"

My friend rolled her eyes and sighed. "I thought there were no challenges tonight?" She directed the question to my date, who rubbed a hand over the back of his neck.

"Upper-tier challenge only," he murmured, giving me a clear shut-the-fuck-up sort of look. "Sorry, Carls."

She glanced between me and Heath, and I wrinkled my nose. I

was definitely not "upper tier" and was now realizing that I shouldn't be participating at all. But it seemed harmless enough...right?

Carly nodded slowly, then mimed zipping her lips shut. "I'm going to go schmooze with the elders," she told us, gesturing for her date who had been chatting with someone else. "Have fun, you two. Don't get caught, and for god's sake, Ash, don't lose."

I narrowed my gaze at Heath when she walked away. "What does that mean? Don't lose?"

Sheepish didn't begin to describe his expression. "Ah, well, this one is less of a prize incentive and more of a...hmm...well, let's just say the motivation is to not lose rather than just to win. Don't worry, though, we've got this."

Another tray floated past, held aloft by a straight-faced waiter, and I spotted two little ducks floating in the champagne. One red, one white.

"Sorry, Carter," I muttered, snagging both glasses and handing one to Heath. "Cheers."

He tossed his head back with a laugh, then clinked glasses with me before taking a long sip of our duck-spiked champagne. Amid our duck game, Heath took his time to introduce me to various rich and powerful guests as opportunities arose. It quickly became obvious that the point of the Devil's Backbone Society was not just to play silly games to entertain bored rich kids. It was to make important connections and build alliances that would see the younger generation of DBs rise to the highest seats of world power later in life.

Every now and then, he'd guide me out onto the dance floor, where he proved to be a surprisingly strong lead as he whirled me around the room with that sexy smile on his lips. Carter seemed to be everywhere, constantly watching us. Watching me. I didn't hate it, though... In fact, every time I caught his eye, I found myself desperate to know whether he'd done anything about his mother's issues.

When Carly grabbed me to chat about her date, Heath excused

himself to give us privacy to "girl talk" and my friend rolled her eyes. "Totally code for needing to pee. He's just too fancy to admit it."

I snickered, snaking another duck-spiked glass of champagne from a passing waitress. For some reason, the white ducks were in the champagne flutes more than they were on food, and I was starting to get seriously tipsy for it.

"So…what do you think of Edmund?" Carly asked, sipping her own drink as her gaze drifted over to the handsome man in question.

I followed her line of sight and hummed thoughtfully. "Well, having barely exchanged more than a few words with him, I can't speak to his personality…but he seems nice?"

Carly snorted a laugh. "Okay but hot, right? We're not here for his conversation, babe, just appearances. And his dick. Oh my god, you should see that thing. It's—" I choked on the sip of champagne I'd just taken, and she paused to pat me on the back. "You okay?"

"Yep," I croaked. "Isn't this your first date?"

She shrugged and smirked. Bloody hell, no wonder she and Royce got along so well.

"Uh-oh, here comes trouble," she groaned under her breath, her eyes darting past me.

My shoulders stiffened, expectations of Jade or Paige about to tip a drink over me filling my head, so I was shocked speechless when a strong hand gripped my waist.

"There you are. I've been looking everywhere for you," Nate said in a weird voice, making my spine straighten even further. His fingers squeezed my waist, like a silent plea to play along, and I turned to find myself face-to-face with his bow tie. Fucking tall men were putting a kink in my neck.

"Nathaniel, you can't be serious," a woman scoffed, making me realize he wasn't alone. Carly's squeak of surprise beside me put me on edge, and I met the woman's gaze cautiously. She was beautiful, elegant, and ice cold. But at the same time, very familiar. Why did she look so familiar, like we'd met before? Maybe just because she looked like Nate? Carly muttered a quick excuse and slipped away like she was made of smoke. *Traitor.*

A brittle smile tugged up my lips. "You must be Nate's mom," I said, offering my hand. "I'm—"

"My girlfriend," Nate blurted out, cutting me off before I could say anything more. "Ashley is my girlfriend and things are very serious, which is why you need to stop suggesting I get back with Paige, Mom." Another squeeze at my waist, hard enough that it hurt, and I subtly dug my elbow into his ribs in return. Clearly he needed help getting his mother off his back, but I owed him nothing, so he needed to sweeten the fucking deal if he wanted cooperation.

The woman—Jocelyn, I think Heath said her name was—stared at me like I was a bug to be squashed, not even attempting to cover her irritation.

"Ashley," she repeated. "What an interesting coincidence. You seem to have recovered well from your little hike in the woods last semester."

I blinked at her in confusion, then the penny dropped. That was why she looked familiar. She had picked me up on the side of the road and driven me back to campus after the society left me for dead in the forest. "Professor Reynard?" I said with confusion, recalling her name. "I didn't realize you were…"

Her answering smile was brief. "I didn't realize you were dating my son, or I'd have checked in to see you got adequate medical care that day. Seems you were okay, though?"

"No," Nate snapped, seeming genuinely angry, "she wasn't."

Another elbow in his ribs made him jerk his gaze away from his mother so he could scowl at me. I tipped my head back to meet his eyes, trying to silently ask what the fuck he was doing. His own eyes widened slightly, like he was just as confused as I was, and his lips parted.

"Sorry, it was Ashley?" his mom interrupted, reminding me that we weren't alone. "Nathaniel, doesn't your father's whore secretary have a daughter named Ashley?"

Shock rippled through me and I gasped out loud. This bitch just called my mom a whore? Did she not know Mom and Max were married now? Or she did know and not care? Either way, I could see where Nate's sour attitude toward me and my mom had come from. If Jocelyn had been speaking like that in front of her son for any length of time, it was unsurprising that it'd sunk in.

"Does she?" Nate murmured, fingers digging into my waist again. "I don't recall. Anyway, I really should spend some time with my girl-friend…" The attempt to extract himself from his mother's attention was painfully clear, but she didn't take the hint, staring at the two of us even harder. Like she was trying to see through the deception with X-ray vision.

"Nonsense, Nathaniel, I want to get to know your new girlfriend some more. Is this a new relationship, dear? Because rebounds are very—"

"Nope, not new," Nate snapped, cutting her off. "In fact, it's very serious. Right, sweetheart?"

Jocelyn's sharp gaze shifted to me, waiting for me to reply, so I swallowed back the urge to leave him in the shit and forced a smile to my lips. "Sure is," I murmured. "I've spent more time at Nate's place than my own dorm lately." Which was true. Except that time was spent in his friend's bed.

Her lips pursed, annoyance etched across her beautiful features. "Well, how nice for you." She drew a breath, then shook her head slightly. "Ashley, dear, I do hope you aren't offended, but I was just pointing out to Nathaniel that plans were already put in place for his engagement to Paige, and although I'm sure you're a nice girl… you're a rebound, darling. Nothing more. Certainly not the woman he'll marry."

My jaw dropped at the woman's blatant audacity. Was she hearing herself?

Nate certainly was. "Well, that's where you're wrong, Mom. Ashley and I have actually spoken at length about our future, and Dad already considers her a daughter, so I think it's about time you drop the Paige plans. Don't you?"

Again…true. Just not for the implied reasons. Jocelyn and Max must really not be on speaking terms at all for her to be so very in the dark about her son's life. Regardless, I had no words for how to contribute or corroborate or…anything. So I just leaned into Nate and tried to look like I actually liked him. Or even tolerated him. His hand shifted from my waist to my stomach as he held me closer, like we were genuinely in love, and all I could think about was how much of a dick he'd been earlier in the week. What had he called me, again? Nevaeh Bicycle?

Thinking of that saw me tilt my head back to peer up at him. The shadow of his black eye remained, just barely concealed with makeup. Vain prick.

"What?" he murmured, eyes narrowing. Then he added a quick, "Sweetie?"

I smiled back, the first genuine smile since he'd started this weird little act. "Nothing, sugar-butt. Just thinking about that lovely afternoon we had at your place on Monday." Then I reached up and pressed my thumb into the bruised skin beside his eye. "Just a loose eyelash." I pretended to blow it off my thumb while his bruised eye twitched ever so slightly.

"Jocelyn Reynard, is that you?" a tuxedoed man called out, striding over to us and spreading his arms wide for a hug that Jocelyn didn't reciprocate. "My dear, you seem to be aging backward."

Nate's mother offered a chiming laugh, patting the heavy-set man's chest lightly. "Oh, Bernard, you are too kind. You remember my son, Nathaniel, don't you?"

The man who eyed Nate had a rosy glow to his cheeks and a certain glassiness to his eyes. "Of course, how could I not? And who is this lovely creature on your arm, Nathaniel?"

Jocelyn answered before either Nate or I could get a response out. "Oh, Bernard, this is Ashley," she purred, sending Nate a challenging glance. "His future fiancée, apparently."

Jesus fucking Christ, this was getting out of hand now. Right as I was about to open my mouth and put an end to the craziness, Nate dipped his head to whisper frantically in my ear. "Bernard is the head of the Devil's Backbone elders council. Please just...shut up."

My jaw snapped shut, unease rippling through me. Before I could make any different decision, though, the intoxicated old man roared a cheer and clapped Nate on the shoulder. "Fiancée!" he exclaimed. "Well, congratulations, boy! Let's get a drink to celebrate."

Before I could even blink, Bernard had ushered Nate away and left me standing there in shock as his mother eyed me up and down.

"You two don't have me fooled, Ashley," she murmured, shaking her head. "You're little more than a distraction. But by all means, let's see how far my son is willing to take the charade. Congratulations on your engagement, dear." She clinked her glass against the champagne flute I hadn't even realized I was still holding, then walked away as she took a sip.

Dumbstruck, I raised my own glass and gulped the alcohol...only to choke on the tiny duck I'd forgotten was floating there.

Fuck an actual duck, what had Nate roped me into now?

Chapter Nineteen

January 10

I've been soaking up all the time Ashley will give me during the day, totally fucking up both our study schedules by luring her into my bed with my almost obsessive appetite...not that she's been complaining. But nights are a different story. I'm still too messed up from what happened last semester, and I don't trust my sleeping self not to hurt her. So I insist she sleep in her own dorm, knowing Royce will be there to keep her safe.

    The nightmares are back, and I'm too scared to tell anyone. The only saving grace is that my video feed proves I haven't left my bed at night. They're just nightmares...for now. But they're growing in intensity and it's bleeding into my decision-making during waking hours. My temper is so much shorter, and I'm quick to violence. I don't hate it, either. I finally feel...alive.

H. Briggs

What the fuck just happened? Nate's mom was a bitch for one thing, but that lined up with the professor who'd given me a lift back to campus while hypothermic and barefoot. She'd suggested I visit the hospital, yes, but she hadn't insisted on it or—to my knowledge—given my well-being a second thought after dropping me off. Surface-level humanity only.

A chill raced down my spine and a sour dread twisted my guts as I glanced around. Nate was some distance away, being patted on the back by a group of older men who reeked of wealth, but he caught my gaze with a frown set on his brow.

Whatever he was trying to say, whatever question his eyes were asking, I didn't understand. We were not on the same page, nor could I read him like I could Heath. Or even Carter, for that matter. Nate was a fucking enigma and seemed to be working off a totally different narrative than the rest of us.

I glanced down at the duck I'd nearly choked on, sitting innocently in my palm now, then sighed and slipped it into my purse. My eyes were stinging, which meant my makeup was probably running thanks to my near-death experience, so I abandoned my flute on a nearby table and glanced around for the restrooms.

"Ash, you good?" Carly called out as I passed by her and Edmund talking with an older woman who dripped jewels.

I gave her a quick nod and flashed what I hoped was a reassuring smile while gesturing to the exit I was heading for. Hopefully it was clear I was just heading to the bathroom to freshen up and clear my head because I really badly just needed a minute alone. Picking up the pace, I slipped out of the party and headed down the corridor, away from the elevators.

Farther along the hall, I spotted a sign for the restrooms. Then I recognized the two glittering-gowned women heading into the ladies' room and froze in my tracks. No freaking way was I getting stuck in a closed space with Paige and Jade after Nate told his mom we were practically engaged. Fuck that for a joke.

Instead, I bypassed the ladies' room and headed for the disabled access bathroom instead.

"Spark!" Carter called out from the direction of the party, heading my way with a scowl set across his brow. My breath caught in my chest at the look on his face, and my pulse thundered so hard I was growing light-headed.

I needed a fucking minute to myself, so I waved back and ducked into the disabled restroom before he could catch up. Just a moment after I flicked the lock, he knocked on the door.

"Spark, are you okay? I just heard about your engagement to Nate. What the—"

Oh no, word was spreading that fast? "I just need a minute, Carter," I called back. "Too much champagne, you know? Also, for the record, Nate's lost his fucking mind. Can you please ask what the hell he is doing?"

His chuckle soothed something inside me. "Noted. I'll wait for you, though. Nate painted a hell of a target on your back just now, and Paige is lurking around somewhere."

I groaned, leaning my hands on the vanity to stare at my reflection. I really needed to get Nate alone and ask him to his face what the fuck he was thinking. But right now he was being congratulated on a harmless lie that had somehow escalated at the speed of fucking light into a fake engagement.

No, not somehow. Nate's mom was responsible for that shit, and she didn't seem even slightly remorseful for it. No wonder Max had divorced her.

I ran the tap while I peed, knowing Carter was standing right outside the bathroom door and not wanting to imagine him listening. Right as I flushed, I heard him answer a phone call and sighed. I'd bet money Heath and Royce had heard the gossip by now and were trying to find us.

After washing my hands, I checked my own phone and noted the expected missed calls. And a text message from Nate.

NATHANIEL ESSEX:

> Sorry. That got out of hand. I owe you one.

Rolling my eyes, I typed out a quick reply.

ASHLEY:

> One? You're joking. You owe me about six million. What the fuck, Essex?!

His reply cleared up nothing.

NATHANIEL ESSEX:

> Yeah, I know.

Frustrated, I tossed my phone back into my clutch and grabbed some toilet paper to fix the mascara smudges at the corners of my eyes. Then I took a deep breath to calm my racing heart before unlocking the door.

As anticipated, Carter was still waiting outside leaning against the wall opposite the restroom I was using. When I started to open the door, his head snapped up and the blank expression on his face made me freeze.

"Carter?" I squeaked just a split second before he rushed forward, slamming the door open fully and shoving me backward. I stumbled, shocked, and he kicked the door shut as he advanced, forcing me to back up.

Panic whipped through me faster than lightning, and I put my hands out to hold him at arm's length. Or tried to. "Carter, stop!" I gasped as he swatted my hands aside and grabbed me by the throat. His eyes remained glassy and unfocused, his every muscle tense like his own body was fighting against his brain with every movement.

"Stop!" I pleaded, clawing at the hand around my throat.

It had no effect, as he shoved me against the bathroom wall beside the mirror and his fingers tightened around my throat. Holy fuck, was he going to kill me? This wasn't him. This wasn't Carter... Someone was pulling his strings. Someone wanted me dead, and Carter was nothing more than a weapon.

Tears streamed from my eyes, the running makeup stinging and making it hard to see, but there was no mistaking the nefarious intent when he started gathering up my full skirt with his free hand. He wasn't going to kill me...not immediately, anyway.

"Carter," I whimpered, clawing at his hand pinning my throat to the wall. "Please, Carter, don't do this." For a moment, through my tear-blurred eyes, I thought I saw a flicker of something pass across his blank expression. For just the briefest moment, I thought I'd gotten through to him.

Then his fingers found the satin of my panties and ripped them clean off my body with a stinging jerk. I screamed then, fucking terrified of what was about to happen. It was Carter, and fuck if I didn't just about turn myself inside out with desire when we were together, but he wasn't here with us right now. This was someone else entirely and that thought twisted my stomach into agonizing knots.

Dark spots danced across my vision. I only had seconds to act before I passed out...then I'd be totally at the mercy of whoever was controlling Carter, and god only knew if I'd wake up again. So I lashed out, slapping him across the cheek as hard as humanly possible, letting my nails dig in and raking four red slashes in his gorgeous face.

"Carter!" I pleaded, sobbing. "Come back to me! Don't do this! Carter, please, don't hurt me!"

The dark spots got darker, and gut-wrenching resignation washed through me. I'd failed, and Carter would never fucking forgive himself when he eventually snapped out of it. If he ever did. Fuck, what if he was keyed to kill himself afterwards, just like…

Abruptly, he released me and I crumpled to the floor in a puddle of midnight-blue couture as Carter stumbled back a couple of steps.

"Spark?" he croaked, horror saturating that one word.

I lay there a moment, gasping for air and shaking so hard, I thought for a second I was having a seizure. But I only gave myself the briefest moment before blinking back the tears and holding out my hand to him.

"I'm okay," I whispered, my own voice rough.

The sound of both our harsh, gasping breaths filled the room for a tense second, then Carter skidded to his knees in front of me, reaching out with trembling hands.

"Spark?" he moaned. "Did I…? Oh my god, no…" His hands dropped away before he could touch me, and he pushed away like he was scared to be so close to me.

"It's okay," I tried to reassure him, despite the way my heart galloped in my chest and my whole body pebbled with gooseflesh. "I'm okay. You stopped, Carter. You stopped. I'm okay."

I was not okay. I'd thought I was going to die, or be raped, or both. And all at the hands of a man I lo—that I cared deeply for. Knowing it wasn't him only made it marginally better.

Carter was deathly pale, his hands shaking as he fumbled for his phone, shaking his head over and over, like he wanted to somehow erase what had just happened out of his head. If he even remembered? Or maybe he'd just put two and two together once he snapped out of it.

"They're coming," he mumbled, seemingly unable to meet my eyes as guilt and disgust oozed from every pore. "They'll know what to do."

I didn't need to ask who he meant, because the door burst open a second later to reveal a panic-stricken Heath. He took one look at

145

me huddled in the corner before launching himself at Carter with murder written all over his features.

"Stop!" someone screamed, but it was as effective as holding up an umbrella against a tsunami.

Utterly useless.

Chapter Twenty

Heath has had Ashley at our apartment all damn week. Only ever during the day, when the two of them used to study in the campus library. I was rarely home at the same time—thank fuck—but I could smell her shampoo when I came home in the evenings. Shampoo...and sex. Fucking hell, just the lingering scent of her got me hard.

I need to sort shit out with my mother before Spark gives up on us. Trouble is, Portia's dodging my calls. Like she knows I plan on offering an ultimatum. It's so damn tempting to ignore the threats and do what I want, but it's not just my future on the line. Not just my freedom at stake. At this point, I'll do just about anything to keep Spark safe, even if it breaks my own heart.

Jan. 10
C. Bassington

Heath's fist connected with Carter's face as my scream echoed through the bathroom and I scrambled to intervene before he could kill Carter. Because Carter wasn't fighting back at all. He was just taking it, like he wanted the shit kicked out of him as penance for what had happened.

"What the fuck?" Royce exclaimed, skidding to a halt and smoothly blocking Heath's next swing before it could meet Carter's face. "What just happened in—" He cut off with a sharp inhale as his gaze took in me on the floor, his focus shifting to my throat where I could feel the bruise of Carter's hand already swelling up, and then snapped to the side.

I followed his line of sight and groaned when I saw what he'd spotted. My ripped panties.

"You motherfucker," Royce breathed, one eye twitching in fury as he turned to face Carter full-on. A flash of light alerted me to the sudden appearance of a knife in his hand. Where the fuck had that come from? Was he serious?

"Stop it!" I shrieked, genuinely terrified of what might happen next. Stumbling and tripping on my full skirt, I lurched up from the tiled floor and wrapped my arms around Carter to create a human shield. I trembled all over, but nothing could make me move when both Royce and Heath looked like they were ready to castrate their friend on the spot.

Carter shuddered in my koala embrace and a low moan rolled out of him. "Spark...Ashley...let them. I deserve it."

"Shut the fuck up, Bassington," I snapped back. "We all need to calm the fuck down and discuss what just happened like rational adults." I glared over my shoulder at Royce when I said that, and the stare he sent back sent a shiver down my spine. I'd never seen him so dark before, and it tightened something in my chest.

"Ashes, he hurt you," Heath croaked, utterly horrified with whatever he was seeing. I had a fair idea, since my eyes still burned with fresh tears spilling over and my throat ached from my near strangulation.

I shook my head firmly. "We need to get out of here. Now. All of us. Call Nate and get my car, Royce. We'll meet you downstairs."

Royce's jaw tightened and he shook his head firmly. "I'm not leaving you alone."

"I'm not alone," I snapped back, frustrated and angry and down-right scared. "Heath, get the claim ticket from my purse, please. Royce, I swear to fuck, if you don't do what I am asking—"

"What?" he barked back, pure fury radiating from his pores. "If I refuse to leave you alone with him right now, what the fuck are you going to do, Squirrel?"

"Ban you from sleepovers for starters," I replied, unable to think of much else that would matter to him. "Never let you drive the Firebird again, perhaps?"

His brow dipped in a scowl, and I had to guess one of those two utterly empty threats had struck enough of a nerve because he snatched the valet ticket from Heath and stormed out. Not before casting one long, scathing glare Carter's way, though.

"You too, Heath," I said in a shaking voice. "Find Nate, please. We will meet you at your apartment."

"No," he replied, sounding like he was struggling to keep himself from falling apart. "I'm sorry, babe. I don't care what you threaten me with. I won't leave you alone with Carter right now. Please don't ask that of me."

"He's right," Carter said softly. "I don't want to hurt you, Ashley...not again."

I clenched my teeth so hard, it hurt my jaw, and I released my human-shield hug to give us both a bit of breathing room. "Carter Bassington Junior, if you call me Ashley one more time instead of Spark, I will use Royce's little knife to cut the name into your arm so you never forget it. Am I clear?"

He blinked at me, stunned. Then he nodded slightly. "Yes, ma'am," he murmured. I narrowed my eyes in a warning glare, and he amended his response. "Yes, Spark. Understood."

I gave a firm nod and glanced at the mirror to check my appearance before we left the restroom and caused a stir. Or more of a stir than we'd probably already caused with the screaming. "Fuck," I muttered, seeing firsthand the mess my makeup was. "Heath, can I trust you not to punch Carter again while I clean up my face?"

The scowling man in question just leaned his shoulders against the closed door, folding his arms over his chest in a clear message. No, he wouldn't hit anyone, but he also wasn't taking his eyes off me for even a second.

Good enough. I grabbed some toilet paper and tried my best to clean up the dark tracks of mascara and eyeshadow staining my cheeks, wincing at the red marks ringing my throat. Against my pale skin, they were hard to miss.

Neither Heath nor Carter said a damn word as I pulled the pins out of my up-do and arranged my hair down over my shoulders in an attempt to mask the signs of assault so we didn't become the talk of the society before making it out of the hotel.

"Good enough," I murmured, swiping on a fresh coat of lipstick and grimacing at my reflection. "Come on, let's get out of here." I tried to ignore the persistent tremor in my hands as I clipped my purse closed and tossed all my used tissues.

Heath held open the door for me, and I grasped Carter's arm firmly in mine to ensure he came with us and didn't try to slink off and play in traffic. Or hang himself. Guilt did crazy things to someone's mind, as Heath had already proven.

We made a brisk line to the elevators, not making eye contact with anyone and thankfully making it without running into Paige or Jade…or Nate's mom. Fucking hell, I'd hate to try to explain that.

To my relief, Royce already had my car waiting in front of the lobby door with the engine running. I gave Carter a firm push to the back seat, waiting for him to climb inside before pushing the seat back into position.

"Are you coming with us?" I asked Heath as I placed my hand on the passenger side door.

He nodded, jaw tight and brow furrowed. "I'll bring Carter's car and meet you there."

"Good thinking," I murmured, then hesitated. "It wasn't him, Heath. He wasn't—"

"I know," he admitted with a heavy sigh. "I figured as much when you literally put your body between him and Royce. Be careful, Ashes. If it can happen to Carter…"

I swallowed hard, nodding my understanding. If it could happen to Carter, it could happen to anyone. "Drive safe, okay?" Because all I could think about was Daniel Mahoney and the implication that he'd deliberately crashed while hypnotized.

Heath leaned in and brushed a kiss over my lips, which I leaned into with a small moan. I was hurt, yes. But I wasn't broken.

I slid into the passenger seat, too tired and shaken to argue with Royce about who was driving, and Heath leaned down to glare at him through my window. "Keep our girl safe, D'Arenberg," he ordered without even the slightest hint of teasing.

I expected Royce to shoot back a snarky remark or flip Heath off or something, but he just gave a grim nod and shifted the car into drive, pulling us out of the valet zone at speed.

No one spoke for the entire drive back to the apartment, and Royce parked my car in the guest spot beside Heath's Ducati like it was my permanent space. I knew we needed to discuss what had happened and clear the air that Carter hadn't hurt me, that he hadn't been in control of his actions. But I was exhausted and barely found the energy to stand upright as we rode the elevator up to their floor.

Royce unlocked the front door, and I forced my feet to carry me over to the kitchen to retrieve two ice packs from their freezer—one for Carter's face and one for my throat. Fucking hell, what a night.

Carter accepted the ice pack, staring at it in genuine confusion

151

before heading outside to their extensive balcony area, where Lady had a doggy paradise set up.

Royce stared at me for a long moment, his brow dipped in what seemed like a permanent scowl. Then he swiped a hand through his blond hair, messing it up as he muttered a curse. He jerked the freezer open again and pulled out a bottle of liquor to pour us both a heavy-handed shot.

I didn't even sniff it or question what we were drinking. Just accepted the glass from him and knocked it back in one swallow. It burned on the way down, and I gagged a little, but then it spread that fiery warmth through my belly, and I held my glass out for a refill.

Royce obliged, watching me intensely as I swallowed the second shot and coughed with the afterburn.

"Are you okay, Squirrel?" he finally asked in a rough voice.

I wet my lips, tasting the sweet alcohol lingering there. He watched me do it, his expression tight and troubled. "I'm okay," I murmured finally, testing the truth of that statement aloud. "It wasn't him."

The deeper meaning of that statement seemed to strike Royce like a hammer and he flinched. "Fuck."

I nodded my agreement. "Yeah. Exactly."

Royce glanced toward the balcony, where we could just make out the curve of Carter's hunched shoulders as his head hung low. Pained sympathy and guilt tracked across Royce's face as he considered the implications of that statement. "Fuck."

In response, I grabbed the bottle of booze—spiced rum, I saw on the label—and refilled both our glasses. "Yup." Because what the fuck else could I say?

Royce groaned, scrubbing his hands over his face like he wanted to erase all the murderous thoughts he'd been having about his friend. I handed him his glass and we took the shots together.

When the front door opened a minute later, I was already starting to feel myself relax into the fuzzy warmth of intoxication. Obviously, that wouldn't fix the problems at hand, but for right now, for facing the guys and explaining everything that'd happened? I'd take the liquid courage and alcohol blanket.

Nate's wide eyes landed on us in the kitchen, then snapped down to my throat where I held the ice pack. Then back to my undoubtedly puffy, tear-stained face.

"Who the fuck hurt you, Layne?" he demanded, oozing violence and rage.

Here we went again. This was getting old.

Chapter Twenty-One

January 11

Carter thinks he's the only one who can woo Ashley with pretty dresses and shoes? Wrong. I've had her in my bed all week, no way am I gritting my teeth while he dresses her in red for another society event. It's required a hell of a trade with Royce to get his help, but I'm confident she'll be in blue tonight.

It's a dick move, undercutting Bass like this, but a guy's gotta do what a guy's gotta do when love is on the line. Ash is my end game. I feel it in my bones. I just need her to see it too.

H. Briggs

It took the rest of the bottle of rum—shared between all of us, in fairness—and several repeated conversations before we finally cleared the air on what'd happened with Carter and me in the restroom. I stuck firm in my belief that he was one hundred and fifty percent not under his own willpower, which directly contradicted what Nate's mom had told them about hypnosis. Unless, of course, her idea of drug influence played a part.

Then we needed to circle back around to how Carter had been triggered. I remembered the phone call he'd taken right before it all went down, and a check of his phone records revealed it was a private number call.

"I don't think you'll be shocked to hear who that call came from," Nate said with a groan, looking up from his laptop. He'd grabbed it the moment I mentioned Carter getting a phone call and had spent the last twenty minutes sitting on the floor with his laptop on the coffee table, tracing who'd made the call.

Dread rolled through me, and I rubbed the bridge of my nose. "Dr. Fox?"

Nate shook his head. "Nope." He spun his laptop around to show us the result he'd zoomed in on. "Abigail Monstera."

"Great, so our strongest lead is now a ghost," Heath muttered, shaking his head. "We really should have seen that one coming."

I rolled my eyes, frustrated. "Obviously it's not actually her. It's someone who knows I had her diary. Right? It has to be whoever stole the diary from my room, messing with our heads. Nate already traced her number back when I got those texts about Paris, and it's disconnected. So clearly this is just someone with better hacker powers being a smartass."

Nate's lips quirked up in a smile. Admittedly, we were all a bit tipsy at this stage. "Hacker powers?" he teased. "Is that like...invisibility or shapeshifting?"

I narrowed my eyes and extended my middle finger.

"Why Abigail, though?" Heath mused aloud. "I don't remember anything particularly different about her, do you guys?"

Royce yawned, ruffling Lady's fur as she rolled on her back to expose her belly. "I remember she was hazed pretty harshly by the inner circle at the time. Remember Dirk had a real vendetta against scholarship students?"

The other guys all nodded and murmured their agreement, but I was out of the loop. "Who's Dirk and why does he hate poor people?"

"Dirk Fitzpatrick," Nate said, answering my question. "Used to be the DB leader when we were freshmen. He was a real elitist snob who perpetuated the idea that Nevaeh students should never be associating with lower-class citizens. Thinking back, there's every chance some of the initiations and hazing were taken too far with a few students."

I frowned, thinking it over. "But…you never saw it happen yourselves? You'd have stopped it if you did…right?" I really fucking hoped so. For all Nate's faults, I really didn't believe he'd stand by while anyone was truly bullied simply based on their bank account.

His brows shot up and he met my eyes with a hard stare. "What do you think, Layne?"

"After the stunt you pulled tonight," Carter said quietly, speaking up for the first time in almost an hour, "I doubt you want to hear what Ashley thinks of you."

Royce let out a low whistle, glancing between Nate and me with a lopsided grin. "Was this to do with how I saw you two all cozy while talking to Jocelyn?"

"You didn't hear?" Carter shook his head slowly, clicking his tongue. "Nate and Ashley got engaged tonight."

Heath's jaw almost hit the floor and I threw my hands up in the air. "We did nothing of the sort. Nate was just bullshitting to get his mom to back off. Irrelevant. Can we circle back to Abigail please? Can you guys remember anything useful as to why she's so involved in this hypnosis shit now? She *is* dead, right?"

"Uh, yeah?" Royce replied, scratching the back of his neck and looking confused as hell. "They found her body in Lake Placid, didn't they?"

I shrugged. "From what I researched, they had to ID based on dental records. Seems suspicious, doesn't it?"

"I dunno," he sighed. "That would mean she faked her death,

which I don't think is anywhere near as easy as books and films make it out to be. I think…it's more plausible that someone knows you found her diary and is now fucking with your head. All our heads, to be fair. We need to look into Dr. Fox more. He's definitely involved."

Heath nodded. "Agreed."

Carter huffed a sound of agreement as well, then gathered up the empty glasses to carry them to the kitchen. "I'm going to get some sleep," he muttered to everyone and no one at the same time, then disappeared down the hallway with his shoulders hunched and his steps dragging.

Everyone remained silent as he left and then exchanged worried glances when his door clicked shut.

"I hate to be the one to say it," Royce said quietly, breaking the silence. "But I don't think he should be alone right now." His quick glance at Heath said everything he wasn't saying out loud. If guilt and paranoia could drive Heath to suicide based just on fragmented memories of bad deeds, what could Carter be pushed to with firm evidence of what he'd done?

Nate grimaced, swiping a hand over his tired eyes. "Royce's right."

He started to get up from his seat on the floor, but I got up faster. "I've got it," I said quickly. "You keep doing the hacker thing. Find us someone to hold responsible, please."

Nate's brow dipped in a frown as Heath and Royce both made sounds of protest but I was already halfway out of the room. Carter had flinched when our hands brushed earlier, and it hadn't escaped my notice that he wasn't meeting my eyes at all. Nothing good could come from letting him beat himself up over hurting me, and no one could absolve him of that guilt better than me.

I tapped lightly on Carter's door, then let myself in when I got no response. A quick glance around told me he was in the shower, so I closed the door behind myself and made my way over to his bed. For as much time as I'd spent in the guys' apartment, I'd never actually been in Carter's room.

It was tempting to snoop around and look at the small collection of framed photographs displayed on his wall, but he hadn't invited me into his space. So I sat my butt down on the edge of his bed and tucked my knees up to my chest. I'd stripped out of my gown not long after getting back and was wearing one of Heath's hoodies and a pair of his boxer shorts with the waistband rolled several times. I'd grabbed the shorts so I wouldn't be bare-assing it on the sofa with all the guys while we talked.

Carter took ages in the shower. Ages. Long enough that I got sleepy and laid my head down on his pillow while waiting for him. Then the moment my eyes shut, I was struck by a flash of terror. What if he'd drowned?

Acting on instinct and panic, I clambered over his bed and burst into the attached bathroom, fully ready to administer CPR or mouth-to-mouth or...something.

"Ashley?" Carter exclaimed in confusion, looking up with water streaming down the hair flopped in his face. He was alive. Not drowned. Just sitting on the floor of the shower with the water beating down on his broad back so hot, his skin was red and steaming.

I blinked a couple of times, wondering why I'd been so sure he needed my help. "Um, I was worried. You were taking a really long time..."

He swiped a hand over his face, pushing his soaking, ink-black hair back from his forehead. "I didn't know you were waiting."

I bit the edge of my lip, embarrassed. "I was worried," I said again.

The surprise and confusion melted away from Carter's face, replaced by darkness and regret. "I'm fine," he muttered, his head dropping low once more to break our eye contact.

I frowned, because the dismissal was painfully clear. He didn't want my concern, nor did he want my company. Well, tough shit. No way in hell was I letting him take on the guilt of what'd happened under hypnosis.

Drawing a deep breath, I stepped farther into the bathroom and tugged off the hoodie I was wearing, tossing it on the floor. That motion was enough to jerk Carter's head back up from the pool of despair he was currently drowning in.

"What are you doing?"

I huffed a frustrated sigh, pushing my borrowed shorts off. "Joining you, obviously. Make some space."

Stunned, he stood up to allow me access into the cubicle, but his every muscle was tensed up and his jaw clenched as I brushed against him. I took my time, getting my hair fully soaked under the spray before turning to face him.

"Carter," I said softly, "you keep calling me Ashley and I don't like it."

His head bowed again, water-drenched hair falling over his forehead. "I don't deserve to call you anything else. Ashley…" He reached out, his thumb tracing over the dip of my throat where I'd already noticed a bruise darkening.

I swallowed, leaning into his touch. "You didn't hurt me, Carter," I told him earnestly. "One thing I am absolutely certain of when it comes to you? You'd never hurt me like that. Not physically. My feelings, yeah, sure, you're pretty brutal there, but this? It wasn't you any more than it was Heath or Royce or Nate or fucking me for that matter. So don't you dare feel guilty for something you had no control over."

He shook his head, rejecting my logic. "I understand what you're saying…but it doesn't change facts. I hurt you. Me. These bruises were left by my hands. How can you not be terrified to be alone with me right now, Ashley? I am."

Tilting my chin up, I cupped his face in my hands to force him to meet my eyes. "I'm not scared of you, Carter, because you stopped. You snapped out of it when you realized you were hurting me. No matter how firmly the hypnosis had its claws into your head, you stopped."

Self-hatred and guilt radiated through his deep blue gaze, but I wasn't accepting that. Not now, after all we'd been through. Rising up on my toes, I brushed my lips over his to show him in action what I was trying to get across with words—that I trusted him implicitly.

A pained moan escaped him as he whispered my name, but I didn't want to hear it. Every Ashley on his lips was cutting me like a knife, and I'd do anything to bring us back to Spark.

"Carter," I breathed, kissing him again. "You don't scare me."

He kissed me back, unable to help himself as his hands found my waist and gripped me tight. A small moan slipped between us as he pressed me to the shower wall and deepened our kisses until my head swirled with desire. The hard length of his cock trapped between us said he was equally affected, but he seemed satisfied to simply kiss me.

Tough luck, buddy. I want more.

"I should scare you," he whispered against my lips as I hitched a leg up around his waist to pull him closer. "You should simply be with Heath and not give me a second thought." He meant more than just tonight's incident, but that wasn't new information. His hot-and-cold act of the past weeks was exactly that: an act. He wanted me just as much as I wanted him.

"That's the problem," I confessed as I snaked a hand between us and gripped his erection. "I think about you all the time…even when I'm with Heath."

His breath hitched, understanding exactly what I was implying. "Fuck," he whispered in a hoarse voice, his dark lashes fluttering as I stroked his cock. "Fuck…Ashley…"

My grip tightened and he hissed a sharp inhale. Then a little chuckle. Hope surged in my chest, sure that I must be finally getting through to him. "Carter, I'm not tall enough. You're gonna need to pick me up because if I don't get this dick inside me within the next three seconds, I'm going to—"

My sentence cut off with a squeak as Carter hoisted me into the air and slammed the full length of his huge cock into my pussy. It hurt, but in the best way.

"Holy shit," I gasped, my fingers clawing at the back of his neck for balance as my body spasmed with the sudden intrusion.

His answer was a bruising kiss that stole the very air from my lungs and turned me into a puddle of goo in his arms. My hips rocked, and I moaned into his kisses, begging him to fuck me.

"Is that what you wanted?" he asked in a dark whisper, his lips still against mine as he slowly withdrew just the slightest distance before thrusting back in.

A whimper escaped my throat as I nodded. "Yes," I hissed, then bit his lower lip. "Fuck me until you remember who the fuck I am."

His next thrust was hard enough to knock my head against the tile and I laughed, to which he just shook his head with disbelief. Still, the tiniest hint of a smile curled the corner of his mouth, and I'd take that as a win.

"As if I could ever forget," he growled, pinning my hips to the tile as he increased his pace. His mouth found mine again as he fucked me under the shower spray, doing exactly what I asked for.

Deep in my chest, an acidic puddle of fear and anxiety tried to eat away at me, but the intense waves of arousal and euphoria Carter was shoving into me quickly smothered it.

Regardless of what might have happened, we won. We. Won. And we'd come out stronger for it.

Dr. Fox—or whoever the hell was playing ghost—had no fucking clue who they were messing with, and we sure as shit wouldn't break so easily.

Chapter Twenty-Two

0530: WOKE UP PER BODY CLOCK. VERIFIED WITH MY PHONE SENSORS THAT I HAVEN'T SLEEPWALKED AT ALL DURING THE NIGHT.

0730: WOKE UP AGAIN WHEN ASHLEY SLIPPED OUT TO SHOWER. SHE HAS HER FIRST SHIFT BACK AT THE COUNTRY CLUB TODAY.

0830: TOOK HER FOR BREAKFAST AND COFFEE BEFORE SHE LEFT TO START WORK. TRIED TO SUGGEST I DRIVE HER, BUT SHE REFUSED. STUBBORN WOMAN.

0930: WENT HOME TO SHOWER AND CHANGE CLOTHES. I REALLY NEED TO START KEEPING MY STUFF IN ASHLEY'S DORM, JUST TO SAVE ON GAS.

1000: NATE CHALLENGED ME TO A FEW ROUNDS OF COD. THAT'LL TAKE MY MIND OFF THINGS...

1600: HEATH OFFERED ME HIS 1971 PLYMOUTH HEMI 'CUDA CONVERTIBLE TO SWITCH OUT ASHLEY'S DRESS FOR THE PARTY TONIGHT. IT WAS AN OFFER TOO GOOD TO REFUSE, AND CARTER NEEDS TO BE HUMBLED. I STASHED HIS RED DRESS IN HER CLOSET AND LAID OUT HEATH'S BLUE ONE. PART OF ME DEBATED SWAPPING IT FOR ANOTHER COLOR ENTIRELY, BUT NOT ALL OF US HAVE CONNECTIONS WITH LUXURY DESIGNERS.

1830: SQUIRREL LOOKS AMAZING. UTTERLY BREATHTAKING.

Aches in all my muscles were what eventually pulled me out of sleep, and I cracked my eyelids to check if the sun was up. Carter must have sensed me wake up, because his arms tightened around me and his lips trailed sleepy kisses up the back of my neck.

"You know this is the first time we've actually slept together?" he murmured, his lips tugging on my earlobe. I moaned lightly and rocked my ass back against him. He was already so hard, it made my insides turn to quivering jelly. My everything ached, but I still wanted him to fuck me again.

He chuckled, one huge hand cupping my breast and his fingers tweaking my nipple as I gasped and rubbed against him like a bitch in heat.

"Again?" he teased, already dipping a hand between my legs. "Four times last night wasn't enough? Spark, you're insatiable."

I moaned as his use of my nickname woke up all my nerve endings and hooked my leg over his hip, making it easy for him to thrust into me from behind. Easy position-wise but certainly not easy for the tight fit it caused. I cried out as he bottomed out, his own breath coming in a satisfied grunt.

"I could stay like this forever," he confessed, lips against my ear as his arm banded around my waist. He held me so close, so firm, like he never wanted to let go. "This is where I feel most at home, balls deep in your sweet cunt."

Words failed me as he started to move, splitting me apart as he rocked that huge dick deep inside my body. I was boneless and relaxed with the residual sleep in my limbs, little more than a puppet for him to do with as he pleased as his pace increased while his teeth grazed the curve of my neck.

I cried out as another orgasm started to build in my core, and he pumped faster to push me over the edge. His teeth indented my skin as I came, and I didn't hold back my moans of ecstasy as I crested and fell in the most addictive way. Carter didn't come with me, though, slowing his motions to ride out my climax, then flipping me onto my belly.

He hitched my hips up in the air, his palm meeting my bare ass with an audible slap that made me squeak. It was quickly followed by a delirious giggle, though, as he massaged the cheek he'd slapped.

"Fuck, Spark," he moaned as he parted my cheeks and repositioned himself between my legs. "I want to fuck this so bad, I actually had a dream about it." His thumb pushed into the hole in question, and I moaned, writhing. "You want me to, hmm? Dirty little Spark."

I grinned, my cheek in his pillow. "Not without lube, I don't." And we had very quickly discovered he didn't have any last night. Carter had sheepishly admitted that he didn't bring hookups home with him, so he wasn't prepared. It was cute, even if it was also frustrating because yeah…I did want that.

He gave a growl, then slammed his hard cock back into my pussy with ferocity. His thumb stayed where it was while he fucked me into oblivion, and I came again before he pulled out and spilled his cum all over my ass. Then he used two of his fingers coated in his own seed to fuck my ass until I screamed another earth-shattering orgasm.

It was a totally different sort of climax, and I was beyond excited to know what it'd be like with his dick.

I collapsed back into his bed, utterly boneless and exhausted as he fetched a warm washcloth from the bathroom to clean me up like the gentleman he was. Then, to make extra sure he'd done a good job, he used his tongue to clean me up even more. Fuck…Carter Bassington was determined to make me forget all our other issues and it was working.

After coming on his face, I must have passed out. Or fallen asleep. Or a combination of the two, because the sun was high in the sky by the time I woke again to the smell of freshly brewed coffee.

As tempted as I was to head straight out to the kitchen and guzzle the coffee, the moment I stood up I winced. I needed to rinse at minimum. Considering how much water we'd used in the night, I kept my shower brief, then dressed in one of Carter's black T-shirts that was long enough to cover my ass before heading out of his room.

I tiptoed past the other boys' rooms, unsure if they were still asleep or even home, and found Carter in the kitchen cooking up an omelet. Shirtless, in just a pair of loose black shorts. It was like a thirst trap made real.

"Smells delicious," I commented, hugging him from behind and letting my fingers run over all the ridges of his body. Fuck, he was cut.

He turned the gas burner off and tipped the omelet out onto a plate before turning to face me. Then he hoisted me up onto the island counter and kissed me like my mouth was the only thing keeping him alive.

"Mmm, what's for breakfast, Bass?" I asked, unable to wipe the smile from my lips when he eventually eased back.

"I'm so tempted to say you," he murmured, swiping his tongue over his lips like he was savoring the taste of me. "I could lay you out right here on the island. Maybe drizzle some maple syrup over those lush folds and lick it all up again." His hand slipped beneath my T-shirt, and he gave a pained moan when he realized I was bare-assed.

I grinned, all too tempted. "I doubt your housemates would appreciate it if we did that." Then I paused to think about it. "Maybe Heath would…but Nate would probably feel the need to douse the kitchen in bleach."

Carter smirked, shaking his head before turning back to grab the plate he'd just deposited his gourmet omelet onto. "For you, Spark." He held it out, but I frowned when I spotted the bandage on his forearm. I hadn't seen it before, but in my defense, I had also been thinking about less PG-13 options for a snack.

"What happened to your arm?" I asked, setting the plate aside and grasping his hand in mine. "Did you burn it? Cooking shirtless is hot and all, but not the safest attire for a chef."

His chuckle was fucking sinful perfection. "No, I didn't burn it. Don't worry, Spark, it's just a scratch. Coffee?"

The quick way he slipped loose of my hold and averted his gaze made me suspicious, so I slid off the counter and followed him to the coffee machine. "Show me," I demanded, my gut telling me not to let this drop. Not after the night we'd just had.

His head hung in defeat, that messy, black hair hiding his eyes for a moment. He knew better than to argue with me, though, so just held out his arm while I quickly unwound the bandage and peeled back the bloodied gauze.

"Carter!" I exclaimed, my jaw damn near hitting the floor when I inspected his wound. Or wounds, as it were. "What the fuck did you do?"

His eyes locked on mine, full of intensity. "Exactly what I needed to do, Spark," he replied in a dark voice. "Exactly what I deserved."

Speechless, I stared back at him a moment, then flicked my gaze back down to his bloody, sliced-up forearm. *Spark*. He'd cut my nickname into his arm just as I'd threatened to do if he didn't stop calling me Ashley. What had I said to him last night? That he needed to remember who I was? Well, now he'd never forget.

"You're insane," I whispered, bringing my gaze back to his.

He shook his head slightly, his lips curling at the corners. "I'm in love."

My brows shot up so hard, I worried I'd lost them. "Excuse me?"

"You heard me, Spark," he murmured, totally ignoring his own injuries as he cupped my face in his hand. "I'm yours now. It's permanent."

I blinked stupidly, my mind like static. Shock would do that to a girl. "What about your mom?"

He lifted one shoulder in a shrug. "I'm dealing with it."

"What about Heath?" I narrowed my eyes, asking the question I was much more concerned about. "I'm still with him and—"

"We're both team players. I reckon we can make it work," Carter replied, having clearly already thought this through. "In fact, I bet you'd have a lot of fun with a little teamwork."

Oh. *Oh.* He meant… My cheeks heated and Carter's smile spread wider, having received confirmation without me even saying a word. Holy fuck, was this happening?

Wetting my lips, I tried to search for the right words to respond, but he saved me by crushing a ferocious kiss against my mouth. I melted into him, letting him claim my lips entirely as my head whirled with the implications of what he was offering. Not just a sexual three-way—he was offering so much more.

Love. He was offering love, just as Heath had.

It scared me.

"Um, speaking of Heath…is he home?" I asked as I redressed Carter's arm with shaking hands. "We should, um, talk. About things. Clear the air."

Carter hummed his agreement, waiting patiently for me to finish his bandage, then he kissed the top of my head. "He's not home. None of the guys are. But I can find out where they're at if you want?"

He grabbed his phone from the charger it was plugged into and I peered over his shoulder as he brought up an app called Where's

Wally. Once it was loaded, he clicked Heath's name and it brought up a map with a GPS marker.

"Oh shit," Carter muttered, quickly swiping back to check Nate's and Royce's locations too. I vaguely noticed my own name was on the list but filed that away to discuss another day. Carter seemed genuinely worried right now.

"Where are they?" I asked. "What's at the corner of Lemontree and Eighth?"

Carter groaned, scrubbing his hands over his face before pushing away from the counter. "We need to get dressed," he told me with a grim look. "They're at Dr. Fox's house."

I gasped. They were at Dr. Fox's house? Willingly…or not? I guess we were about to find out.

Chapter Twenty-Three

THIS SHIT WITH CARTER HAS SHAKEN US ALL SO MUCH MORE THAN
ANYONE SHOWED TO ASHLEY. NO ONE WANTS TO SCARE HER, AND I GET
IT. BUT I KNOW MY FRIENDS...I THINK THEY'RE GOING TO DO SOMETHING
RECKLESS. ROYCE IS A LOOSE CANNON, AND SOMETHING SNAPPED IN HIM
TONIGHT. I'M WORRIED HE WILL DO SOMETHING HE CAN'T TAKE BACK.

N. ESSEX, JANUARY 12

Carter drove like the devil himself was chasing us down, and it only
served to fill me with overwhelming levels of dread for what we
might find at Dr. Fox's house. The most solid theory I came up with
on our way over was that he'd become frustrated that his hypnosis
of Carter failed and was retaliating by turning the other guys into
mindless zombies by whatever means necessary.

The whole drive, all I could picture was finding the three of them
limp and lifeless, drool running from the corners of their mouths
because their brains had been fried.

When we arrived, Carter put his hand out to stop me leaping

from the car. "Wait," he ordered, jaw tight and eyes dark. "We don't know what we'll be walking into. Just…can you please wait one minute while I take a look around? Please?"

If it'd been an outright order, a demand, I'd have told him to go fuck himself and leapt out of the car. But he was genuinely asking and using manners, and that in itself was so unlike Carter, it stopped me in my tracks.

"One minute?" I repeated, anxiety damn near choking me.

Carter nodded firmly, his expression grim. "One minute, that's all I'm asking, Spark. Just let me work out what we're dealing with before putting yourself in the firing line. If you got hurt again…"

I swallowed hard, biting my lip. He had a valid point after last night. So I kissed him quickly, told him to be careful, then damn near crawled out of my own skin with nervousness while he got out of the car and headed toward Dr. Fox's house.

He was casual about it, hands tucked in his pockets and posture relaxed as he strolled up the path as though he were just stopping by to ask for an extra-credit assignment or something. I chewed the crap out of my lip while watching him knock on the door and peer through the window.

For a moment, I wondered if this would be an anticlimactic endeavor and no one would be home. Maybe the guys had been here and already left? And maybe the tracking app was malfunctioning or something? We hadn't tried calling any of the guys on the drive over, because Carter had pointed out that if they were in danger we could be tipping our hand to Dr. Fox.

Right as Carter turned back to where I waited in the car, spreading his hands wide with confusion, the door jerked open and a hand shot out. That was all I could see from where I sat. Just a hand darting out, grabbing Carter's hoodie, and dragging him into the house with one swift movement. Then the door slammed shut once more, and my stomach dropped clean out of my asshole.

"Fuck!" I exclaimed aloud. "Carter!" As if he could hear me from my position inside the car across the street. Fuck waiting the rest of the minute I'd promised, he was clearly in danger, and I was the only one left who could save him. Them.

It took several tries to unbuckle my seat belt and get out of the car. Then I nearly lost the way-too-big shorts I'd borrowed as I sprinted across the road and up the pathway. Not bothering to knock, I threw open the front door and burst inside with zero plan and even less skill.

I barely made it two steps inside the house before colliding with a hard chest, and a pair of strong arms banded around me like iron shackles. Holy fuck, this really wasn't my finest hour.

"Let me go!" I shrieked, only to find a hand clamped over my mouth.

"Shhhh!" someone hissed, and the door closed firmly behind me.

The sheer audacity of my captor and possible murderer to shush me? *Oh hell no, not on—*

"Layne, cut it out," Nate growled, hauling me away from the front door. "Stop acting like we're trying to kill you, and I'll let you go."

Oh. Shit. My "captor" was Nate and I'd just been shushed by an exceptionally amused-looking Royce. Well, it was still rude.

Nate must have sensed the fight evaporating from me because he released his hold on my body a moment later and peeled his hand away from my mouth. "You good?" he asked when I wobbled and spun around to face him.

I took a moment to glance between him and Royce, then nodded shakily. "Yup. Sorry, I thought you were... Someone grabbed Carter and I thought he was... Um, what the fuck is going on?"

Nate squinted at me, folding his arms over his chest. "You thought Carter was in mortal peril so you decided the best course of action was to come bursting in here armed with your sharp wit and cutting sarcasm? Well-thought-out plan, Layne. That wasn't stupid at all."

I glowered, embarrassed at how accurate his summation was. "Fuck you. Where's Heath and Carter? And Dr. Fox? Why are we in Dr. Fox's house without him? This feels illegal."

Royce scoffed at that. "Illegal barely scratches the surface, Squirrel. You shouldn't be here, though. Someone needs to get you back to campus, asap."

Outrage saw me give a squeak of protest. "What? Why?"

His answering grimace was full of dread. "Plausible deniability, babe. Best if we drop you off to spend the day with Carly. Maybe go to the mall or somewhere lots of people will be able to provide an alibi."

"An alibi?" I exclaimed, confused as fuck. "What for? Breaking and entering?"

The sound of arguing echoed from deeper inside the house, and I gave Royce a puzzled look before heading that way. I needed to see Heath and Carter for myself to know they were both okay, and these guys were acting suspicious as hell.

"Uh, that's not a good idea!" Royce called out after me, while Nate tried to grab my arm to stop me again. I dodged his hand and picked up the pace. Either he was going to have to tackle me, or I was going to find out what the hell was going on in Dr. Fox's house.

The arguing was definitely Carter and Heath; I recognized their voices as I drew closer. Or it was largely Carter asking *what the fuck* with increasing levels of confusion and outrage, while Heath snapped back about not needing a lecture.

"Bass failed to mention he'd brought Ashley along for the ride!" Nate called out, seeming to feel the need to warn them I was approaching.

Sure enough, Carter dashed out of what I guessed was the kitchen, intercepting me in the hall. "Spark, baby, you said you'd wait in the car. We just have a little situation here."

I scowled, now one hundred percent sure something suss was going on. "For one minute, yes. One minute is up, Bassington. What the fuck is going on? I thought you were all dead but this—"

"Ashes, I really think it'd be best if you went back to campus!" Heath called out from the kitchen. "Nate, can you drive her back? Please? Carter can help me deal with this."

Carter wheeled around, shaking his head despite the fact Heath couldn't see him. "No, Carter cannot. Carter is in enough trouble as it is without calling in any more favors from that person."

Okay, I was annoyed before, but now that Carter was speaking both ambiguously *and* in third person? Something was seriously fishy. With his back turned, I ducked past him and continued on in the direction Heath's voice had come from. Carter gasped and grabbed for me, but he was too slow.

I'd already seen it.

"What...the fuck?" I asked in a strangled whisper, taking in the sight of blood splattered everywhere. All over the walls, the cabinets, the fridge, the floor...Heath. Holy shit, Heath was *covered*. And I had to assume the source was the very lifeless body on the tile floor.

Heath gave me a sheepish grimace, gesturing weakly to the corpse. "So, um, this isn't ideal. It'd really be preferable if you'd let Nate drive you back to campus now so no one connects you with this..."

"Wait, what do you mean?" Royce spoke up, joining us in the kitchen and gingerly picking a clean patch of tile to stand on. Now that I paid attention, he was also splattered in blood but just nowhere near as much as Heath. "Carter, we figured you could call your guy and—"

"I can't," Carter growled, shaking his head. "He's not my guy, he's my mother's. And since she's currently threatening to pin my last cleanup on Spark...I'd prefer not to hand over even more ammunition."

I gasped so hard, I nearly choked on my own saliva. That was why he'd been so weird about his mom?

The other boys seemed just as shocked as I was by this information, all of them speaking over each other to the point I couldn't make out what anyone was truly saying. The gist of it was that they weren't fucking happy, though.

"Okay, enough!" I shouted, needing to be heard over them all. "Enough. We can untangle that mess later. Right now…let's deal with this. Um. What happened?"

The boys exchanged cryptic looks, then Royce leaned his butt against a clean patch of counter and stuffed his hands in his pockets. "We came over to ask Dr. Fox some questions."

That was it. That was his whole explanation.

I waited a moment longer, thinking surely he'd elaborate a little more on the subject, but nope, that was it. My eyes narrowed, and I glared daggers his way. "Thank you, Roycey, very informative. Heath?" I turned my gaze to my blood-soaked lover, who was looking seriously pale and sweaty. "Jesus, fuck, someone grab a bucket before he vomits on the evidence?"

Carter snagged a fruit bowl from the table and dumped the fruit out before sticking it under Heath's face.

"I'm okay," Heath informed us with a weak cringe. "I'm okay. Promise. Just…the smell just hit me." He gagged but somehow managed to hold back his vomit as he clamped his lips together. "I just…I'm going to sit down for a second." He took the fruit bowl with him as he stumbled to the corner of the kitchen and slid down the cabinets to sit on his ass.

Confused and worried, I turned to Nate for answers. I was seeking honesty and logic from Nate of all people. Hell must have been preparing for a snowstorm.

"Royce isn't wrong. We did come looking for some answers," he confirmed, speaking cautiously as his gaze traveled across his three friends before landing on me. He stood there in the doorway with his stance balanced and his arms folded across his chest like he was taking charge. Thank fuck too, because someone needed to. "We maybe didn't approach it in the most diplomatic way, but after what happened to Carter, we weren't really thinking the consequences through."

Royce scoffed at that, a loopy grin on his lips. "I'd say this played out fairly similar to what we theorized."

"And what if we'd been wrong?" Nate exploded, glaring death at Royce and giving me a pretty clear idea of who'd initiated this field trip. "If we were wrong—and we easily could have been—then we'd all be getting arrested for assault and god only knows what else."

"Instead of murder?" Carter asked, tilting his head as he stared down at the body on the floor. "Somehow I'd think assault would be the lesser crime here."

"It was an accident," Heath muttered from his seat on the floor, looking miserable. If I hadn't already guessed purely based on how bloody he was, that confirmed for me who'd done the deed itself. Honestly, I was shocked. Of the four of them, Heath would have been my last guess for committing murder.

Nate ran a hand through his hair, messing it up a little as he blew out a breath. "I'm not sure we can call it an accident when you repeatedly bludgeoned a restrained man, bro. There's literally nothing left of his face."

Oh. Wow. That…explained the mess.

For some reason, I glanced around the kitchen until I spotted what must have been the murder weapon. A granite duck figurine.

A startled laugh escaped me, and I clapped a hand over my mouth to hold it in. "Sorry," I muttered. "It's not funny. Sorry. I just… You used a duck? What is with you guys and waterfowl?"

175

Chapter Twenty-Four

She's mine now, and I'm never letting her go. Can I share
her with Heath? We'll see, I guess.

Jan. 12
C. Bassington

Nate, Heath, and Carter stared at me like I'd grown another head,
but at least Royce snickered under his breath, grinning as he met
my gaze.

"Purely coincidental, Squirrel," he assured me as he rubbed his
jaw. "Funny, though. I hadn't even noticed."

"Can we circle back to the dead guy?" Carter asked, gruff and
demanding. I liked when he used that voice in the bedroom, but
right now it felt like a scolding, so I pouted a bit. "How'd you all go
from questioning him to Heath becoming a murderer?"

Heath huffed a sound, still looking deathly pale. "I thought there
would be a cool membership card that you'd give me, Bass."

Carter rolled his eyes like he was at his wit's end. It also sort of suggested the guy in Paris wasn't Carter's first slipup, and I filed that information away for later. "You're an idiot, Briggs," he muttered, sighing. "I'm guessing he did something or said something that triggered a dormant hypnosis?"

Heath grimaced, and Royce snort-laughed.

"This wasn't done under hypnosis," Nate replied in a grim voice. "Triggered, yes, but only into normal human rage. Here, I recorded the whole thing just in case we needed documentation later." He pulled out his phone and tapped his thumb over the screen until he located the video in question.

On the little recording, Dr. Fox—I had to assume—was tied to a dining chair in the middle of the kitchen we currently stood in. A noticeably cleaner kitchen.

"You can probably fast-forward through most of it," Royce suggested with a shrug. "I'm thinking it's maybe more important to deal with this first and dwell on reasons later?"

Carter grunted. "Good point."

Still, I took the phone out of Nate's hand and pressed play. In the interest of time, though, I did as he suggested and skimmed the first part, pausing only when I saw Heath grab the duck off a shelf. Then I rewound enough to hear Dr. Fox's gloating confession that not only had he been messing around in Heath's head for months but that he'd also planted the idea of suicide when Heath had started remembering some of the hypnosis-induced acts he'd partaken in.

"Wow," I muttered aloud, pausing when Heath in the video reached for the duck again. I didn't need to watch the rest; the outcome was painted all over the kitchen right now.

"That's it?" Nate asked, frowning at me with an intensity that made me uneasy. "*Wow*? That's your whole reaction to this?" He waved a hand at the dead body—rapidly cooling, I'd bet—and shook his head with disbelief. "Just...*wow*?"

I handed his phone back and shrugged. "What do you want from me? Hysterics? I don't know if my acting skills are totally up to the task, but I can give it a go once we get this sorted out, if you'd like?"

He stared back, incredulous, before muttering something under his breath about psychotic women and something about how he should have known I was unhinged.

Whatever. Nate's opinion of me meant very little with how big our more immediate problem was. No way in hell was I losing Heath to a murder conviction when what he'd done was only one step further than self-defense. Sort of.

"Okay, we need to cover this up," I said, parking my hands on my hips. "Without giving Carter's bitch mother any excuses to force him into some kind of medieval marriage contract. Crap, your car!" I snapped my fingers at Carter, gesturing to the street where we'd left his very recognizable Koenigsegg Gemera. "Go. Move it. Quick. Where did you guys park?" I directed the question to Royce, since Nate was still staring at me like I'd revealed myself as a blue alien. Carter silently went to do as I'd instructed.

Royce shook his head. "Two blocks away. And we already checked which neighbors have security cameras, so we'd know which ones needed to be wiped later. Um, not that we intended this ending, but it seemed the smart thing to do."

"He made us dress as Mormons," Heath informed me, still seated on the floor but looking marginally less pale. "We rode bikes and everything, just to knock on people's doors."

I bit back a laugh at that mental image. "What did you say? Do you have any clue what Mormon missionaries even say in those door-to-door pitches?"

"No clue," Royce replied with a grin. "Do you? No one actually lets them get the whole pitch out before slamming the door, so all we needed was the suit, bike, and a polite hello, to sell the act. Anyway, only two neighbors had cameras, and Nate reckons they'll be easy to wipe."

"Kinda wish I'd seen that," I muttered, then ruffled my hair with my fingers, thinking. "Okay, so Nate, you can handle the security cameras? That just leaves…this. Um…and we can't rely on Carter's shady cleanup guy because he answers to his mother, who sounds like the devil incarnate. Uh…your DNA is probably all over the house too. None of you are wearing gloves."

Royce and Nate both looked down at their hands, and Nate whispered a curse. *Idiots*.

"You seem…very calm about this," Heath commented, wincing as he looked at his own hands. Then he pushed to his feet and crossed to the sink to rinse them under the tap. "I'm not saying that as a bad thing. Just surprising."

I shot him a wobbly grin because, internally, I was barely holding it together. "All those years of true-crime podcasts had to come in handy one day. Now, I am assuming there're no pig farms nearby?"

"You're not serious," Nate said in a strangled voice. "That's not a thing."

"Yes, it is," I countered. "They don't eat clothing or shoes, so you'd have to strip him. And they would shit out teeth eventually, but otherwise it's proven to be effective."

Royce was already on his phone, shaking his head. "Nearest pig farm is a five-hour drive from here and commercially run, so I doubt they'd be cool with us feeding the piggies some chopped-up psychologist for dinner."

I tapped my fingertips against my lips, thinking it over again. "It also wouldn't erase all the evidence here."

"We could set it on fire," Heath suggested, scrubbing the blood from his fingernails with a dish brush. "Fire would get rid of DNA and fingerprints and shit. And it would be appropriate, considering how he made us burn down the old science hall."

A silence filled the room as we all considered that option, broken only by Carter returning to join us. He was sweaty and puffing slightly, and I trusted he'd parked far enough away to not have it be an issue.

"What are we thinking about?" he asked, looping an arm around my waist and kissing my hair. The bandage on his arm had a few dark splotches and would need to be checked once this was all over.

Crazy fuck.

"Arson," Nate replied, scowling.

Carter nodded thoughtfully. "It would clean the scene, for sure. Good thinking, bro. We'd need to stage it as a break-in gone wrong, though, because even fire can't disguise the blunt force trauma in Dr. Fox's skull. Doable, though."

After a little more discussion, we decided on our plan. Ideally, we needed to wait to set the fire until after ten p.m., when most of the neighborhood would be asleep, but we didn't want to risk anyone finding the body in the meantime and didn't want any discrepancies to come up between time of death and the fire. So, after sending Nate and Royce back out into the neighborhood with their bikes to deal with door cameras, we started dousing the kitchen and the corpse with accelerant.

When we were satisfied that we'd done all we could to cover our tracks—including untying Dr. Fox's restraints and wiping down every surface that might have fingerprints—we left via the back door. Carter then smashed the glass from the outside to stage it as a break-in and tossed in a lit match.

As casually as we could, considering I was barefoot and wearing men's clothing four sizes too big for me, we walked the three blocks back to Carter's car. None of us spoke, not even as we watched the plume of smoke start rising up into the sky. It was like we were all holding our breath, waiting as the minutes ticked by before a well-meaning neighbor would call the fire department.

By some dumb luck, either no one noticed or the fire department was busy, but a full half hour passed before the trucks came flying around the block with sirens screaming.

"They'll be lucky to find any evidence at all now," Carter murmured as we drove back to their apartment. "It only takes five minutes for a house to become fully engulfed. At this stage, I'll be shocked if they even find Dr. Fox's skeleton."

"Mmm, I wouldn't be so sure," I replied, googling how hot a fire needed to be to turn bones to ash. "The fire would need to be burning at 1400 to 1800 degrees Fahrenheit for three hours to fully cremate him, and house fires on average sit at 1100 degrees but can in some situations reach 2000 degrees. I'm not saying it's not possible. I guess it depends how long they take to put it out?"

Carter glanced over at me quickly before returning his eyes to the road, saying nothing. Heath started laughing in the back seat, though.

"Here I was thinking you'd be the useful one in covering up crimes, Bass," he chuckled, "but it seems you've met your match."

Another glance from Carter, but this time it was a whole hell of a lot more heated. "Damn right I have."

Well, fuck. That did funny things to my insides, so I bit my lip and turned to look out the window for the rest of the drive. It wasn't until we were parking that another thought struck me.

"Nate can clear our search histories, right?" Because I'd just been googling how hot crematoriums run in comparison to house fires, and Royce had searched pig farms. It wouldn't take a genius to hold us accountable for murder based on those breadcrumbs.

Heath grinned, looping an arm over my shoulders as we waited for the elevator. "He can, for sure. But I love that you thought about it."

"You love everything about Spark," Carter murmured as the doors slid open and the three of us stepped inside. "Not that I can blame you."

Oh wow, that took a serious turn. "We should, um, we should probably have a conversation…the three of us. Maybe it can wait until we aren't waiting for the police to knock on the door, though."

Heath tilted his head thoughtfully. "I don't know; there's no time like the present. Besides, how else will we work out where you're sleeping tonight? Because you're not going back to the dorm."

181

My jaw unhinged slightly. "I'm not?" I squeaked with an edge of protest. I didn't like being told what to do…but under the current circumstances, maybe it wasn't the worst idea to hang out with the guys for a bit. "Well, good luck getting Nate to agree with that." Because he'd been less than impressed whenever he found me hanging out with Heath during the week.

Carter and Heath both grinned at that, though.

"Why would he have any objection, Spark?" Carter asked in a teasing voice. "You guys are engaged after all."

I groaned, smacking my forehead. I'd almost forgotten about that too.

Chapter Twenty-Five

January 13

I didn't go to Dr. Fox's house with the intent to kill him. At least...I don't think I did? Royce maybe had murder on his mind, but I could see how triggered he was by thinking Carter intentionally hurt Ashes. Still, Nate was with us and he's usually the voice of reason so I figured we would just tie Dr. Fox up and force a confession then turn him over to the police.

I just never expected him to confess that much. To freely admit he'd pushed me into suicide and to sound so fucking smug about it. Like he knew we were decent people and would never actually hurt him. Well. I guess I proved him wrong.

Shit. I really shouldn't be writing this all down. Talk about damning evidence. I'd better rip this page out and destroy it, to be safe.

H. Briggs

The idea of talking out our odd little three-way relationship was actually a lot worse than the reality of it. Both Heath and Carter had already come to terms with it on their own and had just been waiting for me to come around. They were both shockingly mature about the whole thing, but I had to wonder if their own brother-love played a part in that adjustment.

The arguments only started when it came down to where I would sleep. Apparently, they were both okay with the poly-relationship in theory but weren't willing to sacrifice their own desires to keep the peace. Eventually, when things started to get really heated, Nate stepped in and put his foot down.

Which was how I found myself waking up Monday morning in Nathaniel Essex's bed. Thankfully, without the devil himself, but still. Weird. His sheets smelled distinctly of him, but fortunately there were no feminine perfumes to betray Paige's presence. Small mercies, considering everything.

I still had no clothes of my own, unless I was willing to put on my ball gown from Saturday night, so after I showered in Nate's bathroom—not wanting to wake the rest of the apartment up—I wrapped myself in a towel and tiptoed out to the kitchen in search of a phone charger. I needed to debrief Carly on all the things that wouldn't get us arrested on a phone-tap.

"How'd you sleep?" Nate asked from the living room, and I jumped so hard, I nearly dropped my towel. "Sorry, figured you saw me." He gave me a side-eye as he folded the sofa-bed mattress back into the cavity of the couch.

"I didn't. Um, not bad…all things considered." I winced as I said it, thinking back to everything that'd happened in the last two days. It was enough to turn me gray.

Nate hummed a sound of understanding as he neatly folded the quilt and stacked it beside the pillows he'd used. "You don't always sleep well after covering up a murder? I do."

I shot him a sarcastic smile. "Ha-ha, very funny. I was exhausted, okay?"

He snort-laughed at that. "Not surprised."

Christ. Now I was blushing like a fucking virgin, thinking about how he'd probably heard Carter and me rocking each other's bones all damn night after the party. Clearing my throat, I turned back to the kitchen and made a beeline for the coffee machine. Coffee would make everything more tolerable.

"Do you want coffee?" I asked, remembering my manners considering not only was I intruding in his apartment but I'd literally stolen his bed.

Nate huffed, striding across to the kitchen area of their open-plan apartment. "I'll make it. You get dressed. The last thing I need is to have Carter come out here and start fucking you on the countertop."

Just when I thought I couldn't blush any harder, my cheeks proved me wrong. "I'd love to, but my full-length ball gown seems a bit overkill for Monday morning breakfast, don't you think? I was just going to text Carly and ask her to send some stuff over."

"Royce already did," Nate replied with a heavy yawn, gesturing to the dining table. Sure enough, there was one of my duffel bags, full—presumably—with my clothes.

I left the kitchen, holding on to my towel with one hand, and went to grab the bag. "Thanks, that's useful." The bag was heavy, literally bursting at the seams with how much was stuffed inside. "Did he think I was staying for a month or that I was super indecisive?"

From the corner of my eye, I saw Nate roll his eyes. "The first one," he muttered, then pressed the grind button on the coffee machine to drown out any further conversation.

Taking the hint for what it was, I carried my heavy bag back through to his bedroom and quickly changed into a pair of jeans and a form-fitting white T-shirt. Royce had even remembered to include bras and panties, which was surprising. Most guys I figured would totally overlook those minor yet significant aspects of an outfit.

Once dressed, I zipped up my duffel and parked it just beside Nate's door, unsure where else to store it for the time being. I had a really strong feeling I wouldn't be heading back to my dorm again tonight but obviously couldn't kick Nate out of his room again... It was a debate for after coffee.

"Coffee's ready," Nate announced when I reappeared in the kitchen. "Are you hungry?"

My stomach rumbled, totally betraying me before I could say no. "Yes, but I can grab something on my way to class." I checked the time on my phone, which was now charging on the counter beside the coffee machine. I still had ages before my first class, so I could probably meet Carly somewhere for food.

Nate shrugged. "Suit yourself." He flipped open a cabinet door and waved a hand at the assortment of syrups inside. "Have at it, sweet tooth."

He scooped up his own coffee, then disappeared down the hallway and into his bedroom. A moment later, the static hum of the shower started up and I nearly choked on my tongue when I realized I was mentally picturing him getting undressed.

What the fuck was wrong with me?

Trauma must have been fucking with my head. Although, weirdly, I was nowhere near as shaken up from the weekend as I probably should have been. We'd literally covered up a murder...a murder committed by my boyfriend. One of them, anyway, not to say the other had clean hands.

I was starting to think maybe I had a type.

"Good morning, Squirrel baby!" Royce greeted me with a sleepy smile as he strode into the kitchen...shirtless. Were they all allergic to clothing these days? "Oooh, coffee for me? You shouldn't have." He swiped my coffee from the countertop where I'd been topping it up with toffee nut syrup and took a gulp.

"Hey!" I protested as he gagged. "That's mine, thief."

"How the fuck do you drink that? It's pure sugar." He handed it straight back and nudged me aside to prepare his own without the sweeteners. "You look fresh this morning. Sleep well?"

I sipped my own caffeinated concoction and nodded. "I did, surprisingly. Thank you for the clothes. You saved me having to do the walk of shame back to my dorm in a borrowed T-shirt and shorts."

Royce quirked a brow, raking his gaze down my outfit, then shrugging. "You're welcome."

I pursed my lips, watching him make his coffee in silence. "You sure packed a lot of clothes for just one night, though…"

His lips curved in a smile, but he just shrugged again and continued preparing his latte. Carter was the next one awake, scuffing his feet into the kitchen while legitimately still looking half-asleep. His messy black hair was all in his face, but he somehow locked on me like a homing pigeon and scooped me up in a hug that lifted me clean off the ground.

"Good morning, Spark," he growled with a sleep-husky voice, making me tingle all over. "I missed you in my bed last night."

Royce made an exaggerated gagging sound as Carter's mouth found my neck and I let out a little moan. Shit, could anyone blame me? It felt good and Carter was mind-blowingly hot. Scorching. I was actually starting to worry about the future of my degree because, goddamn, it'd be tempting to just stay in bed with him and Heath twenty-four seven.

"Before this turns into an NC-17 scene, can I please remind you that you're late for your finance lecture, Bass?" Royce tapped his wristwatch pointedly, and I marveled at the fact he'd put his watch on but not a shirt. Priorities.

Carter groaned, still not putting me down. "I don't want to go," he grumbled, face still buried in my neck. "I'm gonna stay here and eat Spark's pussy all day."

Oh. Wow. Um…I was okay with that.

"Good luck with that," Royce replied, not taking Carter seriously,

"Squirrel and I have Philosophy class at ten, and Carly's expecting us to meet her for breakfast in half an hour."

Carter's arms tightened around me for a moment, then he lowered me back to the floor with a frustrated groan. "You're such a cockblocker, Royce," he muttered as he released me, then punched Royce in the shoulder on his way out of the kitchen once more. Presumably to get ready for class.

In his absence, I propped my hands on my hips and squinted at Royce. "You're talking to my best friend behind my back? Rude."

Royce gasped, looking mortified. "What? I thought I was your best friend. Double rude. Anyway, Carly helped me pack up your clothes last night so we made plans then. I grabbed your laptop from your room, but did you need anything else for classes?"

He raised his coffee mug to take a sip, and I could swear his biceps flexed way more than that motion called for. Come to think of it, should abs all be so very defined while relaxed?

I frowned suspiciously. "Are you flexing right now?"

His lips tilted in a grin. "Are you checking me out right now? Thirsty Squirrel."

Fuck me dead, I was blushing again. Talk about selling myself out. "Are you going out like that? It's a cold day. You might consider a shirt at the very least."

Smug fuck just grinned wider. "Because you're having a hard time containing yourself and that rapidly growing attraction to my sexy body? I get that a lot. But yes, I suppose I should get dressed."

He took his coffee with him to get ready, and rather than hanging out alone in their kitchen, I decided to sneak in and wake Heath up.

His room was dark and quiet when I slipped through the door, and I held my breath as I tiptoed closer to his bed. He was fast asleep, one arm dangling out, and I nearly changed my mind. Then that arm shot out and grabbed me, hauling me into his embrace as I squealed in surprise.

"Mmm, good morning," he mumbled, wrapping his whole body around me like an overgrown octopus. He was sleeping in just a pair of boxers and by the feel of things, I'd interrupted a very good dream.

"You scared me," I admitted with a laugh. "I thought you were asleep."

"I was," he moaned, "but this is much better." His hips rocked that hard length against me, and I cursed my fully dressed state of being. "Why are you wearing so many clothes, Ashes?"

"Such a good question," I replied with a heavy exhale, arching my back as his hand slipped beneath my sweater. "I'm supposed to meet Carly in half an hour, I think."

Heath paused, then rumbled a happy sort of sound. "Plenty of time. I'll take it." Then my sweater somehow teleported from my body to his floor. So weird. Oh well, may as well send my jeans to keep it company.

Carly would be fine waiting when this was my excuse. Royce... well, too bad.

Chapter Twenty-Six

I'M SO FUCKING CONFUSED. EVERYTHING FEELS SO INCREDIBLY OUT OF
CONTROL RIGHT NOW, AND THE ONLY THING REASSURING ME THAT WE
AREN'T BEING MANIPULATED OR HYPNOTIZED ON THE REGULAR IS ALL
THE CAMERAS I'VE SET UP TO RECORD OUR EVERY MOVEMENT. BREACH OF
PRIVACY? ABSOLUTELY. BUT I'D RATHER INVADE MY FRIENDS' PRIVACY THAN
RISK MORE GAPS OF TIME IN OUR MEMORIES. MORE MYSTERIOUS BRUISES
AND SCRATCHES OR MORE ACHINGLY REALISTIC "NIGHTMARES" GIVING
GLIMPSES OF WHAT WE'VE DONE.

TROUBLE WAS, THOSE CAMERAS CAPTURED EVERYTHING...IN EVERY
ROOM OF OUR APARTMENT.

DOES THIS MAKE ME A PERVERT? UNDOUBTEDLY YES. BUT STILL, I
HAVEN'T TOLD ANYONE ABOUT THE SURVEILLANCE AND I HAVEN'T TURNED
THE CAMERAS OFF. I TRY TO TELL MYSELF IT'S FOR ALL OUR SAFETY. BUT I
NO LONGER BELIEVE MYSELF.

N. ESSEX, JANUARY 14

Somehow—don't ask me how because I was still confused—the guys convinced me that I needed to stay with them a little longer. I mean, I'd seen it coming a mile away when Royce packed half my closet into my "overnight" bag, but the whole sleeping arrangement conundrum led me to think it was only temporary.

Apparently, I was wrong.

"This is getting silly," I muttered the following weekend when I padded barefoot into the kitchen. Nate had just woken up on the sofa bed again and looked like he'd had a shitty night again. "You need your room back. I can just bunk in with one of the guys so you can stop sleeping out here."

Nate yawned heavily, stretching his arms over his head and making my brain short-circuit for a hot second. Bloody hell, these guys were inhuman.

"Nope," he said, seeming happy to leave it at that as he went to work folding up the bed linens.

Frustrated, I went to help, as I'd done the last few mornings. "You're being childish, Nate. It's not going to cause World War Three if I crash with Carter for a night. Or shit, Royce has been sleeping in my bed for months. What difference would it make if I repaid the favor?"

Nate shot me a confused scowl. "In your bed? He said he was sleeping on an air mattress."

I blinked a few times, then nodded slowly. "Right. Same thing. So I could sleep on an air mattress here, or we can keep it very easy and I sleep here on the sofa bed, or…crazy idea…I just go back to the dorms and stop causing issues?"

"Nope," he said again, taking the folded quilt from my arms and stacking it with his pillows. "You have work this morning?"

I rolled my eyes, irritated at the blatant change of subject. "Yeah, I've got a double shift to cover someone who called in sick. I've got a few minutes before I need to leave, if you want me to take Lady over to the park?"

"Nah, Carter can do it. She's his dog. Give me five minutes and I'll drop you off." He said it so fucking casually that I wouldn't have thought twice about it coming from anyone else. But Nate? Alarm bells went off.

"Why?" I asked as he started to head toward his bedroom, which I'd been inhabiting all week. "Why are you being so nice, Essex? This isn't like you. Are you—"

"Ha-ha, funny," he snarked. "I'm not hypnotized. I'm very clearly just preemptively banking good karma for any future conflicts that may or may not arise."

Weirdly, I couldn't tell if that was a joke or not. With Nate, it was hard to tell.

As tempting as it was to sneak in and wake Heath up—early morning snuggles were fast becoming our thing, like how late-night showers with Carter were becoming a thing—I didn't want to be late for work. So I filled Lady's water and fed her breakfast while waiting for Nate, then headed down to the parking garage with him a few minutes later.

"I don't know why I keep letting you guys drive me places," I admitted out loud as we got into his enormous truck. "I have my own car, and it works just fine."

Nate just shot me a sidelong glance, then focused on reversing his huge vehicle out of the parking space. "Some might say," he murmured thoughtfully as he kept his focus on driving, "that you've been relying on yourself for so long that maybe you subconsciously enjoy the feeling of being taken care of in little ways."

I scowled. "I'm not an invalid, nor am I some kind of weak woman desperately seeking a man to lighten her mental load."

He rolled his eyes. "Is that what I said? Fuck, woman, stop trying to put insults in my mouth. It's not a fucking bad thing; it's just psychology. How old were you when you got your first job? And I don't mean a pennies-on-the-dollar job. I mean one where you contributed to household bills."

My jaw tightened. "Fourteen."

Another sidelong glance. "Seriously? Doing what?"

I cleared my throat, feeling uncomfortably vulnerable being so honest with Nate. "I was doing deliveries for a pharmacy, actually. For elderly folk who couldn't leave their homes but needed their medication."

This time his glance was sharper. "In Panner Valley? How were you getting around?"

"Bicycle," I admitted grudgingly. "It wasn't dangerous, if that's what you're implying. It was just blood pressure medication and crap like that. Not narcotics." At least…I didn't think it was. Admittedly, I'd never paid a hell of a lot of attention to the exact prescriptions. I'd just delivered them.

"In Panner Valley," Nate repeated, dumbstruck. "And Carina was okay with this?"

I gave a short laugh. "Carina didn't know. She thought I was earning money through after-school tutoring."

"Fucking hell, Layne," he muttered, shaking his head. "You're proving my point here. No one is forcing you to accept rides to and from work or campus; you're simply accepting because subconsciously you need a break from being so damn independent all the time." He paused, like he was letting that kernel of wisdom sink into my stubborn brain. Then he shrugged and grinned. "Or maybe in the back of your mind, you're aware that your Firebird is worth more money with fewer miles on the clock."

I chuckled. "Yeah, that's probably it."

We were both quiet for the rest of the drive across to the country club, and when we arrived Nate, asked what time I'd be finished. I wasn't totally sure, so said I'd text our group chat when I needed a lift back.

Work was busy. It was a Saturday, and despite the cold, the spa bookings were back-to-back from opening till closing. The small saving grace to the long hours was that country club clients tipped really well and the club didn't take a cut.

By the time I showered in the staff locker rooms and changed out of my uniform, I was wrecked. Every muscle in me ached, and I realized as I headed for the exit that I hadn't texted the guys for a lift home.

"Dammit," I mumbled, fishing out my phone. It'd be quicker and easier to get an Uber, but then that'd be a cut into my pay for the day... I should have driven myself.

"Need a ride?"

The question startled me, and I looked up from my phone to find Royce leaning against the door of his car all wrapped up in a coat and scarf but still looking cold as fuck.

"How long have you been waiting?" I exclaimed, hurrying across to him and touching my fingers to his pink cheek. "Fuck, Royce, you're frozen!"

"I'm fine," he replied with a grin. "But you really took your sweet-ass time getting out. Your manager said you were finishing at six?"

I threw my hands up. "Yeah, because I didn't know you were out here waiting for me or I wouldn't have spent twenty minutes blow-drying my hair after the shower. Give me the keys. I'm driving."

His brows shot up, but he did as he was told, dropping the keys into my open palm. "Yes, ma'am."

"Idiot," I mumbled, circling around the hood of his Bugatti to take the driver's seat. "Hello, darling," I whispered to the car as I stroked the leather steering wheel.

"Stop dirty-talking my car, Squirrel," Royce complained as he strapped himself in and blasted the heat. "It's making me jealous."

I grinned and jokingly moaned when the engine roared to life. The panicked stare Royce shot my way made me laugh out loud, but I focused on not crashing his three-million-dollar car as I eased out of the parking space.

"Can I take the long way home?" I asked, trying not to sound as gleeful as I was feeling behind the steering wheel of a supercar.

"Squirrel, you can drive us to Mexico if you want," he replied with a lopsided smile. "I should have given you my keys months ago. How was work?"

"Long, exhausting, but good," I replied honestly. "Clients were all super polite and tipped well, which makes it all worthwhile." My stomach rumbled and I grimaced. "I did miss my lunch break, though. What are we doing for dinner?"

"Heath's cooking enchiladas, I think." He tugged off his coat, having probably warmed up enough, then shifted in his seat so he was almost facing me while I drove. "You look good driving my car. I could get used to being a passenger princess."

I smiled, glancing at how relaxed he seemed. "I'll order you a crown online."

"Speaking of driving places...I was wondering if you have any plans tomorrow?" He sounded cagey all of a sudden. Less confident.

I glanced over, curious. "Um, just working on my humanities assignment. And I should probably move back into my dorm, since none of us have been arrested or even questioned by police all week. Why?"

He raked his fingers through his hair, seeming nervous. "I need to visit my mom and I was wondering if you wanted to come with? It's a whole-day mission, though, so if you need to work on assignments—"

"I'd love to come!" I cut him off. "Are you kidding? I've got two weeks before I need to hand that one in. It's not urgent. Where does she live? Why have I never heard you mention your mom before?"

Royce gave a soft laugh, swiping his hand over his face. "Ah, well...I don't see her super often. She lives in Hastings...or more specifically in Clearview Correctional Facility."

Shock saw me jerk my gaze to his for a moment before I remembered I was driving and jerked my eyes back to the road. "Oh. She's...a warden?"

Royce grinned. "No, Squirrel. She's an inmate."

Well, fuck. "Oh. Um. What did she do?"

He drew a deep breath and released it with a heavy exhale. "According to her? Nothing. According to the state? Mass homicide so…she's in there for life. Fun fact, I was actually born in prison."

My jaw dropped. "What? Royce, you ass, you can't give me mind-blowing information about yourself while I'm focusing on not hurting your sexy car! What the fuck?"

He chuckled. "Yeah, well, I can give you my whole sad story while we're on the road tomorrow, if you want?"

"Um, yes," I enthused. "Yes, please. Fuck, Royce, I feel like I don't even know you." I frowned, flicking my eyes to his briefly. "Not in a bad way. Just…I dunno. I'm a crappy friend for never asking about your story."

"Nah," he replied, relaxing in his seat once more. "You've just had a lot going on. But…things are different now. Right?"

I wet my lips and nodded. "Sure feels that way."

For the rest of the drive home, we chatted about lighter topics, like Carly's new boyfriend, and laughed about the whining voicemail Paige had apparently left on Royce's voicemail during the week. Then when we arrived back at the apartment, we walked right in on what seemed to be a fairly intense argument between Carter, Heath, and Nate.

"Um, hi?" I said when everyone shut right the fuck up after we opened the door. "What's going on?"

Nate shot a pointed look at Carter, who had his arms folded firmly across his chest with a stubborn-fuck expression on his face. "Go on, Bass. Tell Layne what you did. See what happens."

My eyes narrowed in suspicion. "Carter…what did you do?" Because he'd already cut my name into his flesh—which was thankfully healing well with daily tending—so what could possibly be worse?

Suddenly, Carter seemed a little less confident, his gaze shifting from me to Royce and back with an edge of nervousness. "Maybe we can talk in private, Spark?"

Heath scoffed. "Yeah, right. I want to watch her slap the shit out of you. To be clear, Ashes, I told him this was a bad idea, and he did it anyway."

"Wow, really just hanging me out to dry," Carter grumped. "Pricks. And you said it was a good idea earlier in the week."

Heath held his hands up in a defensive gesture. "I said it was a good idea *if Ashley agreed.* I never said go ahead and do it without consulting her. That's your grave to lie in, you dipshit."

"Someone start explaining!" I shouted, losing my patience. Then, as I snapped, I noticed the suitcases lined up neatly in the hallway. My suitcases. "What the… Carter, what did you do?"

He huffed a frustrated sigh. "I canceled your dorm room and it got reassigned, so we needed to move all your stuff today before the new student moves in. Carly helped."

As if somehow Carly helping made it all okay. My eye twitched as I looked from my suitcases to Carter and back again at least a half dozen times, then squeaked a strangled "Sorry, what?"

He forced an uncomfortable smile. "You live here now. Surprise!"

Chapter Twenty-Seven

0530: WOKE UP PER BODY CLOCK AND CHECKED MOTION CAMERAS. NO SLEEPWALKING, ONCE AGAIN. STARTING TO THINK MAYBE WE'RE IN THE CLEAR?

0600: QUIETLY HIT THE GYM ON THE THIRD FLOOR WHILE EVERYONE WAS STILL ASLEEP. FUCKING NATE WAS SNORING ON THE COUCH. HE'S BEEN WEIRD THIS WEEK, AND HIS INSISTENCE AT LETTING SQUIRREL TAKE HIS ROOM REEKS OF ULTERIOR MOTIVE.

0730: MADE IT BACK INTO MY ROOM RIGHT BEFORE ASHLEY'S ALARM WENT OFF. NOW TO SHOWER AND LOOK SLEEPY WHEN I HEAD OUT TO SAY GOOD MORNING.

0800: STUPID NATE MUST HAVE TAKEN SQUIRREL TO WORK BEFORE I GOT OUT OF THE SHOWER. HIS TRUCK IS GONE BUT HER FIREBIRD IS STILL IN OUR GARAGE.

0900-1600: HELPED CARTER AND CARLY PACK UP ASHLEY'S DORM ROOM. SHE'S GOING TO KILL HIM, BUT AT THE SAME TIME I'M NOT MAD ABOUT HAVING HER MOVE IN WITH US. WE JUST NEED TO CONVINCE NATE TO CHILL THE FUCK OUT A BIT.

R. D'ARENBERG, JANUARY 20

"I'm going to have to kill him," I declared for what was possibly the fiftieth time already, and we'd barely started our drive to Hastings. "That's the only solution. I have to beat him with a marble duck."

"Too soon," Heath groaned from the back seat of my car. He was squashed in there like a sardine but had insisted I take the passenger seat since Royce had begged to drive again.

I turned in my seat to flash him a grin. "Sorry. Okay, then I'll stuff sixty-seven tiny ducks down his throat and make him choke on them. Death by duck just seems really appropriate."

"Just deny him sex," Royce suggested with a sly smile. "He'll very quickly learn his lesson."

"I'm on board with that idea," Heath agreed enthusiastically. "And am more than happy to keep you plenty satisfied so it's not a hardship on you."

"You're such a gentleman, Heathcliff," Royce teased, glancing at him in the mirror.

I laughed, shaking my head. "You guys are cruel. Death by duck seems more humane." But it didn't fix the problem. I was homeless thanks to Carter's stubborn sense of entitlement. He'd known perfectly fucking well I wasn't going to be okay with this, so he'd waited until it was absolutely too late to do anything about it.

I'd spent far too long the night before trying to reverse his actions, but it was all to no avail. It was the weekend, and the campus admin wouldn't get my emails until Monday morning, which was when my room's new occupant would be moving in. So unless I wanted to try to have her evicted—which would be a dick move since she was an innocent bystander in this mess—I didn't have many options.

"I can't make Nate sleep on the couch forever," I grumbled aloud. "I'll have to find somewhere else." But Prosper City was way out of my price range, and the waitlist for the dorms was insanely long. Hence my room getting snapped up so quickly.

"Carter can figure it out," Royce said, reaching out to pat my knee reassuringly. "It's his responsibility. And in the meantime, you can come sleep with me again. My bed is like double the size of your dorm bed, so we wouldn't even need the pillow wall."

I smiled and tried not to blush thinking about all the mornings I'd frantically rebuilt the pillow wall after waking up tangled up in Royce's arms while he slept soundly. "Thanks, roomie, that's a great idea. Nate looks half-dead from lack of sleep at the moment too. The sofa bed must be awful."

Heath gave a thoughtful hum in the back seat. "I think it's less about the sofa bed and more about the fact he's waking up at every little creak and sound throughout the night, worried one of us is being sleeper-cell activated. And when Lady is snoring and scratching and whining, it means he isn't ever really sleeping."

That made me feel even worse. I shook my head firmly. "Well then, that's that. He's getting his room back tonight, no arguments."

Heath changed the subject, asking about one of my assignments that I'd been working on, and I shifted gears into my academic mind to answer him. It wasn't until we stopped for gas a while later that I fully realized Royce's hand was still resting comfortably on my knee. I liked it there too.

The drive to Hastings took us a little over three hours, then we needed to wait for visiting hours to start and spent way too long signing in as guests. I asked Royce at least a dozen times if he was sure he wanted me to actually come in with him, since Heath wasn't coming in with us, but Royce insisted he wanted me there.

When we were finally granted access—after an invasively thorough pat down—I recognized Royce's mom without even needing him to point her out. She was definitely where he got his looks from, because even in prison scrubs and no makeup, she was beautiful. Her platinum-blond hair was pulled back in a high ponytail, and her green eyes sparkled when she saw her son.

"Royce, sweetheart," she said as we sat down on the other side of the glass. "It's good to see you. And you must be Ashley?"

"Hey, Mom," he replied with genuine warmth. "Um, yeah, way to be a creep before you're introduced, but yes, this is Ashley."

Startled, I glanced at Royce with confusion. "You told your mom about me?" He'd mentioned on the drive up that he spoke to his mom every week by phone and visited once a month, but I hadn't expected that I'd been a topic of conversation along the way.

His mom laughed, but it was a kind laugh. "Oh, honey, you're all he talks about these days. It's so nice to finally meet you, though. I'm Kathryn, but you can call me Katie." She gave me a wink, and I struggled to see how this woman was in jail for life after being found guilty of murdering six people. She seemed so…normal.

Then again, Ted Bundy hadn't seemed like a serial killer either, right?

Royce had turned a peculiar shade of pink and gave a weak laugh as he rubbed the back of his neck. "Mom, don't be a shit stirrer. I tell you about all of my friends."

Katie nodded slowly, eyes wide. "Right, yes, of course. All your friends." Then she gave him an exaggerated wink, and Royce made a strangled sort of noise in his throat. "I can imagine my son has given you next to no information about me, Ashley, so you're most welcome to ask questions if you'd like. I'm excited to get to know you as well!"

Meanwhile, Royce looked like he wanted the floor to swallow him whole, so I grabbed his hand in mine out of view and squeezed his fingers. "Um, yeah, he really hasn't said much," I admitted, "but I don't want to waste your visit time. I know you only see each other once a month."

Katie shrugged, and Royce shifted his hand in mine to lace our fingers together. I could tell that this wasn't easy for him, despite how chill he seemed with her.

"Yes, that's true. But it's also nice to meet someone new. We don't get a lot of that in here. Royce mentioned you're focusing on social studies at Nevaeh? How are you liking that?" She seemed genuinely interested, and I found myself nervously talking about my degree and the classes I was enjoying the most and the least.

Katie smiled when I mentioned my political history professor, Dr. Harris. "Oh, you're kidding me. He's still teaching? Does he still spit on the front row during lectures?" She shuddered, and I gaped in surprise.

"You went to Nevaeh too? I didn't know...and yes, oh my god, the spitting is insane! Front row basically needs raincoats."

She snickered with amusement. "Yes, I was a student there..." She shot a pointed look at Royce, who responded with a one-shoulder shrug of apology. "If I didn't already know the lengths Michael went to trying to pretend I never existed, I might be offended, Royce."

He sighed, his fingers tightening on mine for a moment. "Sorry, Mom. Old habits die hard." Then to me, he quickly explained, "My father doesn't tolerate any mention of my mom. If not for my Uncle Henry—Mom's brother—I'd never have been able to know her at all."

Stunned, I tried to pull my thoughts together. For one thing, Royce's dad sounded like an absolute piece of shit who had probably been beating him as a kid. But at the same time, I had a hard time matching that concept up with Katie.

"Did you meet Michael at Nevaeh, Katie?" I asked cautiously, not wanting to pick open old wounds.

She pursed her lips, all traces of warmth washing out of her eyes. "Yes. We were in a club...of sorts. I was a freshman, on scholarship. He was one of the inner-circle postgrad students."

"Oh, you were in the Devil's Backbone?" I asked, not second-guessing my question until both Katie and Royce flinched. Then she turned a furious glare on her son, who seemed to slink down in his seat a little bit.

Somehow, I suspected I shouldn't have said that.

"Royce..." she sighed. "You promised me."

"I'm sorry," he mumbled. "You know how they are...and with all of us as legacy children, it was—"

She waved a hand, cutting his excuses off. "I'm well aware. I just hoped… It doesn't matter. Yes, Ashley, we were in the society together, and before you think it was some tragic love story, it wasn't. We flirted a bit, but Mike flirted with a lot of girls. My darling boy here was just the by-product of way too much vodka at one of those ridiculous duck events." She offered a smile his way to soften that little blow.

I frowned, trying to piece it all together. "So…it was a one-night stand? And then…?"

"And then a week later I was being arrested for the murder of six society initiates," she said in a cool, matter-of-fact voice. "People I was friends with, people I had no prior disagreements with, and people I would never have thought about hurting in my wildest dreams. And yet, when I was put on trial the prosecution somehow had video surveillance footage that showed me butchering them all with an ax while they slept."

My jaw dropped. "Holy *shit*." It was the best I had.

Katie gave a sad smile. "Yeah. Pretty much. There was no arguing with that kind of evidence, and everyone just figured I'd blocked it out in my mind because of how violent it was. Or that I'd had a temporary mental breakdown or something. Either way, here I am. But for what it's worth…I know I never would have done such a horrible thing. Not of my own free will."

That. That right there sent a chill down my spine. I glanced at Royce and he was already looking back at me with the same recognition in his eyes. I swallowed hard, my heart racing in my chest… Had Katie been one of the first hypnosis victims twenty-four years ago?

How old was Dr. Fox, though? Katie was only in her early forties by my math, and Dr. Fox had seemed like he was into his sixties. Maybe he was a teacher back then too?

"You didn't have any professors called Dr. Fox, did you?" I asked with dread.

She frowned, thinking. "Not that I remember? It was a long time ago, though. Why?"

Royce squeezed my hand, and I shook my head. "No reason. Sorry. So, Royce was born in prison? That definitely explains his blatant disregard for rules." I said it with a teasing smile, a lame attempt at lightening the mood, but she went along with it and shifted our conversation to how she managed to forge some semblance of a relationship with her only child while serving a life sentence.

It was full-on. When our time was up and we left, my heart weighed a thousand pounds for the childhood Royce had endured. It once again validated why he was so close with the other boys and why Max seemed to play the guardian role in all of their lives—someone had to.

"Thank you for coming with me," Royce said quietly as we made our way back out of the prison still hand in hand.

I leaned into him, releasing his fingers so I could loop my arm around his waist. "Anytime, friend."

He inhaled sharply, then let it out with a heavyhearted sigh as he murmured "friend" under his breath with an almost heartbreaking edge of disappointment.

Chapter Twenty-Eight

January 21

Carter seems to enjoy pissing Ashes off. We all warned him that it needed to be her choice to move into our apartment, but he just went ahead and bulldozed over her anyway. Not to say I disagree with the outcome, I just think he was a moron for his approach.

Fuck it, not my problem. I'm more than happy to reap the benefits while he's in the doghouse.

H. Briggs

Heath had been waiting in my car the whole time we were visiting Royce's mom and had brought his laptop and textbook along to work on his assignments. I had—reluctantly—given him my keys if he'd wanted to go to a diner or something, but he'd opted to stay put.

"I'm starving now though," he admitted when I commented on that fact.

"Same," Royce agreed, grinning as my Firebird roared to life. "Let's grab lunch before we head back."

I checked the time on my phone and quirked a brow. "Lunch at four in the afternoon? I mean, sure. Why not? Do you know anywhere nearby?"

It was a silly question, given that Royce had been visiting his mom in this town every month for basically his whole life. He took us to what he described as his favorite eatery, where the gray-haired waitress recognized him with a warm greeting and escorted us to a booth in the back.

She offered us menus, but Royce declined, announcing we'd all have his usual. Whatever that was.

"If she comes back with something weird, I'm not eating it just to be polite," Heath stated, draping his arm along the seat back behind me.

Royce gave an exaggerated gasp. "You mean you don't like puffer fish sashimi smothered in bat excrement? Since when did you have the palate of a six-year-old, Briggs? Live a little."

I grinned, because clearly he was teasing. He *was* teasing...right?

"So how was Katie this month?" Heath asked, changing subject. "She ask about me?"

I whacked him with the back of my hand. "You did not just imply what I think you implied, Heathcliff Briggs."

He chuckled. "Just joking, obviously. But I bet she loved meeting you, Ashes. Did she think you guys are dating?"

"Yes," I confirmed, rolling my eyes with a smile. "And Royce trying to insist we're friends only seemed to make it worse."

Royce's jaw tightened and he shrugged. "Doesn't really matter what my mom thinks we are. What did you think about her story?"

The humor faded away as I drew a deep breath. "I can see why you brought me to meet her, for sure. I wonder if there's some way to prove whether she was under hypnosis or something?"

Royce shook his head. "There's not. I've spent years with my uncle, trying to find all the evidence surrounding her arrest and the murders…there's nothing useful. It's just her word against a mountain of proof and our new gut feeling that hypnosis could be involved. Which, again, how do you prove it?"

"We can't exactly just ask Dr. Fox now, can we?" I agreed with a groan.

Heath winced. "Sorry, that's my bad."

Royce's lips tilted with a lopsided smile. "Bro…*my bad?*" He snickered, shaking his head at—I had to assume—Heath calling violent murder *my bad.*

A food runner appeared then, delivering three huge burgers with mountains of fries and three enormous Cokes.

"Mmm, real Coke shits all over Pepsi," Royce hummed after taking a sip.

"They're the same thing," Heath replied, picking up his burger in both hands and licking his lips. "Now this is the sort of puffer fish sashimi I can get on board with."

Royce picked up a fry and threw it at Heath. "They are not the same thing, you heathen. Squirrel, please tell me you're on my side with this?"

I nodded enthusiastically. "One hundred percent. In fact, I just became twenty percent less attracted to Heath for not immediately knowing they taste different."

Heath just laughed, licking grease off his thumb. "Liar, you love me."

And then I choked. Fucking infuriating men needed to stop saying things that panicked me while I was eating or drinking. Thankfully, it was just a droplet of Coke that I'd inhaled, which probably wouldn't kill me…but my face burned all the same. Didn't help that both Heath and Royce were looking at me like I couldn't be trusted to eat solid foods without adult supervision.

The thing was, though, I still didn't feel totally comfortable or secure in this relationship with Heath or Carter. Not secure enough to go tossing my heart out for everyone to see and stomp on, that was for sure. Regardless of how true Heath's statement might have been.

Royce seemed to take pity on me, asking Heath instead about his classes, and the two of them carried the conversation while I quietly enjoyed my burger. It was a great burger, so Royce had good taste. Once we were finished, Royce paid the bill and must have tipped heavily because the waitress shook her head in disbelief, then hugged him. He patted her back and murmured something about seeing her again next month as we left the diner.

"Want me to drive?" I offered, despite the fact it was my car. Royce just scoffed and slid into the driver's seat like it was his second home, leaving me to roll my eyes in amusement. "I guess not. I'll sit in the back, then."

Before Heath could insist he was fine back there—he absolutely was not with legs that long—I clambered in and got comfy.

"I suppose you do fit a little easier," Heath admitted, pushing the passenger seat back into position and sliding in. "I forget how little you are sometimes."

"He means because you've got big-dog energy," Royce informed me with a smirk in the rearview mirror. "You act like you're six foot sometimes. Not a little yappy dog, like Jade."

I scowled, not so sure if that was a compliment or an insult. Heath saved me the need to respond by turning on my stereo and spending the next half hour arguing with Royce over what radio station they should listen to.

At some point, I curled up in a ball and went to sleep. Long drives always made me so tired.

"Watch out!" Heath's startled shout jerked me out of deep sleep a split second before the car swerved sharply, then crashed to a stop like we'd just hit something. Hard.

"Fuck!" Royce exclaimed. "He came out of nowhere! Shit, Squirrel, you okay?" His seat belt unclicked, and he all but climbed between the seats to check on me, and I groaned as I

208

rubbed my head. I'd smacked it somewhere in that abrupt stop, and it throbbed.

Royce swatted my hand away and grabbed my head between his hands to check if I was bleeding, but I was pretty sure it was a minor bump at worst.

"What happened?" I asked, batting his fussing hands away. It was dark outside, but given the time of year and how late we'd left the diner, that wasn't surprising. "Where are we?"

"Deer," Heath replied, sounding a little pained. "We hit a deer. Or he hit us. Jumped out of the bushes with exactly zero warning."

I gasped, shoving Royce out of the way and gaping at the dense spiderweb of cracks that my windshield had become. Horrified, I heard a little whimper escape me. "My car…"

Royce winced. "I'm so sorry, Squirrel." He popped open his door and climbed out, then leaned in to lever the seat forward to let me out to survey the damage. When I saw the full extent, I nearly fainted. My shattered windshield was far from the worst of it, and I wanted to vomit when I saw how twisted and caved in the front end of my beautiful car was.

"I'll get it repaired." Royce tried to placate me as I circled the car, wringing my hands with anxiety. "I know a guy that will do an awesome job getting this back to how it was. You won't even know anything happened when he's done."

He was attempting to be reassuring, and I appreciated it. But even my inexpert eyes could see this might be a total write-off. Fucking hell, Dad was going to be so disappointed. Tears pricked at my eyes, and I swallowed hard to hold them back. It was an accident. Obviously it was an accident. But…my car!

"We had to get off the freeway about a half hour ago because of a truck roll-over," Heath said, rubbing his chest with obvious discomfort. "So we're firmly in the middle of butt-fuck-nowhere right now."

"With no cell reception," Royce groaned, checking his phone. "Fucking hell. Squirrel, I am so sorry."

I shook my head, fighting the urge to cry. "It was an accident," I croaked. "And you handled it better than I probably would have. We're all alive, right? Though…Heath, are you okay?"

"Yeah," he wheezed. "I'm good. Seat belt probably left a mark, that's all. We just passed a town not long back. We could start heading in that direction?"

They both looked at me for confirmation, but I just shrugged. "Fuck if I know. Yeah, that sounds like our best option if there's no reception out here. And"—I glanced around in dismay, thankful that the huge moon provided some light—"it doesn't look like the busiest road, so we could be here for hours if we wait for another car."

Royce leaned back into the car and fetched my handbag, which he passed to me, then grabbed Heath's laptop bag and looped it over his own shoulder before locking the doors. A little pointless, considering the car couldn't be driven anywhere, let alone stolen, but still it made me feel a little better to have the keys in my bag once more.

"Come on, then, let's get walking. How far back do you think that town was, Heath?" Royce turned the flashlight on his phone as he led the way back down the road in the direction we'd just come. "It wasn't crazy far, was it?"

"Nah, only about five or ten minutes maybe?" Heath grimaced as he rubbed his chest, then took my purse out of my hand and looped it over his arm. It was cute but so unnecessary.

"It's not heavy," I laughed, holding out my hand to take it back.

Heath shook his head stubbornly. "What kind of asshole do you take me for? Even a five-minute drive could take us over an hour to walk. Hopefully we can get cell reception before we go the whole way, though."

As if the universe was laughing at us, the walk took the better part of two hours, and we still had zero bars when we arrived on the outskirts of the little town. It was weird, and I'd spent far too much of those last two hours detailing all the different ways we could be picked up by a serial killer and brutally murdered.

"You're a bit sick, you know that?" Royce asked as we approached the run-down motel with a flashing neon Vacancy sign. "Don't get me wrong. It's hot. But also now I see why you were so clear-headed last week with the, um, situation."

With covering up the murder Heath had accidentally committed, he meant. It was a valid point.

"I'm just saying, this feels like one of those scenes out of a Hitchcock movie. If the shower curtain is one of those plastic things, I'm not going in there alone. Just so we're clear." Then I frowned and swiveled my head to stare at him. "Did you just call me hot, Roycey?"

He held my gaze unflinchingly. "Yeah. What of it?"

"I'm always happy to share the shower with you, Ashes," Heath offered with a grin. "Even if it is Carter's thing. I'll put on a fake British accent and everything."

Why the fuck that got me all tingly inside, I couldn't say. Maybe it was exhaustion. I just laughed and gestured for them to enter the little reception office ahead of me—just in case there was a chainsaw murderer hiding behind the counter.

As it was, there was no one behind the counter at all, but the bell chime of us entering brought a plump woman out of the back room within a minute.

"Good evening." She greeted us with a tired smile. "Looking for a room?"

"Yes, please," Heath responded politely. "Two if possible?"

She shook her head with a grimace. "Sorry, not tonight. That crash on the freeway has everyone diverting through our town, and we're almost at full capacity already. I can offer you one room or point you in the direction of Motel Seventy-Seven, about an hour's drive south of here."

"One room is fine," I said quickly. "We actually hit a deer on the road south of here, but there seems to be no reception to call a tow?" I checked my phone again, in case something had changed, but nope.

211

The woman nodded. "Yes, that'd be because of the crash. The truck literally collided with our cell reception tower and took the whole damn thing down. Landlines still work, though, if you need to make any calls. As for a tow truck, my cousin Larry can sort you out in the morning."

"That would be amazing, thank you," I replied, mustering up my best smile.

Heath sorted out paying for our room—thank fuck he had cash, since the internet was also down—and the woman handed us over the key. It was hanging on a big, plastic heart key ring, and she winced as she passed it across. "It's our honeymoon suite, but I only charged you the standard room rate since there's just one bed. It's big, though, and there's a sofa."

Honeymoon suite? Who the heck was honeymooning at the Lucky Star Motel in the middle of nowhere? "I'm sure it will be fine," I murmured.

She nodded thoughtfully. "Well, the minibar is fully stocked, but if you want food, I'd suggest checking out the Drunken Cactus down the road a little ways. Their kitchen is only open until ten, though."

We thanked her, then went in search of our honeymoon suite. It wasn't hard to locate, and once Heath unlocked the door with the key on the big heart, I had to do a double take in case my eyes were messing with me.

"Oh, wow," I chuckled, stepping inside and gaping at the enormous heart-shaped bed. "I mean...she wasn't lying about it being big enough, but how on earth would they get sheets to fit that?"

Royce waggled his eyebrows as he crossed over to the head of the bed, where there seemed to be a coin slot. "If this thing vibrates, we've probably all died in that car crash and stepped into such a wacky afterlife. Heath, bro, got any quarters?"

Heath sighed but stuffed his hand into his pocket to pull out a handful of change, which he handed over. Royce inserted four into the coin slot, then twisted the lever.

Nothing.

"Aw, man. Anticlimax from hell." He pouted and flopped down on the nonvibrating bed.

Heath laughed and poked around at drawers and cabinets until he found the minibar, then gave a little cheer. "She wasn't exaggerating about the minibar being stocked up, though! Shots, anyone?"

He held up a handful of tiny bottles and the grin on his face was way too infectious to say no to. And really, after nearly dying in a car crash, I think we deserved it.

I took one of the little bottles from him and cracked the lid, then waited for the boys to do the same before offering mine for a toast. "To the deer," I announced, clinking bottles with them both.

"To the deer," they responded, and we all drank in unison.

Chapter Twenty-Nine

EVERYTHING WAS QUIET THIS WEEK. ALMOST TOO QUIET? NO ONE
SLEEPWALKED, NO ONE TRIED TO KILL ASHLEY...AND TO MY RELIEF, NO
POLICE CAME KNOCKING ON OUR DOOR. I CASUALLY ASKED AROUND
CAMPUS ABOUT WHY DR. FOX MISSED HIS CLASSES BUT WAS TOLD HE'D
TAKEN EARLY RETIREMENT. WEIRD, NO QUESTION ABOUT IT. IT SEEMED
LIKE SOMEONE WAS COVERING UP HIS DEATH...BUT WHY? AND WHO? IF
ANYTHING, IT ONLY MADE ME MORE SURE WE WERE ALL STILL IN DANGER.
　　　THAT, MORE THAN ANYTHING ELSE, WAS WHY I SUPPORTED CARTER'S
IDEA TO MOVE LAYNE IN WITH US.
　　　FOR SAFETY.

　　　　　　　　　　　　　　　　　　　　　　　N. ESSEX, JANUARY 21

Several little bottles of tequila later, we realized the landline phone in
our room didn't work, so the boys did fifteen rounds of rock, paper, scis-
sors to decide who'd venture out to use the office phone to call Carter
and Nate. Heath lost, and I sweetly suggested he pick us up some food
while he was gone, so we didn't survive on baby liquor bottles alone.

Something about being in a motel room immediately made me need snacks. Even if I wasn't remotely hungry, I needed to have snacks just in case.

"How are we going to make this sleeping arrangement work out tonight?" Royce pondered, eyeing the heart-shaped monstrosity that I sat on the tip of. "I don't know how well a double pillow wall will hold up on that shape."

I giggled, already feeling the alcohol going to my head. "Can I tell you a secret?"

Royce's head whipped around from where he'd just started browsing the minibar again. "I love secrets. Tell me."

I pursed my lips, debating if this was going to totally fuck up our arrangement…and I really didn't want to fuck it up, but on the other hand, I no longer lived in the dorms and Royce no longer had any reason to sleep over with me, so really, it was a moot point… right?

"You can't tease me about it," I warned, already feeling my cheeks heating with preemptive embarrassment. "Promise?"

"I would never," he replied with a wide, toothy grin. Now I had his full attention, and panic started to set in. If I were sober, maybe I could rapidly change gear and make up a lie to tell instead, but nope, my brain wasn't braining that hard.

"Sometimes the pillow wall disappears in the night, and I wake up snuggling you like you're my favorite teddy bear," I blurted out, then clapped both hands over my mouth.

Royce's mouth widened in shock, and his eyes sparkled like he was desperately holding back his laughter for my sake. Fuck, he was kind. And sexy. Why was my best friend so damn sexy?

"Whaaaaaat?" he asked in a scandalized voice. "How often is sometimes, sneaky Squirrel?"

I winced, shifting my hands to cover my eyes and block out that intense green gaze that seemed to be stripping back my layers like I was an overripe onion. "Okay, all the time. Like every night. I usually wake up before you and put the pillows back in place so things don't get weird."

My eyes were still covered by my hands, but I sensed him shifting closer. "Why would it get weird?" He peeled my hands away from my face, and I scowled at his grin.

"Because we're friends, Royce, and you gave me so much grief when you caught me checking you out after the shower, so I thought—"

"Ah, see, I knew you were checking me out!" He sat back on his heels, smirking like a fat cat. "But what if I don't want to be friends anymore?"

Panic whipped through me, and I gave a startled noise of protest before my brain caught up and reminded me that statement could go two ways. "Wait. What?"

He shrugged, seeming a little nervous, which didn't add up. Royce didn't do nervous. "I don't like the friend zone, Squirrel. I kept thinking maybe if I flirted with you enough…but I'm starting to think I really need to take a hint and move on."

My mouth flapped open and shut a couple of times, and I blinked like a fucking owl. "Excuse me?"

He sighed heavily, then got to his feet. I watched, confused, as he grabbed the notepad and pen off the little writing desk and scribbled on it.

Then he returned to where I sat in a puzzled, frozen state and handed me the paper. "Here, I'll put it in writing so there's no miscommunication."

Squinting, I looked down at the note.

I LIKE YOU.
I THINK ABOUT YOU NAKED ALL THE TIME.
I WANNA BE MORE THAN FRIENDS.
I MIGHT ALREADY LOVE YOU.

My heart raced as I read it about a dozen times, then looked to Royce who was back on his knees again, waiting for my reaction.

"Are you fucking with me right now?" I asked, dumbstruck.

His brow dipped, and he shook his head. "No...but I'd quite like to fuck you right now if that was on offer. Just figured since you're being honest about the pillow wall, I'd get this off my chest as well."

He was being casual and lighthearted about it, but the intensity of his stare said otherwise. As did the bead of sweat on his temple. My breathing quickened as I thought through the implications of what he was saying.

"If this is just about sex—"

"It's not!" he quickly interjected. "I mean this in the nicest possible way, babe, but if I just wanted sex, then there are plenty of less complicated options on campus. You're...a whole hell of a lot more than just sex."

I wet my lips, my heart racing so hard, it physically hurt. "I mean, you're not wrong..." Considering I already had two boyfriends and now lived in their apartment. Oh, and we'd covered up a murder together. Things didn't get much more complicated than that.

"What if I told you I was the one destroying the pillow wall every night?" He dipped his head but glanced at me through his long lashes. "Because every time I did, you would snuggle into me almost immediately, and I liked to pretend for a couple of hours that you were mine."

What the fuck?

"You sneaky shit!" I exclaimed in a shocked whisper. "Were you awake every morning when I panic-pillowed?" His smirk said it all, and I clapped my hands over my flaming face all over again with a groan. "Oh my god, I hate you."

"Do you, though?" he asked with genuine curiosity. "If I kissed you...would you kiss me back? Or slap me for stepping out of the friend zone?"

My breath caught in my chest, and butterflies on crack erupted in my belly. Was this that afterlife shit Royce joked about? We'd actually died in the crash, and now this was all an alternate reality within which Royce was actually attracted to me? If so…I was okay with it. This was a happy place to be.

I removed my hands to stare at him in stunned disbelief. "I still don't know if you're messing with me," I admitted, "but why don't you try it and find out?"

His green eyes widened for a moment, like he was shocked to hear my answer. Maybe he'd fully convinced himself—much like I had—that our attraction was purely one-sided. But then he closed the gap between us, his long fingers sliding into the back of my hair as his forehead rested on mine…but he stopped short of kissing me.

"I'm scared," he confessed in a whisper, "that I won't be able to go back to being friends after I kiss you."

"Good," I replied, bringing my hands up to cup his face. "I don't wanna be your friend anymore, either." Then I closed the gap between us, our lips brushing in the softest caress imaginable.

Royce froze, and I almost second-guessed myself before remembering he'd started this. So rather than pull away in embarrassment, I leaned in to kiss him more purposefully and was rewarded by a small—but very manly—moan as he kissed me back.

His fingers flexed against the nape of my neck as his tongue coaxed my lips apart, and my whole damn body flushed with the heat of desire. I'd quietly fantasized about kissing Royce dozens of times, but the fiction paled in comparison to reality. He kissed like a fucking incubus, making my nipples instantly harden and my pussy clench with anticipation. It was almost shocking how thoroughly my body responded, but at the same time…I wasn't surprised.

Royce wasn't some hot-guy hookup. He wasn't a stranger. He was…Royce, and I was just as attracted to his personality as I was his body, which added so many extra layers to the sizzling chemistry between us.

"Holy shit," he gasped sometime later as he broke away for air, his fingers still firm against my skull like he was scared to let me go.

"Squirrel…Ashley…I really, really don't want to stop at just a kiss, but—"

"But fucking nothing," I growled, then bit his lower lip and reveled in his slightly helpless moan. "You kicked this door down, Royce. There's no putting it back on its hinges now."

His chuckle did unspeakable things to me, and I squirmed a little as he kissed my throat. "Did you just call me unhinged, Squirrel?"

"I guess I did," I laughed in response, leaning back and raising my arms as he stripped my sweater over my head. "Is this going to cause issues with Heath and Carter?" Because crap, as if I didn't have enough on my roster—but he did know them a lot better than I did.

Royce's smirk was pure mischief as he trailed his fingers down my bare rib cage and I arched into his touch. "I think it'll cause more issues with Nate, but that's an acceptable risk in my opinion."

I hadn't even thought about that, but it was a good point. I could imagine he'd be pretty annoyed that all three of his best friends were now fucking his barely tolerable stepsister. Oh well. Too bad, so sad.

"Nate's a big boy. He can get over it," I muttered, tugging on Royce's T-shirt. "Take this off." He did as I ordered, giving me a full view of all those smooth, tanned muscles, and I grinned with a shake of my head.

"What?" he asked, squinting suspiciously.

I chuckled, pulling him in to kiss again. "You were totally flexing the other day," I whispered between kisses, and his lips curved into a smile against mine.

"And you were checking me out again," he accused, "so we're both guilty."

He had me there. Rather than deny it, I just reached for the waistband of his jeans and pulled him onto the ridiculous heart-shaped bed with me. "You sure you wanna do this?" I asked in a breathy voice as I worked the tight button of his jeans open and dragged down the zipper. "We really can't go back to the friend zone once you've had your dick inside me."

Royce sucked in a sharp breath as I teased his hard length through his thin boxer briefs. "Squirrel, baby, I can safely say...I never want to be your friend again." Then his mouth was back on mine in a friendship-destroying kiss that sent my head spinning, and in a matter of seconds, all our remaining clothes disappeared.

"Holy fuck," I gasped as my hand wrapped around his impressive cock and encountered metal. "You pierced your dick? Of fucking course you did, Royce."

He chuckled, a deeply sexy sound as he rocked into my hand and tugged my earlobe with his teeth. "Sure did. You'll love it too."

The arrogance should have been a massive turnoff, but it really wasn't. Instead it just made my insides tighten up with anticipation and my fingers tighten to stroke him harder. It wasn't just one piercing, either, but I'd have to wait until later to get a better look. Right now I was too damn desperate to get him inside me.

"Show me," I urged, spreading my legs wider and guiding his tip right where I wanted it.

He pushed up on his elbows just enough to glance down, watching the moment of entry with a low groan as I gasped at the unfamiliar sensation of his piercings. He took it slow, pushing in at a controlled pace while my inner walls spasmed and rejoiced to welcome him inside, an orgasm already starting to swirl and build deep within my core.

"Oh my god," I whimpered when he finally thrust the last inch inside with a soft grunt, then claimed my mouth in another one of those all-consuming kisses that made me feel hot and tingly all over. Then...then...he started to move with those piercings all too noticeable, and I instantly came. Not a small orgasm, either—it was a screaming, panting, thrashing sort of climax.

Shocked and a little embarrassed, I moaned a little *what the fuck*, to which he just laughed and kissed me again.

"Told you," he murmured against my lips with a hint of a growl. "But you're mine now, and I'm only just getting started."

Holy possessive crap. This was a side of Royce I was unprepared for, and a panicked voice in my head started screaming that maybe… maybe…I already loved him too.

Chapter Thirty

Royce asked if we were all cool with him taking Spark to meet his mom. On the one hand, I think it's a great idea. Knowing what we know now, Katie's situation seems all the more suspicious. I think Ashley would love to meet her too. But selfishly, I don't want him stealing her for a whole day when I have a crapload of ass-kissing to do. She's big mad at me right now, but I know I can talk her down—the makeup sex will be so worth it.
   Maybe I can finally fuck that sweet ass of hers...

Jan. 21
C. Bassington

One thing I very quickly learned about Royce was that he had endurance and patience. He was more than happy—downright gleeful at some stages—to hold back his own release for the opportunity to see me fall to pieces over and over again until I genuinely suspected I wouldn't be able to walk ever again.

"Can I tell you a secret?" he murmured, kissing my hair as I gasped for air in the wake of another intense climax. We were both sweaty and tangled up in the heart-bed sheets, but his pierced cock was still rock-hard where it was buried deep in my pussy.

Unable to form words, I just jerked a nod in response.

"The soundproofing in our apartment kinda sucks," he informed me, lazily playing with one of my nipples as he spoke. We were in spoon position, with one of my legs hooked up over his hip. "And Carter's en suite shares a wall with my room. So sometimes, when you two are loud or I'm listening hard enough, I can hear everything you two are doing…or saying…"

My eyes snapped open, and I drew in a sharp breath.

Royce chuckled, a dark sound. "Oh yes, you know exactly what I'm talking about, don't you? Has he done it yet?" Then he groaned. "Fuck, the way your cunt just clenched around me is unbelievable."

I wet my lips, trying to find my voice as nervous anticipation filled me in dizzying waves. "Not yet," I replied in a husky voice.

"Good," he murmured, his fingers tweaking my nipple as he rocked his hips. "Can I?"

Holy shit. Royce really wanted to destroy me for anyone else, and I wasn't even the slightest bit mad about it. Not even fully thinking through the logistics, I nodded. "Yesss…"

His whole body seemed to tense and flex at that one word, then he abruptly withdrew and climbed off the bed.

Right as I was about to protest, he shot me a sharp look over one of his perfectly toned shoulders. "Get on your knees, Squirrel. Ass in the air for me."

Stunned and more than a little fuzzy-headed from all the orgasms, I rolled to my belly and did as I was told. My reward was a sharp gasp and moan from Royce as he returned with whatever he'd grabbed out of the minibar. Then a moment later, I understood.

"That's a really well-equipped minibar," I panted as he slicked lube down my crack and into my tight hole with two firm fingers. Royce wasn't here to play, and I was all for it.

He hummed a laugh. "It's the honeymoon suite, Squirrel. Would you expect anything less?" He dropped the little bottle of lube onto the sheets, then the crackle of a packet hinted that he was putting on a condom. Probably to protect his piercings, which was not a bad idea. Then he was gripping my hips and forcing that broad tip inside without any further preamble.

A strangled scream escaped my throat at the intense stretch—so much more than Carter's fingers—and Royce froze in place. "Don't stop!" I exclaimed, arching my back into a deeper bend.

He hesitated only a second before his fingers dug into my flesh harder, gripping my hip bones as he worked more length into my ass with panting gasps. "Tell me if it's too much," he ordered in a gruff voice, still a goddamn gentleman even with his dick in my asshole.

"More," I demanded instead. "Give me more."

I moaned as he did as I asked, even though it hurt. It was a hurt that I could quickly become addicted to because it was so very closely linked to pleasure, and I just knew I'd be coming harder than I'd ever thought possible before we were done.

"Oh my god, Squirrel," he gasped as he pushed deeper. "You feel fucking incredible. This ass was made to be fucked. You like the edge of pain, don't you?"

I didn't respond because I figured my moaning and panting sort of spoke for itself, but then he slammed in the rest of the way, and I screamed. He grabbed my hair in one hand, wrapping it around his fist and jerking my head back as my body bowed beneath him.

"I asked a question," he growled.

Fuuuuck. "Yessss," I hissed, my eyes nearly rolling back in my head. "I love it."

With the most impeccable timing, the motel room door opened right then, and Heath stomped through carrying a bag of takeout boxes and a scowl on his face. I gasped, panicked, but with Royce's dick buried between my cheeks and my hair in his fist…there wasn't much chance of hiding what was going on in his absence.

"Uh, give us a minute?" Royce suggested with an edge of humor.

"Look, I gave you as long as I possibly could," Heath snapped, depositing the food onto the table and tugging off his coat. "But it's freezing out there, okay? You wanna try standing outside in the freezing cold with the hardest dick known to man and see how long you last?"

Royce held his grip on my hair, keeping my head tilted back at an almost uncomfortable angle as he started to rock his thick, pierced cock in my ass. "Five more minutes," he grunted.

Heath tossed his coat onto the sofa, then turned to glare at the both of us with blazing eyes. "I gave you nearly two hours, dickhead. You want me to—" He broke off, his brows shooting up and his mouth rounding in an O. "Bro. Carter's gonna murder you."

Royce withdrew farther this time, then thrust back in hard enough to make me *oof*. Then an embarrassing little mew escaped me, and my face flamed.

"Tough shit," Royce murmured, his free hand stroking my rear end. "He had plenty of time."

Heath met my eyes with a considering look, and I licked my lips. Blame it on the position he'd caught us in, but at this stage, I figured there wasn't anything to be lost by shooting my shot. "Heathcliff… are you just going to watch? Or are you going to come over here and fuck my mouth?"

Royce barked a startled laugh, his hips pumping that thick cock in a series of shallow thrusts while he chuckled. "If you don't—"

"I'm not an idiot," Heath snapped back, already tossing his shirt aside and unbuckling his jeans. "You have no idea how hard it was not to stand outside jerking my cock like some kind of Peeping Tom, creepy fucker."

He didn't bother taking his jeans off, just tugged them down enough to free his huge cock and knelt on the heart bed close enough to reach my mouth. Slick precum already beaded on his broad tip, and I licked my lips eagerly as Royce tugged my hair harder. Heath fisted himself and tapped my lips with the salty tip. "Open wide, beautiful girl. This won't be gentle."

"Good, she likes it rough. Don't you, dirty girl?" Royce thrust hard, and I cried out just a split second before being muffled by Heath's cock stuffing into my mouth. I relaxed my jaw, taking him in and swallowing, eager to relax my throat around his girth, and he rewarded me with a gasping curse.

It was a lot. A lot. And Heath hadn't been lying when he said he wouldn't be gentle. I wasn't sucking his cock—he was fucking my throat. Equally as hard as Royce fucked my ass. All I could do was brace my hands on Heath's thighs and hold on for dear life between them as they pounded into me from both ends. Tears streamed from my eyes, and my muscles screamed with exertion from the position, but if anyone tried to stop, I probably would have lost my damn mind with frustration.

Then Royce released his grip on my hair and reached around to thrust his fingers into my pussy.

I shattered.

The noises that I made as I came, and came, and came would probably haunt me for the rest of my life, but I was no longer in control of my own body. Liquid gushed between Royce and me, and he grunted curses, body trembling as he finally allowed himself to finish.

Heath was just a split second later, shooting his hot load straight into the back of my throat as I desperately tried to swallow and not choke.

It was safe to say, I was a boneless fucking mess. The guys had to manhandle me under the sheets, and it felt like hours before my head stopped swirling and my breathing slowed to normal. All the while, the boys got cozy on either side of me and turned on the TV to some sports game while they ate the nachos Heath had picked up.

226

"So, um, Heath…" I said when I finally recovered enough to find my voice. "I take it you're not mad about this development?"

He looked down at me, licking queso from his fingers. "Not even a little bit. As funny as it was to see Royce stuck in the friend zone so long, I also know how he feels about you. There's something comforting to know you have other protectors…just in case."

I swallowed hard, heaviness settling over our warm, fuzzy scene. Just in case? He meant just in case something happened to him. Or any of them. He was saying he was glad I had backup boyfriends in the event one of them died.

Talk about a morbid dampener on the mood, but at the same time he was only speaking the truth. I blew out a breath and sat up from my snuggled position between them. "I think I might take a shower." Because I was sweaty and sticky and that was no way to sleep.

"Want company?" Royce offered with a suggestive brow waggle.

I smiled, shaking my head. "I'm pretty sure you already broke me, so no." Because also now I was thinking about everything that'd happened so far this year with the society and hypnosis… Was it all over now that Dr. Fox was dead?

Fuck, I hoped so. Now, more than ever, I hoped it was over. The thought of losing any of my guys made my chest ache painfully, and I found tears sliding down my face as I showered.

I couldn't afford to lose any of them. What the fuck did that say about me, that I couldn't just be satisfied with one? Maybe Nate was right. I was a hypocritical slut after all, because I would quite legitimately commit murder myself if anyone tried to get between us now.

Even Carter…although he'd better grovel hard before getting back into my panties.

Chapter Thirty-One

I slept like the dead, barely moving an inch after falling asleep between the guys as they watched the end of their sports game, until I woke up. As it was, I woke to Royce hastily lubing up my asshole before stuffing his rock-hard, pierced cock inside with one forceful thrust.

"Holy shit," I gasped, my eyes popping open with the sudden intrusion. His hand clapped over my mouth to muffle any more noise as he fucked me hard from his big-spoon position. The running shower clued me in to Heath's whereabouts, and I relaxed back into Royce's embrace…if it could be called that.

I was still so sleep fuzzy that I didn't even try to fight it when my orgasm stole through me, then Royce triggered an encore by finger-fucking my pussy at the same time as he came, grunting and gasping into my tangled hair.

Then, all of a sudden, with no warning at all, the bed started violently vibrating.

"What the fuck?" Royce exclaimed, but I was incapable of doing anything but lying there, laughing so hard tears rolled from my eyes while he frantically tried to find the off switch on the stupid thing. "I guess it does work after all," he commented with a bemused smile when the ancient thing stopped jiggling.

I yawned and chuckled as I snuggled back into the pillow, fully ready to go the fuck back to sleep.

A few minutes later, a knock sounded at the door, and I cracked my eyes open just long enough to see Heath, fresh from the shower and wrapped in a towel, go to answer it.

"…tow is heading out now to pick up your car," I vaguely heard the woman from the reception desk saying to him. "…keys… address of where to deliver it?"

"Yeah, one second. I'll ask my girlfriend," he replied, closing the door and turning to look at me. "Oh, hey, you're awake."

I rolled my eyes. "Like I had a choice." I elbowed Royce, who just laughed smugly. "Keys are in my bag there." I gestured to where my handbag sat beside the sofa. "Can they just tow it to your place? I'll need to transport it to my mechanic back in Panner Valley."

"What's the business? I'll make sure it's taken straight there." Heath fished out the keys, then grabbed his phone to google the exact address when I told him where I wanted it to go. He passed the info along to the motel manager, then turned back to us with a rueful shake of his head. "Reception is back, in case you were curious, but also, we need to get up. Nate will be here to pick us up shortly."

As much as I wanted to stay in bed all damn day, it was a Monday, so we all had lectures to attend. And I for one did not want Nate catching the three of us taking a trip to Paris. So I groaned and complained but also dragged my ass into the shower and denied Royce access while I freshened up.

We had just enough time to grab some bitter black coffee at the pancake shop across the road before Nate pulled up in his beast of a truck with Carter in tow.

They all did the manly bro-hug/handshake business, and I trailed along behind, sipping my disgusting coffee and trying not to gag with each swallow.

"...sure no one got hurt?" Nate was asking when I refocused my attention on the guys.

"Yeah, we were lucky Royce managed to swerve; otherwise, the fucking thing would have hit the side of the car right where Ashes was sleeping," Heath replied, shaking his head. "Though, I'll admit, when he swerved into the buck, I thought he was insane for a moment."

Carter scowled at me, his gaze scanning me from top to toe, then his eyes narrowing at Heath suspiciously.

"We're fine," I growled, officially grouchy from lack of sleep and the bitter coffee. "Can we just go please?" I tried to brush past them to get into the truck, but Nate caught my arm in his.

"You sit in the front. The three stooges can take the back."

Confusion made me blink, then I jerked a nod. "Okay, sure, whatever." I was too tired to argue, instead just circling around the front of the truck to get to the passenger door. Then I groaned a little as I hauled myself up on the running board to get inside and spent way too long trying to find a comfortable position to sit.

"Are you sure you're not hurt?" Nate asked, making me freeze. "You were walking a bit stiff and seem...uncomfortable right now."

"I'm fine," I snapped, forcing myself to sit back in my seat as normally as I possibly could while attempting to ignore my aching bits. Avoiding eye contact, I buckled my seat belt and folded my legs. Totally normal. Nothing to see here.

From the back seat, Carter groaned. "God damn it," he cursed, punching Heath in the shoulder. "We had an agreement."

"Ow, dickhead," Heath protested, punching him back. "Don't get mad at me!"

Carter gasped, and I glanced over my shoulder to see him staring at Royce in shock. "No! You?"

Royce just grinned like a fucking Cheshire cat, not even the slightest bit guilty. "Me, motherfucker. You snooze, you lose."

Christ. Was this how it was always going to be? Boys were stupid.

"What the hell is going on?" Nate asked in bewilderment as he started up the truck and headed out of the little town. "What are you all talking about?"

"Absolutely fucking nothing," I snapped before anyone could go explaining in great detail about how Carter had just put two and two together and not only realized Royce and I were fucking but also that Royce had fucked my ass so hard, I was walking funny. *Great. So great.*

Reaching out, I turned on Nate's sound system and cranked the volume up enough that no one could talk. Much better.

He only tolerated it for about twenty minutes, but that was long enough for the boys in the back seat to get the message that we would not be openly discussing our sex lives in front of Nate. Not today, when I was in this mood, anyway.

"So how bad was the damage to your car?" Nate asked after turning the music down a few notches. "Can it be fixed?"

I grimaced, thinking of the twisted metal of my front end. "I don't know. Maybe not. The cost to repair a vintage car like mine...not to mention sourcing the parts..." I sighed heavily, propping my elbow on the door. "If anyone can do it, it's my mechanic, Rex."

"It's your dad's car, isn't it? Is he going to be upset?" Nate—for once—wasn't being a jerk about it. He sounded genuinely concerned, which was confusing.

"Probably. He told me to sell it years ago, but I was too attached to the memories." Now it was probably only worth as much as the parts would sell for. Damn it.

"I'll fix it, Squirrel," Royce promised from the back seat. "And in the meantime you can drive my car."

I flashed him a grin over my shoulder. "As tempting as that sounds, I definitely can't afford to scratch your Chiron. It's fine. You guys seem to love playing chauffeur anyway, right?"

"Anytime, Spark," Carter replied, and I had to remind myself I was still mad at him. Sexy bastard.

I pursed my lips, remembering how I was technically homeless now and definitely couldn't squat in Nate's room forever. At the same time, I couldn't just bed-hop between the other guys each night like some kind of freeloading whore. Maybe one of the girls at work needed a roommate?

"Do you think we will make it back in time for my humanities class?" I asked, checking the time on Nate's dash. My class wasn't until ten, but I had no clue how far we were from Nevaeh, thanks to the detour last night.

"Maybe," Nate murmured thoughtfully. "Do you have work tonight as well?"

I nodded, a little thrown off that he remembered my schedule. Then I heaved a sigh at the idea of working a massage shift while walking like a cowgirl. *Damn it, Royce.*

Nate fiddled with the stereo while the guys chatted in the back seat about some society party coming up. Part of me wanted to listen, but at the same time, I was just tired. Nate finally decided on a playlist that was oddly relaxing piano music set to a rain background. At first I found it a strange choice, but then my eyelids started drooping, and I lost the energy to question anything.

I often found sleeping in cars horribly uncomfortable, my neck always ending up with a kink from my head flopping around, but I slept deeply on the drive back to Nevaeh. Dimly I registered that we'd arrived home, but before I could shake off the heavy blanket of sleep, someone lifted me out of my seat with strong arms.

"Shh, go back to sleep," Heath whispered, kissing my hair. I relaxed into his hold, despite the nagging feeling that I should be awake for...something? Couldn't be that important, surely. Sleep was a better idea.

I didn't remember getting into the apartment or being tucked into bed, but when I eventually woke up some time later, I was a hell of a lot less cranky. Which meant I'd probably slept for far too long during the day.

Blinking sleep from my eyes, I glanced around with confusion. Where the hell was I? This wasn't Nate's room, it was...I wanted to say it was Carter's, but that didn't seem right either. The sheets and bedding were unfamiliar, not his usual dark-gray-and-crimson vibes. Instead they were a soft sage green and the quilt was subtly floral. Feminine.

"What the shit?" I muttered, sitting up to glance around the room with more focus. The furniture was still Carter's, but all of his personal belongings had been removed. Instead of the signed sports memorabilia on the dresser, there was now a makeup mirror and vase of flowers.

Sliding out of the huge bed, I padded over and pulled open the top drawer. Gone were Carter's socks and underwear, and instead it was full of my own panties. Shocked, I looked through the rest of the drawers, then crossed to the closet to find it also stocked with all my things and none of his.

Had Carter moved me into his room? Sure seemed that way. But where were all of his things? Another glance around had me spot a folded note on the bedside table, and I sat on the edge of the bed to read it.

Spark, you needed the rest, so Royce is getting notes from your class for you. I'm sorry for being a pushy fuck, but I hope you like your new room. Text us if you need anything.

—Eternally yours, C.B.

I groaned, knowing full well I couldn't stay mad at him for long. It was a very sweet gesture to give me his room, but it couldn't be a permanent solution. Maybe Carly would want to get an apartment with me? I should ask her.

Yet when I reached for my phone to text her, I hesitated. Nate's words echoed through my head, suggesting that maybe deep down I liked being pushed into this arrangement. That I really wasn't as mad as I pretended to be, because I enjoyed living with the guys.

"Fuck," I whispered aloud. Because I hated that Nate was right. I was happy with them...all of them. For better or worse, but hopefully now it would just be better. Dr. Fox was gone, and the hypnosis was over.

Right? I just couldn't shake the feeling that I still needed to watch my back, though. That maybe it wasn't so simple. Maybe we weren't ready to live our happily ever after just yet...

Chapter Thirty-Two

February 15

As badly as Carter handled the situation with Ashes moving in, I'm glad he did it. I love having her here. I love smelling her shampoo wafting out of her bathroom in the morning; I love hearing her happy hum while making coffee; I love being able to bend her over the arm of the sofa when we're the only ones home. Between the four of us, we have all shot down her every attempt to find other living arrangements, and it seems like she's stopped trying. We've got a good thing going on...even if not everyone wants to admit it just yet.

H. Briggs

Valentine's Day was stupid. Actually ridiculous. Carter, Royce, and Heath had filled the entire apartment with so many red roses, I worried whether they'd left any for the rest of the town to buy. Nate had been conspicuously absent—giving us privacy—but it'd cast an odd mood over the evening.

Carly had been sulking about me moving out of the dorms, so we were having breakfast together at the apartment before I needed to head to work. I'd picked up extra shifts to make up for taking the weekend off, since we had a society thing coming up.

"Your mom is calling," she informed me while I attempted to flip pancakes. I was useless at cooking pancakes but wanted to try nonetheless.

I glanced over at where she was holding my phone out and wrinkled my nose. "Let it go to voicemail," I said with a grimace. "I have a feeling she found out about my car somehow. It'll be a lecture about how I should have sold it years ago."

"You sure?" Carly asked with a frown. "Looks like she's tried to call a few times. It could be something important."

I shook my head. "Honestly, I'm sad enough about the Firebird without her piling the guilt on top right now. I'll call her back another day."

Carly shrugged and declined the call. A few minutes later, though, Nate appeared from down the hall with his phone to his ear and a frustrated scowl on his handsome face.

"Yeah, just a minute. I'll put her on," he said, then held out the phone to me. "Carina wants to talk to you."

My jaw nearly hit the floor, and I shook my head. "What? No. Nate, what the shit?" My protests came in strangled whispers so Mom wouldn't hear. "How does she know I'm here?"

He shrugged, sweeping a hand through his hair. "Fuck if I know. Morning, Carly."

Carly gave him a small nod in response. They'd both been trying hard to get rid of the awkwardness, which was nice. I hated feeling like my friend might be uncomfortable visiting due to their history.

"Nate," I hissed, gesturing to the phone in his hand. "Tell her I'm not here. Because why would I be here?" Because in addition to not telling my mom that my car had been totaled—Rex had declared it totaled a week ago, much to my agony—I also hadn't told her that I'd moved out of the dorms. Call me crazy, but I doubted she'd like to hear that I was not only living with my boyfriend, but I was also living with my other two boyfriends...oh and my stepbrother. Couldn't forget that complication.

He just rolled his eyes and brought the phone back to his ear. "Carina? Yeah, uh, she's not here. Sorry, I thought she was visiting Heath, but I guess not." He paused, listening, then blanched and met my eyes with a guilty expression. "Ah. I see. Yes, let me just... I'll put Ashley on, shall I?"

I gaped at him in outrage as he physically grabbed my hand and placed his phone into it, wrapping my fingers around the device with an apologetic grimace.

"Sorry," he whispered. "I can't deal with her gentle parenting voice. It creeps me the fuck out."

Rolling my eyes, I extended my middle finger to Nate, then brought the phone to my ear with a sigh. "Hi, Mom. Sorry I missed your call. I was just—"

"Oh save it, Ashley," Mom replied with a growl of frustration. "You were dodging my calls and we both know it. I can't believe I had to call Nathaniel to get ahold of you."

I rubbed at the middle of my brow while Nate nudged me aside to rescue my burning pancake. "Yeah, sorry. I was just visiting Heath."

She gave an irritated sound. "Uh-huh, sure. Is there something you've forgotten to tell me? Something important that I should know?"

I cleared my throat and looked to the ceiling for some sort of divine courage. "About the car?"

A short pause. "Car? What about the car?"

"Oh." I blinked rapidly, changing gears. "Nothing. Wait, what is this about? You sound pissed off at me, and if it's not about the car then—"

"What happened to your car, Ashley?" she demanded, and I mentally cursed my own big mouth for not letting her lead the conversation.

"Um, I hit a deer a couple of weeks ago. It's not a big deal. I just thought that's what you were calling about. But it's not, so... what's up?"

"You—" She sounded horrified, then huffed a sharp sigh. "I was calling to ask why the hell Max's boss just congratulated him on his son's engagement?"

My blood ran cold, and I locked eyes with Nate at the stove. *What the fuck?* I mouthed the words at him and he gave a helpless shrug.

"Oh, really?" I hedged, scrambling for a casual brush-off. "That's weird. He never mentioned anything. Maybe someone misunderstood something?"

Mom gave an angry grunt. "I'm sending a picture to Nate's phone. I'd like you to tell me why his lovely fiancée looks so very familiar, Ashley, and I swear to coffee, if you lie to me, you will regret it."

The phone vibrated in my hand, and I reluctantly looked at the screen. Sure enough, someone had snapped a photo of Nate and me at the society party. It'd been taken right at the moment where I'd pressed my thumb into his black eye, but it looked awfully like an intimate caress to anyone who didn't know. Nate's hand was on the small of my back as he looked down at me, while my head was tipped back and my hand on his face... Yeah, okay, it didn't look great.

I flashed the phone screen to Nate with a frantic gesture, and he just winced.

Real fucking helpful.

"Mom, it's not what it looks like," I hurried to say when I brought the phone back to my ear. "Nate's mom was—"

"Jocelyn was there? I knew that looked like the back of her head. That..." Mom blew out a long sigh. "That explains a lot. Okay, tell me the truth, Ash."

I rolled my eyes, sending Nate another middle finger before explaining exactly what had actually happened, from Jocelyn pushing Nate to get back with Paige to his white lie about us dating, then how Jocelyn deliberately snowballed the whole thing out of control.

When I was done, Mom was silent for a moment. Then she gave a little laugh. "Bloody hell, yeah, that sounds like her. Okay, so to be clear…you and Nathaniel are not engaged, nor are you romantically involved at all? Because, honey, Max and I would have some things to say about that."

"No!" I exclaimed. "Definitely not. Nate and I are…not like that. At all. Not even the littlest bit romantically involved, I swear." Nate's brow dipped as he watched me, probably trying to work out what Mom was saying on the other end. If I were nice, I'd have put the call on speaker.

Mom's sigh was pure relief. "Okay, good. So the rumor I heard about you living together was also just a rumor, yes?"

Ah shit. "Ummmmm, well…" I rubbed my eyes and shook my head. This was a guilt trip I really didn't need, and I suspected she would launch into a whole safe sex talk about me dating three guys, and it was way too early for that shit. So I did the most mature, adult thing I could think of. I grabbed a packet of chips from the pantry and crinkled the bag right beside the phone. "…breaking up…bad reception…call back later…" Then I hung up.

She immediately tried to call back, but I just tossed the phone to Nate like it was a live snake. "Not it," I grumbled. "You started this mess. You need to clean it up."

He caught the phone, then handed me the stack of perfectly golden pancakes he'd somehow managed to salvage from my mess. "Let me know when you're ready. I'll drop you at work on my way to campus."

I murmured a thanks, then fetched syrups and whipped cream from the fridge before noticing the way Carly was staring. "What?"

Her brows shot up. "What do you mean *what*? What was all that?"

I split the stack between our plates and handed her some cutlery. "I already told you about that stupid engagement lie."

Her laugh was scandalized. "I'm not talking about that. I'm talking about that." She gestured to the pancakes and then the direction Nate had just disappeared. "You guys are...comfortable. I thought for sure things would be awkward as fuck seeing as he's the odd man out in your orgy palace but...the vibes were not awkward. At all."

I shrugged, not seeing the problem. "We're mature adults, Carls. We are capable of moving past our prior differences."

She snort-laughed, digging into her food. "Still not what I meant but sure, okay. Anyway, speaking of your orgy palace...how's Roycey?" Her smile turned smug, and I rolled my eyes. Ever since telling her that Royce and I hooked up, she was insufferable.

Apparently she'd known he was into me for months and I missed all the hints. I thought she was full of shit, but she was not letting up on the smugness.

"Someone said my name?" the sexy devil himself asked, strolling out in just a pair of loose basketball shorts and looking like a whole fucking sex dream come to life. He jerked a nod of greeting to Carly, then swept me up in a hug that took my feet clean off the ground and made me squeal.

"Mmm, good morning, Squirrel," he growled, burying his face in the crook of my neck as he pinned me to the door of the fridge. "I missed you this morning. Why'd you need to creep out so early?"

An embarrassing little moan slipped out of me as he kissed my throat, and I smacked his shoulder. "Dammit, Royce, not in front of Carly."

"Don't stop on my account," she smirked, spearing another forkful of pancakes. "You two are fucking adorable together. Puts me in a good mood for the day."

"See, babe? Carls doesn't mind." Royce crushed his lips to mine in a breath-stealing kiss that nearly succeeded in making me forget we weren't alone.

240

Reluctantly, I peeled myself away and slid out of his grip. "Quit it," I scolded, my face burning with embarrassment. "Carly and I are having breakfast, and then I have work. What time do we need to leave tonight?"

"Oooh, for the DB weekend?" Carly asked. "Edmund and I are heading off around lunchtime after tutoring."

I nodded, my mood souring. When the guys had told me about it a couple of weeks ago, I'd been adamant that we shouldn't go. But they'd been very convincing that the danger was over. It'd been nearly a month since Dr. Fox's "disappearance," and nothing had come back on us. No police inquiries, no suspicious surveillance… nothing. By all appearances, we'd gotten away with murder.

More than that, Heath's nightmares had drastically improved, and no one had any suspicious hypnosis incidents that we could track. So for all intents and purposes, it did seem like life could return to normal, like maybe I could start to enjoy my time at Nevaeh and in the Devil's Backbone Society…

So for that reason, I'd agreed to attend the weekend event in Napa Valley.

"I think just whenever Squirrel finishes work," Royce answered, stealing a pancake off my plate. "Three-ish?"

I nodded. "Yep, should be. Are you picking me up?"

Royce pouted and shook his head. "Carter called dibs. Nate, Heath, and I are expected to be there to help set up some shit. Inner-circle business." He rolled his eyes dramatically, and Carly clapped her hands over her ears. "Calm down, Carls. I'm not sharing secrets. Anyway, can I drop you at work?"

He sidled up closer, the flirty smile on his face implying he wanted to do more than just drive me. Tempting. Very damn tempting. But I had a long shift on my feet and really didn't need to be walking around with cum-soaked panties.

"Nah, you're fine. Nate said he'd drop me off before class." I stole my plate back and nudged him away. "I'll see you tonight."

Royce gave an exaggerated sigh, then grabbed a handful of my hair to jerk my head back and kiss me thoroughly. "Fine," he growled between kisses. "I'll be counting the minutes."

He disappeared, adjusting his shorts as he went, and Carly gave me a pointed look.

"What?" I asked, scowling.

She shrugged. "Nothing." But her smile said it wasn't nothing at all. Probably reading way too much into me sticking with Nate's taxi services. She just loved seeing connections that didn't exist, I was sure of it.

Chapter Thirty-Three

AS MUCH AS I FEEL WEIRD SAYING THIS...THINGS MIGHT FINALLY BE GETTING
BACK TO NORMAL. ABSOLUTELY NOTHING WEIRD OR BAD HAS HAPPENED
IN ALMOST A MONTH. I'VE BEEN KEEPING A REALLY CLOSE EYE ON ALL
THE DBS AT NEVAEH, NOT JUST MY FRIENDS. NO ONE SEEMS TO HAVE ANY
UNEXPLAINED BEHAVIORS LIKE WHAT HAPPENED WITH DANIEL MAHONEY
CRASHING HIS CAR. ZARA IS MAKING A FULL RECOVERY BUT TAKING THE
SEMESTER OFF, UNDERSTANDABLY.
   WE HAVE A DB EVENT THIS WEEKEND, AND I'M ALMOST EXCITED FOR
IT. SO FAR, ALL ASHLEY HAS SEEN OF OUR EVENTS IS DRAMA AND MURDER,
BUT MAYBE THIS WEEKEND, SHE CAN SEE WHAT IT'S REALLY ABOUT. FUN,
FRIENDSHIP, AND EXTRAVAGANT GAMES WITHOUT ANYONE LOSING THEIR HEAD.

N. ESSEX, FEBRUARY 15

Carter picked me up at three o'clock on the dot, and for once all my
appointments had run on time so I was ready and waiting for him out
in the front of the building when he pulled up in that sexy bloodred
Koenigsegg Gemera.

"You ready for this weekend, Spark?" he asked after sweeping me off my feet and kissing me senseless beside his car. "It'll be competitive."

I grinned, slithering out of his arms. "You worried, Bass?"

He barked a laugh, opening my door for me to get in. "As if. I've already paid off the door staff to ensure we end up on the same team anyway, so your win is my win, babe."

I laughed at his blatant cheating while he circled around to climb in the driver's side. He revved the engine, and I squirmed in my seat. It was a solid three-hour drive to Napa Valley, and I'd been thinking way too hard about the logistics of our sleeping arrangements for the weekend. So far, our relationships had been largely one-on-one, with stolen moments in showers and sneaking between beds late at night. But in the interest of maintaining some kind of balance in our living situation, I was yet to go all in with the three of them at the same time.

It wasn't sustainable long-term, but we all knew that.

"So is this a duck thing?" I asked, trying to hide the fact that I was now thinking about how to get dicked down by all three of my boyfriends, without making Nate uncomfortable in his own home.

Carter shook his head. "No ducks this weekend. It's more similar to that event we did at Royce's place last semester."

I nodded my understanding. "Got it. Gambling with diamonds and playing croquet with priceless prehistoric artifacts."

He grinned. "Similar, yeah. There're society members from all over the state attending, just to keep the competition fierce."

"Do we think anyone will die this time?" I asked, unable to help myself. It was my biggest concern, though.

Carter shook his head with a sigh. "Fuck, I hope not. Anyway, how was work?"

"It was good," I replied with a smile. "Great tippers today. I'll be able to buy a replacement car in no time if that keeps up."

"You know Royce fully intends to buy you one," he told me

with a laugh. "He's just waiting for you to pick one that you like enough."

Yes, I was well aware. He'd made all kinds of insane suggestions too, all worth more than I could possibly earn in several back-to-back lifetimes. But for now I was kind of happy with our arrangement as it was, and they all insisted they didn't mind playing chauffeur.

Which reminded me… "How are things with your mom?"

Carter glanced at me quickly before returning his eyes to the road. "I'm…working on it. Actually I was going to make a suggestion that might sound a bit odd. You know this whole engagement bullshit that Jocelyn started about you and Nate?"

I stiffened, confused where he was going with this train of thought. "Yeah, what about it?"

"Nate mentioned that rumor had circled around to Max and Carina and you got an earful this morning about it." He shot me a grin, and I nodded. "Well…this fix I'm working on with my mother may need a little more time, and in the interim, it's actually buying us time that people think you and Nate are engaged. My mother also heard the rumor and thinks that you're no longer a threat."

I mulled that over for a moment. It was very convenient, that was for sure. No one knew what was going on behind the closed door of our apartment, so if Jocelyn's stupid game was helping me and Carter further our plans, then so be it.

"Okay, well, that's good. At some stage, we will have to have some kind of dramatic breakup, but I see no issues there. I'm sure Nate will do something I can deem worthy of breaking off our engagement for, and in the meantime, you and I are free to continue as we are?"

"Exactly," he confirmed. "If you're okay with that?"

I nibbled on my bottom lip, shooting him a curious glance. "Yeah…are you?"

He pursed his lips, hands tightening on the steering wheel. "You mean, am I okay sharing you with Royce as well as Heath? I'm…

not okay stepping aside and letting them have you. And I'm okay in theory…but in practice, it's taking me a minute to wrap my head around it."

That was fair. And they were all handling the sharing aspect with considerably more maturity than I might have anticipated. If all he needed was time to get used to the situation, then I was more than willing to accommodate. And in the meantime, we were finding plenty of time for just each other. Living together definitely helped.

"Would it be easier if I wrapped my mouth around it?" I quipped, turning his words dirty to lighten the mood.

He shot me a startled glance, then grinned. "You wouldn't. Not while we're driving."

My jaw dropped open in outrage. "I was joking, but now I resent the implication that I would chicken out simply because you're driving. You're a safe driver, Bass. I reckon you can handle it. Unless, of course, you can't?"

One brow quirked, then he released one hand from the steering wheel to unzip his jeans. "Try me." He shifted in his seat just enough to free his cock and fist it.

My eyes widened as he called my bluff. "Sir Carter, already hard? How long have you been hiding that?"

He barked a laugh, returning both hands to the steering wheel as he guided the car onto the freeway on-ramp. "Since the minute I kissed you. It took all my willpower not to try to fuck you on the hood of the car right there outside the club. I could have killed Heath for stealing you this morning."

I grinned, remembering how Heath had quite literally crept in and stolen me—giggling—out of Carter's bed barely fifteen minutes after I bed-hopped from Royce's room.

"It's a long drive," I replied, reaching over to wrap my fingers around his dick. "I can make it up to you."

He sucked a sharp breath, his hands tightening on the steering wheel. His sleeves were rolled up to the elbow, and that motion made the dark lines of scarring stand out on his forearms, making my stomach erupt in butterflies. *Spark.*

Shifting in my seat, I leaned over and wrapped my lips around his smooth head, making him breathe out a strangled curse. "I guess you weren't bluffing," he murmured with a small grunt as I sucked his tip.

"I was, actually," I informed him, then licked his length like a Popsicle, "but now I'm not." I closed my lips around him again and lowered my head to take him deeper into my throat.

A low moan rumbled out of him as I sucked, and one of his hands moved to the back of my head, fingers threading into my hair. "Holy shit, Spark," he gasped as I worked up and down his sizable shaft with my fist making up the difference. The ridges and veins of his cock stood out so hard against my tongue, it was almost like sucking Royce's pierced dick—something I was quickly becoming a big fan of doing.

For a few minutes, the car filled with Carter's soft grunts and moans as he tried to concentrate on driving while I sucked his dick like I wanted us to crash. Then he abruptly jerked the wheel and ground to a forceful stop in the emergency lane.

"What—" I asked, sitting up in confusion as he smacked his hazard lights on.

"Take your jeans off," he ordered, voice rough with need. "Now."

My brows shot up, and I cast a quick glance to the busy freeway flying past us before doing as I was told. Luckily the jeans I'd changed into were a loose boyfriend cut and came off with little effort at all, and Carter slid his seat back as far as it would go, then reclined.

"Get on," he demanded, fisting his slick cock. "If you want me to come, then I expect you to do it too."

Grinning, I climbed over into his lap, taking a minute to figure out where the fuck to put my knees and at the same time not smack my head. Supercars were not made for fucking in. Still, we made it work, and a split second later I was sinking down on Carter's thick cock with a long groan.

"Fuck, Spark," he gasped. "You're so wet already."

Incapable of words, I gripped his shoulders and kissed him hard as he started to move, fucking me from below while I just held on for dear life. There was nothing slow, romantic, or calm about it. We were hard, fast, and dirty as we chased our climax in broad daylight on the side of the freeway. Carter pushed my shirt up and nearly ripped my bra in his desperation to free my tits, then I came hard when he bit one of my nipples hard enough to leave teeth marks.

He came just a moment later, pumping hard up into me as he burst while whispering my name.

It was hot as hell, and I happily would have hung out for a second round, except for the flashing blue and red lights that pulled up behind us. Panic flooded through me and I scrambled off Carter so fast my ass honked the horn twice, then I somehow put my jeans on backward. Whatever, it'd do.

Carter was barely holding back his laughter as he fixed his pants and seat, then rolled down his window right as the police officer approached.

"We all okay here?" the officer drawled, already clearly understanding the situation from just a glance.

Fucking hell.

Carter flashed his million-dollar smile, hands back on the steering wheel like he hadn't just busted a nut inside me thirty seconds ago. "Yes, sir. My girl just dropped her phone between the seats, so we were safely retrieving it."

"All right, then, you drive safe. This is a lovely car." The officer patted Carter's roof, then sauntered back to his cruiser while I nearly died in my seat.

"He totally knew, didn't he?" I squeaked as we waited for the cop car to pull out first before Carter turned off his hazards and flicked on his blinker.

He shot me a sly smirk. "One hundred percent, yes."

248

Chapter Thirty-Four

We all know Spark is nervous about the society weekend event, and it's understandable. The last time we took her to a weekend event, someone ended up beheaded in her bed. This one will be different, though. We've been really hands-on with the planning this time, and Nate has gone above and beyond for security. Besides...Dr. Fox is dead.

To be extra safe, I've bribed the right people to ensure our "random" teams keep Spark with me, so I can keep a close eye on her the whole weekend. All day and night...for safety.

In the meantime, I'm anxiously waiting on news from Royce's uncle. All I need is enough hard evidence to play UNO Reverse Card on my mom, offer some mutually assured destruction, then Spark will be safe. We'll both be free.

That day can't come soon enough, but in the meantime Nate's fake-engagement fuckup is really working in our favor. Who'd have thought? Certainly not me. Here's hoping Ash is okay maintaining the lie a little longer...because Nate's already agreed.

Feb. 15
C. Bassington

The weekend event was being held at an exquisite private vineyard estate where everyone would be staying in house for the two nights and leaving Sunday. As we pulled up, my eyes bugged out at the sheer dollar value of the cars parked on the grass outside the main entrance.

"Obscene," I muttered as Carter parked his Gemera beside a Rolls-Royce La Rose Noire Droptail. "You know how much that car costs?"

Carter gave it a glance and shrugged. "Rolls are old-man cars. Not even a little bit sexy like this baby." He patted his custom-colored Koenigsegg affectionately, and I rolled my eyes.

"Okay, agreed. But still. That's a forty-million-dollar car—Fuck!! Watch out!" I nearly died when he opened his door too quickly and stopped way too damn close to the rose-pink Rolls-Royce. "Christ, Carter, you're going to give me a heart attack. Maybe you should park a little farther away."

"Chill, Spark. I'm not going to scratch it. Come on. Let's head in and get our team assignments before all the good ones are gone." He gestured for me to hop out while he grabbed our weekend bags from his trunk.

I slid out, thankful that I'd turned my jeans around the right way during our last fuck-stop on the way, and leaned into Carter when he draped his arm over my shoulders. "I thought you said teams are assigned at random on arrival?"

"Yep," he confirmed.

"Uh-huh…and didn't you also say that you've rigged it to place us on the same team because you're so completely obsessed with me that you can't bear to be apart for even a minute?" I grinned up at him as we walked across the gravel driveway.

He glanced down with a cocked brow. "Is that what I said?"

"It's what you meant," I replied with a laugh.

Carter leaned down and dropped a quick kiss on my mouth. "I'm sure I meant to say, I rigged us to be on the same team because I'm completely in love with you." He growled those words directly into my ear as we arrived at the front door, and my whole body shivered deliciously in a physical reaction to his confession.

He'd said it plenty of times over the last few weeks, but I had yet to say it back. I was still scared of having my heart broken, despite knowing full fucking well that saying it out loud would change nothing. I knew I was falling way too hard, and if things fell apart, I would be utterly crushed.

"Ashley Layne and Carter Bassington, Nevaeh University," he announced to the door-check staff.

One young man checked our names off a list while another offered a velvet bag for us to pull out the token that would assign our team for the weekend. Right before I could reach in, the other guy nudged him aside.

"I've got it, Chuck," he said, slipping a token directly into my hand rather than letting me take one from the bag. He then did the same to Carter, holding the velvet bag to disguise the motion, and I rolled my eyes.

"Thanks, Bass," Nate said, appearing beside us and clapping Carter on the shoulder as he took the token directly from his hand. "Nate Essex, Nevaeh," he announced, then continued on into the house without waiting to have his name checked off or anything.

"Hey, dickhead, that's my token!" Carter called after him.

Nate turned to shrug and grin. "Just take another, bro. They're random, right? What's the problem?"

Carter glowered, glancing around to take in the amount of attention Nate had just drawn, then sighed heavily. The attendant gave a helpless shrug and offered out the velvet pouch for Carter to draw an actually random token.

"Fuck's sake," Carter grumbled, checking his token as we moved inside toward Nate. "Swap back, asshole."

Nate inspected the token in his hand and smirked. "Nah, I like white gold. What did you get, Layne?"

I held mine up, showing a matching white-gold tile embedded into my token. "Snap."

"What a coincidence," Nate gasped dramatically, giving Carter a knowing look. "What are the odds, huh? Come on. Let's find Royce and Heath to see who else rigged their team color. Oops, I mean who else had a strange coincidence."

I glanced at Carter, but he just scowled and shook his head as we followed Nate through the expansive main foyer of the estate. Curious, I took his token from his clenched fist and peered at the very dark gold of his embedded metal.

"Does this make us enemies for the weekend?" I asked with a bemused grin, placing our tiles together side by side. "How many people are on each team again?"

He'd already explained it to me on the drive, but I'd been largely distracted, so the finer details were hazy. I did remember that there were eight teams, all with metallic color assignments, so there was no option for his classic red.

"Six per team," he muttered, looping his arm around my shoulders again with a sigh. "And yes, unfortunately, my lovely Spark, you're now my sworn enemy until the weekend is over."

The sexy wink he shot me sort of implied he was more than okay crossing enemy lines, though, and my stomach fluttered with excitement. I wasn't mad about this development, even if it did require Nate and I actually work together on the same side for once.

"We're staying in the pool house," Nate said over his shoulder, leading the way outside. Ahead the enormous pool glowed with underwater lights, and delicate fairy lights lit the trees all around. "Figured we could all benefit from a little more privacy this time around…"

As opposed to at the last event, where we'd all shared rooms and I'd found a guy beheaded and naked on the final day? Yeah. Privacy sounded good. I also suspected he meant there was a little more security too, because he needed to input an access code at the door of the pool house when we arrived, and I noted several security cameras facing the front entry.

"Finally!" Royce exclaimed when we stepped inside. "Heath was getting so stressed out, he was considering sending out search-and-rescue to look for your wreckage."

"Oh Heath was, was he?" Heath drawled. "Heath didn't tell you a dozen times that Carter had probably convinced Ash to christen his new car and to stop stressing out like a nervous Nellie?"

Royce just shrugged. "Doesn't sound familiar. Anyway, you're here! What teams did you draw?"

Crossing over to the expansive living room where the boys had set out snacks and drinks, I let Royce drag me into his lap to snuggle as I produced my token. "White gold. You?"

"Aw, man," he groaned. "I'm silver."

"Copper," Heath offered with a pout.

Carter dropped our bags, then joined us with a scowl set on his face. "Black gold," he grumbled. "Nate stole my white-gold token and made a whole scene so I couldn't get it back."

"Just keeping things fair, Bass," Nate replied with a satisfied smirk. "I'm shocked and impressed that you two didn't try cheating as well."

Royce and Heath exchanged a look that suggested they'd tried, and I chuckled. "Well, I'm sure the best team will win. And by best, obviously I mean white gold will win."

"Damn right," Nate said, agreeing and putting out his hand as he moved past me, and I reflexively slapped it for a high five. We were weirdly on the same page already. "We should head over to the ballroom and sort out team color wardrobes, though."

Carter had also mentioned that whatever color you were assigned on arrival, you had to wear exclusively that color for the entire weekend. But since no one knew their teams until they arrived, there would be dozens of boutiques and designers assembled in the ballroom to outfit each guest in their assigned metallic.

"I already handled Ashley's wardrobe," Carter admitted, pouring himself a glass of whiskey from the crystal decanter on the coffee table. "It should be in her room."

"Oh, did you?" Nate teased, flopping down onto the couch beside Heath. "But how did you know what color to get?"

Carter just extended his middle finger and glowered. "Suppose I better go sort myself out, now that nothing I brought will apply to my new team."

Nate looked positively gleeful. "Aw, come on, Bass. We're almost the same size. I can take it off your hands."

Another middle finger from Carter, and Heath whacked Nate's shoulder. "Bro, quit poking the bear. Come on, Bass, I need to hit the wardrobe room too."

Grumbling, they headed out once more, and I wriggled out of Royce's far-too-comfortable embrace. I wanted to see what kind of over-the-top designer attire Carter might have provided for the weekend. "Where is my room?" I asked, glancing around as I stood.

"I'll show you," Royce offered, also getting up and grabbing my bag from where Carter had left it. "I got here a few hours ago so already sorted my shit out."

"Dinner is in half an hour!" Nate called after us as Royce linked his fingers in mine and led me down a wide corridor away from the living space.

The bedroom he showed me to was at the end of the hall and had a huge floor-to-ceiling window overlooking the enormous swimming pool. The water steamed a little in the cool night air, illuminated by all the warm lighting and seeming almost supernatural.

"One hell of a pool house," I murmured thoughtfully as I took in the view. "Uh…no curtains?" Because if anyone did decide to swim— despite the cold—they'd be able to see right into my bedroom.

"One-way glass," Royce assured me. "And if you want to block the light, press this." He stabbed a button beside the enormous bed and the whole window turned black, totally eliminating any light from outside.

I marveled at the glass as he turned it back to transparent. "That's cool. Okay, let's see what Carter's chosen for my themed wardrobe."

"Or…" Royce purred, sitting on the edge of the bed and crooking a finger my way. "We could take advantage of our alone time before the guys get back."

I grinned, both tempted but also aching from my drive with Carter. "Didn't Nate just say dinner is in half an hour?"

Royce shrugged, catching my wrist as I drifted closer and tugging me onto the bed with him. "Half an hour is better than nothing." He rolled us, caging me in with his elbows on either side of my head and his body nestled between my thighs. "I missed you today, Squirrel."

I laughed softly. "You say that every time you haven't seen me in a few hours. It can't possibly be true every time."

His teasing expression sobered as he studied my gaze. "Can't it? You're my obsession, Ashley. Every minute you're not touching me, my heart aches. I love you so much, it literally hurts sometimes. Does that scare you?"

I wet my lips, swallowing hard. "Yes," I admitted honestly.

"Oh well," he responded with a touch of amusement. "Too bad, because that's just how it is for me…and deep down, I think you're only scared because it's the same for you."

He was right. But he spared me the need to reply by forcefully stealing the breath clean out of my lungs with hot, hungry kisses until Nate thumped on our door, letting us know that we needed to go to dinner.

Chapter Thirty-Five

0530: WOKE UP ALONE. I HATE THAT. SQUIRREL SHOULD BE HERE IN MY BED EVERY MORNING, NO MATTER WHAT. I WASN'T EVEN SURE WHO'D STOLEN HER OUT…BUT SOMETHING NEEDS TO CHANGE. SOON. THIS IS DRIVING ME INSANE…

0900: NATE'S ACTING WEIRD. WEIRDER THAN USUAL, ANYWAY. HEATH AGREES THAT SOMETHING ODD IS GOING ON WITH HIM, BUT WE'RE BOTH TOO NERVOUS TO VOICE OUR BIGGEST CONCERN OUT LOUD—THAT HE MIGHT BE GETTING INFLUENCED.

1200: ROAD-TRIPPING WITH HEATH SUCKS. HE'S NOWHERE NEAR AS PRETTY AS SQUIRREL, AND HE WON'T LET ME LISTEN TO COUNTRY MUSIC. HE'S ALL "CLASSIC ROCK" WHICH IS SO PREDICTABLE, CONSIDERING HIS FAMILY. THE ONLY BAND I'M VAGUELY OKAY LISTENING TO IS TORCHED.

1800: CARTER AND ASH SHOULD BE HERE BY NOW. SHE FINISHED AT THREE, AND IT'S A THREE-HOUR DRIVE. THEY SHOULD BE HERE. WHY AREN'T THEY HERE? DID SOMETHING HAPPEN? I NEED TO CHECK THE INCIDENT REPORTS FOR THE ROUTE THEY'D HAVE TAKEN FROM NEVAEH.

2100: WE JUST GOT BACK FROM DINNER, AND I PROMISED TO SLEEP IN MY OWN ROOM SINCE WE ARE NOW OFFICIALLY ON

DIFFERENT TEAMS...BUT WE ALL KNEW I WAS LYING. JUST GOTTA
SLIDE INTO SQUIRREL'S BED BEFORE HEATH AND CARTER BEAT ME
TO IT.

R. D'ARENBERG, FEBRUARY 15

Anticipating a fierce competition day, I opted to skip the after-dinner party and make it an early night. My forearms ached from my long massage shift, and my eyelids had been dropping even as I tried to eat my dinner. The boys had all straight-face promised to stay in their own bedrooms too.

Needless to say, I was not shocked to wake up in Royce's arms with my face buried in the crook of his neck sometime just after dawn. I'd forgotten to black out the giant window, but it was kind of nice to see the sun glowing on the horizon.

"What time is it?" I mumbled, knowing full well he'd already be awake. Since he'd confessed to destroying our pillow walls, I realized he woke up every morning at five thirty on the damn dot without an alarm. It was weird as hell.

"Early," he replied, stroking my hair. "Sleep a little more, Squirrel baby."

"Mmmkay," I agreed, relaxing against his chest and enjoying the way his fingers teased through the lengths of my hair and brushed my bare back. Despite the boys telling me they'd let me sleep alone, I'd gone to bed naked. It was just a hunch.

The soft click of the door opening woke me up again sometime later, but Royce didn't tense under me, so I could guess it was one of two people.

"Well, well, well," Heath murmured, "this is against the rules, I'm sure of it. Consorting with rival teams? What would the judging panel have to say?"

"They can shove their opinions up their asses," Royce whispered back, his chest vibrating with a laugh. "What are you doing creeping in here, Heathcliff? Last I checked, you're also not on Ashley's team this weekend."

Heath huffed a soft chuckle. "Came to see if you broke the rules, obviously. Those boxers aren't silver, by the way."

"Shut up," I grumbled, not opening my eyes. "Ashley's still sleeping."

Heath took that as an invitation to slide into bed on my other side, snaking his arms around my waist and pulling me into his embrace. "Are you sure? You look awake to me." His hands roamed over my body, then he sucked a breath. "Ah, loophole in the rules. Not wearing team colors at all."

Humming happily, I snuggled into his bare chest and relaxed back into sleep while the two of them spoke very softly about the game we were set to play today. I was sort of paying attention but mostly just letting the deep rumble of their familiar voices wash over me like some sort of weirdly niche meditation music.

For once, we weren't clamoring to fuck as many times as possible before the sun fully rose. We were all just content to lie there comfortably, enjoying one another's company. All that was missing was Carter.

I wondered if maybe he just needed the right motivation—much like Heath walking in on Royce balls deep in my ass that first night. Maybe he just needed to try it on for size before deciding group scenes weren't his thing?

It was something to think about, anyway.

Eventually, we all got up and joined Carter and Nate for breakfast in our shared living space. Whoever had bribed the organizers to give us the pool house deserved a crisp high five. The number of unfamiliar faces at dinner last night had been overwhelming, but even worse were the familiar ones.

Like my white-gold team member—Paige.

So I was immensely grateful that we could eat breakfast and fully caffeinate in the privacy of our little crew before needing to join everyone else for the day's activity.

"This seems...wrong," I admitted after emerging from my room fully dressed for the activity. "Doesn't it?"

Carter's deep blue eyes sparkled as he took me in from head to toe, shaking his head slightly. "Fucking hell, Spark. How do you always look so...incredible?"

I rolled my eyes, feeling self-conscious. "It's the dresses, not me. This one is gorgeous, by the way. Same designer?"

He grimaced. "Yeah. You're stunning, babe. But you still look better in red."

Royce scoffed, coming out to join us while messing with his silver bow tie. "You mean she looks better in bed? One hundred percent agree. Damn, Squirrel, you look positively—"

"Bridal," Nate finished for him, eyeing me with a scowl. "You look like you're dressed for a wedding. What the fuck, Bass?"

Carter just shrugged. "I was working with white gold. What did you expect?"

"At least you gave me practical shoes," I added, lifting the skirt of my floor-length ball gown to show the pair of white-gold-and-crystal-embellished sneakers he'd set out with my dress. Looking around at the guys in their metallic-hued tuxedos and stiff leather dress shoes, I was thinking I'd gotten the better option, even if my full skirts would hamper my ability to run.

White-gold opera gloves covered the majority of my arms and the dress had a high neckline, but Carter had also provided a gorgeous cashmere coat in the same color, in case I was cold.

"You're a walking target with all that fabric," Nate grumbled, swatting a hand at my huge ball-gown skirt.

I rolled my eyes. "As if you're not. Have you looked in the mirror, Essex?" Because his white-gold suit was awfully close to white-white and would show every speck of dirt just as easily as my dress would.

"You wanted that team—quit complaining," Carter said with a smirk. "Spark, babe, we'll try to take it easy on you."

Royce grinned, casually wrapping my hair around his fist and tugging it to tilt my head back for a kiss. "I won't. But you'll love it anyway."

I groaned, kissing him back, until Nate gave Royce a shove. "Let's go before you horny bastards distract my teammate." He grabbed my gloved hand in his strong grip and all but dragged me out of the pool house behind him.

Other attendees were already gathering out on the lawn behind the estate, all richly attired in evening wear within the eight metallic shades chosen for the teams. It was an absurd sight, but considering there were no dinosaur bones in sight, I supposed it could always be worse.

The officiants and judging panel all wore the anonymous metallic masks and black robes that I recognized from previous Devil's Backbone events, and I shivered when I looked at them. All I could picture were the ones who'd abducted me from Nevaeh and dropped me half-naked in the forest to die.

I had to remind myself multiple times that these masked, robed people were not those ones. It was a hard reality to wrap my head around, though.

It took ages for all the teams to assemble and become fully equipped for the event itself. Safety goggles were handed out to everyone, and rules were read twice over before anyone was handed their loaded gun.

Paige—also dressed, shockingly, in a bridal gown—glared daggers at me through her safety goggles, but Nate shifted his position to block her line of sight while speaking with another of our white-attired teammates. Whether it was accidental or not, I was relieved for the physical barrier between us.

"Okay, we have five minutes to talk strategy before the starting bell," Nate said a moment later, gathering the rest of our team around so he didn't have to speak loudly. The bronze team was right beside us, and we didn't need to go giving away our plan. "Gregory, you're in charge of getting our egg to one of the defendable towers. Everyone will be going for the closest, so I want us to aim for the farthest at the westernmost point of the vineyards. Kara, you have our flag, yes?"

The girl in question, who wore a fully sequined gown with a dramatic split up her thigh, nodded. "Sure do." She patted her chest, where she'd stuffed our team flag for safe keeping.

Nate nodded. "Excellent. You stick to Gregory like glue and lay claim to that tower the moment you get there. Paige and Russell will flank you as guards, while you make your way across. Clear?"

Paige gave a frustrated sound. "What about you?"

"Layne and I are on attack. We're targeting the silver team first, then copper, then black gold." I snorted a laugh, and he jabbed me with his elbow. "You four are tasked with defending our egg. Am I clear?"

"That's a terrible plan," Paige argued. "Just the two of you on attack against the other teams? You don't stand a chance. One person should be able to defend our tower, and everyone else can spread out for—"

"Paige," Nate snapped, "shut up."

"Listen to Nate," Russell, a tall, dark-skinned guy, muttered to her. "He knows this game better than the rest of us."

Paige's cheeks pinked, clearly hating being overruled, but her furious glare snapped to me like this was all somehow my fault.

"The second that bell tolls, it's a free-for-all," Nate told us in a serious tone, ignoring his ex-girlfriend's hurt feelings entirely. "I want you four to sprint. Am I clear? Don't try to shoot the other teams straight up. Just go. We will lay cover fire. Got it?" The four he spoke to all nodded, even Paige eventually. Then Nate quirked a brow at me. "You understand, Layne?"

I nodded as well. "Yep. Got it, boss."

An odd expression skated across his face, then he shook it away. "Just don't get hit. They may just be paintballs, but they still hurt like a motherfucker without armor. There are going to be some nasty bruises tomorrow."

"Understood," I replied, checking that my gun was loaded and ready to fire. I hadn't played paintball in years but still vividly remembered how much getting hit at close range could hurt, so I'd be doing everything possible to avoid that. One shot did not automatically disqualify players, but they would count as points for the other team. And with the paint in our matching metallic colors, it would be easy to tally.

The part that made me most nervous was the egg that each team had been given to protect. It was heavily jeweled and looked a whole hell of a lot like a Fabergé egg. I didn't want to know whether they were real, so I hadn't asked. In this case—especially if any were damaged—ignorance was bliss.

Then, we were out of time. The bell rang, and chaos erupted.

Chapter Thirty-Six

February 16

Both Royce and I tried to bribe the door attendants when we arrived, to hand Ashley a matching token for either of us. The fuckers took our money and apparently went right ahead with their prior arrangement to line her up with Carter. Except Nate beat him at his own game, which was funny, but at the same time, what the fuck is Nate playing at? He's been acting so suspicious for the last few weeks. Now I'm worried he's got something awful planned for Ashes.

Not deliberately. I don't for a second think he would ever harm her knowingly. But I can't help wondering if someone is messing with his head. It would explain all his weird behavior lately.

Fuck, I hope not. But the only other explanation is that he's developed a massive crush on my girl, and that's too insane to be true.

H. Briggs

Thank fuck I had some prior experience with a paintball gun and wasn't a terrible shot to begin with because some of the players were just downright terrible.

Screams and laughter rang out all through the vineyard as people dashed between vines and dove behind the man-made barricades that'd been set up purely for this game.

To my shock, Nate and I seemed to make a good team. The two of us picked our way through the vineyard obstacles with coordinated precision as we searched out the silver team's base to steal their egg.

"On my count," he said as the two of us crouched low behind a barricade about half an hour into the battle, "make a run for it across to that tower. I think I see a silver flag and no one guarding it. I'll lay cover fire if I see anyone pop out, okay?"

I jerked a nod, checking my ammo. We'd used a lot of paintballs already, but every team could reload if they wanted to lose five points. We weren't that desperate just yet. "Got it," I confirmed.

"Three...two...go!" Nate gave me a little shove, and I tucked low as I sprinted across the open space, holding my breath as I ran.

Several shots sounded, but nothing hit me as I dove for cover behind the next obstacle and came face-to-face with bitchy and bitchier.

"Paige, what the fuck are you doing here? You're supposed to be guarding our team's tower!" I exclaimed, shifting my gaze between her and Jade, who was dressed in glittering black gold.

Paige's pretty face twisted in a sneer. "And you're supposed to be back in Panner City, whoring yourself out to sleazy businessmen for happy endings, and yet here you are. What the fuck do you think you're playing at, telling everyone you're engaged to Nate? No one is dumb enough to believe that. He doesn't even like you."

Ah. I should have known that stupid lie would find its way back to her. And although it was on the tip of my tongue to correct her...

Nah, fuck that.

"Oh, honey, jealousy is such an unattractive look on you," I said sweetly and with a heavy dose of condescending bitch. "I can assure you, it wasn't me who told everyone that we're engaged"—technically true—"but I can see how this is hard for you to swallow. Although I'm sure not many things are."

She blinked a couple of times with confusion, then glanced to Jade, who squinted at me with disdain. "Whatever, trailer trash. You don't even have a ring on."

I held up my gloved hands, turning them to inspect. "Are you sure?"

Paige snarled an angry sound, then grabbed Jade's paintball gun and shot me right in the stomach with a sparkly-black paint bullet. It hit me like an actual punch in the gut, and I almost doubled over from the force of it and the shock that she was willing to sacrifice the game over her jealousy.

Just then, Carly came skidding around the corner with her silver gown fluttering in the breeze. "Whoa, what the hell?" she exclaimed, looking from me to Paige and Jade, and then the gun in Paige's hand. "Oh, hell no, you did not."

Then, without waiting for explanations or excuses, Carly fired two shots, one at each of them. The first hit Jade in the chest and she cried out like it was lead, not paint, and the second…well, I wasn't totally sure if Carly had terrible aim or fantastic. It hit Paige square in the face, and along with silver paint splattering all over her face, so too did a burst of blood from her nose.

The scream she let out drew more attention than just nearby players—and Nate, who came sprinting breathlessly around the corner with a panicked look on his face; it also drew a masked, robed referee.

"Carly…fucking hell," the masked man groaned. "Disqualified. You too, Paige. We saw you shoot your own team member. Jade, you're out as well for letting her use your gun."

Paige, sobbing and wailing about her supposedly broken nose, was all too happy to leave the game. Jade scowled and pouted but went with her friend without any protest. Carly looked like she was ready to throw punches, though, until the referee grabbed her arm, jerked her close, and muttered something in her ear.

Instantly, all the fight disappeared out of her, and she gave a meek smile up at him. "Okay," she simpered, batting her lashes. "I'll go. See you at the party, Ash!"

I gaped after her, then turned to Nate in confusion as the referee disappeared once more. "Was that Edmund in the robe and mask?"

Nate quirked a brow, then gave a short laugh. "No. It was actually his older brother, Spencer. He graduated from Nevaeh last year."

I nodded slowly, taking that information on board. Interesting reaction Carly just had to her new boyfriend's brother, but shit, who was I to judge right now?

"Oh, look!" I brushed past Nate and stretched up on my toes to snatch the silver flag from the little tower. "I guess Carly was their defender. Crap, now I feel bad..."

Nate scoffed, taking the flag from me and stuffing it inside his pocket. "Don't. It's still Royce's team too, remember? Surely you want to beat him?"

I grinned because...yes. Yes, I did.

"Fucking hell," he sighed, staring at the wide patch of sparkly black staining the middle of my stomach. "That dress is probably ruined now. Carter's mom would have an actual aneurysm if she saw."

I wrinkled my nose. "What's it got to do with her?"

Nate huffed a laugh, shaking his head. "Do you and Carter ever talk, or is this whole thing just about sex? Actually, don't answer that. It's a Portia Levigne Couture dress, Ashley. Portia is Carter's mother. He changed all the sample size specs to your measurements last semester, so literally all her new concept gowns are perfectly made to measure for you."

My jaw dropped. "Are you joking? That's—"

"Kinda creepy? I know. Watch out!" he barked at the same time he grabbed me, spinning us around so the paintball, fired from some distance away, hit him in the back rather than me in the head. "Go!" He shoved me, and we both took off running for shelter while the next paintball flew wide and hit a tree to our left.

I dove behind the closest structure, feeling the skirt of my dress rip as I did so, but Nate was right behind me.

"Copper?" he asked, trying to look over his shoulder to see who'd hit him.

"I think so?" I replied. "Copper or bronze maybe?"

"Bastards," he growled, then glanced back the way we'd just come from. "Shit, we didn't check if the silver team left their egg undefended, and now either bronze or copper could be moving in on it."

"So let's go back and check," I told him with a shrug. "Winning eggs is the best way to win the game, right? So we don't want to let that one slip through our hands."

Nate poked his head out from our barricade, then immediately jerked it back as more paintballs splattered to our left. "Copper," he said with a chuckle. "Their base must be close, and they've possibly left it undefended to see what all that screaming was about from Paige." He pursed his lips, thinking for a moment. "Okay, let's double back to check the silver tower very quickly, then go find copper. Ready? Go."

In unison, we took off running at a crouch, guns at the ready as we went. Satisfaction rippled through me as I heard a yelp when one of my shots landed. Then all of a sudden, Nate tripped over something and went tumbling with a grunt of pain, and I hesitated.

"Go!" he ordered when a shot splattered the vines behind us. Whoever was shooting had shitty aim but that might not last long if we were sitting ducks. "Keep going!"

His inability to immediately get back to his feet suggested he was either caught on something or injured, but at the same time, he was a big boy, and it was only paintball. So after the next copper splat landed so close it splattered my glove, I did as I was told and ran for cover.

The next barricade I went to duck behind was already occupied by a pair of pewter team players who were way more interested in trying to eat each other's faces than actively playing the game. So I shot them both with a white-gold paintball and laughed as I sprinted out through the vines once more, searching for the silver tower. Somehow, I'd become all turned around and lost sight of it.

Ducking around the end of a vine row, I slowed my pace as I approached a big old oak tree. Maybe I could climb up and get my bearings from a higher viewpoint?

"Well, well, fancy meeting you here," a deliciously familiar voice purred as I rounded the trunk looking for a foothold.

A grin curved my lips as Heath appeared from the other side of the wide trunk, looking like some kind of fashion model in his copper suit with his paintball gun strapped across his chest.

"Have you been following me, Heathcliff?" I accused, narrowing my eyes suspiciously. My gun also hung from its strap at my back, and I briefly considered taking a dirty shot at close range.

It'd hurt, though, so I quickly decided against it—especially considering I knew Heath would never do that to me just to win. Royce or Nate? Different story. But Heath was too honorable, so I couldn't resort to sneaky tactics now.

"Where's Nate?" he asked, sliding a hand around my black-gold splattered bodice and pulling me close. "I saw you two were working well together…"

I shrugged. "We're adults and on the same team."

Heath swiveled us, pressing my back to the tree trunk as he leaned his elbow on the bark. "But we're alone now, right?"

"Mmm, isn't it against the rules to fraternize with opposing teams this weekend?" I teased, already tilting my head back and silently begging him to kiss me. Somehow my fingers had found their way under the leather of his belt and I was pulling him closer with magnetic desperation.

"Aren't rules meant to be broken, Ashes?" he replied, his smile pure evil as he dipped down to deliver the kiss I wanted. Instantly I wanted more, moaning into his kisses as I slipped my hands under his shirt to touch hot skin. What was probably only ever meant to be a quick make-out started to turn hot and heavy when I grasped his hard shaft through the designer suit pants and he ground against my palm.

Then a shot sounded, and Heath jerked.

"Thanks for the distraction, Layne," Nate drawled, shooting Heath a second time as he limped closer. "But we have a game to win. Come on." He held out his hand to me, and I bit back my laughter as I offered Heath a sympathetic smile.

"Sorry, babe," I giggled, smacking a quick kiss on his cheek. "Rain check."

Then I took Nate's hand and let him pull me away from my white-gold-spattered lover, laughing as we ran back into the maze of the vineyard. Nate was right—we had a game to win. And neither one of us was a gracious loser.

Fucking Nathaniel Essex and I were scary alike in some ways.

Chapter Thirty-Seven

I'M STILL LAUGHING ABOUT CARTER'S FACE WHEN I STOLE THAT TOKEN OUT OF HIS HAND. CLASSIC. HE THOUGHT HE WAS SOOOO SNEAKY BUT APPARENTLY FORGOT WHO THE FUCK HE WAS DEALING WITH. NOTHING SLIPS PAST ME IF I HAVE ANYTHING TO SAY ABOUT IT. AND IN THIS CASE, I'M BEST POSITIONED TO KEEP ASHLEY SAFE. ALL THREE OF THEM ARE SO FOCUSED ON HER MAGICAL VAGINA, THEY WOULDN'T SEE A THREAT COMING EVEN IF IT SLAPPED THEM IN THE FACE WITH A WET FISH.

IT KIND OF MAKES ME MAD WHEN I THINK ABOUT IT. DO THEY EVEN LIKE HER AS MUCH AS THEY'RE PRETENDING? OR IS IT JUST ALL ABOUT THE SEX FOR THEM?

IT FUCKING SUCKS THAT I'M QUESTIONING MY FRIENDS' MOTIVES LIKE THIS. THEY'RE LITERALLY THE BEST PEOPLE I KNOW. BUT STILL...THEY'RE ALSO GUYS. AND ASHLEY IS HOT AS HELL.

N. ESSEX, FEBRUARY 16

The rest of the game turned into a bit of chaos with friendly fire increasing with every passing minute as people got bored or competitive. After some time and plenty of annoyance from me, Nate admitted that his ankle might be sprained. He'd only been limping since the moment he'd fallen, but every time I mentioned it, he tried to gaslight me into thinking I was imagining things.

Dick.

Eventually, he caved and agreed that, yes, he was limping, and yes, he was in some "small measure" of pain, so I parked him up in the stolen silver tower—where we had found their egg after all—and used him as bait to pick off any other players who came for an easy shot.

Our finest moment was when Carter tried to lure me into a quickie in the bushes, and I swiped both his flag and egg, then left him with blue balls. *Sucker.* Nate had laughed so hard at that one, I'd done a full double take. I couldn't remember ever hearing him laugh genuinely.

When the bell tolled, I insisted Nate lean on me so I could help him trek back across the acres of battleground to see the final scores. We had no clue if our team had successfully defended our egg and flag, but we'd undoubtedly taken a hit for Paige being disqualified.

Paint-covered players all trickled back onto the patio, where servers were already roaming with trays of champagne, and Nate snagged a pair of full flutes for us.

"Sit down," I ordered, pointing to a vacant seat by a little garden table. "Take the weight off your ankle. I'll get some ice."

"Stop fussing, Layne," he growled. "I'm fine. It wasn't that bad." Still, he sat down where I had pointed, and that in itself told me he was in pain. If it were really fine, he'd still be stubbornly on his feet or doing a tap dance just to prove his point.

I just arched a brow, then plucked a bottle of wine from an ice bucket on the nearby cocktail table. "Excuse me," I said politely to a passing waitress, "could I trouble you for that napkin?"

She shrugged, handing me the linen napkin folded over her arm. I laid it flat on the table and dumped a pile of ice out of the wine bucket, then wrapped it up in a little package.

"This is unnecessary," Nate grumbled as I sank to my knees in front of him and lifted his injured foot up into my lap to apply the ice to his ankle.

I glanced up at him with a grin. "You don't like feeling like the damsel in distress, Essex? You're lucky you're so fucking heavy, or I'd try to carry you out just to emasculate you further."

He scoffed and his lips twitched like he was trying really fucking hard not to find me amusing. It was a losing battle—he just hadn't realized it yet.

"Whoa, what happened, Cinderella?" Royce asked, sauntering over to us. He was covered in so many different colors of paint, I could barely make out his silver tuxedo, but the grin on his face said he'd had a great time nonetheless. "Squirrel, babe, I don't think a glass slipper will fit his stinky foot."

"Don't tease," I scolded. "That's my job. Nate sprained his ankle out on the battlefield."

"Oh, baby!" Royce threw himself into Nate's lap dramatically, knocking the chair over and spilling the both of them onto the pavers in a tangle of ruined designer suits and spattered paint.

Nate groaned and cursed between bursts of laughter, trying to shove Royce off while his friend smothered his face in kisses. "Get off, you overgrown child. Fucking hell, I actually needed that ice!"

"Did you?" I chimed in, sitting back on my heels as I waited for them to scrap it out on the ground. "Weren't you just saying it was overkill?"

They wrestled a little more before Royce helped Nate right his chair and get seated once more. I arched a brow at him in question, offering the makeshift ice pack, and he took it with a muttered thanks before applying it to his own ankle propped up on a second chair.

"Have you guys seen Carter or Heath?" Royce asked, swiping a couple of water bottles from a passing waitress and handing me one.

"My team totally flaked this challenge. Carly got disqualified for something and lost both our egg and flag. Totally useless."

Nate and I exchanged a smirk because we'd already handed off the spoils of war to one of the masked, robed referees for safe keeping.

"There they are," I said, seeing the two handsome devils heading over to us, grinning and jostling each other as they debated who'd been hit with more paint. I rose back to my feet and brushed off my full skirt, which was an entirely pointless gesture considering how filthy I was. Not only was I splattered with several colors of metallic paint but I was also covered in mud, grass stains, and crushed grapes. My hair probably looked like a fucking albatross had started nesting season judging by how tangled it felt.

"Spark! How the hell are you so untouched right now?" Carter exclaimed, scanning me over from top to toe. I was hardly untouched, but the only direct hit I'd taken was the one from Paige in my stomach. All the other splatters were just that: splatters.

I laughed, shrugging. "Teamwork, obviously."

"Also I'd be cautious challenging her to *Call of Duty* anytime soon," Nate added with a smirk. "Layne is a closet sniper."

Heath, Royce, and Carter all looked at me in surprise and I offered an innocent smile. "I used to go deer hunting with my dad when he was home from work. He was pretty strict about making sure I put in the hours at a rifle range to ensure I was capable."

"I suddenly don't feel good about the black-gold win," Carter admitted with a grimace, running a hand over his scruffy jaw. He hadn't shaved in a couple of days, and it was a good look on him. "Even if we did get both the pewter team's egg and flag."

"Wow, nice work," Nate drawled, barely hiding his sarcasm. "That'll be hard to beat."

Carter narrowed his eyes in suspicion. He obviously knew we'd stolen his egg and flag, but he didn't know about the other wins we'd clocked. A moment later, a loud crack rang out and the sky above us erupted with fireworks. It was midafternoon but cloudy enough that we could still see the display well enough.

"Congratulations, white-gold team!" one of the masked referees announced over a loudspeaker. "Winners of this game with an impressive score of 8,283 points. Each qualifying team member has won fifty thousand dollars. Honorable mention to black-gold team, who came second with, er, 3,612 points."

Carter gaped at Nate and me in shock. "No! How?"

I was still hung up on the prize announcement that had just been made, though. "Did he just say fifty thousand dollars? American dollars, not Japanese yen?" The guys were all so casual about wealth, it was probably the equivalent of a Starbucks gift card to them, but to me? This was huge. "Wait, he said qualifying members. What does that mean? Am I not…? Not me, right?" Because surely there was some sort of buy-in or membership fees or something that qualified someone to win.

Heath gave me a puzzled look, shaking his head. "Were you disqualified at any stage of the game?"

"No…"

"Then you get the money. Disqualification means you're out of the game and ineligible for prizes. If you played and your team won, then you get the prize." Heath looked so matter-of-fact about it. Like it was just that simple. I didn't even know what to say.

I was so overwhelmed, tears burned in the back of my eyeballs, and I did the only thing I could think to do: I launched myself at Nate in a huge hug. He stumbled but caught me with arms around my waist, steadying us before we toppled over.

"Thank you," I sobbed into his paint-covered jacket. "That pays off a huge chunk of my debt."

He awkwardly patted my back, body stiff like he was unfamiliar with the sensation of being hugged. Which I knew couldn't be true because Max was far from distant as a parent, and I was sure my mom had forced plenty of her motherly affection on him in the last year.

"I don't know why you're thanking me," he replied with an uncomfortable laugh. "It was teamwork, right?"

Still, I squeezed him tighter. I didn't want to say it out loud, but if I'd ended up on literally any other team, I would not be walking away with fifty grand this weekend. Nate was the only one more interested in winning the game than getting his dick wet. And while I loved the sneaky make-outs behind vines, I loved financial freedom more.

Finally, sensing he was as uncomfortable as he could possibly get, I released Nate from my hug.

"If you have debts to pay—" Carter started to say, his brow set with a confused frown.

"Don't," I snapped, shaking my head. "I don't want or need any man to support me." But I was more than happy to win the money fair and square, and I was 100 percent confident that was what'd happened here. We'd won, no questions asked and no charity offered.

Royce smacked the back of Carter's head. "Bro. You'd think you'd know her better than that by now." He extended a hand to me, and I took it, letting him pull me away from Nate. "Come on, Squirrel. Let's head into the party. The games aren't over yet!"

He tucked my arm through his, guiding me to walk with him across the patio, where paint-splattered players were in full party mode already. The other guys followed, and Royce glanced at me a couple of times, but his tight jaw suggested he was holding something back.

"What's on your mind, Roycey?" I asked as we approached the main estate.

He huffed a small sigh. "I feel the need to explain...none of us knew what the prize for winning would be. Sometimes it's just bragging rights or something stupid like a life-size crystal giraffe, so we don't ever really take the games seriously."

I nodded slowly, guessing at the point he was trying to make. "So if you'd known there was so much money at stake...?"

"I'm glad Nate was on your team for this one," he said softly. "Sometimes I think we forget what sort of real-world impact these prizes might have…and we forget that you weren't raised like the rest of us assholes, with such a casual indifference toward money."

I gave a small laugh, shaking my head. "That's true. Weirdly, I'm also glad I was on Nate's team this time. I'm sure that's a statement I'll never say again, but for today it's true."

We'd paused behind a small crowd of guests, and as we moved forward, I realized what the holdup was. Everyone was stripping.

"Um…?" I blinked up at Royce in confusion, and he smirked.

"Dry cleaners," he said, gesturing to the uniformed staff taking paint-ruined dresses and suits from the guests. "They get the clothing cleaned and then donated to a charity that provides formal wear to impoverished high schools for their students' proms."

That…was actually a really lovely idea, and I noticed guests were handing over their entire outfits, shoes included, stripping right down to underwear. In lots of cases, girls were just going full bare-chested as they collected a cocktail and continued on inside.

I bit my lip, suddenly very aware of the fact that my dress had enough structure in the bodice that I'd not worn a bra. So if I took it off, I'd just be in a tiny pair of white-gold lace panties which barely covered the crack of my ass.

But for charity? It would be a dick move to keep the gown. Especially since I hadn't paid for it myself. So I sucked up my modesty and turned to let Royce unzip the back of my gown when we reached the front of the line.

As I slipped out of the dress, a man's shirt dropped over my head, still partially buttoned up.

"Oh, um," I started to say, before recognizing the manly cologne scenting the fabric, and threaded my arms into the long sleeves. "Thanks, Heath." I turned to smile at him, and he brushed a quick kiss on my lips.

"Anytime, Ashes," he replied, then continued stripping down to his briefs.

It only then clicked in my brain that we weren't heading back to our rooms to change; we were just staying as is. Practically naked. Somehow I suspected the evening was going to turn real dirty, real fast.

Chapter Thirty-Eight

Fucking Nate. I should have just let him make a scene and taken my token back...but at the same time, I'm pretty confident he will take good care of Spark during the game. As much as he pretends she irritates him, a blind man could see how soft he is growing toward her these days.

He knows how much she means to us, and as such, he won't risk her safety. Maybe he's finally starting to think of her as family? She is technically his stepsister, and he always wanted siblings.

It's just paintball. What's the worst that can happen?

Feb. 16
C. Bassington

The party—if we looked past the fact everyone was in their underwear at best and all but naked at worst—was surprisingly normal. Sure, it all had the Devil's Backbone air of excess about it with shots being handed out in glittering crystal shot glasses and poker chips made of precious metals, but if you squinted really hard, it would just be a regular college party.

Carly and I played—and won—about four games of cocktail-pong, where instead of Ping-Pong balls, we needed to toss tiny resin ducks into the opposing teams' brightly filled martini glasses, and Heath seemed to make it his mission to ensure we both had plenty to eat from every possible canapé that roamed past.

Wearing Heath's shirt made me so comfortable, I was actually enjoying myself for a while. Until I glanced over to see a girl called Serafina eating foie gras like she was starving, and a chill of unease ran through me.

"You okay?" Nate asked as I abandoned Carly and Heath to head over to the bar for some water. Maybe I was too drunk?

I nodded but couldn't wipe the confused frown off my face even if I tried. I requested my water from the bartender, then turned to Nate, who was watching me with narrowed, suspicious eyes.

"I'm fine," I murmured, taking a sip of my water.

"Liar," he accused softly, quirking a brow. "What happened?" He was seated on one of the tall cocktail stools, his injured ankle propped up on another and a tumbler of whiskey on the coaster beside his hand. He wore nothing but a pair of white-gold boxers, but I doubted he was getting many complaints. Nate spent a lot of time in the gym, and it fucking showed.

Forcing myself to shift my gaze away, I looked back in the direction I'd just seen Serafina scoffing her fatty duck liver. "Um, you know that girl who is always asking people to sign her PETA petitions outside the science department? Serafina?"

Nate nodded slowly. "Yeah, she's a third-year DB. Really heavily involved in anti-cruelty to animals organizations. Why?"

My mood soured even further, hearing him confirm what I already knew. "I just saw her eating foie gras. Like shoveling it in as if she'd never tasted anything more delicious in her life."

He wrinkled his nose. "That doesn't sound right. Maybe it wasn't her you saw? There are lots of people here from other universities. Could it have been someone else?"

I nibbled the edge of my lip, unsure. "Maybe."

"Or maybe it wasn't foie gras? There's heaps of weird mushroom and tofu canapés going around as well." He grimaced like he'd accidentally tried one of those and wasn't a fan.

I sighed, nodding. "Yeah, you're right. I just thought—"

"You thought maybe she was hypnotized to act against her free will," he finished for me with an understanding smile. "I get it. I've been overthinking a lot of shit lately too. But, Ash, Dr. Fox is gone." He carefully avoided saying *dead*, and I appreciated that fact.

"I know," I groaned, rubbing my forehead. "It just feels wrong to move on with our lives, doesn't it? Like we should have gone to the authorities with what we knew. But then I'm also fully aware of how fucking insane we would sound if we tried to report it. Hypnosis? Come on. Even we struggled with the concept when Heath suggested it."

Nate blew out a long breath, then reached out to grab my shirt and pulled me closer so he could speak softly. "I get it, and I agree. But we also can't let this rule us, Ash. Dr. Fox is gone, and so is the hypnosis-experiment shit. It's okay to relax, and it's okay to be happy."

Logically, I knew he just didn't want to be overheard, but my stupid pulse was racing at how close we were all of a sudden. Like my dumb-ass lizard brain thought he was going to kiss me.

Where the fuck had *that* thought come from?

Shocked and puzzled by my own thoughts, I found myself locking gazes with Nate's whiskey-brown eyes and searching for…something. Hatred, disgust, pity, or irritation—any of the emotions I was more comfortable seeing in his eyes. But I found none of those, and that rocked me harder than I was really prepared to admit.

Confusion rippled through his expression as I held his gaze, and

I bit the corner of my lip nervously. He broke eye contact, his gaze dipping to my mouth, and I sucked in a shuddering breath before forcefully ripping myself away.

"Um, you should have ice on that ankle," I murmured, gesturing to his elevated foot.

Nate cleared his throat, swiping a hand over his hair. "Yeah, I did. It melted."

"I'll get you some more," I offered, putting another step between us as I backed away.

He shook his head. "Nah, it's fine. I was going to head back to my room anyway." He awkwardly hopped off the stool and tested weight on his bad ankle with a grimace.

I was just about to insist he let me help him when Carter swaggered over looking like some kind of fae prince with his jet-black hair and ink-covered muscles. "You need a hand, Essex?"

"Nah, I'm good," Nate replied, then took a limping step and winced. "Okay, fine. But don't even fucking think about carrying me bridal style."

Carter grinned and faked like he was going to scoop Nate up in his arms, making his friend punch him in the chest. "Ow, fuck, bro, I was kidding. Come on. I'll get you tucked into bed. You coming, Spark?"

Carly was gesturing for me to come back and play another dumb game with her and Heath—what looked to be horseshoes with solid-gold horseshoes—so I shook my head. "I'll stay a bit longer."

Carter cupped my face, tipping my head back to kiss me briefly, then promised to be back in no time. He offered Nate his shoulder, and the two of them exited the party arm in arm wearing nothing but their boxer shorts. *Hot.*

Okay, Ashley, where the fuck did that thought come from?

I groaned and shook my head. More water. I needed to sober up if I was actually thinking about Nate in any kind of sexual context.

No surprises, the horseshoes were indeed made of solid gold.

The excess of wealth was actually sickening, but at the same time, I was more than willing to reap the benefits when I won the society's games. We played for a while, and my switch to water definitely helped us win against the sloppy drunk girls wearing just bronze micro-thongs.

Carter returned sometime later and tugged me away to hand me a little velvet box. "Nate asked me to give you this," he said quietly, glancing around. "We had a little run-in with Paige on the way back to our accommodation and...we both think this is a good idea."

Confused, I opened the box he'd given me and inhaled sharply. "Oh."

"And not that I like this part, but Nate did have a good point when he said we should tone down the PDA at these events. Word travels fast around the society—even if members have long since graduated." Casual as anything, he took the diamond ring out of the box and slid it onto my ring finger.

I swallowed hard, eyeing the enormous jewel sitting in ornate claws. "I guess once a DB, always a DB, huh?"

Carter smiled. "Something like that. Do you like it?" He held my hand in his, looking down at the ring thoughtfully. It was a large, brilliant white, oval-cut diamond encircled by a baguette diamond halo for a stunning sunburst effect, and weirdly suited me, as though it'd actually been chosen with me in mind.

"I do," I admitted. "It's fake though, right?" Because buying an actual diamond ring for your fake fiancée was absurd.

Carter just laughed, then got pulled away by some guy who begged him to go play life-size chess. I returned to Carly and Heath, and Heath's gaze immediately snapped to my new jewelry. He pouted a little, but it was with a resigned sort of nod. Apparently this was something the guys had already discussed among themselves...

"Damn it," Royce hissed when he joined us, grabbing my hand in his to inspect the ring. "Guess he made it official, then."

I rolled my eyes and gave him a shoulder bump. "Shut up,

troublemaker. Want to escort me back to my room? For safety, of course."

His grin spread wide and his gaze turned heated. "Oh, well, if it's for safety, then how can I refuse? Heath!" he called out to where Heath and Carly were gathering our horseshoes. "I'm walking Squirrel back to the pool house."

"I'll come too," Heath replied, handing Carly the heavy pile of horseshoes. "See ya, Carls."

She rolled her eyes but sent me a knowing smirk. "Sleep well, Ash."

"Oh, I will." I grinned back, despite knowing full damn well very little sleep would be had. Now if only we could grab Carter on the way to make it a proper party...

Chapter Thirty-Nine

0530: WOKE UP WITH SQUIRREL IN MY ARMS. PERFECTION. EVEN IF HEATH'S FOOT WAS TOUCHING MINE, I COULD PUT UP WITH IT IF IT MEANT NOT WAKING HER UP.

0900: MUST HAVE FALLEN ASLEEP AGAIN. SQUIRREL SLIPPED OUT TO VISIT CARTER, AND I KNOW THIS BECAUSE I WOKE UP TO THE SOUND OF HIS HEADBOARD SMACKING THE WALL AND HEATH SNUGGLING ME LIKE I WAS LITTLE SPOON. THE FUCKING AUDACITY, I AM NOT LITTLE SPOON.

1000: CONVINCED ASH TO DRIVE HOME WITH ME. I LIKE BEING HER PASSENGER PRINCESS, AND SHE LOOKS SO HAPPY DRIVING MY CAR. I NEED TO SORT OUT THAT REPLACEMENT CAR FOR HER THIS WEEK, ONCE HEATH FINALLY PAYS UP ON OUR DEAL.

SHE'S GOING TO LOVE HER NEW CAR, BUT I'M FULLY PREPARED FOR HER TO PUSH BACK. MY SQUIRREL HATES BEING HANDED ANYTHING, AND ALTHOUGH I LOVE HOW FIERCE AND INDEPENDENT SHE IS...I WISH SHE'D LET US SPOIL HER LIKE SHE DESERVES.

R. D'ARENBERG, FEBRUARY 17

Royce let me drive his Chiron the whole way back to Nevaeh and didn't even try to mess around while I was driving like I'd done to Carter. He was perfectly content to just enjoy the drive from his own passenger seat and play DJ with the radio station. It was nice, and the whole time we had the added safety of knowing both Nate's and Carter's cars tailed us like fucking Secret Service.

If anyone hit a deer, we'd all be there to help out.

We got back to the apartment in the early afternoon, and I immediately set up my laptop and textbooks on the dining table. As fun as the weekend had been, I wasn't going to risk failing my classes. Heath happily joined me, while Royce and Nate parked on the couch to play video games with the sound turned down far enough it wouldn't bother us.

Carter had to go and collect his dog from Mrs. Brown, the lady downstairs who pet-sat for him on the regular, then ended up taking her to the groomers for a blowout—the dog, not the pet-sitter. When he returned home, Lady looked like the pampered princess she was with a shiny new bow in her fur. Red, of course.

After some hours of working on my assignment, I was starving and my back ached.

"Can we get Chinese?" I suggested, abandoning my homework to join the guys on the sofa. Heath had already finished the project and joined Royce in an intense game of *Mario Kart*. "I've got a craving for beef and broccoli with fried rice."

"Shit yes." Royce enthusiastically agreed, tossing down his controller and grabbing his phone. "I'll put the order in."

The guys took turns telling him what they wanted, and he added all the dishes to his shopping cart before asking me if I wanted anything else. My eyes were already bugging out at how many dishes they'd ordered, so I just laughed and shook my head. "Maybe some fortune cookies. But otherwise I think you've done the whole menu already."

He grinned and shrugged, then submitted the order. "Bass, come with me to pick it up."

Carter sighed but handed his controller to me. "Fine. Let's go in your car, though. I don't want my leather smelling of MSG for days."

"Because then it wouldn't smell of Ashes anymore?" Heath teased, and my face heated with embarrassment as I glanced Nate's way.

Carter seemed totally unashamed, though, laughing as he pulled his shoes on. "Yep, exactly. C'mon, Royce, let's go. Now we've started talking about it, I'm starving."

The two of them left, and within a few minutes, Heath's phone dinged with a calendar reminder.

"Crap. I've got an online therapy session in five minutes," he muttered, checking the notification. "Don't let Royce eat all the sweet-and-sour pork. He's a fucking pig."

Nate snorted. "Pun intended?"

"Funny guy!" Heath called over his shoulder as he carried his laptop to his bedroom to set up for his therapist appointment.

Alone all of a sudden, Nate switched the game over, then arched a brow at me. "Well?"

I glanced at the screen to find he'd swapped from *Mario Kart* to *Call of Duty*. "Uh…I don't know how to play."

His lips curled in a lopsided smile. "Great, gives me an advantage. Just don't die, Layne. Easy as that."

Grumbling under my breath about crappy instructions and how he must really need the head start, I slouched down on the sofa to concentrate on the game. After I died for the third time, Nate gave an exaggerated sigh and actually explained more about the game and objective and strategy.

Only then was it a fair fight, and I started racking up some kill points myself.

We only played for about half an hour before the guys got back with food, but the whole time, I couldn't help feeling like Nate was watching me. Every time I tried to catch him, though, he was engaged with the screen so I figured maybe I was imagining things. Which was entirely possible.

"Bass, check it out," Royce called out, carrying the stacks of food to the coffee table. "Nate's getting his ass handed to him in COD."

Carter chuckled, shaking his head. "That's a first. Put a movie or something on while we eat."

Nate didn't comment on his subpar gaming performance and used the remote to turn off the console and select a movie.

"Heath has a therapy session," I told the guys, picking through the boxes until I found the sweet-and-sour pork, "so we're saving this one for him."

Royce pouted. "All of it?"

"Yes, all of it," I scolded, swatting his hand as he tried to take it from me. "Eat one of your other sixty-five thousand options."

Carter fetched plates and forks from the kitchen, and I stared at them in horror as they dished up the food. "What the fuck are you doing?" I asked when the shock faded enough to let me speak.

"What?" Carter replied, clearly confused.

I grabbed one of the twenty sets of disposable chopsticks that had been included in the bags and snapped them apart. Then, holding his gaze, I opened a box of stir-fry and snared a baby corn directly from the container with my chopsticks.

"Takeout does not involve silverware and dishes, you animals. Eat from the fucking box like a real man." I demonstrated by delivering the baby corn into my mouth and was delighted to see laughter bubbling up on his otherwise-stoic expression.

Royce reached over and grabbed a set of chopsticks for himself, then proceeded to use them like stabbing instruments to pick up a piece of Mongolian lamb, and I stared in disgusted fascination as he dropped it twice before eating it.

"Fucking hell. Never mind, just use a fork." I wrinkled my nose and tried not to watch as he tried to manipulate the chopsticks between his fingers. "Christ, Roycey, for a man so good with his fingers, I expected you to know how to use chopsticks."

His eyes snapped to mine, his brows hitched, and I only then realized I'd said my inside thoughts out loud.

"And there goes my appetite," Nate grumbled, pushing up from the couch but taking a box of food with him as he disappeared down the hall to his bedroom.

"He's just cranky because he hasn't gotten laid in ages," Royce informed me with a knowing smile. "And now that he's fake engaged to you, none of the other girls at Nevaeh are an option or it'll get back to Paige."

Crap, I hadn't even considered how that snowballed lie might be impacting his actual sex life. For a moment, I felt a little bit bad about it, then I remembered that he was the one who'd started the farce in the first place, specifically to get Paige to leave him the fuck alone. So really, it was entirely of his own making.

The three of us settled in to eat and watch a movie, with Heath joining us after his therapy session. When he realized I'd saved the whole box of sweet-and-sour pork, he kissed me so hard, I almost forgot we were meant to be eating.

A few minutes after that, Nate announced he was going out and slammed the front door before anyone could ask him where he was going.

I frowned after him, concerned that perhaps he was starting to feel uncomfortable in his own home with all of us being so cozy on the sofa and said as much to the guys.

"Maybe," Heath agreed thoughtfully, "but I wouldn't read too much into it. He was looking at real estate the other day, searching to see if there were any five-bedroom properties near campus."

"Really?" I squeaked, floored that he wasn't searching for studio apartments to get the hell away from my man-harem.

This was apparently not such shocking information for the guys, as they effortlessly shifted into another topic of conversation while I sat there dwelling on the fact that maybe Nate wasn't so annoyed with me after all.

We were all so exhausted from the weekend, I had to wake Royce up to send him to bed before the movie even finished. Heath, yawning heavily, half dragged Royce down the hallway and went to bed himself after kissing me a dozen times.

"You." I pointed to Carter. "My bed. Now." He grinned like I'd just offered his very favorite dessert, and I laughed. "To sleep. You're wrecked as well, and I don't care how snuggly Lady is, you can't be comfortable on the fold-out every night."

"Hey, no arguments here," he replied, already stripping out of his clothes before even getting through the bedroom door, "so long as you're in here with me, Spark."

I groaned, shaking my head. "Tempting, really fucking tempting, but I need to finish another assignment tonight or I'll fall behind schedule. I'm going to go make a coffee and stay up late to get it done."

"Or…" he said with a sly smile, reeling me in with his fingers hooked into the waistband of my jeans, "hear me out. You come to bed with me now and get a really good rest so you're fresh to work on it in the morning."

Goddamn, he was hard to say no to. Which was probably why I found myself making that coffee almost two hours later, with blankets draped over the coffee machine to muffle the sound and avoid waking everyone up.

"What the fuck are you doing?" Nate drawled from somewhere behind me, and I nearly jumped out of my damn skin.

I whirled around to find him standing there looking more than a little disheveled and perplexed as he eyed my blanket soundproofing. "You scared the crap out of me!" I exclaimed in a strangled whisper. "When did you get home?"

"Just now," he replied. "Why are you awake and…making coffee?" He squinted down at his watch like he was second-guessing what time of day it was. If I were a betting kind of woman, I'd say that Nate was drunk. Or tipsy at the very least.

"I need to finish another assignment tonight," I said quietly, willing my heart to stop racing from the fright I'd just had. "And I'm fucking exhausted from the weekend so…coffee. Where have you been?"

I didn't intend it to come out as needy as it sounded and winced when I heard myself, but Nate didn't seem to notice. He just leaned against the island counter and stuffed his hands into his pockets with a sigh.

"I went to meet up with a girl," he muttered, shifting his weight between his feet like he was testing that sprained ankle. He'd been limping a little today but nowhere near as bad as the day before.

I cleared my throat, turning back to the coffee machine. "Oh yeah? Have fun?"

Fuck. Why did I sound like that? I sounded…jealous.

"Not really," he admitted, sounding irritated. "Because apparently I can't get my fake fiancée out of my head."

"What?" I squeaked, spinning around to stare at him in shock because surely I'd just misheard or misunderstood. He just scowled back at me like I was the source of all the bad things in his life, and a shiver ran down my spine. "Because you're worried Paige will hear you're cheating on me?"

He rolled his eyes like that was the dumbest statement in the world, then pushed off the counter and closed the gap between us, his hands braced on the counter behind me for balance and our faces way too damn close. Even with the significant height difference.

"Yeah, Layne," he said with heavy sarcasm, "because of Paige. God forbid you accept the fact that it isn't my slutty ex-girlfriend buying up all the real estate in my head these days."

My breathing hitched and the implications of what he was saying thundered through my chest. "Nate…how drunk are you right now?"

He inhaled deeply, his eyes closing for a moment before he shook his head. "Nowhere near drunk enough." Then he cupped my face in one hand and tilted my head back. I had a chance to push him away right then, but I didn't move. I didn't push him away, and when his lips met mine, I fucking gasped like some kind of sex-starved bodice-ripper heroine.

He took that as the encouragement it was and deepened his kiss with a near-frantic enthusiasm. Our tongues twisted together, the smoky taste of whiskey filling my senses as he kissed me like he wanted to climb right inside my heart and never leave. He moaned, seemingly hungry for more but then...

I was *kissing Nate*. What in the fuck was I thinking?

Panicked, I shoved him away and gasped for breath. "Nate, what the hell?"

He stared back at me in shock, like he was as confused as I was about what'd just happened. Then his expression darkened in a scowl once more. "Don't flatter yourself, Layne. I just needed to see what all the fuss was about. I'm not exactly lining up to take a turn through your revolving bedroom door anytime soon, if that's what you're worried about."

I sucked a sharp breath, his words striking like knives after kissing me with such intensity and sincerity. He hadn't been faking, and that was not a hate-kiss.

"You're drunk, Nate," I said, reminding myself as much as I was him. "Go and sleep it off before you say or do something you'll regret."

His eyes narrowed and he swiped a hand over his mouth. "I'm not drunk."

"You are," I scoffed. "You reek of whiskey."

Anger and frustration flared in his eyes. "And you reek of Carter."

Shocked outrage saw me bark a laugh. "Well, that'd be because I just spent the last two hours with him fucking me in about twelve different positions all over my room. Maybe when I finish my assignment, I'll activate that revolving door and see whether Heath or Royce wants a turn, seeing as apparently I'm a slut like that." I was shaking. Actually shaking. "Go the fuck to bed, Nate, before you do any more damage."

My eyeballs were hot, but I desperately didn't want him to see me cry, so I turned back to the coffee machine to finish making my espresso.

He was silent for a long, tense moment. Then he just muttered a quiet curse and left the kitchen. From the corner of my eye, I caught him scrubbing his hands over his hair with frustration as he disappeared down the hallway, but I didn't relax until I heard the click of his bedroom door shut.

Then, and only then, did the tears start falling.

Chapter Forty

March 6

Something has happened between Ashes and Nate. We're all sure of it even though neither of them will admit it. They're avoiding each other to the point of ridiculousness ever since we got back from the society weekend in Napa. Whatever Nate did or said, he clearly felt awful about it. He is all sad eyes and small gestures at the moment but clearly hasn't found the balls to straight up apologize.

    I wish he would. It's been three weeks and they can't seem to be in the same room together, which is making our apartment feel like the floor is covered in eggshells.

    We may need to stage an intervention soon and get to the bottom of things.

H. Briggs

Things couldn't keep going the way they were. I'd thought that surely when Nate woke up the next morning, he would have no memory of our kiss or that he'd be mortified at his drunk behavior, but no. First thing that next morning when I yawned, he made a snarky remark about my "busy night" and it all went downhill from there.

I was hardly blameless. Every time he lashed out, I jabbed back, totally unable to roll over and take the insults that were completely out of line to start with. Then, around two weeks after our war of words began, he said something that really struck a nerve.

Which was why, three weeks after Napa Valley, Carly and I were attending an open house for a rental near campus. It was high fucking time that I moved out of Nate's apartment.

"You sure the guys are on board with you moving out?" Carly asked as we toured the small two-bedroom unit while the agent waited, looking bored, in the hall. "You did discuss this with them, right?"

I shrugged, avoiding eye contact. "Uh-huh."

Carly groaned, smacking her forehead. "I knew this was too good to be true."

"What? No, they're totally fine with it," I lied with a forced laugh. "So fine. Very supportive. This place seems good, right? Only a five-minute walk to campus, so we can save on gas, and bedrooms are, um, big enough for a bed." Sort of. Just. A small bed. The prize money from Napa had cleared my student loans from Panner Valley entirely so I could actually afford rent if I picked up an extra shift at the club.

Carly didn't reply, and when I turned around to look at her, she had her phone in her hand.

"What are you doing?" I asked suspiciously.

She quirked a brow, then brought her phone to her ear as she held up one finger to tell me to wait.

"Hey, friend," she sang when her call connected. "I just thought I'd let you know that the apartment Ash and I are currently looking at seems great and we're probably going to—"

"Carly!" I cried out, reaching for her phone to try to snatch it away, but the lanky bitch just put it on speaker and held it up way too high for me to reach. "Carly, not funny!"

"You're doing what right now?" Royce's voice echoed out of the phone, and I glared daggers at my way-too-tall friend. "I must have heard you wrong. It sounded like you're looking at an apartment with my Squirrel, but that can't be right because she lives here. With me."

"Oh, really?" Carly replied, giving me a loaded glare. "So she didn't discuss moving out? And you are not—what did you say again, Ash?—very supportive of the idea? Huh. How weird. No one could have seen that one coming."

"Pin your location," Royce growled. "I'm on my way."

The line went dead and Carly winced. "Ooh, girl, you're in so much trouble. Roycey seems like a spanker too."

"You're an asshole," I groaned, scrubbing my hands over my face. "Why don't you wanna live with me?"

Her response was to wrap me in a huge hug, resting her chin on my head. "I do, Ash. It would be so much fun being roomies, but I also don't want to sign a lease and then find myself scrambling to find a new roommate when the guys inevitably drag you back into their lair. Or worse, get you knocked up."

A panicked laugh bubbled out of me as I shook off her hug. "Not going to happen. Thank fuck for my good friend Mirena."

She just shrugged. "Okay, well, you're still wearing that engagement ring, so what's a girl to think?"

Instinctively, I clasped my hands together to cover the ring in question. I'd tried to take it off about a hundred times in the last three weeks and for some reason kept finding reasons not to. My current flimsy excuse was that if it was real—and I suspected it was—I didn't want to risk losing it by leaving it lying around my room.

At the same time, it was satisfying to flash it in Nate's face when he was being a grade-A fuckface, just to remind him that he'd started the lie so had no one to blame but himself.

"You still didn't have to sell me out to Royce, though. Some friend you are," I grumbled, picking up my handbag from where I'd left it on the counter and exiting the apartment.

We both thanked the real estate agent and made watery promises to think about it before heading down the seven flights of stairs to the street.

"Look, I figured you'd rather Royce than Carter, and you definitely didn't want Heath laying on a guilt trip with the big puppy-dog eyes," Carly said with a laugh as we both puffed our way down the stairs. "Royce seems like he'd let you off with a light spanking. Carter would probably have you tied up and edged for hours."

I stopped dead in my tracks as I thought that over, then nodded. "You're probably right. Good call."

"You're welcome," she snickered, nudging me to keep walking. "Also, no way in hell were we taking a place with this many stairs and no elevator. My calves are burning already."

"Think of how good your ass would get, though," I said, "and no need for a gym membership, so that's another win."

Carly just laughed as we reached the lobby and stepped out onto the sidewalk just seconds before Royce's Chiron came flying around the corner and screeched to a stop right beside us.

"Get in, Squirrel!" Royce barked through the open passenger side window. "Now."

My jaw dropped in defiant outrage. "I'm not just leaving Carly on her own because you've got your panties in a bunch. You don't have enough seats for all of us."

I couldn't be sure with how shadowed his face was within the car, but I could feel his eye might be twitching in anger. It almost moved me to do as I was told, but a bigger part of me wanted to dig my heels in for the sake of it.

"Ash, babe, I love you, but I really don't want to get in the middle of this," Carly said with a grimace. "I'll grab a cab. Oh look, there's one now. Taxi!" She hailed the passing cab and basically sprinted across the road to dive in the back seat.

"Chicken!" I yelled after her, and she blew me a kiss from the window as the taxi started driving once more. I still made no move to get in Royce's car, though, folding my arms and glaring at him in the driver's seat.

He stared back at me for a tense moment, then gave a frustrated sigh and got out of the car. Anticipation filled my core like a thousand butterflies as I watched him stalk around the hood of his sexy vehicle, and I started to second-guess my decisions.

"Squirrel," he said in a dark voice, clearly attempting to rein in his temper for the sake of getting what he wanted, "please get in the car."

"Make me," I retorted, completely losing control of my bratty side despite knowing full damn well I was playing with fire.

To absolutely no surprise at all, Royce had his hand in my hair and my back pressed against the side of the car in less than a breath of time, my head jerked back so firmly, I whimpered. "Squirrel, if you don't get in the damn car in the next ten seconds, I will bend you over the hood and fuck your ass right here in broad daylight while all the nice people passing by watch."

I gasped, already hot and flustered with desire. "You wouldn't."

He crushed himself against me, pushing a little moan out of my throat as his hard length ground against my abdomen. "Try me," he replied, ghosting a kiss over my lips. "Ten...nine..."

I tried to move and do what I was told, but he held me firm, fingers tangled in my hair and hips pinning mine to the car. "Royce, I can't move," I protested with a laugh. "Not fair."

He just shrugged, his lips curved in an evil grin. "...eight... seven..."

"Royce!" I whined, squirming in his iron grip. As tempted as I was to call his bluff and have him actually follow through on that threat, I really didn't want to be arrested today.

"...six..." He was full chuckling now, and it loosened his grip on my hair ever so slightly.

Then right when I was going to kiss him to break his concentration, his phone rang loudly in his pocket. "Hold that thought," he murmured, pressing a finger to my lips, then reaching to answer the call.

"Royce," Nate's voice echoed from the speaker, audible at the close distance. "Are you with Ashley?"

Royce huffed a sigh. "You already know I am, stalker. What's up?"

"You need to come home. Both of you. Something's happened." He didn't explain further, just ended the call and expected us to both jump at his command.

I was right on the verge of saying Nate could get fucked, but Royce's shift in mood told me he was taking that call a lot more seriously. He released me in an instant and popped open the passenger door, making a smooth transition from sexy-scary soft-Dom to gallant gentleman.

With a frustrated sigh, I slid into my seat and waited for him to take the driver's side again before complaining. "How does he know the exact perfect time to cockblock us?" I grumbled, because it was far from the first time he'd managed to interrupt us over the last few weeks.

Royce arched a brow in curiosity. "Oh, you totally wanted me to do it, didn't you? Dirty little Squirrel. If it helps, I don't have any lube on me, so probably would have only fucked your cunt."

"Ah, I see, so you deal in empty threats now? Good to know." I tried to shove Nate out of my head and plot more ways to make Royce angry.

He groaned and ruffled his fingers through his sunshine hair. "Right. Now I need to start carrying lube in my glove box. And maybe some handcuffs, just in case."

I squirmed in my seat but kept my mouth shut for the rest of the drive. Hopefully Nate's little drama was something easily resolved and we could continue with our empty threats in the privacy of my bedroom.

Sadly, that was not the case.

"Cameron McIntyre was just found dead," Nate announced once we arrived home. Heath and Carter were already there, Carter seated on the floor to scratch Lady's belly, and Nate was pacing the living room like he'd been mainlining coffee straight into his veins. "Her body was pulled out of Lake Placid. One of the girls who raised the alarm said she looked badly beaten and had dark bruising around her throat, but my guy in the Prosper PD said they're already listing cause of death as suicide by drowning."

My eyes widened in horror, despite having no idea who Cameron was. I had to assume she was a DB initiate... And from how distraught Nate was, maybe she was an ex-girlfriend?

"Cameron McIntyre?" Royce repeated, sounding nauseated. "That's the girl who took Squirrel's room in the dorms, right?"

Well, fuck. That...was a good reason to panic.

Chapter Forty-One

I'M SO TOTALLY SCREWED. AS IF THE PAST THREE WEEKS WEREN'T BAD
ENOUGH WITH ASHLEY.

AS SOON AS I TOLD EVERYONE ABOUT CAMERON'S SO-CALLED SUICIDE,
I KNEW I'D HAVE TO CONFESS TO THE CAMERAS I HAD SET UP. WHICH IN
TURN WOULD MAKE EVERYONE FEEL LIKE THEIR PRIVACY HAD BEEN INVADED
AND UNDOUBTEDLY CEMENT ASHLEY'S DECISION TO MOVE OUT.

BUT I DON'T WANT HER TO MOVE OUT. I DON'T WANT TO KEEP
FIGHTING WITH HER, BUT I ALSO KNOW IT'S EASIER LIVING WITH HER WHEN I
KNOW SHE HATES ME. WHEN SHE'S SOFT AND KIND, WHEN SHE'S FRIENDLY
OR FLIRTY...THE LINES BLUR TOO MUCH. IT'S BETTER TO KEEP HER ANGRY, SO
I DON'T PUT EITHER OF US IN ANOTHER UNCOMFORTABLE SITUATION.

SO SUE ME. I LIED ABOUT HOW MANY CAMERAS I'D PLACED. I ONLY
FESSED UP TO THE ONE MONITORING THE FRONT DOOR, BECAUSE THAT
FOOTAGE WAS ENOUGH TO PROVE NONE OF US HAD MYSTERIOUSLY
SLEEPWALKED THE NIGHT CAMERON WAS MURDERED.

I SHOULD TAKE THE OTHERS OFFLINE, BUT THIS RECENT DEVELOPMENT
MAKES ME THINK WE STILL NEED THEM.

FOR SAFETY.

N. ESSEX, MARCH 8

A loud crash followed by a groan of pain made me rush from my bathroom dripping wet and wrapped in just a towel a few days after the news of Cameron's death broke. Panicked images of Heath hanging from the ceiling fan filled my head as I raced to the living room, only to find Carter rolling around on the kitchen floor, holding his thigh in pain.

"What happened?" I exclaimed, glancing around to see a chair knocked over and a box of lightbulbs on the counter. "Did you…did you just nearly kill yourself trying to change a lightbulb, Sir Carter?"

His answer was just another pained groan. "I think I pulled a muscle," he admitted pitifully. "The chair slipped while I had one foot up on the counter, and I think I just did the splits. My body isn't made to do the splits, Spark. It hurt."

Giggles erupted from me as I tucked my towel under my arms, then offered him a hand to help him up. "Come on, handyman Bass. I'll massage it out for you. Go lie on the sofa. I'll grab some oil and put some clothes on."

"Or you could skip the clothes. Nate just left for the gym." He waggled his eyebrows, then winced as he tried to put weight on his leg. "Ow, holy shit."

Laughing, I pushed him toward the couch and went to grab my oils from my room. I started to pull out some clothes but then realized he made a good point: Nate wasn't home, Heath was on a therapy call, and Royce was at class. So I just threw on a short satin robe and made my way back out to where Carter was tugging off his T-shirt.

He'd already put Lady outside, and she was happily chewing on a pig's ear, so I placed my bottle of oil down on the coffee table and smacked his muscular ass. "Take these off, Sir Carter. If you've pulled a muscle, I need to get into your glutes."

"Yes, ma'am," he purred, dropping his boxer briefs and kicking them aside, sitting down bare-assed on the leather couch. "How do you want me?"

I couldn't have wiped the smile from my face if I'd tried. "Lie down." Could I have worked on his hamstrings and glutes with his underwear still on? Sure. But why rob myself of the joy of his naked body when there was no need for modesty? "Ass up, baby girl." I couldn't help myself.

He snort-laughed. "Like this?" He stretched out on his belly and jokingly arched his back to stick his rear in the air, making me chuckle.

"You don't seem injured, Sir Carter," I teased, pouring some oil out into my palm and rubbing them together before laying my hands on his thigh. "Are you sure that wasn't just an excuse to get naked?"

"Like I need an excuse," he retorted, then groaned with pain as my fingers dug into his sore muscle. "Ow. Holy shit, Spark."

I smiled to myself. "Shush. Let me sort out this kink and then we can work on some other kinks."

"Fuck," he wheezed. "Now I'm hard and in pain. You're a cruel woman."

I hummed my agreement but focused on massaging his upper thigh where he'd probably pulled something during his impromptu splits. "It's been a while since you've mentioned how things are going with your mother," I said softly, after some time working on his leg. To give him a reprieve, I switched to his other thigh. "Is she still threatening to have me framed for murder?"

He grunted as my fingers dug into his other hamstring. "No. But only because she's friends with Jade's mother, who has been keeping her fully up-to-date on all the Nevaeh gossip."

"So she's only backed off because I'm supposedly with Nate," I murmured.

"For now," he admitted. "But I'm working with Royce's uncle to build a stalemate against her. Bind her hands, so to speak, so she won't risk pissing me off and losing everything she's built up since my father passed."

I frowned, trying to remember what Royce had told me of his uncle. All I knew was that he'd helped Katie forge a relationship with her son from behind bars. "Is he a private investigator?"

"No, he's a U.S. attorney."

"Oh, I had no idea. That's helpful."

Carter rumbled a small laugh. "Very helpful. He fucking hates my mom too. Actually, he hates anyone associated with the DBS but especially our parents' generation, since they were all involved in what happened to Katie."

"That makes sense," I murmured. "Roll over; I need to get your quads."

I'd slipped into work mode but quickly snapped right back out of it when he rolled over and presented me with his thick, hard erection lying against his tattooed abs. "Oh," I said aloud, blinking like an owl.

"I'm actually feeling tense in a different muscle," he told me with a smirk, wrapping his hand around the base of his shaft. "Any chance you can rub this one?"

I rolled my eyes and groaned at the cheesy line. "What's with you guys and thinking I give out happy endings with my massages, huh?"

He pursed his lips, clearly trying to work out whether he could convince me without inadvertently insulting me. "So…no?"

"I didn't say that." I tugged the tie on my robe and let the slippery fabric drop to the floor, leaving me naked. "If your leg cramps—"

"It won't." He cut me off, eagerly pulling me onto the couch so my knees straddled his hips. "It's so much better already. You have magic hands, Spark."

I narrowed my eyes, even as I braced my oil-slippery hands on his chest. "But if it does—"

"It won't," he insisted, already lining himself up with my center. "Fuck, you're already so wet. Spark, you were totally thinking dirty thoughts about my body that whole time."

I sank down onto him slowly, groaning as his thick girth stretched me out and sent shivers of intoxicating desire zapping through me. "Yeah," I agreed, "you've got a nice body, Sir Carter. I think dirty thoughts about it a lot."

"Fuck," he whispered in a husky voice as my pelvis met his, my body swallowing him whole. "You're perfect, Spark." Then he grabbed my waist and flipped us over in one smooth motion without withdrawing even an inch.

With my back against the couch and my legs around his waist, he thrust deeply a couple of times, and my hips arched up to meet him. "You're not injured at all," I complained with a breathy moan as he fucked that huge cock into my pussy. "You big faker."

He chuckled, kissing my throat as he drilled me with fast thrusts. "Maybe I'm just willing to endure any level of pain to hear those sweet moans and whimpers from you."

"Whoa," Heath said, making us freeze. I tilted my head back and locked eyes with him from upside down. "I didn't realize you guys were home. Did you...want privacy, or...?"

He was shirtless, in just a pair of loose shorts, hair damp like he'd just gotten out of the shower after his therapy appointment. I licked my lips, debating the options, because, on the one hand, Carter wasn't the most team player of my boyfriends, but on the other hand...

"I mean, this is the common living space," I replied with a teasing grin. "If we wanted privacy, then we should have taken it to my room. Right, Sir Carter?"

He grumbled something about playing dirty with nicknames, but he didn't disagree.

"Hmm, I dunno," Heath pondered aloud. "That doesn't sound like an enthusiastic invitation from Sir Greedy Pants. Maybe I'll just sit over here and catch up on current affairs." He dropped into the armchair beside the sofa we occupied and flicked on the huge TV. His eyes were not on the screen, though.

Carter's hips rocked a few times, thrusting shallowly as he seemed to think it over. "Do you want Heath to join in?" he asked in a husky whisper, his question for me and me only. "Do you want us both to fuck you at the same time?"

My pulse thumped so hard, I was sure he could feel it against his lips on my throat. "Yes," I admitted without any hesitation. "I really, really do. But only if you're okay with it."

"I am," Heath offered, his hand inside his shorts despite his claim to be watching the news. "If anyone was curious. I'm okay with three-ways. Just ask Royce."

Carter groaned, his teeth sinking into my nipple for a moment. "Fine," he growled. "But Heath has to wipe down the leather before Nate gets home."

"Deal," we both replied.

In seconds Heath had kicked his shorts across the room, and the two of them manhandled me until they had me right where they wanted me.

Heath groaned as I sank down onto his huge dick, my tits in his face as his head rested on the back of the sofa. "See, Ashes," he murmured, cupping my breasts in his hands as I rose and fell a couple of times to work him in deeper, "if you didn't live with us, how could we do this in the middle of the day?"

They'd all been giving me no end of grief after Royce told them what I'd been doing with Carly the other day. Apparently they were taking every opportunity to show me the benefits of our current arrangement…and this was definitely one of them.

"This oil is safe to use, right?" Carter asked, holding up my massage oil just a moment before I realized what he meant.

Almost panting with excitement, I nodded. "Yeah. It is."

"Good," he murmured, then drizzled a heavy amount down my crack. "What was it you said to me before?"

Nervous laughter bubbled out of me as I leaned deeper into Heath, mentally preparing myself for a very unexpected configuration. When Carter had asked if I wanted them to fuck me at the same time, I had just assumed he would be fucking my mouth. But this was also a more than welcome turn of events that I was more than enthusiastically inviting.

Heath waited patiently, his tongue flicking my hard nipple playfully as Carter got himself sorted, taking a few attempts to work out where to put his legs to both balance and reach where he needed to reach, but eventually he worked it out and started the important work of pushing his oil-slicked cock into my tight asshole.

"Fuck," I hissed as he forced the tip inside with a grunt. Heath was far from slim in the trouser-snake department, and it meant that my core was already well occupied regardless of which entry was used. But I, for one, was more than willing to push the limits. What was the saying? Fuck around and find out?

"Breathe, Spark," Carter coaxed, his fingers stroking down my spine as he pushed deeper. "Holy shit, that feels so good."

Heath sucked my nipple into his mouth, teeth teasing me with the edge of pain and causing delicious trembles to erupt through my whole body. I gasped and moaned, trying to rock between the two of them as Carter forged ahead.

He grunted, grasping my hips to hold me still as he made a few thrusts to work the rest of the way in, then pushed me down so that Heath was also completely inside.

I was…just missing Royce now. Shit, maybe I did have issues.

"Please," I panted, so overstimulated I felt like a lit firework with an undetermined length of fuse. "Please…fuck me."

"You heard her," Heath said, his fingers threading into my hair as he pulled my face down to kiss.

Carter hissed as he rocked out and thrust back in experimentally. Then Heath did the same, bucking his hips up from beneath and making me squeal. Then they somehow managed to coordinate their busy schedules and thrust at the same time, which made me scream against Heath's kisses.

"Oh, I liked that noise," Carter admitted. "How many of those can we get before she comes?"

Too many. The answer was too fucking many, and yet at the same time, not enough…

Carter bit my shoulder as he came on the tail of my orgasm, then Heath immediately gasped a curse and blew his load as well.

"What the fuck?" Heath moaned, his face buried in my hair as I turned to jelly between them. "Dude, I fucking felt you coming. That was messed up."

"Bad messed up?" I mumbled with curiosity. "Or good messed up?"

"I don't totally know," he admitted, then started laughing as Carter peeled himself off my back and stood up to stretch.

Just then, the front door clicked open, and I froze, anticipating Nate had caught us fucking on the couch again.

"Oh, come on!" Royce exclaimed instead, and the tension flooded out of me in a wave so intense, it left me lightheaded. "Fuck, you guys, where was my invite? Squirrel, baby, encore?"

"Nah, I'm wrecked," Carter said with a hint of amusement. "I haven't nutted that hard in years. I need a shower and a gallon of water to rehydrate."

Heath chuckled as I slid off his lap. "Fuck, I hear that." He put up his open palm, and Carter slapped it in a crisp high five. "Maybe a nap too?"

Royce glowered, having already pulled off his shirt. "You guys suck."

The two of them chuckled, grabbing their discarded clothes before heading out of the living room. I was slicker than a waterpark from our combined releases but also wasn't that mean…so I slithered off the sofa and onto my knees. "Nah, they don't. But I do."

Royce's brows shot right up, then a huge grin curved his lips. "Fuck, I love you."

Chapter Forty-Two

The guys are more than just friends to me. They're my family. My real family, instead of whatever the fuck my mother plays at during holidays and public appearances. They've always been there for me, no matter what. But never, never in all my years had I actually considered sharing my girl with them.

Until Spark. She's the definition of that name, igniting a fire within me that I hadn't ever thought possible. Melting my ice and softening my brittle edges, while lighting up every goddamn room she enters. Everything good in my life right now is because of her. My Spark.

If I were an outsider looking in, I'd think we'd all lost our minds. But being in it, being in her alongside my best friends? It was pure bliss.

I think, maybe, I regret agreeing with the guys that she'd have to choose between us at the end of the school year. Maybe this thing could actually work? God knows I can't fathom losing any of my

friends, but at the same time, I don't think I'd
survive losing her.

Mar. 8
C. Bassington

My day started off on the wrong foot from the moment my eyes
opened. I was alone in bed—something that very rarely happened these days—and the sheets beside me were cold. While
uncommon, it wasn't unheard of for the guys to get up early and
hit the gym or make breakfast, but I had the whole day off from
both classes and work so had been really looking forward to a
lazy sleep-in.

No one was in the kitchen, and a quick peek into Royce's and
Heath's rooms told me neither of them was home. *Damn.*

With a deflated sigh, I went back to the kitchen and set about
making my own coffee. It wasn't that I was a horny bitch and needed
to get off at least once before coffee... Okay, it wasn't *only* that, but
it was the startling realization that I had grown so accustomed to
never being alone that now I was at a loss for what to do while alone.
And if I was honest, a nagging sense of dread and panic clawed at
my chest at the unknown.

It was dumb. Logically, I could see that I was being a fucking
needy, codependent bitch. Intellectually, I could appreciate the fact
that just a week ago, I'd been looking at apartments to move into
without the guys and therefore would be alone a hell of a lot more
than now.

Logic was a dick.

I sent a text to our group thread, asking where everyone was, just
in case. What if they were in trouble or sleepwalking or needed help?
It was better to seem needy than regret it later.

Their replies pinged almost instantly, and the relief washing through me was so intense, my hands trembled.

"Pull it together, Ashley," I scolded myself as I opened the thread.

CARTER:

> You were fast asleep. I ducked out to get you an almond croissant from the new bakery.

HEATHCLIFF:

> At the gym with Royce, back soon!

ROYCE:

> LOL…ducked out. Good one, Bass. Quack.

CARTER:

> You're such a child. No croissants for you.

I giggled as I read through the thread and swiped away an incoming call from my mom. I loved her, but I was still half-asleep and pre-caffeine. Besides, I was more interested in the text thread promising baked goods.

ASHLEY:

> See if they have an apricot custard danish?

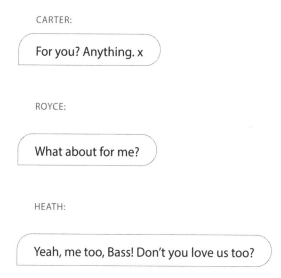

CARTER:

For you? Anything. x

ROYCE:

What about for me?

HEATH:

Yeah, me too, Bass! Don't you love us too?

Carter's response was a middle finger emoji, and I chuckled, then swiped away another incoming call from my mom. She still didn't technically know I was living with the guys, and I'd dodged her questions effectively enough that I also hadn't fessed up to being in a relationship with all three guys.

So yeah, call me crazy, but I had a feeling she would find out sooner or later, and I badly didn't want a safe-sex talk about group sex. Not with my mom. Not when we already suspected her, Max, and my dad had something more than friendship going on when Dad was in town.

Gross.

Footsteps scuffed down the hall, and I glanced up to see Nate sleepily making his way out of his bedroom looking like he was modeling for a pajama brand and the bed hair was really artfully styled.

His phone was in hand, and he yawned as he squinted at the screen.

"If that's my mom calling," I said quickly before he could answer, "I'm not here."

He rolled his eyes and showed me the screen as he drew closer.

It wasn't my mom; it was his dad. That made me frown in concern. Had something happened? I gave him a nod, and he answered the call on speakerphone, placing it on the countertop between us.

"Hey, Dad," he said in a husky, sleep-thickened voice that sent a shiver through me. "What's up?"

"Nate, is Ashley there at the apartment with you? Carina has been trying to call and can't get ahold of her." Max's voice was clipped and tense, but it wasn't an angry or disappointed-parent sort of voice. Instead, he sounded almost scared.

Nate arched his brows at me in question, and I chewed my lower lip. Then I sighed. What's the worst that was going to happen? I suffer an uncomfortable mom lecture and then move on with life?

"Yeah, Max, I'm right here," I said, saving Nate having to lie on my behalf. "Has something happened?"

The relieved exhale he let out worried me more than anything. Locking eyes with Nate, I knew he was thinking the same: Max was worried as hell about something.

"Carina! She's with Nate. It's okay. She's all right, honey. She's with Nate." Max's voice was muffled, like he'd pulled the phone away from his ear, and all of a sudden I could hear my mom crying. Fucking sobbing in the background.

"Max!" I exclaimed. "What's wrong? Why is Mom crying?"

"Ashley, hon, I think it's best if you come to the house so we can speak in person. Is that okay? I don't know if you have class or—"

"I don't." I cut him off. But even if I did, this would be important enough to skip. "I can leave now so will be there in an hour or so. Is that okay?"

More muffled sobs from my mom, sending chills through me and twisting my gut with anxiety. "Y-yeah. Yes, that's good. Nate, you'll bring her?"

"Of course," Nate replied with a firm voice, all traces of sleep gone.

Max breathed another of those intensely worrying sighs. "Okay, that's good. Nate…please keep Ashley safe. Don't let her out of your sight for even a moment."

Nate and I locked eyes, both equally as panicked about whatever the fuck had our parents worked up. "Understood, Dad," Nate confirmed.

"We'll be fine, Max," I tried to assure him. "Please just look after my mom?"

"She's fine, sweetheart," he said in a gruff voice. "She'll be fine once you get here. Then we can…talk."

With that ominous statement, he told us to drive safe, then ended the call. Nate and I just stood there for a moment, staring at each other in shock. Then I glanced down at the borrowed T-shirt I'd tossed on and scrubbed a hand over my face.

"Um, I'll get dressed. Can you text the guys?" I headed for my bedroom, and he trailed behind me, his focus on his phone screen as I assumed he did as I'd asked, texting the guys.

I grabbed some clean clothes out of Carter's drawers, then glanced at Nate, who'd taken up residence on the foot of my bed. Clearly, he was taking Max's orders seriously and not giving me any privacy, but in the current situation, I found it hard to give a damn. Nate was hardly getting turned on by the quick flash of my tits while I put on a bra, so there was no need to get weird and modest for no good reason.

"They'll meet us there," Nate told me once I was dressed. He grabbed a pair of my sneakers from the closet, then nudged me to his room and placed my shoes down beside his bed. I took the hint, sitting down to get them onto my feet while he quickly changed out of his loose pajama pants and into some jeans and a white hoodie.

I kept my focus on tying my laces and absolutely did not sneak a look at his smooth, muscular ass in the process of changing. Denial was also not just a river in Egypt.

"Let's go," he murmured, grabbing his car keys and wallet as I rose to my feet, shivering with paranoia. I hated that Max hadn't just explained himself over the phone, if only to settle our nerves for the drive. Still, if he or Mom were hurt, he would have said so. I believed that. So whatever had happened, it couldn't be so bad that it wouldn't wait an hour.

We took Nate's truck, peeling out of the parking lot with a squeal of tires and speeding through a yellow light. That told me all I needed to know about how worried he was, despite his seemingly calm exterior.

The silence filled the car with dizzying thickness, and I started running worst-case scenarios in my brain. I kept coming back to my dad. Had he been hurt? Killed? He worked a dangerous job, and we knew it was a possibility one day. That uncertainty had been a major contributing factor in their divorce, I was sure of it.

But then why would Mom have been so panicked about where I was? It didn't make sense.

"Hey," Nate said, cutting through my spiraling thoughts as he took my hand in his, threading our fingers together to squeeze mine firmly. "They're okay, Ash. You heard them both on the phone. They're acting weird as hell but they're fine. Just take some deep breaths, all right? We'll be there soon."

I hadn't even registered the fact that I'd started crying until then. With my free hand, I swiped the tears from my cheeks, then tried to calm my breathing. Hyperventilating helped nothing and would only distract Nate from driving.

"I'm okay," I whispered. "Sorry."

He said nothing back but also didn't release my hand for the rest of the drive out to Lake Prosper. When we eventually arrived and he needed his hand back to park, my palm was sweaty but I was a lot calmer.

"Is that a cop?" he asked, frowning at an unfamiliar SUV parked in the driveway.

Alarmed, I eyed the vehicle in question, noting the thicker-than-average radio antenna and suspicious light bar. "Yeah, I think so." Then I frowned, remembering something. "We passed a couple of marked cruisers a minute ago too. What if they came from here?"

He cast me a troubled look, then climbed out of his seat and circled around to open my door before I'd even finished taking my seat belt off.

"Thanks," I murmured on reflex as he offered a hand to help me down from the lifted truck. But then he kept that hand, linking our fingers once more as we headed for the front door.

"Dad?" Nate called out as we stepped through the front door. "Carina? We're here!"

Footsteps echoed against the marble floors, then my mom launched herself at me in a full-body bear hug. She buried her face in my hair, and sobs wracked her petite frame as she mumbled something I absolutely could not make out.

Max was right there behind her, looking like he'd aged ten years, and I sent him a perplexed look as I hugged Mom right back.

"Dad, what's going on?" Nate asked, his fists clenched at his sides after having to release me when Mom pounced. "Is that a cop parked outside?"

Max nodded, running a weary hand over his hair. "Yes. Come inside, kids. We'll explain. Carina, honey, let Ashley go now. You're scaring her."

Mom peeled herself away, sniffling. "Sorry, I'm sorry, I didn't mean to... Ashley Layne, why on earth weren't you answering your phone? Do you have any idea how scared I've been?"

My jaw flapped a couple of times in shock at the sharp left turn into anger she'd just taken. "No," I replied. "I don't know because I have no idea what is going on!"

"Living room," Max said firmly, giving us a push to clear out of the foyer. Frustrated and confused, I sat my butt right on the edge of the sofa, and Nate sat beside me, close enough to touch.

"Ashley, when were you planning on telling us that you moved out of the Nevaeh dorms?" Mom snapped, folding her arms as she stood in front of the coffee table opposite us. "I have to assume you've moved in with one of your boyfriends, but that's a huge life step and something you should have told us!"

Wait, what? "I'm…confused. This reaction is just because I'm living with the guys and forgot to tell you? Mom, I'm twenty-one. I don't actually have to clear these decisions with you."

Mom's eyes widened, and she paled. It wasn't a good expression. It was the kind of face I'd only seen a handful of times in my life, but it came right before a massively excessive punishment. Like the time she found out I'd been caught giving my high school boyfriend a blow job during school hours and grounded me for two months.

"Carina," Max interjected. "Ashley needs context, love. She deserves context." He gave Mom a hard look, then softened his gaze as he turned to me. "Ash, your mom is just lashing out because she's scared. What do you know about the girl who moved into your dorm room? Cameron McIntyre?"

Dread pooled in my gut, and I glanced at Nate nervously. "Um, I know she died a couple of days ago," I admitted in a quiet, cautious voice. "I believe it was ruled a suicide."

Mom let out a loud scoff, throwing up her hands, but Max held up his hand to silently calm her. Or at least tell her to shut the hell up for a minute. I appreciated his involvement.

"We believe Miss McIntyre was murdered, Ashley," Max said softly, picking up a sheet of paper from the coffee table where it had been sitting face down. "We have reason to believe someone intends to hurt you, sweetheart, and Miss McIntyre was a message."

Well, fuck. Words failed me entirely. I turned my face to Nate, meeting his eyes with what I'm sure was a deer-in-headlights sort of expression.

"Why would you think that?" he asked smoothly, his hand resting on the small of my back in silent reassurance. For better or worse, we were in this together.

Max looked really uneasy, then flipped over the page and handed it to us. It was a photocopy of a handwritten note, and I gasped so hard I nearly choked.

Watch your back... You're next.

"This note was pinned to our door, along with a report that stated a female student in her early twenties from Nevaeh was found drowned in Lake Placid. And your room number was scrawled on the report." Max shook his head slowly, his brow creased in concern. "We thought this was you, sweetheart. We thought you'd been killed by..." He trailed off, glancing over his shoulder to my mom.

She was crying again, tears tracking from her puffy, red eyes, but she nodded firmly. "Tell them," she croaked. "They need to know."

"Killed by who?" Nate pushed, equally as alarmed as I was.

Mom sniffed hard, trying to pull herself together. "My stalker," she said. "I'm being stalked and threatened, and it's recently started to escalate. We think you're now being targeted, Ash."

What the fuck?

I exchanged another panicked glance with Nate, then looked at the photocopied note again and shook my head. "I don't understand. How did you know Abigail?" Because that note was in her handwriting—I'd know it anywhere.

Mom and Max now looked just as confused as I felt. "Who's Abigail?"

Chapter Forty-Three

0530: FOR ONCE, I'M NOT THE FIRST ONE AWAKE. HEATH'S ALREADY IN THE SHOWER AND ASHLEY SEEMS TO BE IN THE HALF-ASLEEP DAZE OF SOMEONE WHO SLEPT LIKE CRAP. I GET IT, SINCE I WAS ALSO PLAGUED BY NIGHTMARES AFTER EVERYTHING THAT WENT DOWN WITH MAX AND CARINA YESTERDAY.

CARINA HAS BEEN DEALING WITH A STALKER FOR YEARS. NEARLY A DECADE. AND SHE NEVER TOLD ASHLEY ABOUT IT, WHICH EVERYONE COULD SEE KNOCKED SQUIRREL AROUND.

IT'S ALL SO CONFUSING. WHAT DID THE HYPNOSIS AND DR. FOX HAVE TO DO WITH CARINA'S STALKER? WAS IT ALL A COINCIDENCE? WE NEED TO FIGURE IT OUT, OR WE'LL ALL END UP LOSING OUR SANITY ALONG THE WAY.

R. D'ARENBERG, MARCH 9

We all stayed the night at Max and Mom's house after going over the information a dozen times. We couldn't tell them everything—we couldn't admit that Heath had accidentally murdered Dr. Fox or that we'd covered up the crime with arson and a staged break-in. We certainly couldn't tell them that Carter nearly raped and killed me under the influence of hypnosis.

One thing I was absolutely certain of was that the handwriting on Mom's note matched Abigail's diary. But I didn't have the diary anymore, so all I could offer was my firm confidence in my memory of the cursive scrawl.

I could see Mom didn't believe me. Or maybe just that she suspected I was simply remembering wrong…and maybe I was. Memories were weird like that. But when I woke up the next morning, I just had a gut feeling that someone else might verify my claims.

"Katie's been in prison for twenty-four years," Nate said with a heavy sigh as we drove up the freeway toward Hastings. "Dr. Fox wasn't even teaching at Nevaeh when she was a student, and Abigail wasn't born yet. I don't see how this can help."

"I'm with Nate on this one, Squirrel," Royce admitted from the back seat, where he was sandwiched between Carter and Heath. "As sure as I am that she got tangled up in some hypnosis crap, there's no way to prove it."

I threw my hands up in exasperation. "Okay, but *how* did she get involved in hypnosis? She was in the Devil's Backbone, right? So are we. There's got to be a connection, and she's literally the only person I can think of that might give us honesty. Your dad seems oblivious, Nate, and—"

"Well, yeah, because we gave him nothing to work with. Maybe if he knew more, then—"

"Then he'd be totally okay with the fact we are all accomplices to murder ourselves?" I snapped, cutting him off. "No. He wouldn't, and neither would my mom. At least Katie can't judge us." Not that we could go confessing to shit while visiting her in maximum security prison.

Everyone was quiet for a moment, and I chewed the edge of my lip nervously. The anxious twist to my gut hadn't let up since the moment I'd heard Mom crying on the phone and only seemed to be getting worse.

"This is bigger than just Dr. Fox," I said after a while. "Maybe Katie can't give us anything useful, but maybe she can. It's worth trying."

"I agree," Heath offered. "Your gut is pushing this, and I trust your instincts, Ashes."

"I guess worst-case scenario, Royce gets to introduce you as his actual girlfriend and we go for some of those excellent burgers," Carter added thoughtfully. It made me realize that they'd all probably done the trip to Hastings with Royce plenty of times before. They really were good friends to one another.

Nate was quiet, his jaw clenched and his knuckles white on the steering wheel, but I didn't push the issue. We were all tightly wound right now, and the last thing we needed was a three-hour drive filled with bickering.

Thankfully, the conversation in the back seat shifted to sports, which then somehow circled around to the Nevaeh women's basketball team and how Jess was doing in recovery after being hit by a car. She had a long recovery ahead, but by some miracle, Zara—the passenger in the car—was doing well. She'd transferred to a different university for next semester, which wasn't surprising.

"Are we all coming in?" Heath asked when we arrived at the prison just ten minutes before visiting hours started. We'd parked in the half-empty lot and all got out. "Is that allowed?"

Royce shook his head. "Three people maximum, remember?"

Nate tossed Heath his keys. "Go for a drive if you want, but for fuck's sake, don't hit a deer." He grabbed my hand in his and started striding for the entrance without any hesitation or question about who the three people visiting Katie would be.

"You need to stop manhandling me, Essex," I muttered when we approached the foyer.

He glanced down at me, the very corner of his mouth curving up.

"Do I, though?" As if to emphasize his point, he squeezed my fingers and directed us toward the reception counter with Royce taking the lead to get us checked in.

We all handed over our IDs and patiently submitted to the metal detectors and various checks before being led through into the same visiting room Royce and I had met Katie in last time. It was a lot quieter than when we'd last experienced it, and I suspected that was thanks to it being a weekday.

After being directed to some seats, we waited while a guard fetched Royce's mom, my foot bouncing anxiously until Royce clamped a firm hand on my knee.

"Breathe, Squirrel," he murmured, his frown full of concern. "You're going to send yourself into a panic attack at this rate."

I hadn't even noticed I was panicking, but now that he pointed it out…yeah, okay, I needed to chill the fuck out. I had enough time to take a few slower breaths before Katie was led into the room by a bored-looking guard and her handcuffs attached to the table as before.

"Twice in one month. This is unexpected," she said by way of greeting with a smile on her lips. "Hello, Nathaniel, lovely to see you. And you again, Ashley. What's going on?"

Clearly, she was sharp enough to know we hadn't made the drive simply to visit for visiting's sake. A small wrinkle bunched her brow as she eyed the three of us in concern and focused her attention on her son.

"We have some sort of confusing questions we want to ask," Royce admitted with a grimace. "Um, I guess first things first, do you recognize this handwriting?" He pulled out the photocopy of Mom's threatening note and flattened it on the table for Katie to see.

Katie peered at it, frowning as she inspected the paper. Then she sighed and shrugged. "It's just a messy scrawl. It could be anyone's. It looks vaguely familiar, yes, but probably because most people my generation have a messy scrawl. This note seems sort of threatening, though, or maybe a warning? Where's it from?"

I jerked my gaze to Nate in surprise. "Could it be a warning? We hadn't considered that."

"Ashley, honey, is someone threatening you?" Katie's frown was deeper than ever. Somehow, despite never actually raising her son, she was more maternal than some other moms I'd met. "If you need help—"

"I'm okay," I quickly replied, not totally believing that statement anymore. "But we just wanted to run a few ideas past you. If that's okay? Only because we feel like there have been a few things happening recently that seem way too coincidental with how you ended up in here and maybe... I dunno. Maybe they're not just coincidental?"

Katie blinked a couple of times, then nodded. "Anything I can do to help. I'm an open book. What things are we talking about?"

I chewed the edge of my lip, nervous as hell, but Royce saved me by answering himself. "Hypnosis things," he muttered, only just loud enough for his mom to suck in a sharp breath. "And it seems to be tied to the society somehow."

Katie wet her lips, shifting in her seat. "I see."

"Also we wanted to ask if the name Hyperion means anything to you?" Nate added, surprising me. I'd almost forgotten all about that breadcrumb we'd found in Dr. Fox's office.

"Hyperion," Katie repeated, looking thoughtful. "It seems familiar. Let me mull that over while you tell me more about this hypnosis stuff."

"We sound insane, don't we?" I whispered, my face heating with embarrassment. "I swear we aren't. Things have been happening..."

"You don't sound insane, Ashley," Katie said with a serious set to her lips. "I know you need to remain vague, but has anyone been hurt?"

I glanced at Royce, and he gave his mom a silent nod.

Katie exhaled heavily, her shoulders sagging. "Okay. Um, Nathaniel, would you mind terribly if I spoke with Royce and Ashley alone?"

Nate stiffened in surprise, his fingers squeezing mine where he had grabbed my hand under the table. "Why?"

Royce shook his head. "Mom, this concerns him too. All of us, actually. There was an accident at Nevaeh recently. One of the society members drove into a bunch of students, then crashed into a wall. It killed him and injured several others, but his girlfriend said he was in a trance. Like he had no control of his own actions." He was offering evidence that couldn't incriminate us, but I could see Katie wasn't convinced. Her sad eyes darted to Nate again, and her lips tightened.

Nate huffed a sigh. "I'll go," he muttered. "If that's what it takes to get answers." He released my hand and stalked back out of the visiting room with stiff posture, the tension basically radiating off him.

Once he was gone, I turned to Katie in confusion. "Why?"

She gave a troubled sort of smile. "Because it's not the sort of thing I feel he wants or needs to hear, honey. I mentioned last time you were here that Michael and I didn't really know one another all that well before I got pregnant? Well, that wasn't strictly true. Sorry, Royce baby, close your ears. Mike and I had been casually dating for a few months. Nothing serious, and his family would never have approved of him dating a scholarship student, but I did have genuine feelings for him. I believe he felt the same. He certainly confided a lot in me. About his life, his family, his friends…"

Royce rubbed at his brow, shaking his head. "I don't get it. What's this got to do with Nate?"

Katie huffed. "Mike and Max were best friends. Them, Rhys Briggs, and Edward Bassington. I suspect they still are?"

Royce and I exchanged a look. "Yeah, except Carter's dad died when he was eight."

Katie blinked a few times, like she hadn't known that fact. Then she shook it off. "Well, Mike used to confide in me a lot. One of the hot topics back then was Max and his girlfriend, Jocelyn."

323

A chill ran down my spine at the mention of Nate's bitch mother. "What about them?"

"Jocelyn was a ladder climber of the worst kind. She came from money herself, but it just wasn't enough. Neither was her relationship with Max, and she was forever trying to snag Mike for herself as well—except of course, he was secretly seeing me." She was trying to walk us to whatever point she was trying to make, but my mind was already whirling like a tornado as I processed the information.

Royce seemed just as frustrated and impatient. "What does that have to do with anything?"

Katie pursed her lips, seeming to debate whether to continue for a moment. "Jocelyn's father worked for the military on a project called Hyperion. I remember it because Mike suspected she was using her father's military connections to conduct research on her own master's thesis."

Oh fuck. I felt like I was going to vomit.

"What, um, what was her thesis about?" I croaked, my head already swimming as all the blood drained to my feet.

Katie grimaced. "I think you already guessed, Ashley. Jocelyn was deeply involved in exploring the limitations and uses of hypnosis."

Fuck a goddamn duck. I should have seen that coming.

Chapter Forty-Four

March 9

None of us wanted to believe what Katie told Royce and Ashley. Nate obviously rebelled against the suggestion that his mom was somehow involved in all the hypnosis, but so did Carter and J. Sure, she wasn't the warmest mother on earth, but she wasn't evil. We'd all known her our whole lives, and aside from being fairly absent since the divorce, she still loves Nate. No way in hell is she fucking around inside our heads and literally killing people just for giggles.

We all know her. She's not a murderer.

Then again, I'd like to say the same about myself and unfortunately it simply isn't true anymore.

Shit. Maybe it is impossible to truly know a person...

H. Briggs

It'd been two weeks since our visit with Katie and her shocking revelations about Jocelyn. Nate had been understandably horrified when we relayed the information and lashed out. As harsh as he was in his insults, it was painfully clear that, underneath it all, he was scared and hurt. So I bit my tongue and, for once, didn't bark back.

He needed time to process the information. We all did. But while I thought we would all think it over and see that, yes, Jocelyn was a very valid suspect...the guys all seemed to dismiss the idea as being far-fetched and illogical after very little reflection at all.

It led to a lot of arguments, and I hated that. Everyone was walking on eggshells by the time I broached the idea of me moving into my own place again.

I wasn't sneaky about it, but Carter lost his shit and got into a fight with Royce. It escalated until Heath and Nate were dragged into it, leaving me to abandon the idea entirely, purely out of fear they were actively going to come to blows. The strain in the apartment seemed to escalate after that, with Heath withdrawing, Royce always on the edge of irritation though he tried to hide it, and Carter? Carter either wanted to fuck it out or just storm off to the gym. Apparently talking wasn't something anyone wanted.

Not even me.

So when Nate handed me an invitation to his birthday party over coffee one morning, I was left gaping after him—particularly when he added, "No excuses, Ash. You need to be there."

No excuses. I hadn't been making excuses to Mom or Max since they'd confessed to Mom's stalker or whatever they were. The person who'd harassed her for years. I had called Dad because I wanted to know what he knew, but he was out in the field, so all I could do was leave him a message.

Somehow I was utterly unsurprised to discover Nate's birthday was another extravagant party hosted at a lavish mansion in Prosper Heights. Carter had once again provided me with one of his mother's obscenely expensive—and stunning—dresses, but this time it was a full-skirted cocktail dress in pristine white with the one shoulder strap creating a huge bow.

"No red tonight?" I joked as he zipped me into the luxurious garment.

He gave a gruff moan. "I wish. It's a black-and-white party, and since it's Nate's birthday, I figured we should play along. You look amazing in everything. I'm just biased toward red."

"Do you guys always have these huge parties for your birthdays? I feel like the last real birthday party I had was when I was nine. Some girls from school came over for a sleepover, and Mom made us all cute little tent beds in the living room." I smiled at the fond memory as Carter brushed a kiss over my bare shoulder.

He laughed softly, his breath warm on my skin as I turned to face him. He was still shirtless, and when he raised a hand to fix a loose curl in my hair, the scarring on his forearm caught my gaze. Snatching his wrist in my grip, I kissed the inside of his wrist, right over the *k* of Spark.

It'd healed cleanly—thank goodness—but the scarring wouldn't fade anytime soon.

"You're still insane, you know that?" I murmured, then traced the letters with the tip of my tongue. I'd done it dozens of times before, and it always elicited the same reaction from Carter—heavy eyes, quickened breathing…usually followed by him tossing me over his shoulder or onto the bed or against a wall or…

"I know," he replied with a sexy smirk. "Still in love too."

Fuck. Same.

He groaned a little as he reluctantly pulled his arm out of my grip, forcing himself to grab his shirt from the hanger to finish dressing. "But no, to answer your question, we don't do birthday parties every year. This is just because Nate is turning twenty-five."

I dragged my eyes away from his toned, tattooed flesh and checked my makeup in the mirror instead. My lipstick had smudged ever so slightly so needed fixing. "Is twenty-five a big deal? Does he come into his magical powers and shift into a dragon or something?"

Carter scoffed. "Have you been reading Royce's romance books again?"

I shrugged, because yes. They were really good and giving me a weird sense of comfort in our unusual relationship dynamic.

"Twenty-five is typically when we rich kids get access to our inheritances, unless the older generations are particularly strict or old-fashioned and add additional clauses to the trust requirements. Nate's grandparents weren't dickheads, so he just has to be twenty-five to inherit an obscene amount of wealth."

"I'm guessing your family falls into the dickhead category?" I asked with a grin, because his mom wanted to frame me for murder. Clearly she was a dickhead of the highest degree.

Carter smiled back, buttoning his black shirt. "Yes. Very firmly. So does Royce's, for that matter. I definitely wouldn't expect any sort of party for his twenty-fifth in June."

"Are you guys talking about me?" Royce asked, letting himself into the bedroom with a drink already in hand. We were getting ready in one of the bedrooms of the rented mansion and intended to stay the night after the party, so no one needed to drive. I'd insisted Nate take the master suite, since it was his birthday, and found a bedroom on a whole different floor for the rest of us, so he didn't need to hear us getting down and dirty later.

"Always," Carter drawled. "We can't stop talking about you, Roycey baby. You're just so darn interesting."

Royce shrugged. "Seems legit. I'd believe it." Then he swept his gaze over my short dress and high heels. "Damn, Squirrel, you look like a fucking present waiting to be unwrapped."

I glanced down at the giant bow and wrinkled my nose. "Good point. I hadn't thought of that."

"I'm okay with it," he quickly added. "It just means I'll be thinking about unwrapping you later."

Carter shot me a dark look that said he fully intended to beat

Royce to it, and I bit back a smile at their competitiveness. It was all in good nature these days.

"Help me with this," Carter murmured to Royce, gesturing to his black silk tie. He'd gone the full black route on his outfit, as had Royce. From what I'd seen of Heath earlier, he was in a black suit with white shirt and tie. I wondered if Nate was in all white. God, then we'd look like we'd dressed to match.

Royce fussed with Carter's tie, making sure it was sitting perfectly before picking his drink up once more and offering me his arm. "Shall we, Squirrel?"

I tucked my hand through his and let him lead the way out of the bedroom. The party had already started downstairs about half an hour ago, but Carter had delayed me in the bathroom, fucking me over the vanity when I was meant to be doing my makeup.

Heath and Nate were easy to find, lurking near the bottom of the stairs like they were waiting for something. They both looked incredible in their suits, but rather than being in all white, Nate had gone with a black shirt and pants with a white velvet jacket. It was a good look for him.

"Finally," Heath teased as we reached them. "We were taking bets on how long you guys would be after Royce disappeared up there to find you."

I grinned, resisting the urge to kiss him. We'd massively dialed down the PDA in public since I was still Nate's fake fiancée—something Mom had been more and more suspicious about recently despite my continued assurances it wasn't real.

"Happy birthday, Essex," I said instead, offering him a polite friend hug. He leaned into it, his hand on the small of my back. I had his birthday present clutched in my hand, and as anxious as I was to get it over and done with, I asked, "Can we talk for a moment in private?"

He raised a brow in question as he drew away from my hug, then glanced to the small, gift-wrapped box in my hand. "Sure. Heath, sort us out some cocktails? We'll just be a minute."

Ignoring the guys' curious glances—because I hadn't discussed this gift idea with any of them—I let Nate lead me away and through the main living area, where dozens of sharply suited guests already stood around drinking, chatting, laughing, generally enjoying the party. More than just college students too—I recognized several older guests from the last Devil's Backbone party.

"In here," Nate murmured, ushering me into a bedroom just off the main living areas. A glance around said it was the room being used for gifts, with stacks of professionally wrapped boxes lining the floor. "Is this private enough?"

He closed the door behind himself, and I drew a deep breath as I crossed to the foot of the bed and sat down, mainly so I wouldn't pace nervously. "Yeah, this is fine. Sorry, I meant to find the time to speak with you before the party but, um, got distracted."

"I heard," he muttered, almost under his breath, and my face flamed. I really, really needed to learn how to shut the fuck up during sex. "It's fine. I also wanted to discuss something with you tonight."

My brows rose in surprise as he pulled a thick fold of papers from the inside of his jacket pocket but didn't make any moves to hand them to me. Odd. He seemed...nervous.

That made two of us.

"Okay, I'll go first," I offered with a weak smile. "Firstly, I wanted to apologize for the last few weeks. After we met with Katie...I'm sorry for accusing your mom of being some kind of deranged psychopathic puppeteer. Loads of people have studied mental manipulations in the academic sphere. That alone isn't evidence enough."

Nate sighed and came to sit beside me. Not so close to be uncomfortable but close enough that we could speak a little more intimately, not yell apologies across a chasm of space.

"I appreciate your apology, Layne, but it's not necessary. You haven't had a great first impression of my mom, and with the shit that's happened, it's entirely understandable you'd be suspicious. But at the end of the day, she's my mom. She would never hurt me, and whoever is doing all this? They don't care who is hurt. Just look at Heath."

I nodded silently because it was the same discussion we'd all been having since speaking with Katie. The guys all just wanted me to trust that they knew Jocelyn well enough to know if she was a murderer. I wasn't going to argue with Nate on his birthday, though.

"Well, hmm." It was the best I could give, because although I was sorry for being an asshole, I still thought Jocelyn was fishy as hell. "Anyway, I had a really hard time trying to think what I could get you for your birthday since you have everything you could possibly want already."

Nate gave a short laugh with a bitter edge to it. "Not everything."

I rolled my eyes with a touch of frustration, figuring he was probably dreaming of some obscure one-of-a-kind yacht or something. "Okay, well, I can't afford to get you anything you can't already get for yourself, so I just…" I trailed off, majorly second-guessing my choices. "Fuck. Okay, look. My best idea for a birthday gift was to move out of your apartment and give your space back. But you saw how that discussion went the other day."

This time his laugh held more warmth. "Yeah, I think you and I both need to accept the fact you're never leaving."

"Well, this was the only other thing I could think of." Before I could lose my nerve, I handed over the small gift box I'd been holding on to. "Technically it's a gift from my mom too."

Max and Carina weren't attending the party tonight, as Max had been called away on some urgent business in New York and Mom had gone with him. Probably for the best, so we didn't have to be on our best behavior in front of our parents.

Nate gave me a curious look, setting aside his folded papers to open the gift. "Oh, it's a watch?"

Embarrassment flooded through me at his confused expression, but I forged ahead nonetheless. "It's… I mean, yes. It's a watch. But obviously not like the watches you guys wear, so don't feel like you have to ever take it out of the case or anything, but it was my grand-father's watch. Um, Mom's dad, I mean. He used to say it was his lucky charm and that all the best things in his life happened while he was wearing that watch. He wanted to pass it down to his grandson, but I was it for Mom. Until she met Max."

Nate was silent for the most intensely heavy moment, staring at the old-fashioned watch in its wooden case. When he looked up at me, his eyes were shiny.

"Thank you," he whispered, shaking his head slightly in disbelief. "This is… No one has ever given me something so thoughtful."

I shrugged, super uncomfortable now. "You're welcome. Carter said twenty-five is a big deal for you upper-class fucks, so I figured a new Xbox game just wouldn't cut it as a gift."

A chuckle escaped him as he looked back at the watch in dis-belief. Then he unclipped the white-gold Patek Philippe watch he wore and swapped it for my grandfather's Omega Seamaster.

"You don't have to wear it," I insisted again, with a small laugh to see his obscenely expensive timepiece tossed aside.

He looked up at me from tightening the strap. "Yes. I do. I want to see if your grandfather's luck is still lingering." The intensity of his gaze as he said that sent a shiver over my skin, and my mouth went dry.

"What, um, what do you mean?"

It was a dumb question. I'd know that look in his eyes anywhere. It was the same that night after Napa Valley, right before he'd kissed me. He was so drunk then, I'd pushed him away because he wasn't in control of his actions. But he seemed totally sober now.

Oh shit. Was Nate going to kiss me?

Oh shit! Did I want him to?

Chapter Forty-Five

I'M WORRIED ABOUT ASHLEY. WE ALL ARE. SINCE CARINA ADMITTED TO
HAVING A STALKER—POSSIBLY THE SAME AS WHOEVER WAS MASQUERADING
AS ABIGAIL—SHE'S BECOME INCREASINGLY OBSESSED AND PARANOID. KATIE'S
SUGGESTION THAT MY MOM HAD ANYTHING TO DO WITH THE HYPNOSIS
ONLY MADE EVERYTHING TEN TIMES WORSE.

SHE'S NOT GOING TO LET IT GO. THAT MUCH HAS BECOME PAINFULLY
CLEAR. ASHLEY WILL DIG AND DIG AND DIG...UNTIL SOMEONE ELSE WINDS
UP DEAD. I'M SO SCARED IT WILL BE HER NEXT TIME. IF DR. FOX COULD PUSH
HEATH TO ATTEMPT SUICIDE ON THE MERE SUSPICION HE WAS BREAKING
THE MANIPULATIONS, WE ARE ALL TERRIFIED OF WHAT THE FUTURE MIGHT
HOLD FOR ASHLEY IF SHE DOESN'T STEP BACK A BIT.

SOMETHING'S ABOUT TO BREAK, AND I'M STARTING TO THINK HER
HEART IS THE SAFEST OPTION. AT LEAST THAT COULD BE REPAIRED...ONE
DAY. BY SOMEONE MORE DESERVING THAN US.

N. ESSEX, MARCH 10

Nate leaned in but stopped just short of kissing me as he inhaled a sharp breath. His eyes closed, his brow was drawn with tension. Clearly, we were at a crossroads.

"Layne," he murmured softly, "I wish—"

I cut him off by closing that gap between us and crushing my lips to his. Sure, he might shove me away and make another disparaging comment about my revolving door, or maybe…

"Fuck," he groaned against my lips, and then all of a sudden, his hands were in my hair and his tongue was in my mouth as he dragged me into his lap. My knees straddled his waist, my short skirt bunched up as he pulled me closer.

It was like we were made for each other, our mouths moving in perfect synchronicity and our bodies melting into one another as his hands shifted from my hair down to my thigh, then up to grasp my ass in two firm handfuls.

A little moan escaped me as his fingers dug into my flesh, pulling me closer still as his hardness swelled beneath my crotch. Without even consciously thinking about it, I found my hips grinding down on him like I wanted the clothes to evaporate.

One of his hands shifted from my butt to my core, stroking me through the thin fabric of my panties. I shivered with desire and he groaned against my kisses. No question he could feel how soaking my underwear already was, and just a bare moment later, his finger teased the edge of the elastic and slipped beneath to touch my flesh.

"Holy shit, Ash," he murmured as I tossed my head back, my spine arching at the intense pleasure his touch sparked. I'd very quietly been wanting him to touch me like that for way too fucking long. Way longer than I would ever admit. His teeth scraped the skin of my throat as he touched me more forcefully, pushing my panties aside to get better access as his finger delved into my pussy.

A low groan rolled through him as he pushed his finger deeper, and a shudder ran through my whole body. "Fuck," he gasped, adding a second finger as I gripped his tie with my fist and held on tight as my hips rocked on his thrusting digits. "Oh my god. Yes, like that. Fuck my hand, Layne."

Helpless to do anything other than exactly that, I yanked hard on his tie and claimed his mouth with mine once more as I chased down my unexpected but very welcome climax. It wasn't difficult. The intoxicating scent of Nate filled my senses as his expert tongue branded his kisses on my soul in a way that could never be erased.

When I came, it wasn't a screaming, dramatic affair. It was clenching, whimpering, and shared breathing as the heady sensation of euphoria washed through my whole being. My toes tried to curl in the platform heels I wore, and Nate's free hand clutched me tight against him like he didn't want it to end. He jerked and shuddered as I finished, kissing me deeper than ever as I damn near strangled him with his own tie.

For a few moments, we just stayed in place. Breathing hard. Then he kissed the bend of my neck and said my name in a way that sent a cold wash of dread rolling through me.

"What?" I snapped, already withdrawing in anticipation of his rejection. Again. Just like that night after Napa…

"Stop it," he growled, grabbing the back of my neck before I could clamber off his lap. "Hear me out, Ash. Please. This isn't the same thing as that night I was drunk."

I shook my head slowly, studying his whiskey eyes with my heart breaking. "You can't keep doing this to me, Nate. You can't keep pretending there's something between us and then—"

"No one is *pretending* here, Ash!" he barked. "I feel it. Trust me, I fucking feel it so damn hard, it hurts, but that's the problem. What I feel is too much, it's too big, and I'm scared…" He trailed off but didn't break eye contact with me to hide his emotions. "I'm terrified that I don't have the capacity or the emotional depth to give you what you need. I can't fucking share you, Ashley. Don't you get it? If you were mine…you'd be mine. And I know you'd never be able to give me that because you're already in love with the three best guys I know."

It was too much. Too painful. I closed my eyes in a vain attempt to hold my tears at bay, but it was no use as they squeezed out nonetheless. There was nothing I could say back, though, because how the fuck did I argue that fact? It was, after all, just that. Fact.

Nate exhaled heavily, pulling me in until our foreheads rested against one another. "Ashley...things have changed so much since we first met, but I can safely say right now, with my whole heart, I never wanted to make you cry. I have tried to walk away a hundred times. I've tried...but it was always pointless. I needed you to know."

I swallowed hard, trying desperately to get a fucking grip and not melt down. He was being honest with how he felt, and I couldn't tell him he was wrong. Just because his friends were okay with sharing me didn't mean he also had to be on board.

"I understand," I whispered, my voice choked with emotion. Reluctantly, I slipped out of his arms and off his lap, taking several steps away to create some physical space and breathing room. "I'm sorry. I can't...I can't change how things are."

He leaned forward with his elbows on his knees, the most distraught expression cutting his face. "I would never ask you to. Not you or them." His own voice was as rough as mine, and I needed to turn my back to save from spilling more tears.

"Can I just have a minute alone?" I croaked, my throat tighter than a bow string. "Please? I'll... I just need a minute."

Nate gusted a heavyhearted sigh, then must have stood up because, a moment later, his hands rested ever so softly on my upper arms and his lips brushed the bend of my neck. "I'm so sorry, Ash. I'm so fucking sorry I can't be what you deserve."

Christ. I could handle his insults, I was prepared for his cold indifference or disrespect, but this heartfelt devastation and open acknowledgment of his feelings were more than I could bear.

"I'm sorry too," I whispered, biting the edge of my lip in a desperate attempt to control my desire to sob.

Nate started to leave, then paused with his hand on the door handle. He breathed a soft curse, and my hope soared. He'd changed his mind.

"Ash, I'm so sorry. I need you to sign some paperwork. I hadn't… This wasn't what I had intended, but it's time sensitive." He crossed back to the bed and located the stack of papers he'd dropped earlier.

I inhaled deeply, putting on my brave face as I turned toward him. "Sure. What is it?"

He offered me a pen and smoothed the papers out somewhat on the end of the bed. It wasn't anywhere near bright enough to really read the tiny print, but at the same time, I didn't want to sit there scouring the document, which seemed to be some thirty-odd pages long.

"A prenup," he said with a sad laugh. "Sorry. It's irrelevant, obviously, but because I come into my grandparents' inheritance at midnight, my lawyers want to ensure that my assets are protected. And since we're engaged…"

I nodded my head. "Yeah, I get it." Because as far as his mother and his lawyers were concerned, I could be a very real threat to his wealth.

"Thanks. I've been meaning to do this for weeks but kept changing my mind." He muttered it like the whole transaction physically hurt.

I shrugged, pretending my heart wasn't actively bleeding from what had just passed between us. Signing a prenup meant absolutely nothing since we had no intention of actually getting married, so I had no issues flipping through the pages and signing everywhere he indicated. He needed to countersign several pages as well, and then it was all done.

Nate almost seemed to be holding his breath when I handed the contract back to him and he folded it back up. "Ashley, I hope you know that I wouldn't—"

"Nate, respectfully." I cut him off. "You've said everything you needed to say. I appreciate where you stand on this, but it doesn't hurt any less. Please just...leave me alone."

His face fell, but he gave a small nod. "That's fair. Do you want me to send Heath in or...?"

"No. I just want to be alone right now. Please. Go and enjoy your birthday, Nate." I went as far as opening the door for him and gesturing for him to fuck off, and he only hesitated a moment longer before doing as I asked.

What the fuck else could he do? He was the one pushing me away, after all. But I was the one already in love with three others. So I guessed we were equally at fault in this case.

Shoving the door shut behind him, I collapsed to the floor to wallow in my heartbreak for a moment. Except I knocked over a stack of presents, and something sounded like it broke when the box hit the floor.

"Shit," I hissed, grabbing the present boxes and hastily restacking. I glanced at the gift card attached to the one that seemed to have broken—then froze in horror.

Happy 25th Birthday, my darling. Love, Mommy

That handwriting. *Oh fuck...* I knew that handwriting.

Bile rose in my throat, and I choked it back, snatching the card off the gift to show the guys as evidence. I needed to show them. We could compare it to the note someone had left Mom and prove once and for all that Jocelyn was involved!

I burst out of the bedroom, blind with panic and focused on finding the guys—or Nate. But instead I ran headlong into a woman dressed in a black gown with a dramatic train. Her toffee-brown hair was tightly coiled to her head and her expression severe as she wobbled in her heels at my assault.

"Ashley, dear, what's the rush? I was just coming to speak with you," Nate's mother said with a glacial-cold smile. Her gaze darted to my hand, where I still wore Nate's ring. "Hmm, I see that hasn't been resolved yet." Then her gaze shifted to my other hand, where I clutched the card she'd written. "Oh, good. You've finally connected the dots. That took a lot longer than anticipated."

My eyes widened as fear stiffened my spine. "So you're not even trying to deny it? You're involved. The hypnosis, Dr. Fox…Heath's suicide?" Horror rolled through me as I thought how vehemently Heath had defended this woman so recently.

She just shrugged. "Why deny it? No one will believe a single thing you say anymore, Ashley. This is my very favorite part of experimental research, when we expand the reach to everyone surrounding the control subject. Buckle up, girl. It's about to get rough."

Then she snapped her fingers in my face, and I collapsed like my strings had been severed, my vision turning black just the moment before my head hit the floor.

Chapter Forty-Six

Royce's uncle thinks I have a strong enough case against my mother to muzzle her for life. Evidence of her embezzling from my trust account, proof of her paying hitmen, footage of her entangled in a romantic relationship with a known war criminal...the list goes on. It's enough to destroy her image, and without her image, Portia Levigne is nothing.

I wanted to tell Spark immediately, but Nate asked me to wait until after his birthday. He was cagey about his reasons, though, and I have a bad feeling in my gut. If he hurts her...I'll kill him.

Mar. 11
C. Bassington

Cotton wool filled my head as I tried to claw my way out of what seemed like the most intense nightmare. But when I finally managed to peel my eyes open and stared at the white ceiling, I couldn't recall a single detail of what the dream had been about—nothing specific, just a horrible feeling of urgency and dread.

My mouth was so dry it hurt, and my eyes were crusty like I'd been asleep for days.

"What the fuck happened?" I murmured, rolling onto my side in search of Royce. But he wasn't there. Neither was Heath or Carter. I was alone. "That sucks," I mumbled to myself, closing my eyes for just a little longer before sighing heavily. I needed to get up and pee, more than anything, but also drink some water and work out what'd happened.

The last thing I remembered was Nate's birthday, getting ready upstairs with Carter…coming down to find Nate and Heath…fucking Nate's hand…

"Oh fuck," I moaned, clapping my hands over my face. He would be utterly impossible to live with after this. Now that he knew how I felt… But he wasn't a dick about it, was he? My foggy memory told me he'd been genuinely broken up about the whole thing and then—

"No!" I sat up with a gasp, the memory of Nate's mom hitting me like a ton of fucking bricks. I needed to tell the guys. I needed to warn them!

Except…I wasn't in my room. I wasn't even in the guest room of the mansion Nate had rented for his party. The bed I'd woken up in was tiny, for starters, barely even a double. And the room was sparsely decorated, with a cheap, impersonal picture of a sailboat on the wall.

Most concerning, though, were the bars over the window.

Alarmed, I rushed to the door and attempted to jerk it open, only to be met with the harsh denial of a lock. The handle wouldn't even turn.

"Hello?" I called out in my panic, knocking on the door. "Is anyone there? Hello?"

Nothing. I tried again and again, and still no one opened the door to apologize for what was clearly a huge mix-up or even offer an explanation, so I turned to assess the room once more.

There, beside the bed, was what seemed to be a call button, like I'd seen in the hospital after my ordeal in the forest last year.

Holding my breath, I pressed the button, then sat down to wait, resisting the urge to pace or scream or, worse, cry. If I was where my gut said I was, I needed to keep my cool.

I counted to three hundred and seventy-nine in my head before the door finally opened and a tired-looking woman entered wearing navy-blue medical scrubs.

"Ashley, it's nice to see you awake," she said in a weirdly impersonal voice. "You must have questions."

"Yes," I agreed, "I do. For one thing, where—"

"I won't be answering them. I'm sorry, but I can take you to meet with your doctor if you'll follow me?" She turned and swept out of the room again, this time leaving the door open like she didn't much care if I followed or not.

Biting my tongue, I hurried after her on bare feet, hugging my oversized gray T-shirt around myself. These weren't my clothes, and fuck if I didn't feel violated as hell for that fact.

"Please wait in here," the woman—maybe a nurse—said, gesturing to what seemed like some kind of holding cell with just a couple of chairs bolted to the floor beside a closed door. "The doctor will be with you soon."

Then she was gone.

"Bitch," I muttered into the empty space, sitting down to wait as a shiver ran down my spine. I was only in a pair of elastic-waistband pants and the gray T-shirt, and what felt like a basic elastic crop top, rather than a bra. Nothing to harm myself with, I supposed.

I counted to six hundred and twelve before the door opened and an older, middle-aged man appeared.

"Ashley, come on in." He gestured for me to enter his office, and I clenched my teeth to keep from screaming and yelling, demanding answers. That would get me nowhere, I was well aware, but the desire was strong. "Have a seat, please."

I did as I was told, playing the part of calm and sane as well as I possibly could under the circumstances. Once I was seated in one of the visitor chairs, the doctor took his seat behind his desk and offered me a bland smile.

"I'm sure you're very confused this morning. You were not particularly lucid when the transport team brought you in last night, but you seem much calmer today so that's great to see. I'm Dr. Marion, and I'll be your primary physician here."

I took a beat, collecting my thoughts. I hadn't been lucid? No shit; I'd been unconscious from whatever Jocelyn had done to me. "Dr. Marion?" I repeated, and he nodded. "You're correct—I am confused. Where are we exactly?"

"Geographically? We're in Montana. This is a very discreet and well-funded psychiatric care facility, where people such as yourself can be given the care and treatment they need, without any prying eyes." He delivered this information as unemotionally as a computer-generated script, and another ice-cold stab of dread sliced through me.

I wet my lips. "I see. And how did I come to be here?" Aside from Jocelyn doing whatever the fuck she did to knock me out, surely the guys had to have noticed her dragging me out of the house? Someone must have witnessed something, considering they'd literally transported me to another state.

Dr. Marion tipped his head slightly to the side, a small flash of pity showing in his otherwise blank face. "Ashley, you were transferred from your previous facility due to an increase in your delusions and the escalating violence you displayed toward staff. It's my understanding that you were sedated for the journey, for safety."

I blinked twice. Previous facility? Is that the lie Jocelyn had told? "Dr. Marion, I believe you have been lied to. I understand you probably have plenty of patients who claim not to be crazy, but in

343

this case, you've been manipulated. I was never in a previous facility, nor should I be here."

He gave a small sigh. "Yes, you're correct. We do hear this a lot." He reached into his desk drawer and pulled out a stack of paperwork, sorting through them to pull out the page he wanted. "But in this case, we have transfer paperwork from your previous physicians along with extensive treatment notes. Most importantly, though, we have the admission document signed by your medical power of attorney."

I shook my head, fast losing my grip on calm. "My medical power of attorney? I don't have one. I am a legal adult. I'm my own power of—" My words cut off in a pained whimper as he placed the document in front of me. The signature might have been unfamiliar a week ago, but having seen it scrawled out so very recently by Nate's own hand... "Nate? He's not—"

The doctor slid another document in front of me. "That's your signature, is it not? On the appointment of the MPOE form naming Nathaniel Essex as legally empowered to make any and all medical decisions on your behalf?"

My heart melted like it'd been doused in acid. "Yes," I whispered in shocked horror. There was no use denying it—that was my signature, just as it was Nate's countersigned beside mine.

That lying, cheating, sneaky...bastard.

Dr. Marion sighed again, putting the documents away. "Ashley, your previous doctor informed me that you have been known to experience regressions, within which you seem to forget what led you to this point. Make no mistake, you do belong here."

I swallowed hard, my pulse rushing in my ears. "I don't. And I don't have any previous doctors. This is all Jocelyn's doing. She's fabricated this entire fucking—"

"Ashley. You are not well." Dr. Marion cut me off with a no-nonsense tone. "You haven't been well for several months, and things only seem to be getting worse."

I shook my head again, panic rising in my chest. "Call him. Call Nate and have him come here to explain himself. He's my medical power of attorney. There should be no reason why he can't come here and tell me face-to-face what the fuck he thinks he's doing. The guys can't possibly be okay with this."

The doctor pursed his lips. "The guys? That would be..." He consulted the notes in front of him, browsing through until he nodded. "Carter and Royce?"

I frowned. "Or Heath. He would never support this insanity, excuse my pun."

"Heath. I see. That would be..." More pages flipped. "Heathcliff Briggs. Ah yes, I see...his suicide seemed to trigger your initial psychotic break. Do you often refer to him as if he is still alive?"

My jaw dropped. "Excuse me? He *is* alive. It was only attempted suicide; Nate saved him."

Dr. Marion gave me another of those pitying looks and my vision went fuzzy for a moment. There was no fucking way he was going to convince me that Heath was dead. This was a sick joke and nothing more. More of Jocelyn's fucked-up head games.

"Ashley...denial isn't helping you here. Heathcliff hung himself in early December, and your mental health took a sharp decline from there. Your parents had you admitted on a psychiatric evaluation on Christmas Day, after you ran out into the snow wearing just a pair of pajamas, then fell through the ice of a frozen pond." He clasped his hands on top of my folder, shaking his head with a sad expression. "I can see we have our work cut out for us."

Agony ripped through my chest as I tried to digest what he was saying. It wasn't true... Was it? I remembered Christmas just fine. Our parents had been all cozy and gross, and I'd gone outside to get some air. Nate had followed, and we'd talked. Right?

Then Heath arrived.

Or had he?

"No, this is all... None of this is true," I insisted, fast losing my grip on the calm I so desperately tried to cling to. "Heath's not dead. Where's my mom in all of this? I'd like you to call my mother, please. I want to speak with her. If anyone should be making medical decisions, it's her."

Another sad look. "Ashley, this pains me. You gave your step-brother medical power of attorney in a moment of lucidity after your mother and his father were confirmed dead in a plane crash last week. Nathaniel is all the family you have left."

I must have blacked out for a moment because the next thing I knew, there was a mint-green-attired orderly offering me a paper cup of water as my head hung between my knees. What the fuck was happening?

"Ashley, this has all been a shock, it seems," Dr. Marion said from where he hovered near the door. "I think it's best if you return to your room to rest."

I sat up, shaking my head. "No. You need to call Nate and make him come here in person to explain himself. I am not accepting this bullshit. Not until I hear it from his lips directly."

Dr. Marion pursed his lips, then nodded. "Very well, if that's what it takes. I will call him and ask if he'll make the journey. In the meantime, you need to return to your room. Cyril, if you could please escort Miss Layne?"

"Yes, Doctor," the orderly agreed, offering me a hand to help me up. I took it, because what in the hell else could I do? Any kind of violent outburst would only see them sedate me, I was sure. My best bet lay in keeping cool until Nate could arrive…then I'd kill him.

Cyril the orderly walked with me out of Dr. Marion's office, and I blinked away the tears building in my eyes. I felt so fucking powerless, and it was an awful sensation. Down the hall, a woman's voice echoed with an uncomfortable familiarity, making me pause in my tracks.

"Miss Layne, we need to keep—"

"One second," I snapped, tugging my arm free of his gentle

grip as I spun around in the direction that voice had come from. A moment later, a pair of white-coated doctors rounded the corner, and I inhaled sharply when Jocelyn locked eyes with me.

I expected her to smirk or wink or…something, but her gaze passed over me like we'd never even met before.

"Jocelyn," I said out loud, starting in her direction. "You bitch, this is too far!"

Nate's mother seemed startled as she frowned in my direction, shaking her head slightly with confusion. "I'm…sorry?"

"That's Dr. Russo," Cyril the orderly informed me, grabbing my arm to halt me in my tracks. "Dr. Sarah Russo."

Nate's mom gave me a worried look, her head tilted to the side. "You must have me mistaken for someone else. I have one of those faces."

Disbelief nearly fucking choked me. "No, you don't. You're Jocelyn Reynard, and this whole fucking thing is your fucked-up little experiment, isn't it? You are behind everything and when Nate—" I broke off then, nearly swallowing my tongue as another horrifyingly familiar white-coated doctor strode around the corner. "H-how is this possible? No…you're dead!"

Dr. Fox met my eyes with a concerned frown. "Have we met?"

"You're dead!" I shouted again, unable to hold my cool any longer. "I saw your body! We burned down your house! This isn't possible!"

Because if Dr. Fox was alive…then what did that mean for everything else that'd happened?

Holy shit. Had it all been in my head?

TO BE CONTINUED…
You're Next
Devil's Backbone #3

347

CAN'T WAIT FOR MORE OF THE DEVIL'S
BACKBONE SOCIETY? DISCOVER MORE HOT
WHY-CHOOSE ROMANCE FROM TATE JAMES
WITH HER MADISON KATE SERIES.

READ ON FOR THE FIRST CHAPTER OF

CHAPTER 1

I shouldn't be here.

If my father knew…

But I would take those risks to witness this fight. This *fighter.*

Music boomed from the speaker beside me, and the crowd got louder. More frenzied and impatient. Adrenaline pulsed through my veins, pushing my own excitement to such a level that I could barely stay still. I started bouncing lightly on the balls of my feet just to keep from screaming or fainting or something.

A grin curled my lips, and I nodded my head to the familiar tune. "Clichéd choice but could have been worse," I muttered under my breath. "Bodies" by Drowning Pool continued to rage, and I pushed up on my toes, trying to catch a glimpse of one of the reasons we'd skipped out on our shitty Halloween party.

"MK, I don't get it," my best friend, Bree, whined from beside me. Her hands covered her ears, and her delicate face was screwed up like she was in physical pain. "Why are we even here? This is so far from our side of town, it's scary. Like, legit scary. Can we *go* already?"

"What?" I exclaimed, frowning at her and thinking I'd surely just heard her wrong. "We can't leave now; the fight hasn't even started yet!" I needed to yell for her to hear me, and she cringed again. She had reason to. In a crowd dominated mostly by men—big men—Bree and I stood zero chance of even seeing the octagon, let alone the fighters. Or if I was honest, one fighter in particular. So we'd climbed up onto one of the massive industrial generators to get a better view.

The one we'd picked just happened to also have a speaker sitting on it, and the volume of the music was just this side of deafening.

"Babe, we've been here for over an hour," Bree complained. "I'm tired and sober, my feet hurt, and I'm sweating like a bitch. Can we *please* go?" She tried to glare at me, but the whole effect was ruined by the fact that she still had a cat nose and whiskers drawn on her face—not to mention a fluffy tail strapped to her ass.

Not that I could judge. My costume was "sexy witch," but at least I'd been able to ditch my pointed hat. Now I was just wearing a skanky, black lace minidress and patent leather stiletto boots.

It was after midnight on October 31, and we were *supposed* to be at our friend Veronica's annual Halloween party. Yet Bree and I had decided that sneaking out of the party to attend a highly illegal mixed martial arts fight night would be a better idea. Even better still, it was being held in the big top of a long-abandoned amusement park called The Laughing Clown.

Like that wasn't an infinitely better way to spend the night than being hit on by a boy with a Rolex and then spending all of three minutes with him in the backseat of his Bentley.

Yeah, Veronica's parties all sort of ended the same way, and I, for one, was over it.

"Bree, I didn't force you to come with me," I replied, annoyed at her badgering. "You *wanted* to come. Remember?"

Her mouth dropped open in indignation. "Uh, yeah, so you wouldn't get robbed or murdered or something trying to hitchhike your way over the divide! MK, I saved your perky ass, and you know it."

I rolled my eyes at her dramatics. "I was going to Uber, not hitchhike. And West Shadow Grove is not exactly the seventh circle of hell."

Her eyes rounded as she looked out over the crowd gathered to watch the fights. "It may as well be. You know how many people get killed in West Shadow Grove *every day?*"

I narrowed my eyes and called her factual bluff. "I don't, actually. How many?"

"I don't know either," she admitted, "but it's a lot." She nodded at me like that made her statement more convincing, and I laughed.

Whatever else she'd planned to say to convince me to leave was drowned out by the fight commentator. My attention left Bree in a flash, and I strained to see the octagon. Even standing on the generator box for height, we were still far enough away that the view was shitty.

My excitement piqued, bubbling through me like champagne as I twisted my sweaty hands in the stretchy fabric of my dress. The commentator was listing his stats now.

Six foot four, two hundred and two pounds, twenty-three wins, zero draws, zero losses.

Zero losses. This guy was freaking born for MMA.

It wasn't an official fight—quite the opposite. So they didn't elaborate any more than that. There was no mention of his age, his hometown, his training gym…nothing. Not even his name. Only…

"Please give it up for"—the commentator gave a dramatic pause, whipping the crowd into a frenzy—"the mysterious, the undefeated, *The Archer!*" He bellowed the fighter's nickname, and the crowd freaking lost it. Myself included.

"Paranoid" by I Prevail poured from the speaker beside us, and by the time the tall, hooded figure had made his way through the crowd with his team tight around him, my throat was dry and scratchy from yelling. Even from this distance, I trembled with anticipation and randomly pictured what it'd be like to climb him like a tree. Except naked.

"I'm going to guess this is why we came?" Bree asked in a dry voice, wrinkling her nose and making her kitty whiskers twitch. Her costume wasn't as absurd as it could be, since most members of the crowd were in some form of Halloween costume. Even the fighters tonight wore full face masks, and the commentator was dressed as the Grim Reaper.

"You know it is," I shot back, not taking my gaze from the octagon for even a second. I hardly dared blink for fear of missing something.

One of his support team—a guy only a fraction shorter with a similar fighter's physique and a ball cap pulled low over his face—took the robe from his shoulders, and my breath caught in my throat. His back was to us, but every hard surface was decorated with ink. We were too far away to see details, but I knew—from my borderline obsessive stalking—that the biggest tattoo on his back was of a geometric stag shot with arrows. It was how he'd gotten his nickname. The stag represented his star sign: Sagittarius, the Archer.

"Ho-ly shit," Bree gasped, and I knew without looking at her she had suddenly discovered a love for MMA.

"They say he's being scouted for the UFC," I babbled to her, "except they said he has to stop all underground cage matches, and apparently he told them to shove it."

Bree made a sound of acknowledgment, but knowing her, she didn't even know what the UFC was, let alone understand what an incredible achievement that was for a young fighter.

"Shh," I said, even though she hadn't spoken. "It's starting."

In the makeshift octagon, the Archer and his opponent—both wearing nothing but shorts and a plain mask—tapped gloves, and the fight was officially on.

Totally enthralled by the potential of the main event fight, I waited eagerly to see how it was all going to pan out. Would it be an even match of skills and strength, spanning all five rounds? Or would it be a total domination by one fighter? I could only cross my fingers and hope The Archer hadn't grown cocky with his recent successes and ended up KO'd in thirty seconds like Ronda Rousey.

The other guy struck first, impatient and impetuous. Watching the way The Archer blocked his attack, then struck back with a vicious jab to the face and knee to the side, I could already tell it would be over before the end of the first round.

"Damn, he's quick," I commented, while my fighter of choice dodged and weaved, not allowing any contact from his opponent. Each strike he blocked or evaded, he returned threefold, until eventually he had the other guy down on the bloodstained mat.

"Is it over?" Bree asked, gripping my arm.

I shook my head. "Not until one of them taps out or you know"—I shrugged—"gets knocked out."

"Brutal," she breathed, but there was a spark in her eyes that said she was having fun.

The Archer's opponent thrashed around like a fish on a hook, just barely holding back the arm threatening to get under his chin. Once the bigger, tattooed fighter got his forearm under there, it'd be all over for the guy whose nickname I hadn't even listened to.

"Come on, come on," I urged, bouncing slightly in my stupidly high heels. "Come on, Archer. Finish him!"

The struggle continued for a few more moments, and then some huge-headed asshole moved into my line of sight. Something happened, and the crowd roared. I could only imagine Archer had locked down his choke hold.

"Yes!" I exclaimed, craning my neck to try and to see. "Oh come on, *move!*" This was aimed at the guy blocking my view. Not that he could hear me.

The commentator started counting. It would all be over in ten seconds if the other guy didn't tap out before that.

"…three…four…five…"

Frustration clawed at me that I couldn't *see.*

"…six…seven…"

Bang!

Startled and confused, I jerked my attention to Bree at the loud noise. Had a car just backfired? Inside the big top? How the hell was that even possible?

"What was that?" I tried to ask but couldn't hear my own voice. My ears were ringing with a high-pitched sound, and everything else was on mute.

Bree was saying something and tugging on my arm, but I couldn't hear her.

What the fuck is going on?

"MK, come *on!*" Her words finally penetrated the ringing in my ears, and I stumbled as she dragged me down from our elevated position and into the chaos below.

I shook my head, still confused as fuck, until Bree's panicked yell sank in.

"Someone just got shot," she told me. "We need to get the hell out of here. Now."

Several more shots—because holy shit, she was right—rang out in the crowded space, and people scattered like bowling pins.

Bree and I clutched each other's hand as we crouched low and made our way as fast as possible to the exit, but we soon realized there was a whole lot more going on than a lone shooter. Between us and the door, an all-out brawl was happening, with at least thirty people swinging punches and kicks. Blood and fuck knew what else flew everywhere. I just barely dragged Bree out of the way when a burly guy in a leather jacket stumbled back from a punch to his face and would have knocked her over.

"We need to find another way out," I told her, stating the obvious as I searched around for another exit. It was a freaking big top, and there must have been almost five hundred people spectating the illegal MMA fight night. The venue had to have loads of other exits. "This way!" I shouted, dragging her behind me as I ducked and weaved through the violent mob.

"MK," my friend exclaimed, tugging on my hand. "Look!"

I followed her shaking finger and saw a puddle of red across the polished concrete floor. A spill of pale-blond hair—the same color mine would be if I hadn't just dyed it hot pink for this costume—and a lifeless hand with chipped nail polish.

"Don't look," I snapped to Bree, yanking on her hand again to get her moving. One girl was already dead, and I sure as shit didn't want to join her.

It only took a few more minutes to get clear of the violent mess inside the big top. The night air held frost, and my teeth chattered as Bree and I hurried away through the dark amusement park.

"Th-that was…" Bree stammered over her words, and I slowed just enough to check that she was okay. Her eyes were wide and haunted, her face pale. She hadn't broken down into hysterical crying yet, so maybe shock was working on our side for once.

If nothing else, it'd hopefully keep her from mentioning why I was so seemingly unaffected by seeing a dead body and all that violence. All that bloodshed.

I locked down the memories of the last dead body I'd seen, stuffing them back into the tiny mental box they'd been in for exactly six years. Halloween was the anniversary of my mom's murder.

"Stay quiet," I whispered to her, my attention on the shadows around us. "We need to get back to your car and away from here."

My best friend, for all her amazing qualities, had zero clue how much danger we were in.

"What's going on, MK?" she demanded, her voice pitched way too loud for my liking.

"Shh!" I placed a hand over her mouth to emphasize my point. We were tucked into the shadows beside a dilapidated sideshow booth, and I frantically searched around us to check that we were alone. "Bree, you need to trust me. That was no random act of violence. Didn't you see the tattoos on those guys brawling? The patches on their jackets?" Her eyes grew even wider above my hand, and her breath came in jerky, panicked gasps. I nodded, confirming what she'd just guessed. "Yeah. Exactly. We're neck deep in the middle of a gang war, and if we don't get the fuck out of here soon…" I trailed off. She knew what I meant. If either gang—the Wraiths or the Reapers—caught us, the consequences didn't bear thinking about. Let's say death would be the easy way out. Bree would probably get ransomed back to her filthy-rich family, but I wouldn't be so lucky. Not because my father couldn't pay but because he'd somehow made an enemy of the Reapers' leader.

Voices came from nearby, laughing guys, and I pulled Bree farther into the shadows until they'd passed us.

"Let's go," I said softly when their chatter faded away.

Bree was right behind me as I started hurrying back toward where we'd parked. More and more people were spilling out of the big top now, so we kept our heads down and tried to blend with a group in costumes. It helped that Bree was still in her sexy-cat outfit and my waist-length hair was hot pink. We just looked like regular girls out for a Halloween party.

I almost let the tension drop from my shoulders around the time we made it halfway through the park, but we couldn't hide with the crowd forever. We'd parked Bree's car in a shed behind the south gate, and everyone else was flowing toward the west one.

Silently, I tugged her hand, and the two of us broke away from the crowd, immediately picking up our pace and hurrying past the broken-down bumper cars.

"This was a bad idea," Bree mumbled, but she stuck close behind me as we jogged—in heels—through the scary-as-fuck park. Why had it all seemed so damn exciting when we'd arrived? Suddenly it was like we were stuck inside a horror movie and any minute now someone would jump out with a knife or chainsaw or something.

Adrenaline pumping through my veins, I rounded a corner without checking first and ran straight into the back of a guy in a full Beetlejuice costume.

"Shit, sorry," I exclaimed, catching my balance on my stripper-esque stiletto heels.

I made to move past him, but a huge hand circled my upper arm. He stopped me in my tracks at the same time as I saw the guy he'd been talking to...and the large, open bag of cash on the ground between them.

"Uh..." I licked my lips and flicked a look from Beetlejuice to the other man. "Sorry, we'll get out of your way."

I tugged on Bree's hand, ignoring Beetlejuice's grip on my arm as I urged her past me on the outside, away from Beetlejuice's leather jacket–wearing friend. It was dark enough that I couldn't make out what patch he wore, but it didn't really matter. They were both bad fucking news.

"What did you hear?" Beetlejuice demanded, shaking me a bit and getting up in my face. His friend just watched. Uncaring.

"Nothing," I snapped back at him. "We were just getting out of here. Some bad shit is going on in the big top."

Beetlejuice sneered, and the leather-jacketed dude snickered. Like they already knew and were happy about it.

"Let me go," I said, my voice firm. "We didn't see or hear anything, and we honestly don't care. There's already one dead girl in this park, and a whole ton of witnesses. This place will be crawling with cops any second now."

Beetlejuice narrowed his eyes at me, his gaze suspicious before jerking a nod. "You saw *nothing*," he snarled, the warning clear as he released me with a shove. "Dumb bitches." This was muttered to his friend as he dismissed us from his presence.

I walked a few paces, not wanting to run while they could see me, but gave Bree a look that practically screamed *hurry your ass up!*

"Wait." That one word hit me like a lightning bolt, and my whole body tensed, my foot frozen in the air. "Don't I know you?"

It was the other guy speaking, and his deep, *familiar* voice sent chills down my spine. He was closer now; I could feel his intimidating presence looming behind me. He was near enough that I could smell the leather of his jacket. He could simply reach out and break my neck if he wanted to.

Panicked, I made a snap decision.

"Bree, whatever you do, don't stop until you get to the car. I'll meet you there." I said this under my breath, but the glare I gave her silenced any protests she might have. "I mean it," I assured her. "Fucking *run*."

She gave me a tight nod, her eyes brimming with fear and determination, then kicked off her heels and disappeared into the night.

"Fuck this," Beetlejuice snapped, and his footsteps quickly faded in the opposite direction. But only his. My creepy shadow hadn't budged an inch.

"Yeah," he murmured, his breath stirring the hot-pink strands of my hair. "I thought I recognized that ass. Now what is a girl like you doing in West Shadow Grove, Madison Kate Danvers?"

I didn't run after Bree because I wasn't a fucking idiot. There was no way I'd outrun this guy in what I was wearing. And now that he knew who I was, he wouldn't just stand back while I took off either.

Instead, I did the only thing that came to my mind.

I spun around and punched him right in the face.

About the Author

Tate James is a *USA Today* bestselling author of contemporary romance and romantic suspense, with occasional forays into fantasy, paranormal romance, and urban fantasy. She was born and raised in Aotearoa (New Zealand) but now lives in Australia with her husband and their adorable crotchfruit.

She is a lover of books, booze, cats, and coffee and is most definitely not a morning person. Tate is a bit too sarcastic, swears far too much for polite society, and definitely tells too many dirty jokes.

Website: tatejamesauthor.com
Facebook: tatejamesauthor
Instagram: @tatejamesauthor
TikTok: @tatejamesauthor
Pinterest: @tatejamesauthor
Mailing list: eepurl.com/dfFR5v